# THE
# COMMISSIONER'S
# DAUGHTER

Joanna Woods

# THE COMMISSIONER'S DAUGHTER

*The Story of Elizabeth Proby*
*& Admiral Chichagov*

THE STONESFIELD PRESS

First published in Great Britain 2000 by
The Stonesfield Press
Peakes House, Stonesfield
Witney, Oxon OX8 8PY

A CIP catalogue record for this book
is available from the British Library.

ISBN 0 9527126 2 8

*The engraving by P. C. Canot reproduced on the endpapers
shows the Royal Dockyard at Chatham in 1793, when
Charles Proby was Commissioner. The Commissioner's House
is the elegant four-storey building on the right, close to the
waterfront. It is the oldest naval building in Britain to
survive intact and has changed little since it was built in 1704.*

Map by Olive Pearson

Typeset in Monotype Bell
by The Stonesfield Press
Printed and bound in Great Britain
by Biddles Limited, Guildford

# Contents

| | | |
|---|---|---|
| | List of Illustrations | vii |
| | Foreword | ix |
| | Acknowledgements | xi |
| | Proby family tree | xiii |
| | Map of Northern Europe in 1812 | xiv–xv |
| 1 | Elizabeth | 1 |
| 2 | Pavel | 25 |
| 3 | Chatham | 48 |
| 4 | Mutiny | 62 |
| 5 | Marriage | 83 |
| 6 | St Petersburg | 101 |
| 7 | The Rise of Pavel | 126 |
| 8 | War | 154 |
| 9 | The French | 169 |
| 10 | 'A Deplorable Caprice' | 184 |
| 11 | The Retreat from Moscow | 201 |
| | Epilogue | 222 |
| | Appendix: The Memoirs | 229 |
| | Notes | 231 |
| | Biographical Notes | 239 |
| | Bibliography | 246 |
| | Index | 250 |

# List of Illustrations

1. Captain Charles Proby. Portrait by Sir Joshua Reynolds. *c.*1765. Elton Hall Collection. Reproduced by courtesy of Mr and Mrs William Proby.

2. Sarah Proby. Copy by E. L. Wager of a miniature by Richard Cosway after a portrait by Sir Joshua Reynolds. Private collection.

3. Charlotte Proby. Miniature by an unknown artist. Private collection.

4. Elizabeth Proby. Miniature by an unknown artist. Private collection.

5. Admiral Vasilii Chichagov. Drawing by an unknown artist, end of the 18th century. St Petersburg, State Hermitage Museum.

6. Catherine the Great. Print after a miniature by an unknown artist. Photograph Mary Evans Picture Library.

7. The Emperor Paul I. Portrait by Stepan Semenovich Shchukin. 1796–7. St Petersburg, State Hermitage Museum. Photograph Bridgeman Art Library.

8. The Emperor Alexander I. Portrait by Baron François-Pascal-Simon Gérard. London, Apsley House, The Wellington Museum. Photograph Bridgeman Art Library.

9. Elizabeth Chichagova. Portrait by an unknown artist. *c.*1806. Private collection.

10. Admiral Pavel Chichagov. Portrait by an unknown artist. Oil on canvas, early 19th century. St Petersburg, State Hermitage Museum.

11. Count Joseph de Maistre. Lithograph by François le Villain after a portrait by Pierre Bouillon. Paris, Bibliothèque Nationale. Photograph Giraudon/Bridgeman Art Library.

12. The Marquis de Caulaincourt. Engraving after a portrait by Baron François-Pascal-Simon Gérard. © Artephot/J. Abecassis.

13. John Joshua Proby, 1st Earl of Carysfort. Portrait by Sir Joshua Reynolds. *c.*1784. Elton Hall Collection. Reproduced by courtesy of Mr and Mrs William Proby.

14. Count Simon Vorontsov. Portrait by Sir Thomas Lawrence. *c*.1805. The Collection of the Earl of Pembroke, Wilton House, Salisbury. Reproduced by courtesy of the Earl of Pembroke.

15. Military Parade led by the Emperor Alexander I in the Palace Square, St Petersburg. Hand-coloured etching by Benjamin Paterssen. *c*.1803. Ashmolean Museum, Oxford.

16. *View of the centre of the Great Bridge of the Neva.* Etching by John H. Clark after a drawing by Mornay. Illustration for August from 'A Year in St Petersburg', published in London 1815. Stapleton Collection. Photograph Bridgeman Art Library.

17. *The Snake in the Grass,* by Sir Joshua Reynolds. *c*.1788. Elton Hall Collection. Reproduced by courtesy of Mr and Mrs William Proby.

18. The Crossing of the Berezina. Sketch by an unknown artist. Gouache on paper. French School, early 19th century. Musée de l'Armée, Hôtel des Invalides, Paris. Photo copyright © Musée de l'Armée, Paris.

Endpapers. *View of the Royal Dock Yard at Chatham.* Engraving and etching by Pierre Charles Canot after a painting by Richard Paton. Published 1793. © National Maritime Museum, London.

# Foreword

The scene was the crowded foyer of a large and soulless Soviet-era hotel in downtown Moscow. Somewhere in the milling throng of bewildered travellers was my 82-year-old great-aunt Katherine, who had just completed a ten-day package cruise on the Volga from St Petersburg to Moscow. Suddenly I saw her, an indomitable, small figure, as impeccably neat and smiling as if she were in Sloane Square. The only alteration to her appearance was a large plaster on her leg, badly cut when she had been flung across her cabin during a storm on Lake Ladoga. In her suitcase she was carrying a copy of Elizabeth Chichagova's 1802 letter from St Petersburg. This was the starting point of my three-year commitment to the story of Elizabeth and Pavel Chichagov.

Throughout my childhood, there had been occasional references to a member of the family who had married a mysterious Russian admiral called Chichagov, but nobody knew who he was or how they had met. In the late 1960s my parents received a letter from a Hungarian count named Peter de Crouÿ-Chanel, who was the great-great-grandson of Elizabeth and Pavel Chichagov and who wanted to make contact with the family. Through 'Uncle Peter' links were made with a host of charming French and Hungarian cousins, but we learned very little more about the Chichagovs. It was only in 1995, when I found myself living in Moscow and my great-aunt Katherine arrived with Elizabeth's letter, that I realized that there was a story to be told and that I was uniquely placed to tell it.

A few weeks after Katherine's visit, we moved to Paris. Here I was able to contact the Crouÿ-Chanels and embark upon a fascinating odyssey that led from the book-lined splendour of the reading room of the Bibliothèque Nationale in the rue de Richelieu to a lonely cemetery in St Petersburg. Like many other aspiring biographers, I was sustained throughout my search by the belief that I would eventually find a miraculous cache of letters which would tie together all the tantalizing threads that were gradually accumulating in my files. I never did. But the discovery of the correspondence between Elizabeth and her father was a very acceptable consolation prize, which helped me to redress the balance between the abundance of material on Pavel and the very slender pickings on Elizabeth.

At first glance, my heroine is a very ordinary person. Like most women of her period, she lived in the shadow of the men who controlled her destiny, and the challenge of writing her life has been to discern her personality through the often bombastic writings of her father and of her husband. We seldom hear her voice, although her letters to her father are illuminated by the clarity of her reasoning and the certainty of her love for Pavel. Ultimately she emerges as a figure of quiet strength and fortitude – the qualities of unsung heroes and heroines since time immemorial.

Pavel, on the other hand, was briefly a player on the world stage. Had he succeeded in capturing Napoleon at the Berezina, he would have changed the course of history: there would have been no Waterloo. But in a fatal game of chance, Pavel lost everything, and instead of receiving the laurel wreath of which he had seemed assured, he was condemned to eternal disgrace and oblivion.

Throughout the writing of this book, historical accuracy has been a guiding principle, but I have also tried to capture some of the emotional subtext that lurks amongst (and between) the lines of the letters and memoirs on which the narrative is largely based. My dearest hope is that through this blend of history and biography, Pavel and Elizabeth will have ceased to be the shadowy figures of my youth and will have become a reality.

*Note.* In rendering Chichagov and other Russian names, I have used the accepted English transliteration of the Cyrillic form, except in quoted material, where the original spelling has been retained. The name Chichagov was frequently mis-spelt by Pavel's contemporaries when they were writing in French or English. In transliteration, Pavel himself used the French version of his name, Tchitchagoff.

# *Acknowledgements*

In the course of my work, I have been overwhelmed by the support and kindness of a great many people. Foremost amongst those whom I should like to thank in France are the descendants and family of Pavel and Elizabeth, in particular Félix and Jacqueline de Crouÿ-Chanel and Régine de Robien. Without their help and approval I could never have embarked upon the book at all. I am also very grateful for the time and trouble taken by the staffs of the many different libraries and study centres that I visited in and around Paris. Above all, I must thank Soeur Nathalie of the Bibliothèque Slav de Paris at Meudon for her guidance and unfailing patience with my constant visits and requests. In the same context, I should also like to thank Katya Poinsot, Tara Warner, Anastasia Martin-Seglia and Sister Veronika for their help with Russian translations.

On my visit to Russia, I was enormously helped by the good offices of Oleg Vasnetsov, the cultural counsellor at the Russian Embassy in Paris, who facilitated my access to the Chichagov Archives at the Russian State Library in Moscow. My sincere thanks must also go to the Director of the Library, Mr V. K. Egorov, Tatiana Andrianova of International Library Relations and to all the staff who were so helpful to me during my visit. However, without Masha Perepelkina's tireless interpreting and translation skills, I would have been completely lost. Similarly, without the support and hospitality of Philippa and John Larkindale of the New Zealand Embassy, Maree and Geoff Bentley of the Australian Embassy and the organizational abilities of Galina Lavrova, my trip to Moscow would have been far less fruitful.

In St Petersburg I should like to extend my special thanks to the current occupants of the former Chichagov mansion, especially Ludmilla Rodolfova Ferrier for that memorable tram ride in search of the Chichagov abbess. I should also like to thank Vladimir Matveyev and Anastasia Mikliaeva of the State Hermitage Museum in St Petersburg for their help in locating Pavel's portrait.

My debt of gratitude is even greater in England. The book could not have been written without the inspiration of my great-aunt Katherine Proby and the priceless 'nuggets' that she continually unearthed and sent to me from the Elton archives. I have also greatly appreciated the enthusiasm and support of my cousins William and Merry Proby. They have always been unfailingly welcoming and helpful, and the unfettered access that I have enjoyed to the Elton archives, library and portraits has been invaluable.

I am also greatly indebted to the staffs of all the libraries and other institutions in England with which I have been in contact. My special thanks must go to Janet Knight of the Rochester upon Medway Studies Centre, Kathleen Shawcross and Beverly Shew of the Heritage Services at the Central Library in Sutton, Rachel Broomfield of the Devon County Council Records Office and Kate Crowe of the Foreign and Commonwealth Office Library and Records department. There is also Dinah Dean, whose notes, held in the Slavonic and Eastern European Collections of the British Library, greatly facilitated my research. In addition, I am, as always, most grateful to the courteous and helpful staff at the London Library.

I would like to acknowledge my reliance for historical background on Hugh Seton-Watson's *The Russian Empire 1801–1817* and on Anthony Cross's '*By the Banks of the Thames*' and *By the Banks of the Neva*. I am similarly indebted to Philip MacDougall for *The Chatham Dockyard Story* and his other works on Chatham. For the biographical notes, I have relied heavily on the *Great Soviet Encyclopedia* and the *Dictionary of National Biography*.

The brunt of the burden of this literary effort, however, has been borne by two people – my husband, Richard, and my editor and publisher, Simon Haviland (together with his wife, Jenny). Although I suspect that neither had any idea what an undertaking it was going to be, they have never uttered a word of reproach. To Richard I should like to say thank you for his great patience and generosity. To Simon I should like to express my heartfelt gratitude, not only for his tireless guidance and expertise and for the major contributions that he has made to the research and illustrations, but also for his confidence and his commitment.

# PROBY FAMILY TREE

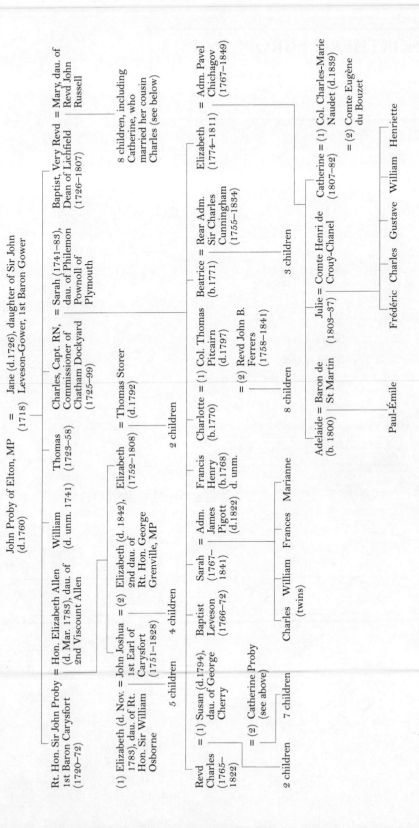

## NORTHERN EUROPE IN 1812

•••••➤ route of Napoleon's retreat from Moscow
(October–December 1812)

➤ movement of the Russian armies

SWEDEN

Christiania

Stockholm

D E N M A R K · N O R W A Y

North
Sea

Öland

Helsingør • Karlskrona

Copenhagen

UNITED
KINGDOM

B a l t i c

Dar

Elton
Great Yarmouth

Texel
Den Helder

Elbe

P R U

Thames
London

Amsterdam

Oder

Berlin

Chatham

Brighton

English
Channel

CONFEDERATION

Leipzig

Dieppe

Erfurt

OF THE

Seine
Compiègne

Prague

Paris

Frankfurt

RHINE

Loire

Karlsruhe

Auster

F R E N C H   E M P I R E

Rhine

Danube

Ulm

Munich

Wagram

Vienna

SWITZERLAND

Geneva   Lausanne

KINGDOM

Chambéry

OF ITALY

Trieste

Rhône

Turin

Venice

Genoa

# CHAPTER ONE

# *Elizabeth*

### 1774–1795

Elizabeth Proby was born at Chatham on 22 August 1774. The date is recorded on a family memorial in the parish church of St Mary's, where she was baptized on 10 October. Like her close contemporary, Jane Austen, she was born into a family of naval officers and into a society peopled by country parsons and country landowners. She grew up in a world where a young woman's life was punctuated by dancing classes and assemblies and largely focused on the prospect of a suitable marriage. Furthermore, the approval of parents or guardians in the choice of a husband was obligatory.

But Elizabeth had a mind of her own and, like that other Elizabeth in *Pride and Prejudice*, she combined a cool head with a passionate heart. It was these qualities that shaped her destiny and separated her for ever from the measured life of rural England which seemed to be her birthright. She was determined to marry the man she loved, in defiance of parental opposition, and by so doing she exchanged the orderly world of Jane Austen for the epic stage of Tolstoy's *War and Peace*.

When Elizabeth was born, her father, Captain Charles Proby, was Commissioner of the Royal Dockyard at Chatham. He had occupied this position since 1771, but before then he had enjoyed an active career at sea. He entered the navy in 1735 at the age of 10 and at the age of 15 he was appointed a midshipman to the *Centurion* under Commodore Anson and took part in Anson's four-year voyage around the world. According to William Clowes, it was Charles Proby who in June 1743 first sighted the fabulous Spanish treasure ship whose capture turned Anson and his men into popular heroes at home:

> At length on June 20th, a midshipman named Charles Proby shouted from his station at the top-masthead, 'A sail to windward!' She was soon seen from the deck, coming down before the wind towards the *Centurion*. It was the long-sought galleon, *N. S. de Cavadonga*. Both ships cleared for action, which lasted an hour and twenty minutes, at the end of which the Spaniard struck her colours. Anson lost only two men killed and seventeen wounded; but the loss of the Spaniards was sixty-seven killed and eighty-four wounded. The

1

cargo of the galleon included $1,313,843, besides 35,682 ounces of silver, and merchandise.[1]

The *N. S. de Cavadonga* was much larger than the *Centurion*, well-armed and carrying 550 hands, compared to Anson's crew of 227, of whom nearly thirty were mere boys. But, as the casualty figures for the encounter demonstrate, with Anson's training and the rigours of over three years at sea behind them, the men of the *Centurion* were of a very different calibre to those aboard the galleon. In the conclusion to his description of Anson's voyage, Clowes makes the following comment and cites the names of several officers, including that of Charles Proby: 'Many of the best men in the Navy, during the Seven Years War, had learnt their first lessons, and gained invaluable experience, during their hard service in Anson's exploring squadron. . . . Anson's expedition was, perhaps, the best example of a naval exploring voyage, forming a splendid and prolific nursery for training the best and most valuable class of naval officers.'[2]

Three years later, aged only 21, Charles was appointed captain. He seemed destined for a brilliant future, but it is possible that an unfortunate incident, shortly after the onset of the Seven Years War against the French, adversely affected his prospects. In 1757, according to the naval biographer Charnock, 'a complaint was preferred against him, by some of the people under his command, of having exercised undue severity towards them.'[3] Charnock states that this charge 'was found utterly void of foundation.'[4] In his entry for Charles Proby, Charnock does not refer specifically to the engagement which gave rise to this incident and which involved two British ships, the *Medway*, commanded by Charles, and the *Eagle*, commanded by Hugh Palliser. In his entry for Palliser, however, Charnock gives the following detailed account of the circumstances surrounding the capture, in May 1757, of the French ship the *Duc d'Aquitaine*:

> The *Medway* shortened sail to clear ship; this gave the *Eagle*, she being clear for action, the opportunity to pass her and begin the attack at two ship's lengths, so that almost every shot took place. After a short but very sharp action, she [the *Duc d'Aquitaine*] struck as the *Medway* came up, having fifty-one men killed, and the number of wounded not ascertained, with ninety-seven shot holes through both sides. Her main and mizen-masts fell just as she struck. The *Eagle* had ten men killed and thirty-two wounded, with twenty-one shot through her sides. The commander of the *Medway* was very unjustly reflected on, for it is certain that nothing but his ship not being clear

prevented his beginning the action, for he afterwards gave repeated proofs of his bravery in several actions during that war.[5]

Charles, as a member of the court martial of Admiral Byng* in January 1757, was well aware of the government's attitude to tardiness. In June 1757 he wrote a letter to Anson,[6] now an admiral, justifying his behaviour and the matter seems to have blown over. This episode may also have been complicated by the prospect of prize money. Crew members of all ships within signalling distance at the time of a capture received a portion, with the captain receiving the lion's share. Palliser, as captain of the *Eagle*, may well have felt that this prize was his alone. In 1758 Charles took part in a successful operation against the French off the Isle d'Aix and he later went on, in 1761, to emerge victorious from a vigorous action with the French ships of war, the *Achille* and the *Bouffonne*.

In 1769 Charles was appointed Commodore and Commander-in-Chief in the Mediterranean, but here too there were suggestions that his performance was not always satisfactory. He was criticized for breaking off an engagement with the enemy and the promotion to admiral never came. Two years later, after thirty-six years of continuous naval service, nearly all of which was spent at sea, he took up a shore position, initially as Comptroller of the Victualling Accounts and then as Resident Commissioner at Chatham. By this time his brother, Lord Carysfort, had been appointed a Lord of the Admiralty and it is possible that his brother's eminence facilitated the rapid switch of positions that occurred between Charles and the previous incumbent of Chatham. Charles's predecessor, Captain Thomas Hanway, became Comptroller of the Victualling Accounts, while Charles took over the infinitely preferable position at Chatham.

There are at least two portraits of Charles Proby by Reynolds; the first is thought to have been painted in 1756 and the other, in which he is magnificently dressed in the recently introduced official naval uniform, in 1765. In both of them, he exudes an air of self-importance. His gaze is cool and his protuberantly rounded cheeks suggest an incipient corpulence. He does not look like a man who would readily inspire affection. From his naval record and from his letters, his greatest qualities appear to have been his diligence and his integrity – both valuable attributes in the commissioner of an important dockyard, but not the stuff of admirals.

* Admiral John Byng (1704–57) was sentenced to death by court martial for neglect of duty and was shot at Portsmouth.

Charles was the fourth son of a well-established Huntingdonshire family. His ancestors had settled at Brampton in the County of Huntingdon at the end of the fifteenth century. However, the first member of the family to achieve distinction was Sir Peter Proby, who served as Lord Mayor of the City of London in 1622 and was at one time Keeper of Queen Elizabeth's Privy Purse. He was also the first member of the family to acquire land in the village of Elton, but it was not until 1660 that his grandson, Sir Thomas Proby, a city merchant, member of Parliament and baronet, became the owner of the manor of Elton. It was he who rebuilt the house which was to become the seat of the Proby family and was the childhood home of Charles Proby.

Charles's childhood was spent in considerable grandeur. Despite its lack of architectural consistency, Elton Hall was an impressive house with a large fifteenth-century chapel. Detached from the chapel, at its eastern end, stood a magnificent crenellated tower of the same period. All around it lay the park, with the family property of woods and farmland stretching for many acres in every direction. Within, apart from the dozens of lesser rooms, there was a fine library, which had been founded by Sir Thomas Proby. Through the family of his mother, Jane Leveson-Gower, Charles was also well-connected, for although she had died when he was only a year old, she had bequeathed to him a legacy of aristocratic kinsmen through the family of her father, Lord Gower.

As a little boy, Charles had accepted the beauty and security of Elton as an inseparable part of his existence. It was only as he grew older that he understood the bitter lot of younger sons and realized that none of this would ever be his. At the age of 10, he was dispatched to the navy to seek his fortune. Meanwhile his eldest brother, John, not only inherited the family estate, but also made a brilliant marriage to the Irish heiress Elizabeth Allen, through whom a great deal of valuable Irish property came into the Proby family. In 1752 John Proby was created an Irish peer and took the title of Baron Carysfort. His son John Joshua, a scholar and a diplomat, was to become an earl.

Elizabeth's mother, Sarah, came from a less illustrious background. Charles had met her not through the social network of the Proby family, but rather through his naval career. However, in the eyes of a naval officer, she had the highest possible credentials, for she was the younger sister of Charles's fellow officer and friend, Philemon Pownoll, whose courage and ability were legendary.

Philemon was ten years younger than Charles and came from a Devon family of naval officers and clerics. Generations of Pownolls attended Oxford, often with the family names of Israel or Philemon. Philemon's father, a naval officer, was also called Philemon – and his father's brother was called Israel. The father was for many years Clerk of the Cheque at Plymouth Dockyard, a senior official who was responsible, with the Storekeeper, for the financial and administrative business of the yard. His eldest son, Jacob, was the Storekeeper.

Sarah was the sixth of the eight Pownoll children and they lived in the village of Stoke Damerel, just outside Plymouth. Her marriage to Charles took place in the village church on 23 September 1758, when she was 17 and he was 33. There is a charming, undated miniature of her (Plate 2) after a portrait by Reynolds painted shortly after the wedding. She looks very young and is wearing a pink dress with a ribbon in her hair. The simplicity of her dress and manner is in marked contrast to the portraits of her husband. She is in three-quarter profile, with her head and eyes to the left. Her thick dark hair is piled high off her forehead and her expression is pensive.

Whatever Sarah's reflections may have been on married life, the star of her brother, Philemon, was in the ascendant. He was serving under Charles as the commander of the sloop *Favourite* during the victorious action in 1761 against the *Achille* and the *Bouffonne*, and in 1762 – in the best traditions of his countryman Drake – he took part in the capture of a Spanish ship with treasure valued at half a million pounds. This was the richest prize of the Seven Years War and Philemon's share is said to have been the staggering sum of £65,000.[7] He promptly invested his newly found fortune in the acquisition of the exquisite estate of Sharpham in the heart of Devon near the village of Ashprington. The estate had over two miles of frontage on the River Dart and Philemon lost no time in employing a fashionable London architect, Sir Robert Taylor, to design a large neoclassical mansion for him on a ridge high above the woods with a commanding view over the surrounding countryside. The gardens were landscaped and laid out in the picturesque style of 'Capability' Brown. As a further sign of his social elevation, Philemon had a portrait of himself painted by Reynolds and one of his wife, Jane, who is depicted as 'Hebe'.

Sarah and Charles had to wait more than six years for the birth of their first son, Charles, on 20 January 1765. There may have been earlier pregnancies, but Charles's continuous service at sea could also explain the long delay in starting a family. Their second son, Baptist, appeared almost exactly a year later and was christened at St Mary's on

26 February 1766. This suggests that Sarah had taken up residence in Chatham before Charles took over the command of the Chatham-based *Yarmouth* in 1766. Five more children came in rapid succession. Another son was born and four daughters, the last of whom was Elizabeth. The move in 1771 to the Commissioner's handsome Queen Anne house at Chatham Dockyard not only provided this expanding family with ample accommodation but also brought considerable status. There were adjoining servants' quarters and a coach house and the ceiling above the main staircase was decorated with an impressive painting of an assembly of gods, which had been taken from the great cabin of the first-rate ship *Royal Sovereign*.

But despite these embellishments, the house had very much the feel of a comfortable family home. There were no cavernous reception halls, but rather a series of charming, low-ceilinged rooms with handsome fireplaces where friends might be entertained in the bosom of the family. The house was flooded with light from its large east- and west-facing windows. To the west there was a view over the busy dockyard to where the towering wooden skeletons of ships of war under construction lay on the slips. Beyond were the waters of the Medway. To the east, however, there was another world. On this side, the windows looked out on a delightful high-walled garden, a haven of peace and beauty in the midst of the constant bustle of the dockyard. In summer, when the air resounded with the shouts of the workers and the noise of hammers and a huge column of black smoke from the dockyard forges hung like a pall over its north-eastern extremities, the garden was full of the sound of pigeons and the scent of roses. The first-floor drawing-room opened on to a long veranda overlooking the garden with a highly polished wooden railing reminiscent of the rail of a ship. This was a place of privacy and calm, where a captain might pace as on his quarterdeck or a couple exchange a kiss.

The upper floors were the domain of the children and were given over to bedrooms, nurseries and schoolrooms. Sarah was fortunate in having given birth to seven healthy children in the space of ten years – many of her contemporaries would have envied her – but she could never blot out the guilt she felt over the loss of their second son, Baptist. During their first year at the dockyard, Charles and Sarah decided to pay a visit to the *Victory*, which had been built and launched at Chatham but, with the end of the war against France, had been placed 'in ordinary' on the Medway until she should be needed. The two little boys, Charles aged 7 and

Baptist aged 6, accompanied their parents. A brief entry under the heading for 'Deaths' in the *Gentleman's Magazine* describes the tragedy: '8 May 1772. Master Proby, son to Commissioner Proby, by falling into the hold of the *Victory* man of war, as he was at play with his brother on the deck, while his parents were in the cabin.'[8]

Elizabeth's early childhood was spent surrounded by a loving circle of brothers and sisters, but above all she was close to her sisters. Her eldest brother, Charles, was soon to be sent off to school at Westminster and then to Cambridge. Her second surviving brother, Francis Henry, was an even more shadowy figure for, like Jane Austen's brother, Edward, he seems to have been separated from the rest of the family and to have taken the name and arms of the Jermy family while he was still a schoolboy at Westminster. Later on he,too, went to Cambridge, under the name of Proby-Jermy, but he did not complete his degree and little more is known of him. It was Elizabeth's three sisters who were her closest companions and friends. The eldest was Sarah, then Charlotte and finally Beatrice and there was also a beloved nurse, Mrs Didham, who was later to share Elizabeth's closest confidences.

Elizabeth's earliest memories would have been of the sounds of the dockyard about her – the ringing of the muster bell, which summoned the workforce at set times throughout the day, the tramp of the marine guards who patrolled the walls and the grind of the wheels in the rope-walk, where thousands of feet of rope were produced annually. There was also the ever-present smell of hemp and tar mingled with the smoke from the forges when the wind blew from the north-east, and the all-pervasive marshy smell of the river that was overlaid with the unmistakable tang of the sea.

The dockyard was like a garrison. It was surrounded by high walls and heavily protected. Admission was through an imposing gatehouse, decorated with the royal coat of arms and defended by a guardhouse of marines. Within the walls was an area of nearly seventy acres, which was covered by the many buildings, slips and docks that were required for the construction of ships. There were also some officers' houses. During the eighteenth century the dockyard at Chatham became the largest employer of civilian labour in the south-east of England. The numbers fluctuated in times of war, but even in 1770 – a peacetime year – the dockyard was employing more than 1,300 people. Outside the dockyard there was a large military presence, which was stationed within the lines of fortifications that completely enclosed a sizeable area of the surrounding countryside and also separated the dockyard from the town. With a naval establishment of this importance, security was a top priority.

The daughters of the Commissioner became well used to passing through what was essentially a huge factory to reach the world that lay outside the dockyard. On Sundays, the Commissioner's carriage would take the whole family to church at St Mary's, which lay at a little distance from the dockyard gates, just short of the town of Chatham, but still within the 'lines'. The churchyard ran right down to the banks of the river, and in 1667 the windows of the church had been shattered by Dutch gunfire during the attack on the English fleet in the Medway. They were repaired at the expense of Samuel Pepys, who was working as Clerk of the Acts to the Navy Board and later became Secretary to the Admiralty. But the girls seldom visited the town of Chatham, which was no place for young ladies. It abounded in public houses and public women anxious to relieve returning sailors of their wages.

Apart from the rougher elements of its naval and dockyard population, there was another, more sinister side to Chatham and its surrounding area. From 1776 onwards, the Medway was used as an anchorage for the notorious prison hulks. The American War of Independence had deprived the British government of its penal colonies. Prisons were becoming acutely overcrowded and old warships seemed to offer an economical and secure alternative. The Medway was regarded as particularly suitable, with its ready supply of ageing hulks from the dockyard. In addition, the inhospitable nature of its surrounding marshlands strongly discouraged any attempt to escape.

The prison hulks rapidly became the hell-holes of the penal system. Prisoners were kept below much of the time, where there was little light or air. Huge numbers were housed in double or triple tiers of hammocks with an average sleeping space of 6' × 20" per man. The prison ship *Brunswick* at Chatham, for example, housed 460 men in these conditions. The food was appalling and there was no occupation of any kind. Not surprisingly, the mortality rate among prisoners was high and earned the hulks their nickname of 'floating tombs'. The bodies of those who died were buried in the nearby marshes. But the Commissioner's little daughters were probably completely unaware of the true purpose of the misty shapes that they could see anchored far away in the middle of the river. Nor were they probably ever told that the reason for the sudden alarms that occurred on dark and foggy winter nights was that some miserable wretch had decided, against all the odds, to make a bid for freedom.

Such was the reputation of Chatham that, although it was on the main coach road from London to Dover, few travellers chose to stay there. Instead they usually broke their journey at the neighbouring cathedral town of Rochester, which had a very different character and boasted several comfortable inns. For Sarah Proby and her daughters, outings to the shops and society of Rochester would have been only a short carriage drive away and would have provided a welcome change from the military atmosphere of Chatham.

The streets of Rochester were lined with elegant buildings, which included the assembly rooms, a circulating library and reading-room and even a theatre. Its ancient and beautiful cathedral, dating in part from the eleventh century, contributed to Rochester's strong ecclesiastical tradition. Before the sixteenth-century dissolution of the monasteries there had also been the Benedictine priory of St Andrew. On a high mound beside the river, and visible for many miles around, stood the ruins of Rochester's magnificent Norman castle, with its four towers and impressive ramparts, still largely intact today. Below it, sailing-ships and vessels of varying sizes plied their trade up and down the river or moored by the arches of the stone bridge, which prevented them from venturing further upstream. Summer boat trips down the Medway from Rochester bridge were a popular diversion.

The American War of Independence led to the resumption of naval hostilities between France and England which were to last from 1778 to 1783. Earlier, in 1773, the First Lord of the Admiralty, Lord Sandwich, had defined what he considered to be the role of the dockyard at Chatham. In a report made after a visit to Chatham by the Admiralty Board, he proposed that the best use for the dockyard was the building and repairing of ships, including those sent from the sister dockyards of Portsmouth and Plymouth. This meant that in time of war, when many ships were damaged, the workload of the dockyard was enormously increased and with it the duties of the Commissioner. Because of Chatham's location, however, and the problems created by the silting up of the Medway, it was no longer suitable as a base for the fleet.

The letter books of Chatham bear witness to the copious correspondence of Charles Proby and to the multitude of his responsibilities. Throughout the eighteenth century there was, on average, a new launching every year at Chatham. In 1774, for example, half of the major ships of war in existence had been built at Chatham.[9] A ship of the line in this the greatest age of fighting sail was a magnificent creature – 'the most honourable thing that man, as a gregarious animal, has ever produced'[10] – but it required large sums of money, years of work and a huge variety of skills and materials, all of which had to be co-ordinated under the authority of the Commissioner.

In his book on the Royal Dockyards,[11] Philip MacDougall notes that a typical 74-gun warship required over two thousand tons of oak, an amount representing four thousand trees. The *Victory*, which had a hundred and four guns, took six years to build and cost £63,176. She had four masts, twenty-seven miles of rigging and four acres of canvas. Everything, from the anchors to the flags, was made at Chatham by its workforce of shipwrights, caulkers, joiners, house carpenters, wheelwrights, plumbers, pitch heaters, bricklayers, labourers, sailmakers, scavelmen, riggers, blockmakers, locksmiths, sawyers, smiths, spinners and hatchellers. Before Charles Proby's time, there had been riots at Chatham, when the shipwrights went on strike over the quantity of 'chips' or bundles of wood that they were allowed to take home from the dockyard. In the summer of 1756 a large number of angry men had gathered outside the Commissioner's house and troops had had to be used to restore order.[12]

In 1775, shortly after Elizabeth's birth, Charles had to deal with his first major conflict with the workforce over the introduction of task work – the Navy Board's term for payment by results. Four hundred shipwrights came out on strike. The strike lasted several weeks but on this occasion there was no armed confrontation and Charles must take some of the credit for the shipwrights being gradually won over to the new method of working.

The dockyards were entirely run by naval officers who were civilian employees of the Navy Board – a body technically subordinate to the Admiralty. The Commissioner was appointed by the Navy Board and nominally a member of it but, as at sea, Charles's relations with his superiors and colleagues were not always happy. He wrote a letter of outraged dignity to the Admiralty when he felt that a senior colleague from the Navy Board was meddling in his business and that he had not been kept sufficiently informed of the details of a proposal to build new barracks at Chatham:

I am thoroughly convinced that your Lordship . . . did not mean, that I should (or think that I would) sit either at the Board or at any of the Out-Posts as a Cypher. . . . I think myself officially treated with disrespect by Commissioner Marsh. . . . his excuses on this head must be very extraordinary ones to convince me of the propriety of his design, as I have already had some reason to suspect his improper interference. . . . I am, My Lord from my present circumstances with a large family etc. in a situation (it may be thought) not to resent injuries, but I cannot be trampled upon.[13]

In 1778 Charles made an application to the Admiralty for promotion to a more active role on the Board. He was anxious to succeed to the powerful position of Controller of the Navy, which carried with it considerable prestige and the privilege, unique amongst the members of the Board, of permission to sit in the House of Commons. He refers wryly again to 'the largeness of my family and the smallness of my fortune'[14] – a not unfounded complaint when one considers that he maintained a considerable establishment, with very few private means, on an annual salary of £500 'with £12 for paper and firing.'[15] The application, however, did not meet with success. Charles's brother, Lord Carysfort, had died in 1772, which left him with little support in high places. He felt this professional setback keenly and he signs his letter to the Admiralty, expressing his mortification, as 'Your Lordship's obliged, disappointed humble servant.'[16]

None of these squalls, however, upset the serene life of the nursery, where Elizabeth spent her days. For her, the dockyard and its activities were nothing but a source of interest and excitement. As a small child she would certainly have witnessed one of the many launchings which took place regularly on the slips just in front of their house. On such occasions, a half holiday was declared and from noon the workshops fell silent, the noise of hammers and lathes replaced by the steady rumble of carriage wheels and the murmur of the gathering crowd. Elizabeth would have heard the constant opening and closing of the front door, which signalled the arrival of visitors, and the rise and fall of her father's voice as he welcomed the various members of the Navy Board and the Admiralty who had come down from London to witness the event.

Since very early morning, Sarah had been busy overseeing arrangements in the house to receive the all-powerful members of the Board, while upstairs her daughters clustered at the nursery window to watch the preparations on the slip. Outside, the huge bulk of the second-rate ship of the line, the *Formidable,* sat on great wooden supports. As yet she had neither masts nor sails, but she was decorated for this patriotic occasion with several enormous flags. The finely crafted timbers of her hull, pierced by three rows of gun decks, gleamed in the August sun and men swarmed around her keel, busily greasing the shipway with slabs of fat.

A small grandstand had been erected for distinguished visitors and there was a band. Beside their nurse in the tightly packed crowd, Elizabeth and Beatrice could have seen nothing but a sea of legs and backs, and so they would have been startled by the crashing sound as the final supports broke away, offering a momentary glimpse of the gracefully curved sides of the ship as she slid down the slipway into the water. The crowd exploded into loud cheers. Dozens of hats were tossed in the air and the two little girls, caught up in the excitement of the atmosphere, began to laugh and shout with the rest.[17]

Unlike many children at this period, Elizabeth and her sisters were never confined exclusively to the nursery. Sarah introduced the family to a daily ritual called 'Tag-Rag letters', which was perhaps a tradition of the Pownolls. It required each member of the family to note in a journal how he or she had occupied their day. Every evening, the family would meet to share their experiences and the children would be encouraged to state their opinions frankly. For Sarah and Charles the object of these occasions was to offer gentle parental guidance and imbue their offspring with a knowledge of the world. Charles took the moral upbringing of his children very seriously and regarded it as his personal domain. Sarah and Charles also strongly believed that there were great educational benefits to be gained by enabling their daughters, as they grew up, to meet as many members of the family and visiting acquaintances as possible. Amongst the stream of aunts, uncles and cousins, their swashbuckling Pownoll uncle, Philemon, must have been a great favourite. Elizabeth may well have envied her older cousin Jane for having such a father, whose presence seemed to fill the house with laughter and fun and who lavished gifts upon his only child. For his part, Philemon observed with approval the happy, closely knit family life of his nephews and nieces and their admirable mother.

By the time Philemon had been promoted to captain, his legendary courage, combined with his popularity with his officers, had given rise to various stories. One of them, cited by the Revd Pownoll Phipps,[18] concerns the fierce action that his ship, the *Apollo*, fought with the French frigate *L'Oiseau* in 1779. During the first broadside, Philemon was severely wounded by a musket-ball in the chest and was bleeding so heavily that his officers tried to persuade him to retire below decks. Instead, however, Philemon tested his lungs on the speaking-trumpet and finding them sound, declared that he would not leave the action. Thereupon, he pulled his shirt tails from his breeches, tied up the wound to stop the bleeding and continued to command the ship as if nothing had happened. Several months later, the musket-ball was said to be still in place. A year later the *Apollo* was once again in action, but this time her captain was killed. He was widely mourned by his fellow officers and by his neighbours in Devon.* A monument was erected to him in the church at Ashprington, but nowhere was he more sincerely mourned than at the Commissioner's house in Chatham.

In his will, Philemon demonstrated his confidence in Charles and Sarah by entrusting them with the upbringing of his daughter, Jane, whose mother had died in 1778 and who, as his only child, was a considerable heiress. But if Jane came to Chatham at all, her sojourn was a short one and in 1783, at the age of 19, she ran away to Gretna Green with a Devonshire neighbour called Edmund Bastard. It is unclear why the couple felt the need to elope, for the Bastards of Kitley were a well-established local family, but Edmund was a younger son and Jane's guardians may have suspected him of being a fortune-hunter. Whatever his motives, he made quite sure of his prize by hiring all the post horses in the district to foil pursuit.[19] The couple went to live at Sharpham, but Charles's later letters to Jane remain cold and businesslike and he did not hand over the large number of 'jewels, trinkets and plate' with which he had been entrusted until six years after the marriage.

For Elizabeth there was a far more terrible loss in store. On 3 August 1783, when she was not quite 9 years old, she lost her gentle, thoughtful mother. The most fitting thing that Charles could think of to say in the announcement of his wife's death in the *Gentleman's Magazine* was that 'she was a sister of the brave Capt. Pownall [*sic*], killed on board the Apollo frigate.'[20] Later he erected in the parish church a memorial to her and to their son Baptist, in which Sarah is described as having 'discharged every duty of Life in an exemplary manner'.

The death of Elizabeth's mother must inevitably have brought the sisters even closer together. Their elder brother, Charles, who had decided to become ordained, was away at Cambridge. There he found his first cousin, Baptist Proby, son of the Dean of Lichfield, who was the same age and who also planned to enter the church. The two boys had much in common and Charles rapidly made friends with Baptist and his

---

* The esteem with which Philemon was regarded locally is demonstrated by the decision in 1786 of Edward Pellew, the future Lord Exmouth, to christen his eldest son Pownoll in his memory.

numerous brothers and sisters. He also visited his older cousin, John Joshua, who was now Lord Carysfort and the owner of Elton Hall, which was only thirty miles from Cambridge. Charles's younger brother, Francis Henry, was still at school and increasingly involved with the Jermy family.

The Proby boys received most of their schooling in London – at Westminster – and although there were local educational establishments in Kent for girls at this time, Elizabeth and her sisters received their education from private teachers at home where, according to their father, they 'had every kind of Master to enable them to fill, with Credit, any Line of Life'.[21] Elizabeth spoke and wrote passable French and she was an excellent musician. She had good handwriting and expressed herself well on paper. The type of education for girls that was available locally is typified by the following advertisement in the June 1769 issue of the *Kentish Weekly Post and Canterbury Journal*: 'Mrs Price, from London, having engaged the House, next door to Mr Hatcher, Carpenter, without St. George's Gate, Canterbury, intends, This Day, being the 12th of June, to open a School for educating young ladies, (Boarders and Day scholars) in English, French and all Sorts of Needlework. Proper Masters to attend for Writing, Arithmetic, Dancing etc.'[22]

However, there is ample contemporary evidence that the range of interests and education for young ladies went far beyond the limited fare of Mrs Price. The cover of the January 1785 issue of the *Lady's Magazine*, which appeared as the female counterpart to the long-established monthly journal the *Gentleman's Magazine*, runs as follows:

The Lady's Magazine; or, Entertaining Companion for the FAIR SEX, appropriated solely for their Use and Amusement. . . This NUMBER contains

1 Cook's Voyage to the Pacific Ocean
2 Manners and Customs of the Inhabitants of Annamooka
3 Arrival at the Hapate Islands
4 A Series of Letters
5 Reprobation of Masks in Theatrical Exhibitions
6 Memoirs of a Young Lady
7 On Good-Nature
8 The Lady's Literary Exhibition
9 The Transformation of Love
10 Thoughts on the approach of Winter
11 History of Miss Harriet Worthy
12 Sur les Moeurs des Anciens & Modernes

13  A Walk by Moonlight
14  The Matron No. 144
15  The Beauties of Dryden
16  Discours à Mecenas
17  The Dangers of Dissipation
18  The Mother-in-Law
19  Of the Variolous Abscess
20  On Innoculation
21  The Novelist
22  Ornithology; or a new and complete History of English Birds
23  An Explanation of the Frontispiece
24  The English Garden displayed
25  Solutions to Enigmatical Questions
26  Enigmatical Question
27  The King's Speech
28  POETRY – Ode for the New Year – The Eye – The Butterfly and Bee –
    Miss— – Lines by an amiable Young Lady – On seeing a Robin-Red-
    Breast hopping about in a Garden – A Shepherd lamenting the Death
    of his Friend Colin – A Rebus – A Love Letter – Twah Si Amn – Rebus
    – An Enigma – A Rebus – A Rebus
29  Foreign News
30  Home News
31  American News
32  Births, Marriages, Deaths

This Number is embellished with the following Copper-Plates, viz.

1. A superb and elegant Frontispiece, designed by Burney, and engraved by one of the most capital Masters. 2. A beautiful engraved Title-Page 3. A new Pattern for working a Frock or Gown; And 4. A Song set to Music by Miss Eliza Turner.

Similarly the breadth of interests of people from Elizabeth's walk of life is closely reflected by the contents of the *Gentleman's Magazine*, which started publication in 1731 and was regularly read by both sexes. It included not only the all-absorbing announcements of births, deaths, marriages, promotions and bankruptcies, but also essays and poems, accounts of events both domestic and foreign, prices of goods and stocks, and advice on gardening.

With the death of his wife, Charles Proby realized that the responsibility for finding suitable husbands for his daughters now lay with him. Unlike their cousin, Jane Pownoll, they had little in the way of dowries. Nevertheless, the Resident Commissioner at Chatham enjoyed considerable prestige in his own domain and Charles took to entertaining young naval and military officers at his house on a regular basis. These evenings of music and conversation, frequently followed by dancing, became the focal point of the girls' lives and there were not many young officers who refused the invitation to pass an evening in the company of the Commissioner's four daughters.

Since the elopement of his niece, Charles's wariness of youthful passion had increased and he felt, more than ever, the need to protect his daughters. He had a horror of what he called 'dissipation', and outings to assemblies and private dances were strictly rationed. In a later letter, Charles makes his views on the dangers of too much dancing quite explicit. The girls were permitted to go to the Assembly in Rochester 'thrice before and twice after Christmas commencing with the King's Accession and ending with his Birthday. The going more frequently and all times during the Season would have been in my opinion, not only totally unnecessary but also calculated to have introduced them into the mania of Dissipation, so destructive of all Domestic Cares and Duties, Virtue in all its species.'[23]

There was also a more personal reason for Charles's reluctance to allow his daughters to attend the Rochester Assembly more than occasionally. After his long hours at his desk, Charles, no longer young, found evenings at the Assembly exhausting. He complains that the balls were 'extended to unreasonable hours and consequently inconvenient to those who live in our neighbourhood.'[24] Furthermore, Rochester society treated naval officers like himself with 'incivility and inattention'. He fumed at a regulation which stipulated that balls could not start before the arrival of the leading lights of the town, and he did not readily forgive the occasion when he and his family party were kept waiting for an hour and a half only to be upstaged by local dignitaries and deprived of their rightful turn to take the floor for the first minuet.

In the years immediately following the loss of her mother, Elizabeth grew up quickly. Because she was largely in the charge of her elder sisters, she was probably allowed to come down to the drawing-room in the evenings far younger than was usual and her musical accomplishments would have ensured her popularity. Her long dark hair had not yet been put up and her large blue eyes were more often than not cast demurely downwards but, as her father was beginning to realize, Elizabeth was already a force to be reckoned with. As the youngest of

four motherless girls, she doubtless often had her own way. Her
approach was quiet and subtle, but like her uncle, Philemon, she stuck
to her guns under fire.

During the summer of 1789, when all of England was watching the
advent of the French Revolution with a mixture of awe and admiration,
Elizabeth was observing, from her frequent position at the harpsichord,
the growing intimacy between her sister Charlotte and an army officer
called Thomas Pitcairn. Charlotte was not yet of age, but as soon as
Charles had given his consent to the match, preparations for the wedding were set in train. The marriage was to take place at the local parish
church of St Mary's, which Elizabeth had attended since early childhood and in whose shaded graveyard her mother lay buried. Three years
earlier there had been a terrible fire which had virtually destroyed the
beautiful fourteenth-century building, but the renovated and enlarged
version was now completed and offered ample space for a wedding. On
23 September 1789, Charlotte and Thomas were married before a con-
gregation of family and friends. The register was signed by Charles and
by two of Charlotte's sisters, Sarah and Beatrice. At 15 years old,
Elizabeth would have enjoyed every moment of this first family wedding
and, glancing around the church where many of Thomas's fellow officers stood resplendent in their scarlet uniforms, she may well have
dreamed of a similar destiny.

Within a year, Elizabeth's eldest sister, Sarah, had also fallen in love.
The object of her affections was Captain James Pigott, commander of
the *Alexander*, who was a naval officer of great ability and the sort of son-
in-law that Charles had always hoped for. Unlike Charles, James moved
up the ranks of promotion with ease and Sarah seemed assured of a
secure future. On 15 March 1791 Elizabeth saw the second of her sisters
walking down the aisle of St Mary's, and on this occasion it was she and
Beatrice who signed the register. Two months earlier, in January 1791,
there had been yet another family wedding. Elizabeth's brother Charles,
who had just been ordained priest at Peterborough, shared a double
wedding in the London church of St George's, Holborn, with a fellow
clergyman, but there is little to suggest that this was a particularly brilliant match. The two brides, who were sisters, were the daughters of a
Mr George Cherry, who is described as 'Commissioner for victualling
H. M. Navy.'[25] Unlike Charles Proby, however, George Cherry does not
feature in the list of administrative officers of the navy drawn up by
Clowes[26] and it seems likely that he occupied a relatively subordinate

position. Furthermore, at a time when girls who had any pretensions to beauty or wealth tended to marry young, the new Mrs Proby's advanced age of 27 sounds suspiciously elderly.

In 1792 Elizabeth was directly exposed, for the first time, to the ordeal of childbirth. Sarah Pigott, who, like Charlotte Pitcairn, had continued to live at her father's house at Chatham for some time after her marriage, was soon expecting a baby. Over the months of her pregnancy, Elizabeth would have watched her sister's changing shape with fascination, observing how her huge stomach now seemed obscenely out of proportion with the rest of her body. Sarah was the first close member of her family whom Elizabeth had seen in this condition and it would have brought home to her the realities of marriage. Sarah was radiantly happy, but Elizabeth was afraid. How could this slender body expel something so large without splitting in two? In the privacy of her bedroom, she may well have gazed at her own slight figure in the mirror and hoped that when her turn came, she would cope with the agony courageously.

Inside the Commissioner's house everyone was focused on the imminent birth. In between the management of the extensive repairs and construction work that were taking place at the dockyard, Charles would have contemplated the arrival of his first grandchild with pleasure. (Of course, the child would not be a Proby, but luckily Charles's wife, Susan, was also expecting a baby in August and that one would bear the family name.) A few days before the birth was expected, a visit from the local doctor created an uproar. He looked at Sarah's distended stomach and asked if he might make an examination. Sarah watched anxiously as he listened to her stomach, pressing and prodding it with his experienced hands. Then he stood up smiling. In his opinion, she was having twins. A few hours later, Sarah went into labour and gave birth to two little boys.

Meanwhile, events on the European stage were taking an increasingly sinister turn, but in England the French Revolution was initially regarded with approval and even seen as a step towards a more enlightened regime. Fox declared that it was 'the greatest and the best thing that had ever happened,'[27] while Wordsworth rejoiced that 'bliss was it in that dawn to be alive, but to be young was very heaven!'[28] Among politicians only Edmund Burke, in his 1790 publication, *Reflections on the French Revolution*, warned of bloodshed to come – a prophesy which proved to be all too accurate. Most people did not envisage another war with France and the government was far less preoccupied with the storming of the Bastille than it was with Spanish imperialism in Vancouver and the expansionist policies of Russia in Turkey.*

Catherine the Great, whose notorious sexual appetites often over-shadowed her more distinguished achievements, was frequently depicted with ribaldry in the English press. Throughout her reign, the relation-ship between Britain and Russia was suspended between strong com-mercial ties on the one hand and a suspicion of each other's intentions on the other. In 1780, in the middle of the war with France and Spain, the Baltic powers, Russian, Sweden and Denmark, had formed a league which they named the Armed Neutrality to resist British warships searching them for contraband of war. While this did not amount to a declaration of war, it did nothing to endear the opposing parties. But apart from such periodic coolnesses, there had been strong links between the Russian and British navies since the time of Peter the Great, who was enthusiastic that the members of his newly formed navy should learn as much as possible from the British. For the British, Russia was a useful source of raw materials. For example at Chatham, the dockyard relied heavily on supplies of hemp from southern Russia. This was shipped, often by shrewd Scottish businessmen, from St Petersburg or Riga and was used for the manufacture of rope in the huge rope-yard.

The onset in 1793 of the Reign of Terror in France jolted the British public into an awareness of the danger that was now looming far closer to home. People were horrified by the guillotining of Louis XVI and the bloodbath of massacres that followed, but this alone would not have driven France and Britain into war. What prompted the outbreak of war was the British reaction to the French defeat of the Austrians in Flanders, coupled with the French announcement of their intention to make war 'against all kings and on behalf of all peoples',[29] their capture of Antwerp, and their declaration of Antwerp and the estuary of the Schelde as open to world trade. The coast of Flanders was uncomfortably close to Britain and Britain protested, upon which the French declared war.

Chatham Dockyard was a hive of activity during the months leading up to the French declaration of war. The French defeat of the Prussians in

---

* The Russians made considerable territorial gains during the Russo-Turkish War of 1787–91. One of the most notable was the capture of the fortress of Ochakov, a key Turkish naval base situated on the north coast of the Black Sea on the bank of the Dnieper estuary. British concerns over Russian victories, in particular the capture of Ochakov, led to a political breach between Britain and Russia referred to as the 'Ochakov Crisis'.

1792 prompted the Admiralty and the Navy Board to start preparations for a war that was becoming increasingly likely. Twenty or more ships were commissioned at Chatham and numerous other vessels brought into service. By 1793, the workforce had grown to 1,800 and the town of Chatham was regularly visited by the press-gangs.[30] Once the war began, with its numerous naval engagements, the dockyard was continually busy with refits and repairs. The *Victory* had been refitted at Chatham in 1789, and in 1793 she became the flagship of Admiral Lord Hood and sailed with the fleet to Toulon. There he burnt the French fleet and departed, leaving the French Royalists at the mercy of their revolutionary compatriots, one of whom was a young artillery officer named Buonaparte.

Meanwhile the Prime Minister, William Pitt, was becoming increasingly concerned about the danger of a spread of revolutionary ideas to England. In 1794 he took the dramatic step of suspending the Habeas Corpus act, so that people could be arrested without trial, and in 1795 a law was passed which made speaking or writing against the government an act of treason. Public meetings without a licence were also forbidden. This curtailing of liberties, which were regarded as rights in eighteenth-century England, and the postponement of long-overdue reforms led to protests by the Whig opposition, which felt that the citizens of England were in danger of losing not only their traditional liberties but also freedom of speech.

The openness of society rapidly disappeared, with the appearance of government-employed spies and even *agents provocateurs*. In London 'Corresponding Societies' were set up by sympathizers with the ideals of *liberté, égalité* and *fraternité* to keep in touch with the French and to share democratic ideas – such as the notion of universal suffrage. In order to circumvent legislation against the formation of national societies, the members, as the name implies, kept in touch with both the French and with each other through correspondence. In early 1796, the political activist and Corresponding Society member, John Gale Jones, set out for the Medway towns, with Rochester and Chatham as his chief destinations. His colleague, John Binns, headed for the equally important naval town of Portsmouth. Jones may have hoped to make contact with some of the ever-growing number of French prisoners on the Medway prison hulks, many of whom were supporters of the Revolution. He almost certainly wanted to talk to naval seamen. He also expected to find people sympathetic to his radical ideas amongst the large workforce at the dockyard, whose recent actions reflected the volatile mood of the nation.

A few months earlier there had been a riot at the weekly market in Chatham over the price of meat, which had been supported by the locally based regiment of militia. At the same time, the six hundred shipwrights of Chatham had come out on strike over the employment of house-carpenters to fulfil some of their duties. The strike lasted nearly a month and the Navy Board was obliged to make concessions to the shipwrights' demands in order to resolve it. Late in 1795, Charles Proby was confronted with yet more problems with his workforce. A bill was pasted on a wall of the dockyard protesting against the laws recently passed by Pitt. The bill claimed that the laws 'completely deprive the People of the Liberty of speech, of *writing, printing, preaching* or *assembly* in any respect whatever to obtain redress of Grievances however arbitrary or oppressive without the presence of a magistrate'.[31] Charles had summoned all the members of his workforce in the early morning and had unwisely attempted to get them to sign a petition to the King in favour of the new laws, but in nearby Rochester, the Mayor had placed a petition opposing them in the guildhall for signing. The next day the workers refused to go to work: instead they occupied the lower spinning house where, despite a personal intervention from Charles, they declined to sign his petition. At noon, they departed in a body for Rochester and signed the opposing document.[32]

Elizabeth cannot have been unaware of these tensions, nor of the potential for violence as the shock waves of the French Revolution began to rock English society. Chatham was dirtier and rougher than ever, and there may have been times when she and her sisters felt uneasy driving through its narrow High Street on their way to Rochester in their father's carriage. Harassed and overworked, Charles had no time to take his daughters to visit London or to make the considerable cross-country journey to his childhood home at Elton. He may have hoped that their elder brother, Charles, now that he was settled with a wife in the prosperous living of Stanwick, would invite the two younger girls, Beatrice and Elizabeth, to stay. At Stanwick Rectory, which was only a few miles from Elton Hall, their Proby connections would gain them immediate entry into local society. Furthermore, their brother Charles was on excellent terms with their cousin, Lord Carysfort.

John Joshua, Lord Carysfort, inhabited a world of wealth, power and politics that was a far cry from the grind of dockyard administration. For Elizabeth and her siblings during childhood, their much older cousin John Joshua would have played a rather similar role to that of

21

their uncle, Philemon Pownoll. In their childish eyes the main differences between the newly rich naval officer and the heir to the Proby and Allen estates would have been age and physique. Both men had the glamour and charisma that come with success.

Like his cousin Charles, John Joshua was educated at Westminster and Cambridge. In 1772, at the age of 21, he inherited Elton Hall, the vast Irish estates of the Allens and the Irish title of Lord Carysfort. At 22 he took his seat in the Irish House of Lords and became a prominent debater. His many-sided talents did not pass unnoticed and honours were heaped upon him. He was elected a Knight of St Patrick and a fellow of the Royal Society. In 1774, the year of Elizabeth's birth, he married another Elizabeth, a raven-haired beauty from County Tipperary who was to bear him six children.

The Commissioner bore a strong physical resemblance to his brother, the late Lord Carysfort, which his nephew, John Joshua, may well have found endearing. John Joshua himself was lean and fine-featured and his Allen blood had endowed him with a Celtic liveliness of speech and gesture that was very different from his cousin Charles's slower pace. With his cousins, too, though he rarely saw them, John Joshua felt the indefinable bonds of kinship. These feelings were doubtless re-enforced as he became more closely acquainted with his cousin Charles. John Joshua's magic world was shattered when his wife, the beautiful Elizabeth Osborne, suddenly died in 1783. His political pursuits and his intellectual and artistic interests lost their savour and his large houses in England and Ireland seemed horribly empty. He desperately needed a change and the unexpected opportunity to visit Russia on a special mission seemed like a godsend.

For over a year John Joshua travelled in Russia or frequented the society of St Petersburg. His visit was never intended to be of such long duration, but, if the contemporary travel diary of an Oxford don is to be believed, he became enamoured of the wife of the Neapolitan Ambassador, the Duke of Sierra Capriola,* and kept delaying his departure.[33] He also met Catherine the Great and cannot have failed to be fascinated by the extraordinary brilliance of the Russian court at that time. It was John Joshua who suggested to the Empress in 1785 that she lacked a proper representation of English pictures in her collection in the

* This was the Duke's first wife, Maria Adelaide del Carretto di Camerano. After her death the Duke married, in 1788, a Russian, Princess Anna Aleksandrovna Viazemskaya.

Hermitage and who, on his return to England, arranged for Reynolds to paint a picture for her and for her favourite, Prince Potemkin. The choice for Potemkin was a happy one, a copy of a picture of Carysfort's own, depicting a voluptuous maiden coyly shielding her face while Cupid pulls the ribbons of her dress to reveal yet more of her magnificent bosom (Plate 17). The choice for the Empress was less successful. The subject was the infant Hercules strangling a serpent and was intended as an allegorical allusion to the exertions of the emerging Russian empire, but the Empress was not altogether convinced of the appropriateness of this portrayal.[34]

When John Joshua finally left St Petersburg, he looked back on his time there with affection and he remained deeply interested in Russia. On his return, he set about courting his second wife. The sharper tongues of London society were quick to make fun of John Joshua's love-making, possibly because the object of his attentions was Elizabeth Grenville, a member of the formidable Grenville family. Her father had been Prime Minister and two of her brothers, George and William, were created Marquess of Buckingham and Lord Grenville respectively. In his description of a London dinner party in 1787, Gilbert Elliot wrote:

> We had another pair of lovers viz. Lord Carysfort and Miss Grenville, who are rather come to a sober time of life for the amusement of courtship, but they did their best. She is much fallen off, though she never was beautiful. When Mrs Sheridan and her sister were singing these words, which they dwelt on a long time 'This may soothe, but cannot cure, my pain' Lord Carysfort fixed his widower's eyes, in a most languishing, amorous and significant manner on his love, who did not seem at all at a loss to understand his glances.[35]

Despite the gossips, John Joshua's efforts met with success and in marrying a Grenville, he became an established member of an all-powerful political elite. Two years after his second marriage, John Joshua received an Irish earldom and was appointed joint guardian and keeper of the rolls in Ireland. He was also sworn in as a member of the Irish Privy Council. But by now he was longing to enter the larger political scene in England and since he was still a commoner in England, he was able to stand for, and won, a seat in the House of Commons.

As he laboured through his enormous correspondence at the dockyard, Charles may have wished that he could launch his two remaining unmarried daughters in the glittering society inhabited by John Joshua and Elizabeth Carysfort. But the tragic death of his daughter-in-law, Susan, giving birth to her second child would have put paid to any plans he may have had to send Beatrice and Elizabeth to Stanwick. He would not have thought it appropriate to send them to Elton alone. He had also heard from his son, Charles, that he was considering remarriage to his first cousin, Catherine Proby, the sister of Baptist. It was clearly not the right moment to impose on him.

Throughout 1795, therefore, it appears that the two younger girls remained at Chatham. Sarah and James Pigott had bought a house at Beddington in Surrey, where they moved with their two sons, but Charlotte, whose married status made her an ideal chaperone, was still living at home. She had no children and there were concerns about the health of her husband, Thomas, but this, as yet, was only a distant cloud. In the meantime, the sisters continued to read and talk, to play music and sing and to entertain young officers, who escorted them to watch military manoeuvres and horse-races on Chatham Lines, and accompanied them on long walks over the hills above the dockyard. Neither Elizabeth nor her family could have guessed how soon the harmony of their family life was going to be shattered.

# CHAPTER TWO

# *Pavel*

## *1767–1795*

In 1774 a precocious 7-year-old boy wrote the following letter to his father: 'I ask your parental blessing and at the same time I inform you that we are all, thank God, in good health and I also inform you, dear Sir my Father, that I can speak French and I am learning how to dance. . . .'[1]

The boy's name was Pavel Chichagov and his father was at that time a rear-admiral and the commander of the fortress and naval base of Kronstadt on Kotlin Island, which lies in the Gulf of Finland about twenty miles due west of St Petersburg. From his earliest years it had been evident to his parents and their household that Pavel was a child out of the ordinary. When, aged 3, he made a miraculous recovery from smallpox, the more superstitious inhabitants of the neighbourhood decided that his escape had been due to the propitious composition of his horoscope, for he had been born on 8 July,* which was the anniversary of Peter the Great's epic victory in 1709 over the Swedes at Poltava. His two elder brothers, however, died and Pavel's complexion was to bear the traces of smallpox for the rest of his life.

At the time of Pavel's birth in 1767, his father was an impoverished naval officer whose family was living, for economic reasons, in one of the least salubrious suburbs of St Petersburg. He had no fortune and had inherited nothing but a few acres of unproductive land near Kazan with about thirty serfs. But though impecunious, the Chichagov family had an honourable record and could be counted among the ranks of the nobility. The family of Pavel's grandfather, Jacob Chichagov, came originally from the ancient merchant town of Kostroma on the banks of the Volga and Jacob had been a companion in arms of Peter the Great. Pavel's father, Vasilii, was one of the first generation of Russians to receive a naval education. He attended the school of navigation in Moscow founded by Peter the Great and was destined for a career in the emerging Russian navy.

* New Style (see also note on p. 231).

It is possible that the Chichagov family owed its noble status to the military service of Pavel's grandfather. During his reign, from 1682 to 1725,* Peter the Great entirely reorganized Russian society. All officers automatically became hereditary nobles and were exempted from taxation, recruit duty and corporal punishment. In return, they and their descendants were expected to serve the state in the armed forces or the civil service. It was also possible for those in the civil service to obtain nobility if they rose sufficiently high – a system which enabled talented people of any background to become members of the aristocracy. Peter drew up a Table of Ranks which showed the exact equivalencies between civil and military ranks and the degrees of nobility conferred by each. Before his reign, the aristocracy had been composed of the boyars – the feudal landowners – and princely families who traced their ancestry to the early kings of Russia before the invasions of the Tartars. There had also always been favourites ennobled at the whim of an absolute monarch. Consequently, although many old and famous names could still be found in the court of Peter, there were many new ones.

Peter's social reorganization should not, however, be mistaken for a move towards a greater sharing of power with the nobles. In Russia this concept had never existed. The monarch was absolute. As landowners had the power of life and death over their serfs, so the Tsar had supreme power over the nobles. Similarly the institutions of central government were entirely controlled by the Tsar. There were no elected representatives, only advisers who were often favourites like Prince Menshikov. Menshikov, who had been the former lover of Peter's wife – later the Empress Catherine I – was the son of a humble stable hand, but he became Peter's closest confidant. Because of his frequent absences on campaign, Peter set up a senate in 1711 which was also to be the supreme court of appeal. Later, in 1722, he created the position of procurator-general – an official who confirmed the decrees of the senate and ensured that laws were enforced – but the Senate only existed to carry out the wishes of the Tsar. Similarly, Peter's division of government administration into various 'Colleges' for Foreign Affairs, War, Navy, Mining and Manufacture, Revenue, Control, State Expenditure, Commerce, and Justice, each with a board and a chairman, was not a significant step towards liberalization.[2]

---

* Peter the Great was crowned Tsar in 1682. In 1721 he assumed the title of Emperor, which was used by his successors together with the traditional Russian title of Tsar.

Because the intervening rulers between Peter and Catherine the Great made only minor concessions to democracy, Catherine's hold over her subjects was as autocratic as that of any of her predecessors. During his short reign, Catherine's husband, Peter III, had released the nobility from obligatory state service except in time of war. Catherine retained this modification, which still allowed for all the previous exemptions. Some nobles retired to their estates, but many preferred the rich pickings at the court of St Petersburg. At the beginning of her reign in 1762, the German-born Catherine was anxious to give Russia, with its barbaric institution of serfdom, a more enlightened system of government. After several years of deliberation, the lot of the serfs was barely changed, but a new charter was produced for the nobles which permitted them to elect local assemblies in the provinces and ordered the establishment of a book in which noble families were recorded. Despite these dispensations, however, the Empress retained supreme authority, which was only very partially shared by her nine-member State Council.

Two years before Pavel was born, Vasilii was appointed by Catherine the Great to lead a Russian expedition to find a sea route from Arkhangel'sk to North America via the Arctic Ocean. The expedition was then to proceed through the Bering Strait to Kamchatka, on the far eastern coast of Siberia. The plans were drawn up by the celebrated Russian scientist Lomonosov, and the three corvettes constructed for the voyage were named after their commanders, Chichagov, Panov and Babaiev. Their equipment was scanty and their path constantly jeopardized by huge icebergs, but the College of the Admiralty nevertheless hoped that some prestigious discovery would emerge from the expedition and were sorely disappointed when Vasilii, having reached 80° N, was forced to turn back without achieving any particular objective. A second expedition was mounted the following year, but the tenacity and courage of the crews were thwarted by the shortcomings of their equipment. In 1768, Vasilii was appointed the commander of the port of Archangel. Two years later he was promoted to rear-admiral and transferred to become first the commander of the naval base at Revel, close to present-day Tallinn, and subsequently the commander at Kronstadt.

Vasilii enjoyed a high personal reputation. His honesty and integrity were unusual attributes in the sycophantic society of St Petersburg and furthermore, in a navy that had few experienced officers, he had good professional credentials. Unlike many of his contemporaries, he shunned social life, preferring to live modestly at home, and he made an appearance

27

at court only when commanded to do so by the Empress. Pavel idolized his father and in return Vasilii seems to have treated his brilliant but highly strung child with great understanding.

Pavel's early years were spent amongst the nurses and servants that abounded in the households of even the most needy Russian gentlemen. His mother, Catherine, was the daughter of a German architect who had settled in Russia. She was twelve years younger than Vasilii, whom she had met when he was 40 and she was the 28-year-old widow of a naval officer. Catherine's independence of outlook was far ahead of her Russian contemporaries, over many of whom the shadow of the Tartars, with their oriental attitude to women, still hovered. In the sophisticated society of St Petersburg, where earlier Peter the Great had forced the old-fashioned nobles to cut their beards and to permit their wives to appear in society, women enjoyed the status of their Western counterparts, but in the more provincial world in which Vasilii grew up, Catherine's Saxon heritage of independence made her exceptional. She had a German love of order and a will for action that contrasted strongly with the more passive approach expected of Russian women. In other ways, as a second-generation immigrant, she was well-integrated with Russian life. Russian was spoken at home and she was a member of the Orthodox Church. The marriage was soon blessed with children and the Chichagovs already had four sons when they lost the two eldest from smallpox in 1770. Pavel and his younger brother, Peter, survived and three more brothers were born in the following years.

At the age of 7, Pavel left the world of the nursery and had his first experience of formal education at the hands of a Frenchman, Monsieur Aumon, who had set himself up as a private tutor in Kronstadt and took weekly boarders. It was also Pavel's first experience of injustice. Before the first week was over, he had been punished for owning up to some trifling misdemeanour in the classroom. He was outraged and refused to return to school after the weekend. Every effort was made to persuade him to change his mind, but he was prepared to endure threats and beatings rather than submit to a master whom he considered unjust. The matter was finally resolved only when Monsieur Aumon was summoned to the house by Pavel's parents and forbidden to inflict any further corporal punishment on him.

Meanwhile Vasilii's career was advancing. His unsuccessful expeditions to the Arctic were forgotten and he regained the favour of the Empress with a successful minor role in the naval war with Turkey, for which he received a decoration. The main honours of Çeshme,* however, went to Aleksei Orlov, the brother of the Empress's favourite, Grigorii Orlov. The lot of the Chichagov family was dramatically improved when Vasilii was appointed to the College of the Admiralty and in 1776 they exchanged the ramshackle naval base at Kronstadt, which had been their home during his period of command, for the stunning capital of St Petersburg. Vasilii was now lodged at government expense and although his salary was still small, this was compensated for by a generous supply of rations to feed the large number of servants that were thought to be appropriate to his rank. Like their colleagues, the Chichagovs doubtless benefited from the universally accepted practice of employing rather fewer servants in order to take advantage of the abundance of rations for themselves. Captains and admirals were also entitled to the use of a boat with a crew for their household shopping, a personal guard of honour and access to subsidized medical supplies.

St Petersburg had been built as Peter the Great's 'window on Europe'. Thousands of workmen died to realize Peter's dream of a European-style city with the maritime potential that he had observed in so many of the great cities he had visited during his time in Europe. But once established on its combination of marshes and islands, St Petersburg grew to be one of the most beautiful cities in the world, adorned with magnificent palaces and churches and interlaced with the winding waterways and canals that earned it the title of the Venice of the North. In winter it was ice-bound for many months, wreathed in mists and locked into a mysterious cold white beauty of its own. In summer the sparkling waters of the Neva and the magic of the gleaming summer nights were unforgettable.

Pavel was sent to board at the prestigious St Peter's school for boys – judged the best in the capital, where most of the instruction was in German. His younger brothers were sent to a cheaper, German-run school, which was considered adequate for the more elementary stage of their education. At the age of 9, Pavel's chief interests were in the excellent food and the abundant free time, supplemented by frequent national

---

* A sea battle that took place in Çeshme Bay on 7 July 1770, during the Russo-Turkish War of 1768–74. On 6 July, the Turkish fleet fled before the Russians and took shelter in Çeshme Bay in the Chios Channel of the Aegean Sea. Subsequent attacks by Russian fireships led to the destruction or capture of the entire Turkish fleet. The Turks lost more than 10,000 men while the Russians lost only eleven. As a result of this battle, the Russians gained supremacy of the Aegean Sea.

and religious holidays. He also discovered a passion for mathematics, but by the end of two years he had already completed the final year and exhausted the pedagogical resources of his teachers. His parents, proud but baffled by the brilliance of their son, had no choice but to give in to his pleas to be removed from school at the age of 11 to pursue, with private teachers, a curriculum of his own choosing. Given his admiration for his father, it was not surprising that Pavel decided to apply himself to studies that would prepare him for a naval career. In his early teens Pavel and his brother Peter enjoyed a short period as ensigns in the Imperial Guard, but his father decided that at 14 Pavel was sufficiently well-educated to take up the appointment of naval adjutant and through the influence of some of his powerful contacts managed to have Pavel attached to his personal suite.

For Pavel entry into the navy was the fulfilment of his dearest wish. He was ambitious and his brief educational experiences had only reinforced his belief in his own abilities. He was convinced that, like his father, he would succeed in his chosen profession. But the deference of his teachers, the awe of his younger brothers and even the well-meant consideration of his parents had done little to prepare this prickly, hot-tempered young man for the rough and tumble of the outside world. The proximity of paternal influence only perpetuated the problem.

One of the Empress's more inspired initiatives to exercise her fleet in peacetime was the annual dispatch of a squadron to cruise in the Mediterranean. In 1782 Vasilii, now a vice-admiral, was nominated to command the squadron of five ships of the line and two frigates which was sent to relieve the Russian squadron that had wintered at Leghorn, on the coast of Tuscany, and was due to return to Kronstadt. Pavel found himself for the first time at sea and was violently seasick, but once he had become accustomed to the ship, he settled down to revel in what was little less than a nautical version of the Grand Tour. The first port of call was Copenhagen, followed by Deal, Lisbon and finally Leghorn. At Lisbon the Admiral and his officers were royally entertained by the Portuguese port authorities with sumptuous meals and excursions ashore, where a dark-eyed Portuguese beauty, whose luxuriant hair reached to the floor, made a lasting impression on the youthful adjutant. From Leghorn, Pavel was able to visit Florence and Pisa and to participate in the social activities prompted by the presence in Italy of a Russian squadron. The Grand Duke Leopold, the ruler of Tuscany, made an official visit on board and was received with all the appropriate honours. The balmy summer evenings were devoted to other amusements – concerts, operas and theatres. Pavel developed a taste for Italian songs and, inevitably, fell in love with an actress.

It was not until the spring of 1784 that Pavel was reluctantly torn away from what he regarded as an earthly paradise and the squadron returned to Kronstadt. The experiences of the previous year had only served to enflame Pavel's passion for the navy and as the ice began to form around Kronstadt and the Russian fleet was, as usual, immobilized for the next six or seven months, he returned home to St Petersburg for further studies. During this time, he became friendly with a young artillery officer called Gur'ev, who was a gifted mathematician and agreed to give him private lessons free of charge.

The long northern winter set in. The Neva froze solid and rapidly became a busy thoroughfare for carriages and sledges. As the days grew shorter, the wealthier inhabitants of the city withdrew to the warmth and comfort of their houses only emerging, swathed in furs, for essential tasks or brisk recreation. The poorer members of the population, who were obliged to remain on the streets by their occupation or through necessity, clustered in heavy sheepskins around improvized braziers and sought by night what shelter they could find from the icy blast of winter.

The Empress had long since left her summer palace at Tsarskoe Selo and the busy winter season of the court was well under way. The reception rooms of the Winter Palace were constantly thronged as the Empress received and entertained an endless stream of officers, officials and nobles from the many different parts of her Empire. There were also large numbers of foreign dignitaries and diplomats, to whom she regularly granted audiences. At 55 Catherine the Great was at the height of her powers. Despite her theoretical support for enlightenment and her well-known correspondence with Voltaire, she now believed that the only way to rule the vast and disparate empire that she had wrested from her husband was by autocracy. Progress in Russia was more readily achieved by a judicious use of the carrot and the stick than by open debate and a division of powers. Since she first came to the throne in 1762 through the conspiracy of the Orlov brothers, who also arranged for the early demise of her husband, Peter III, the Empress's political views had changed, but her personal appetites remained unaltered. The lusty Grigorii Orlov, who had enjoyed her favours for over ten years, had now been replaced by a man of far greater calibre – Grigorii Potemkin. Potemkin, who became a prince and was heaped with honours, fulfilled

a multiplicity of roles for the Empress. He was a brilliant and courageous man and a shrewd judge of human nature. He was initially the
Empress's lover and it is possible that he also became her husband.
When, however, the physical side of their relationship cooled, he
remained as the counsellor to whom she turned for advice over policies and people – she even allowed him to select his successors in her
bedchamber. After his annexation of the Crimea, she constructed a
magnificent palace for him in St Petersburg called the Tauride Palace in
recognition of his achievements in 'Tauris' or Crimea.

As the Christmas season approached, the imperial court was enlivened
by splendid balls and dinners, where the beauty and talent of St
Petersburg society could be found in large numbers. The men were
resplendent in their uniforms and decorations, while the women flaunted
the latest Paris fashions and wore so many priceless jewels that foreign
observers were astounded. The members of the quiet and studious
Chichagov household, however, were rarely seen at these occasions. In the
evenings, the Chichagov boys and their parents would gather around the
high, tiled stove in the sitting-room to talk and read. Perhaps Vasilii also
busied himself with arranging the collection of arms that he had purchased in Italy, while his wife repaired the clothing of the boys. With five
hungry, growing young men as yet dependent on their father's slender
resources, there was never enough money to go round.

The taste of the high life that Pavel had enjoyed during his voyage to
Italy had left him more aware than ever of the modesty of his family's
means. Vasilii doubtless sensed this and he may have tried to instil in
Pavel the belief that personal honour was a far greater treasure than
wealth and that no worldly gains could ever replace dignity and justice.
Vasilii himself embodied many of these values. He was able and wise in
the ways of the world, but he was largely uninterested in money and
influence. As a result, he was well-liked by many people in high places
who were doubtless received, from time to time, at the Chichagov house.
Such guests would have found the modesty and simplicity of their host
particularly congenial after the machinations of life at court. Pavel, too,
would have enjoyed pitting his wits against these older men. He was
fearless in debate to the point of rashness and was not incapable of dis-
rupting an evening's entertainment by flaring up at some slight, real or
imaginary. Probably Vasilii and Catherine ignored these outbursts. As
loving parents, they would have understood the frustration and insecu-
rity that were their origin, but others were less tolerant, and Pavel early

acquired a reputation for intellectual ability coupled with a sense of personal dignity that verged on arrogance.

Throughout the six to seven months of winter, officers and men of the Russian navy were condemned to inactivity. The Baltic fleet was only operational during the short summer season, when the ports were free of ice. In practice this meant that the fleet rarely got under way until July, because even repairs were seldom carried out during the winter. Kronstadt was the key naval base, thanks to its strategic position in the Gulf of Finland, effectively blocking the passage to St Petersburg. Years of neglect had greatly reduced the effectiveness of its fortifications, but in any case the real defences of the capital lay in the surrounding shoals and sandbanks that made navigation, by the uninitiated, hazardous in the extreme. Much of the Baltic fleet was anchored at Kronstadt, but a small part was also kept to the west, in the port of Revel. Revel had the advantage of being ice-free earlier in the year than Kronstadt, but its capacity was limited to about ten ships of the line and a few smaller craft. After the war with Turkey, Russia gained the right to maintain a year-round naval presence in the Black Sea, but in order to accomplish this, Russian ships were obliged to sail half-way around Europe from their home base in the Baltic. This meant that the Russian navy was constantly confronted with the choice between a united force in the Baltic or a force divided between north and south.

Quite apart from the climate and the problems presented by the vast distances between Russia's two spheres of naval influence, the Russian navy suffered from a lack of experienced officers and men. Unlike Britain, landlocked Russia had no maritime tradition; there was no automatic supply of officers and men who had sailed since childhood on merchant or naval ships, nor was there a Russian equivalent to the repository of shipbuilding skills that existed in Britain's numerous naval and civilian dockyards. For most Russians, the sea was an alien element. At the beginning of the eighteenth century, Peter the Great created the Russian navy from nothing and employed large numbers of foreign workmen to build its ships. A high proportion of the master craftsmen were British and there were also some British naval officers, but Peter's real objective was to train Russians in seamanship and navigation so that the fleet could operate without foreigners. To this end, he requested the British government to allow young Russians to serve on British ships and employed a Scottish professor of mathematics to set up the school of navigation in Moscow.

Throughout the eighteenth century, the Russian navy continually looked to the British navy as its model. It was, however, Catherine the Great who tried to combat the shortfall in professional skills by reinstating Peter's practice of placing young Russians for training on British naval ships, and by launching, through her ambassador in London, the first concerted recruitment drive for British naval officers. The result was that between 1764 and 1772 around fifty British officers joined the Russian navy.[3] During the following years, despite the periodic tensions between the Russian and British governments, many more were recruited. Pavel, therefore, as a member of a naval family, grew up in an atmosphere of respect and admiration for the nautical skills of the British, which so far surpassed those of the Russians. For example, it was commonly known that the Russian naval victory over the Turks at Çeshme in 1770 owed much to the brilliant action of Rear-Admiral Samuel Greig, supported by the British captains Dugdale and Mackenzie. It was also known that the two Russian squadrons that composed the Mediterranean fleet had been comprehensively refitted at Portsmouth and at British-held Minorca, before their successful encounter with the Turks. Such superiority does not necessarily engender affection and the Empress was careful to take the sensibilities of her Russian officers into account. For Pavel, the British aroused a curious conflict of emotions that combined profound respect and personal affection with professional jealousy and a sneaking sense of inferiority that frequently manifested itself in tirades against his own countrymen.

It was against this background that the Empress in 1788 decided to appoint Greig, now a full admiral, to command the fleet which was destined for the Mediterranean to participate in the renewed hostilities against the Turks that had created such concern in England. The portion of the fleet that was to remain in the Baltic was placed in June under the command of Vasilii. King Gustav III of Sweden, encouraged by British diplomatic efforts aimed at creating a diversion to curtail Russian expansion in the Black Sea, now confirmed the suspicions of the Empress and declared war on Russia. By June the Swedish fleet was already afloat and the Empress was confronted with a serious threat to national security. Her subsequent actions clearly betrayed her assessment of the relative abilities of Admirals Greig and Chichagov. Greig's departure to the Mediterranean was postponed and he was placed in command of all the ships in the Baltic. Vasilii, on the other hand, was relieved of his command and appointed, once more, as the commander of

Kronstadt. This was a bitter blow to Vasilii and his family and they were further humiliated by the fact that Greig was a foreigner.

Throughout 1788, the Russian and Swedish fleets fought indecisively. The Russians had the worst of it in a major engagement at Hogland. Later, at Sveaborg, they fared rather better, but failed to destroy the Swedish fleet as they had hoped. Greig was deeply disappointed and died of a fever shortly afterwards on board his ship. He was given a hero's funeral and in 1789 the Empress once more gave the command of the sailing fleet to Vasilii, but the command of the newly constructed galley fleet was given to a German, the Prince of Nassau-Siegen. Pavel sailed on his father's ship and was soon to have his first taste of naval warfare. On 25 July, as they approached the coast of Sweden, a small Danish cruiser informed them that the Swedish fleet was close at hand near the island of Öland. Pavel's spirits soared as he envisaged the impending engagement where, at long last, he would be able to see in action the theories that he had studied for so long. But the encounter with the Swedes was a far cry from the fiery engagement of his dreams and produced only a lengthy stand-off between the two fleets, interspersed with sporadic skirmishes. Casualties were light, and bursting guns accounted for half of the 34 killed and 176 wounded on the Russian side. The Empress had also hoped for something better and she sent Vasilii a sharp rebuke: 'We cannot observe, without disappointment, that such a considerable armament and one made at so much cost has not produced the result which we had the right to expect, and we regret to see that the loss of our brave and faithful subjects has not been compensated for by a proportional success.'[4]

Chastened, Vasilii returned to his station. The Empress had outlined a daring plan for a landing, but strong winds made it impossible for Vasilii to carry out her wishes. Meanwhile the news came of a major Russian naval victory at Rotchensalm, where the galley fleet under the Prince of Nassau-Siegen had defeated a Swedish force under the eyes of their King and taken several ships, including the admiral's flagship and 1,400 prisoners. As the summer season ended, the weather grew increasingly unpleasant and every day brought new problems and damage to the fleet. Storms were frequent, forcing many ships to retire, and after several uncomfortable weeks, Vasilii decided to withdraw the remnants of his fleet to Revel and Kronstadt. The Empress and her advisers, however, were dissatisfied and kept Vasilii cruising outside Revel for some time longer. He did not receive the order to disarm until the end of November.

Vasilii and Pavel returned to St Petersburg in low spirits. The family had sustained a tragic loss. Pavel's younger brother, 17-year-old Grigorii, had died just three days before the order for disarmament was given and his mother, Catherine, was plunged in a state of deep depression. She cared nothing for the Empress's displeasure nor for her husband's professional problems, and remained shut in her room weeping for much of the day. The members of the family took it in turn to sit with her, but as soon as she was left alone, the tears returned.

This first experience of real naval life gave Pavel much food for thought. While passionately loyal to his father, he had experienced at first hand the shortcomings of the Russian fleet. As the son of the commander, serving on his flagship, Pavel was uniquely well placed to observe the organization of the fleet at close quarters. In the privacy of his cabin, Vasilii often shared his thoughts and concerns with his son. In Pavel's precise, well-ordered mind, with a love of action so similar to that of his monarch, the desire to reform the Russian navy was born. But at this stage, his chief criticisms were for the chain of command which enabled the uninformed advisers of the Empress to impose impracticable and unrealistic objectives on the fleet. Their ignorance of sailing conditions had caused huge damage and losses by keeping the fleet at sea during the worst season of the year, while the enemy, more wisely, conserved their forces in port. Far away in France a revolution was raging and despite the Empress's efforts to minimize the infiltration of revolutionary ideas into Russia, Pavel was able to become familiar with the works of Voltaire and Rousseau, and became a fervent admirer of the ideals of personal liberty.

During the winter, Vasilii was summoned several times by the Empress. She was concerned by rumours of the strength of the Swedish fleet and feared that it might make an early attack on the ten-ship squadron at Revel before the Russian fleet was prepared. Vasilii's honesty and professionalism reassured her and she never forgot his comment that 'after all, Madame, ten ships of the line can't be eaten up.'[5] On 13 May 1790, King Gustav's brother, Prince Carl of Sweden, with a large fleet comprising twenty-one ships of the line, six frigates and a variety of smaller craft, launched his long-predicted attack on Revel. Vasilii had lined up his greatly inferior force in three rows, as far as possible from the shore batteries, but within the shelter of the harbour. His objective was to trap the enemy between the lines of fire. From the deck of his father's ship, the *Rotislav*, Pavel could make out the pennant of the Grand Admiral, Prince Carl, and those of the vice-admiral, the two rear-admirals and the two commodores, as the Swedish ships jostled for position at the entrance to the harbour. The Russians waited silently. Vasilii had ordered his captains to conserve their ammunition and only to shoot when they were sure that the shots would count. The wind freshened and as the first Swedish ship came into range, she was raked by a line of enemy fire. The Swedish ships were now struggling to manoeuvre in the increasing wind and many of their shots went wide as their ships were thrown from side to side by gale force gusts, but the Russians, anchored in line, were able to keep up a steady, deadly fire. By early afternoon the Swedes had lost two ships of the line and several others had been badly damaged. Fearing greater losses, Prince Carl beat a retreat. Pavel was sent by his father to take possession of the Swedish ship *Prince Charles*, which had been captured.

The Empress was delighted with this action and rewarded Vasilii with the order of St Andrew.* Pavel also received a decoration, which the Empress enclosed with the following letter:

> To Chichagov, Captain of our Fleet, 2<sup>nd</sup> Grade.

> In recognition of your devoted service and skill in directing the ship *Rotislav* at the time of the battle between our fleet and the enemy fleet at Revel, where through your excellent supervision and marksmanship you were the first to remove the topmast from the Swedish ship, thereby incapacitating the ship and causing it to turn into the line of our ships and surrender. For this service, we deem you worthy to receive the order of our military saint, martyr and victor, St George. We therefore create you a knight of this order, Fourth Class, the decorations for which are enclosed. We order you to wear them appropriately and we trust that our favour will encourage you to continue in your devoted service.

> Tsarskoe Selo. Catherine II[6]

For the next three weeks, the Russian and Swedish fleets observed each other uneasily from a distance. More than half the Russian fleet was still at Kronstadt under the orders of Vice-Admiral Kruze, but at last Vasilii heard that Kruze's squadron was on its way to join him. However Vasilii was in no hurry to quit the shelter of his anchorage, guessing that

---

* According to Pavel's memoirs, Vasilii also received a gift of property. This m    . of-erence to the estate at Shklov, near Mogilev, with which he was rewarded by the Empress in her newly acquired territories in White Russia. It seems more probable, however, that Vasilii received the important property at Shklov after the major victory of Vyborg (see pp. 39–40) and that Pavel is either referring to some smaller gift or has confused the dates.

the Swedes intended to place themselves between the two squadrons so that they could attack each one separately. He had calculated, cannily, that Kruze's larger force could better withstand a Swedish attack alone, and he waited until the Swedish fleet was well on the way to Kronstadt before a peremptory command from the Empress obliged him to set sail. As a steady west wind blew him towards St Petersburg, messages began to come in from passing Danish craft that Kruze's squadron had been attacked by the enemy and had retired, with several ships once again badly damaged by the explosion of their own defective cannons. On the morning of 6 June, Vasilii's fleet found itself in view of the Swedish fleet, but with no sign of Kruze's squadron. Vasilii placed his ships between two islands to ensure that they stayed in line and gave the order to pre-pare for combat. Far away, beyond the Swedish line, the distant shapes of ships loomed through the gathering mist, but any hope that they might be the missing squadron were dashed when they failed to respond to the salute of Vasilii's guns. A thick sea mist had now enveloped both fleets and prevented any further action, but when it cleared, the mys-terious ships revealed themselves close at hand as Kruze's squadron. The Swedes, confronted with a combined force, turned tail and headed, to the astonishment of the Russians, for the bay of Vyborg.

No Russian pilot had ever discovered that there was a passage for large ships into the commodious bay of Vyborg, but the Swedes had explored it and prepared it as a place of retreat for their fleet. One by one their ships threaded their way through a narrow passage, between the numerous islands and reefs, and took up a position far down the bay behind the shelter of these natural defences. Shortly afterwards, King Gustav with the galley fleet was observed using the same passage to join his brother in the bay. Without knowledge or charts of these hazardous waters, the Russian fleet could only stand by and watch, but Vasilii immediately set about finding pilots and soon had an effective blockade in place.

While the Russian fleet battled with gale force winds from the west, which threatened to blow them into the enemy lines, the position of the Swedish fleet was also highly precarious. The land surrounding Vyborg was in Russian hands and there was a considerable galley fleet in the port of Vyborg. The weeks passed and as the Russians, between skir-mishes, considered a variety of initiatives, the Swedes began to run low on fresh water and rations. A change of wind to the east finally per-suaded the Swedes, on 3 July,[7] to make a desperate attempt to force the blockade with the aid of fireships. This strategy was to prove disastrous. One of the fireships ran aground in the narrow exit passage and caused extensive damage to its own fleet, while leaving the Russians unscathed. Nevertheless, large numbers of Swedish ships had managed to break through the blockade and were already heading for the impregnable port of Sveaborg. During the chase which followed, the Swedish fleet was reduced to complete disarray and suffered further heavy losses before reaching the shelter of Sveaborg.

Vasilii made a triumphant report to the Empress:

> Apart from the losses of ships of the line, frigates and other ships incurred by the enemy during their departure from the bay of Vyborg, during our pursuit, we captured more than twenty ships of all sizes and many were sunk. We took more than five thousand prisoners, among whom were a rear-admiral and nearly two hundred officers. The number of those who perished on the ships that burned or sank and those that were killed in combat comes to three thousand men. On our side, we did not lose a single boat, but we had seventeen killed and sixty-four wounded, including Captain Travernin, who has since died of his wounds, Captain-Lieutenant Eken, who had a leg removed by the same bullet which killed his captain, and eight other officers wounded.[8]

Pavel was entrusted to carry the report to the Empress, who, having read it, questioned him closely and joked with him over the capture of a luxuriously appointed yacht which was thought to have been intended for the use of King Gustav. Behind her light banter, it is likely that the Empress, wishing to evaluate the potential of her naval officers, was scrutinizing Pavel carefully. He was very similar in build to his father, slim and of medium height, and he had the same ramrod carriage, but there the likeness ended. His face, marked with the traces of his childhood smallpox, still had the roundness of youth and was topped by thick, curling fair hair. His gaze was lively and penetrating and he answered the Empress with a crisp efficiency that was entirely devoid of the nervousness that usually afflicted her subjects during a first audience. When Pavel emerged from the imperial presence, he was informed by Count Bezborodko, the Empress's procurator, that he had been promoted to the rank of First Class Captain and that the Empress had awarded him a golden sword and a thousand ducats for bringing her good news. Vasilii was nominated a knight of the military order of St George, First Class, and rewarded with the gift of an estate.

Pavel doubtless described the meeting in detail to his father, telling him proudly of his latest promotion and of the gifts. The wily Vasilii, who was well aware of the likely outcome of sending his son to the Empress with the news of victory, may have cautioned Pavel not to arouse the jealousy of others by talking about it. But if so, his warning came too late, for Pavel had already been labelled by his less charitable contemporaries as the spoilt son of the Admiral, who had now received the flattering attentions of the Empress on two occasions thanks only to the position of his father.

The victory of Vyborg had a distressing sequel. The Swedish galley fleet, which had been left to the mercies of the smaller ships under Vasilii's command while he pursued the main fleet, sustained considerable damage but had managed to limp into the port of Rotchensalm. The Prince of Nassau-Siegen decided to mount another blockade on the Swedes using the Russian galley fleet and the squadron of Vice-Admiral Kozlanianov. Confident from the recent victory at Vyborg and his own earlier successes, the Prince took few precautions and his force was quite unprepared for the strong opposition that it encountered. The battle raged for over twenty-four hours, until the Russians were forced to retire, with half their men wounded, captured or killed and huge losses to their fleet. Despite this major setback to the galley fleet, the main Russian fleet still had complete control of the Baltic and on 14 August a peace treaty was concluded with the Swedes and hostilities ceased.

The battle of Vyborg changed everything for the Chichagov family. The Admiral was a native Russian hero in a city which had too often had to thank foreigners for its salvation and he became a great favourite with the Empress. As well as giving him a country estate in her newly conquered White Russian territories, she permitted him to select a yacht for his personal use from among the captured Swedish ships. In September Vasilii received, through Bezborodko, a personal invitation from the Empress to attend the celebrations in honour of the recent peace settlements with Sweden and Turkey. The Empress presided over the festivities, which lasted for fifteen days. On the day of the official proclamation of the peace, a magnificently attired crowd was gathered in the immense hall of St George at the Winter Palace. The ladies of the court wore their most dazzling jewels and huge numbers of nobles, clergy and diplomats also attended, but most brilliant of all was the Empress, seated majestically on her gold and silver throne and attended by the imperial family. One by one the honours of war were distributed, and when Vasilii's turn came, he received a golden sword, studded with diamonds, a service of silver and the promise of a parchment diploma recording his achievements. His sons basked in the new-found glory of their father, but their mother continued to mourn for her lost son and grew thinner and paler daily.

For the first time in his life Vasilii was comfortably off and enjoyed a prominent social position. According to a contemporary English observer, John Parkinson, in December Vasilii sat on the left of the Empress at the state dinner for the knights of St George and was the first to be served, by the Empress herself, with the soup.[9] His property brought him a regular income and he had also been decorated with some of the highest honours in the land. In addition he was soon to be awarded the right to a coat of arms. He lived in a handsome house on the north bank of the Neva, within sight of the Admiralty and the Winter Palace, and the Empress had commanded the leading sculptor at the Academy of Fine Arts, Marthus, to create a bust of her favourite admiral to be placed in the Hermitage. The bust bore the following inscription, composed by the Empress:

> The Swedes advanced, three times in strength
> He learned of this, but said the Lord is my defence
> They will not eat us up!
> Soon they were beaten off and his revenge
> Imposed upon the Swedes, captivity or death.[10]

Hand in hand with worldly success, however, came personal sorrow. Catherine Chichagov's unrelieved depression had destroyed her health and in early November 1791, at the age of 53, she died, leaving a desolate household behind her.

For Pavel, the coming of peace brought a sense of anticlimax and his mind constantly revolved around the shortcomings of the Russian navy. The spirited initiatives of the British captains at Vyborg, and through-out the Swedish war, had been in stark contrast to the passive courage of the Russians and highlighted one of the keys to British naval success. The differences in national temperament, however, were not the only problem. The Russians lacked expertise and Pavel set his sights on a visit to England, where he might learn from the British navy at first hand. Vasilii quickly acquiesced to Pavel's proposal that he and his third brother, Vasilii,* should travel to England with Gur'ev as their tutor, in

---

* Vasilii Vasil'evich Chichagov (1771–1826). Some sources suggest that it was Pavel's second brother, Peter, who accompanied him on this journey.

order to further their naval studies. The authorization of the Empress was also gained without difficulty and with the first thaw the trio set sail for England on a British merchant ship from Kronstadt.

The voyage took a month, during which Pavel could not fail to notice the superior seamanship of the British crew, and the speed and perfection of their manoeuvres made him all the more anxious to begin his studies. The party, however, had no clear idea of how to set about acquiring this new knowledge and on landing in England, Pavel immediately began searching in various libraries, convinced that he would discover books from which everything could be learnt. Needless to say, he was disappointed, and it was in a mood of intense frustration that he arrived in London to dine with the Russian Ambassador to Britain, Count Simon Vorontsov.

Vorontsov was 47 years old when Pavel first met him. Unlike the Chichagovs, he came from an old aristocratic family that had enjoyed power for generations. In his own generation, two of his siblings had been closely associated with Peter III. His elder brother, Aleksandr, had been appointed minister plenipotentiary to London by Peter in 1762, but was transferred to The Hague by the Empress in 1764. His eldest sister, Elizabeth, had enjoyed even closer ties with Peter, since she became his mistress. On the other hand, another of Simon's sisters, Princess Dashkova, became an intimate friend and champion of the future Empress during the *coup d'état* in which Peter was deposed. However, through her disapproval of the Empress's liaison with Grigorii Orlov, Princess Dashkova fell from favour and never played an active role at court. Simon, who was one year younger than Princess Dashkova, was for many years the object of imperial suspicion. He felt the unjustness of this bitterly and had spent many years travelling abroad, as well as playing a courageous military role in the war with Turkey, before he was offered, in 1782, a diplomatic post in Venice by the Empress. Two years later, in June 1784, he was appointed to London.

Vorontsov arrived in London a middle-aged widower, with two young children, Mikhail, aged 3, and Catherine, aged 1. He moved into the sober brick house at 36 Harley Street, which housed the Russian Embassy, with mixed feelings. He was deeply affected by the death of his wife and his health was poor. Nevertheless he rapidly acquired an intimate knowledge of the British political scene and was, in 1791, to enjoy one of the greatest diplomatic triumphs of his career. Although he was sometimes accused of having political affiliations within the British government,

Vorontsov's objectives were always the interests of Russia. Thus when Pitt, alarmed by the Russian capture of the Turkish fortress at Ochakov, intended to present the Russians with an ultimatum demanding their withdrawal from the fortress, Vorontsov used every means in his power to combat him. This included allying himself with Fox and the Opposition to force Pitt to cancel the proposed show of British naval force in the Baltic with which Pitt had hoped to support his demands. Vorontsov also contacted influential figures in the City of London and pointed out to them that a deterioration in Anglo-Russian relations could only damage the lucrative trade between the two countries. In addition, he took advantage of the English press to publicize his cause still further. So effective were Vorontsov's methods that in the end Pitt was forced, by popular demand, to abandon his anti-Russian policies.

Vasilii had asked the influential Count Bezborodko to write a letter of introduction for his sons to Vorontsov.[11] Bezborodko liked Vasilii and believed that his appointment was a good one, even if he partially shared Vorontsov's criticisms of Vasilii's tendency to procrastinate.[12] Vorontsov's opinion was less favourable. In May 1791, he had concluded a letter to his brother, Aleksandr, with a cutting comment on Vasilii's performance during the Swedish war: 'They [Admirals Kruze, Kozlanianov, Khanikov and Povalishin] would have done a lot more without Mr Tchitchagoff, who did nothing himself and did not want anyone else to do anything either.'[13]

When the Chichagov boys and their tutor sat down to dinner with Vorontsov, the conversation began with small talk, as their host went through the motions of hospitality. Suddenly he became aware of the angry tone of the eldest of the Chichagov brothers and he turned to look properly – for the first time – at the very heated young man beside him. Perhaps, also, there was something about Pavel's seriousness and youth that reminded Vorontsov of his own early manhood, before age and disappointments had tempered his ardour with pragmatism and patience, and he began to listen with attention.

The problem, it seemed, was that young Chichagov had found no sufficiently advanced books on naval matters, and he had therefore concluded that English naval expertise was greatly inferior to what he had expected. Furthermore, in his opinion, even the lowest Russian naval officer had a wider knowledge than that contained in English naval books. Vorontsov smiled at the absurdity of this assertion, reflecting no doubt that if his own diplomatic efforts had not been so successful,

Vasilii Chichagov, his sons and the whole Russian fleet might well have been obliterated in the Baltic by an encounter with the British. He decided that this opinionated young man needed to be taken down a peg or two. 'You know, Sir,' he replied, 'that the lowest ensign in the British navy knows more than a Russian admiral.'[14]

A deadly silence fell on the table. Pavel's expression froze. What had been intended as a light-hearted reproof by Vorontsov was taken, by Pavel, as a calculated insult to his father. The rest of the evening passed awkwardly. There was no more talk of the navy and Pavel took his leave at the earliest opportunity and vowed to have no further contact with the Ambassador.

Pavel, Vasilii and Gur'ev rapidly decided that their most essential requirement was a good grasp of English. To avoid the temptation of speaking Russian together, they took up separate lodgings and enrolled at different schools. Pavel took a room at Tooting, a few miles south of London, and after three months of hard study found that he was sufficiently competent in English to understand everything that was said to him and to read and speak adequately for his needs. The time passed quickly, but since his occasional visits to London in quest of naval knowledge that would enable him to return to Russia with a wealth of new expertise were always in vain, Pavel felt that they were still not fulfilling the main purpose of their visit.

Finally, in December, the party decided to embark on a merchant ship bound for the West Indies, on which they would, at least, see British seamanship in action. In this voyage Pavel was, once again, sorely disappointed. The captain was an incompetent and the second mate a drunk. Contrary winds forced the ship to turn back at Portsmouth, where Pavel had one of the few genuinely interesting encounters of his English trip. It began unpromisingly at Spithead, when the naval captain in charge of security, which had been greatly tightened with the fear of revolutionary infiltrators from France, insisted that Pavel should come aboard his ship while his passport was checked. But once his credentials were established, he was invited to dine with the officers and he took this opportunity to make his first comprehensive tour of a British warship. This was followed by a congenial evening of good food and conversation. Regaining his merchant ship, he soon decided to abandon the voyage. The news was disturbing. It was February 1793 and Britain and France were at war, creating a real danger of passengers on a merchant ship becoming trapped, for an indefinite period, in some European port.

Therefore, with as much haste as the season permitted, Pavel and his party returned via Rotterdam and Berlin to St Petersburg.

The Empress was highly agitated by the situation in Europe and had ordered the Russian fleet to assemble, in a state of alert, at Kronstadt. She was deeply suspicious of her Baltic neighbours and anxious to make as many preparations as possible. Pavel found his father busy with improvements to the port of Revel, where a barracks for six thousand crewmen was under construction. Further west, at the merchant harbour of Baltischport, work was also under way. For Pavel this was a difficult period. His trip to England had achieved very little and his ambitious hopes of returning as the architect of naval reform were dashed. As a full captain, he was entitled to a ship of his own, but the season was now advanced and all the best ships were already taken. He visited Kronstadt and eyed the ships captured from the Swedes enviously. Several of them were designed by the celebrated Swedish shipbuilder, Frederik Chapman, for whom Pavel had a great admiration. He gazed with longing at the neat lines and cunningly constructed batteries of the *Retvisan*, but for the rest of the summer he had to content himself with an older Swedish ship, the *Sophia Magdalena*. In London the long-standing commercial agreement between England and Russia had been renewed through the good offices of Vorontsov and a convention of mutual opposition to France had also been signed by both countries.

As winter closed in, Pavel sought solace once more in his studies and amused himself, with a few of his friends, in drawing up a memorandum in a satirical vein which listed all the defects of the Russian navy and suggested how they might be remedied. One evening, the idea occurred to him to present this memorandum to the Empress and, without consulting his father, he took it to the house of Prince Zubov, who was now the current favourite and enjoyed regular imperial access. Zubov was an officer in the Horse Guards who had become the lover of the Empress in 1789 at the age of 22. Although he was four months younger than Pavel, he was vastly older in terms of worldly wisdom and sophistication. He read Pavel's light-hearted memorandum and then looked up at him in amazement. 'Does your father know about this?'[15] he asked, and when Pavel confessed that he did not, Zubov suggested mildly that it might be a good idea to ask his opinion before presenting such a paper to the Empress. The memorandum was never mentioned again by either party and Pavel's first attempts at naval reform vanished into oblivion.

As the stance of France became increasingly menacing, the traditional amity between Russia and Britain blossomed. In the face of a common enemy, whose area of influence was expanding daily, Britain and Russia agreed to a further defensive alliance against the French. Flanders had already been overrun and in January 1795 Amsterdam fell and with it the Dutch fleet, which was captured, as it lay frozen fast in the ice, by a force of French cavalry. The British navy, which already had two fleets fully occupied in the Channel and in the Mediterranean, was now required to blockade the French-controlled Dutch fleet anchored in the Texel. A Russian squadron, therefore, was invited to join the British North Sea fleet to assist with the blockade. The Russian squadron was commanded by Vice-Admiral Khanikov, and Pavel, now captain of the coveted *Retvisan*, was a member of it.

A crowd of curious spectators had gathered on the coast to observe the arrival in England of the Russian squadron. Pavel was overcome with patriotic pride. Their squadron, comprising seven ships of the line and several frigates and cutters, made a splendid sight under sail. As they manoeuvred into the harbour and dropped anchor, Pavel noted with satisfaction that several telescopes had been trained on the *Retvisan*. It was only when he arrived ashore, that he realized that many British civilians were expert judges of navigation and the performance of the Russians had aroused more criticism than admiration. Worse was to follow. Through some differences of protocol, the salute returned to Vice-Admiral Khanikov by the British full admiral was, by Russian standards, unacceptable. Khanikov and his officers, already on their mettle in the presence of the British navy, were outraged and Vorontsov was summoned from London to redress the insult. No officer took the matter more seriously than Pavel and he did not hesitate to give Vorontsov the full benefit of his feelings.

Painstakingly, Vorontsov explained that no offence had been intended. In the British navy salutes were according to rank, whereas in Russia they were always reciprocal. Pavel, who had been preparing to defend the honour of Russia with a personal visit to the British admiral, calmed down and thanked the Ambassador sincerely for his clarification. For his part, Vorontsov found Pavel's fiery patriotism heart-warming and, shaking hands warmly, they parted friends. Once harmony had been restored between the allies, a round of courtesy visits began and Pavel was gratified by the interest that the Commander of the Fleet, Admiral Duncan, showed in his beloved *Retvisan*, but at sea there were further troubles in store. Quite unused to the choppy waters and powerful tides of the

North Sea, the Russians found themselves hopelessly slow in comparison with the British. The telescopes of Deal were riveted daily on the
struggles of their crewmen as they failed miserably to match the speed
and efficiency of their British counterparts, and Pavel smarted with mortification as Duncan was required to turn his entire fleet into the wind
to wait for the Russian squadron.

Throughout the summer, the allies sailed together, patrolling the
entrance to the Texel. Despite his frequent humiliations at sea, Pavel
found the British officers charming. They took pains to compliment the
Russians as, with practice, their seamanship improved, and in this stim-
ulating environment, Pavel's ship was soon doing him credit. When
autumn came, and with it the first storms of winter, many of the members of the Russian squadron melted away to pass a tranquil winter in
English ports and harbours, but Pavel remained at his post. Eventually
even Duncan despaired of ever catching sight of the Dutch fleet and
decided to winter at Yarmouth: however, he detached a squadron to continue the watch on the Texel. To Pavel's immense satisfaction, the
*Retvisan* was selected for this duty and before long had, single-handedly,
captured the prize of a rich merchantman from Surinam bound for the
Texel.

The *Retvisan* was the object of Pavel's greatest affections. His mind
continually revolved around how she might be improved and he determined to take advantage of the proximity of excellent British dockyards
to enhance her performance. A timely hurricane in the Medway and a
fire in the galley provided Pavel with a pretext to apply for repairs, the
costs of which were, under the terms of the defence agreement, to be
met by the British government. Pavel, however, was also determined to
upgrade the captain's quarters, which he found very inferior to those on
British ships. Furthermore he knew that the *Retvisan*'s sailing speed
would be greatly increased if she were given a copper bottom. All these
improvements were costly, but Pavel exercised consummate skill in per-
suading not only Khanikov and Duncan that they were necessary, but
also Vorontsov, who kept a watchful eye on the behaviour of his countrymen. The naval dockyard at Sheerness was not equipped to make such
extensive repairs and so in the winter of 1795, Pavel Chichagov dropped
his anchor at Chatham.

# CHAPTER THREE

# Chatham

## 1796

Charles Proby was at his desk working, as usual, at his correspondence with the Admiralty. He had received an instruction to give the ships of the seconded Russian squadron the same status as British ships at the dockyard. Civilities were also to be extended to Russian naval officers where appropriate. There was nothing new in this instruction. Russian ships had frequently been repaired in British dockyards in the past and there were standard procedures. In 1769 the Russian fleet commanded by Aleksei Orlov – which went on to defeat the Turks at Çeshme – had passed through Charles's territory. As the British Commander-in-Chief in the Mediterranean, Charles had been directed 'to show them the most friendly treatment and give them every kind of succour and assistance which they may be in want of, to enable them to continue on their voyage.'[1] The Russian ships were badly in need of help. They had received heavy damage in the Bay of Biscay and many were in poor shape by the time they reached Charles's station in Gibraltar Bay. From there they had sailed on to Port Mahon in Minorca, where they had received an extensive refit from the British.

Most of the ships of the Russian squadron that had applied to the Admiralty for repairs could be handled by the smaller dockyard down-river at Sheerness, which was under Charles's overall authority until 1796, but there was one, the *Retvisan*, which had already arrived at Chatham. Her captain had requested a copper bottom and a complete refit internally. This was going to take months and meant that there would be the usual problems with large numbers of unoccupied Russian sailors drinking in the pubs of Chatham. Charles cannot have failed to reflect on these problems and may not have been overjoyed when one of his clerks announced the arrival of a Russian naval officer who wished to see the Commissioner. The clerk indicated a slight, immaculately uniformed figure standing stiffly to attention in the ante-room. Charles rose to his feet and greeted the officer with courtesy and then invited him to sit down in his office.

The young man introduced himself as the captain of the *Retvisan*. It took Charles several minutes to grow accustomed to his heavily accented English. For his part, Pavel was delighted to have gained admission to the Commissioner with so little difficulty. His experience of life in Russia had taught him the wisdom of going straight to the top. Furthermore, Pavel's social skills had developed considerably over the past two years. Through his father's prominent position he had been exposed to court life in St Petersburg and, although he could still be blunt when he thought the occasion required it, he was now far more polished than the naive young man who had asked Prince Zubov to pass on a memorandum to the Empress. Furthermore, Pavel liked British naval officers and felt at ease with them – sometimes more so than he did with his own countrymen. He saw before him an elderly, white-haired man, clearly not in the best of health, but who nevertheless controlled everything at the dockyard. Pavel was determined to win his approval.

They began by discussing the *Retvisan* and Charles's interest increased when he heard that she had been designed by Chapman. The navy had been keen to lay their hands on a Chapman design for years and since the repairs requested rather exceeded normal requirements, perhaps, in return, their shipwrights might take a copy of the *Retvisan*. Pavel saw no objection and the atmosphere between the two men became warmer. Pavel expressed his admiration for the arrangements at the dockyard and asked if he might be allowed to visit some of the workshops. He was far more serious and professional than most of the Russian naval officers that Charles had met and beneath the courtly, French-style manners, there was a thoroughness that Charles found admirable. The Commissioner was sure that, with a suitable escort, Pavel might observe most of their procedures. As the meeting drew to a close, Charles decided that he liked this young man. Despite his foreignness and his odd pronunciation, he seemed like a gentleman and on impulse Charles invited him to attend the soirée at his house that evening.

Pavel returned to his lodgings, which were located conveniently close to the dockyard in the house of a Mrs Didham. He was in high spirits. His carefully orchestrated campaign to turn the *Retvisan* into the best ship in the Russian navy was about to succeed. He had handled the meeting with the Commissioner with skill and all his requests had been granted. Coming from the absolute autocracy of life in St Petersburg, Pavel saw the continuing goodwill of the all-powerful Commissioner as crucial to his plans and interpreted the invitation to his house as a good omen. Focused exclusively on his naval ambitions, it is probable that he took particular care with his appearance that evening and presented himself with great punctuality.

This was Pavel's first visit to a large private house in England. Vorontsov's residence in Harley Street was the only English house of any size to which he had been invited and there, despite Vorontsov's love of England, the atmosphere was still very Russian. The sight of the well-dressed servant who opened the door and took Pavel's hat before showing him up to the drawing-room may well have caused Pavel to reflect, as he had many times before, on the freedom and independence of the citizens of Britain. In his father's house in St Petersburg, the door would have been opened by an old family serf who probably still wore his native dress from Kazan and whose demeanour mirrored his bonds of life and death to the Chichagov family. British footmen, with their cheerful well-fed faces and careful, deliberate movements, exuded an air of independence and that stalwart sense of their own rights that Pavel had observed and applauded everywhere in Britain. As he mounted the stairs, Pavel looked around him. He was immediately charmed by the intimacy and elegance of the interior of the house at Chatham. It had none of the splendour of the palaces of St Petersburg, but there was a dignified restraint in the furnishings that he found infinitely preferable.

The Commissioner hurried across the room to welcome him. Charles found Pavel's surname almost unpronounceable, but fortunately he could delegate the task of introductions to Charlotte, who, as the senior female member of the family at home, would have acted as his hostess. As Charlotte guided him around the room, Pavel recalled that the Commissioner was a widower and that consequently the entertainment in his house was largely in the hands of his daughters. Charles's financial limitations and the frequency with which he received guests suggest that these gatherings were not on a grand scale. Probably the company consisted of half a dozen or so naval officers, the three youngest daughters of the Commissioner and maybe one or two others. Charlotte, of course, introduced Pavel to both her younger sisters and he found all three of the Proby girls delightful.

In such company Pavel would have had ample opportunity to shine and he was probably regarded by the British naval officers with some interest. Given the rather mixed reputation of the Russian squadron, Pavel's capture of a prize would have caused quite a stir locally. Perhaps he chose, as he does in his memoirs, to describe in detail the cunning with which he rearranged the rig of the *Retvisan* to look like a merchant ship and how he concealed his gun battery with a painted canvas until the moment he loosed a shot over the bows of the unsuspecting merchantman and stopped her dead in her tracks.

After talking to the gentlemen in the drawing-room, the move to the dining-room for supper would have made it possible – and appropriate – for Pavel to divert his attention to the ladies. Pavel had all the instincts of gallantry, although he had very little experience of women. While he was growing up, his parents had possessed neither the means nor the inclination to entertain very much and after the death of his mother, the Chichagov household had been exclusively male. Nevertheless, as the sons of a nobleman, all the boys had been taught to dance and during the past two years in St Petersburg, Pavel must have attended a number of balls and dinners. However, it is likely that even on these occasions, he sought out the company of men. Despite their physical charms, the coyness and the frivolity of the society ladies of St Petersburg would have exasperated a man of Pavel's disposition.

The Commissioner's daughters were quite unlike any girls he had met before. Their manner was very different from that of the Russian court ladies and having spent their lives in the company of naval officers, they were able to talk intelligently on a range of subjects close to Pavel's heart. In addition, all the girls were accomplished musicians and Pavel may well have confessed to a love of music and even perhaps to his weakness for romantic Italian songs.

After supper, they repaired to the harpsichord, where the girls took it in turns to perform, accompanying each other with the tenor viol and the violin. Like many Russians, Pavel had an intuitive understanding of music. His finely tuned ear rapidly distinguished a difference in the quality of Elizabeth's playing and that of her sisters. Her skills on the harpsichord aroused first his interest and then his admiration. Socially, she was the most reserved of the sisters. The expression in her large blue eyes was inscrutable and gave little indication of her thoughts or feelings, but her fingers betrayed her. Pavel was astounded by the emotional range of her playing and sensed there a capacity for passion that was completely concealed by her cool exterior.

On evenings like this, Elizabeth was completely absorbed in her music. Despite her talent, her mastery had been achieved by many hours of practice and she would have been waiting impatiently for the musical part of the evening to begin. Like all serious performers, once she began to play, nothing else mattered. The candlelit room and the surrounding figures faded into a blur as she moved into another world, in which feeling and emotion flowed through the tips of her fingers. She was oblivious to her audience. She was startled back to reality when Pavel asked her, in his broken English, if she would accompany him in an Italian song that he had learnt at Leghorn. She smiled, automatically, and asked for the name of the song. It was one of her favourites. She played a few notes and looked up at Pavel, awaiting his signal. For a fraction of a second their eyes met and then he began to sing. Pavel, too, had practised this song in the past, with a view to singing it in company, and Elizabeth was pleasantly surprised by his voice. It was melodious and well-rounded and he sang with verve. They exchanged glances again at the beginning of the second verse, but they were already in perfect accord.

By Russian standards, Pavel's voice was unexceptional, but then in Russia, song was so much part of the national heritage that musical expectations were high. Amongst the society of St Petersburg, there were many excellent musicians, but the love of music was not confined to those who could afford singing lessons. The boatmen on the Neva sang continually, the household servants worked to the melodies of age-old folk songs and Russian soldiers marched to war in choir. Many of the noblemen of St Petersburg took advantage of the innate musical talents of their domestic staff to entertain their guests – some had even formed their serfs into orchestras. In Chatham, however, Pavel's natural vocal ability and his excellent Italian were exceptional and his performance received a round of applause. When the time came to leave, the Commissioner was warm in his farewells and invited Pavel to attend his evening soirées whenever he wished.

Charles had enjoyed the evening. These days, he left nearly all the organization of the household to his daughters. Charlotte was a perfect hostess and Beatrice and Elizabeth were always a credit in any society. At his age, it was very pleasant to relinquish responsibility when he arrived home and to allow his family to fuss over him. Sometimes he felt more like a friend or even an elderly visiting admirer than a parent, as the girls attended solicitously to his comforts and enlivened the house with music and dancing. He loved all his daughters, but he had a particular affection for his youngest, Elizabeth. She was always so devoted to him and he had grown to depend on her quiet strength that was such a comfort after the long, exhausting days at the office. He was sometimes surprised by his irritation when a young man seemed to be paying her too much attention and found it difficult to conceal his paternal jealousy. Fortunately for his peace of mind, Elizabeth had no serious suitors and seemed totally content with her music and her family.

Upstairs in their bedrooms, the three girls would undoubtedly have chatted about the party and the conversation almost certainly touched on Captain Chichagov. He was probably the first Russian that any of them had met and they were perhaps amazed to find him so civilized – especially as Russia appears to have been known in the family as 'the Land of the Bears'. The image of Russia in Britain at this time was dominated by the exploits of the Empress, but the Proby girls may also have gleaned some knowledge of life in St Petersburg from their cousin Lord Carysfort. Pavel's experiences in the Swedish wars, his acquaintance with the Empress and his knowledge of the Russian court were all subjects of great topical interest and even without his gallant manners and intriguing accent, he would have been an exotic visitor for the sheltered young ladies of Chatham.

As her father had rightly surmised, Elizabeth had never been seriously in love. Several prospective suitors had been kept at bay by her cool manner and her intellectual disposition. Miss Proby was not a young lady to be trifled with. It was true that she loved dancing, but it was the music that attracted her rather than the social encounters. Consequently Elizabeth was not initially in a position to recognize, in herself, the symptoms of love. The weeks passed and Pavel's visits to the house began to occupy more and more of her thoughts. His English was improving daily and he kept the sisters spellbound with his stories of St Petersburg. But he was also highly critical of his own country and frequently compared the autocratic structure of government in Russia unfavourably with the more democratic political system that existed in Britain. Pavel, as a firm advocate of the ideas of Rousseau, assured the sisters that had they ever seen the servitude of the majority of the population of Russia, they would soon share his opinions. On one occasion Pavel's esteem for Rousseau led to a dispute with Charlotte's husband, Thomas Pitcairn. Like many Englishmen, Thomas was extremely wary of Rousseau and believed that it was his philosophy of personal freedom that had cost Britain her American possessions and the King and Queen of France their heads. Charles overheard the argument and lent his full support to his son-in-law.

On the occasions when Pavel and Elizabeth found themselves in conversation alone, a tone of intimacy began to prevail. They talked endlessly of music and marvelled at the coincidence in their tastes. They discussed politics, religion and history. Elizabeth was captivated by Pavel's far-ranging intellectual capacity and the energy of his mind and Pavel was astounded by the wisdom of this young, untravelled girl and her ability to understand him. His nights began to be tortured by the image of her slender figure behind the harpsichord, by the expression in her eyes as they talked and by the sweet, serious tone of her voice. Pavel was no stranger to the torments of physical desire, but with Elizabeth his longing was all-consuming. For him she had, in the space of a few short weeks, become the sum of female perfection.

Elizabeth's emotions would have been complicated by Pavel's foreign nationality. She could never have imagined that she would fall in love with someone who was not English. Yet when they were together, his being Russian became completely irrelevant. He shared all her fundamental moral and philosophical beliefs and his courage and honesty had gained her deep respect. Quite apart from these sober deliberations, the rational, level-headed Elizabeth undoubtedly found herself emotionally stirred by Pavel's tempestuous personality and his fiery temperament, which had found such a perfect foil in her quintessential Englishness. With her natural reserve, she probably did not dare to confess, even to her sisters, the growing strength of her feelings.

Work on the *Retvisan* was continuing apace. Her copper bottom was already fitted and the captain's cabin, in immaculate English naval style, was nearly completed. Pavel's days passed busily and his activities in the dockyard served as a useful distraction from his more personal preoccupations. In London he revisited Ramsden, the famous designer of navigational instruments, with whom he had become acquainted on his earlier trip to England and who, at Pavel's request, created a special instrument for the *Retvisan*. The spring season was approaching and with it the need for the Russian squadron to recommence its naval duties. Pavel and Charles exchanged courteous and businesslike communications on stores, but Charles was having some of the problems he had foreseen with the Russian squadron, nor had Pavel's ubiquitous presence in the dockyard passed unnoticed.

The sight of Russians in Chatham, at a time when many people in Britain were in daily fear of foreign invasion, aroused considerable hostility. The locals were highly suspicious of these odd-looking strangers who seemed to have such easy access to an establishment crucial to national security. In February 1796, during his visit to Chatham on Corresponding Society business, John Gale Jones heard from 'an intelligent young man' whom he met there that

> it was the opinion of many well-informed persons that sending the vessels of that nation [i.e. Russia] to be repaired in our dockyards was only a political manoeuvre of the Empress to gain time and opportunity to inspect them, and to extract information. In this opinion they were the more confirmed by the conduct of the Russian officers, who appeared to be men of considerable penetration and discernment. Upon their first arrival in Chatham they had endeavoured by every possible method to ingratiate themselves with the inhabitants, and by their various observations, and the numerous enquiries they made of the workmen in the various branches of ship-building, had evinced a strong desire to become acquainted with every thing worthy of their notice.[2]

The Russian sailors were also regarded with dislike and Jones's informant related that 'the children pointed at them in ridicule, whenever they passed in the streets, and calling out to them Roos, Roos! And their troublesome behaviour in the various shops to which they had occasion to resort, afforded a strong apprehension that some serious disturbance would take place between the inhabitants and themselves before they quitted the town.'[3]

These sentiments had penetrated the dockyard workforce and on 29 March 1796, Charles felt obliged to write a letter to Vice-Admiral Khanikov at Sheerness to remind him of the dockyard regulations and to tighten up security arrangements: 'That everything may go more smoothly than heretofore between the ships under your command and the officers of this Dockyard, I have taken the liberty to send you the inclosed, from which, I request the favour of you to [issue] such orders to all the ships under your command as you may judge necessary for the purpose.'[4]

A long list of regulations was enclosed, including the prescribed places of landing:

> The officers coming onshore not on duty may land only at the Commissioner's Stairs. . . . As the Russians [i.e. sailors] in this case come onshore in large numbers it may be adviseable for them with the proper non commissioned officers to land and return from Princess Bridge or at the New Stairs between the Dockyard and Ordnance Gun Wharf. . . . As there are no other Foreign officers or men, than those under your command, allowed to be in the Dockyard, which renders it necessary for the officers of all Denominations, or some of them, either by themselves or with men,

to be in their uniforms, to prevent their being taken into Custody as other foreign officers and men would be.[5]

Charles had also become uneasy about the increasingly casual manner with which Pavel and his fellow officers visited the storehouses and workshops and he reminded Khanikov that this was forbidden 'except where required by their duty'.[6] Charles shared some of the feelings of his workforce. Britain had become alarmingly isolated in the war against France. Her Prussian and Austrian allies had suffered severe defeats from the Revolutionary army. The Dutch fleet was fighting on the side of the French and the Duke of York had been beaten in Flanders. Even the usually invincible British navy had met with little recent success. In common with many Englishmen, including the Prime Minister, Pitt, Charles felt that at such a time no patriot should trust a foreigner.

Two weeks later, as the frictions between the Russians and the dockyard workforce continued, Charles wrote a further letter to Khanikov:

> I beg leave to trouble you again with more observations, in addition to those I have already sent, to make the paths pleasanter between your Officers and the Officers of this Dockyard. . . . As some of your ships have neither officers nor men sufficiently versed in the English language to transact business regularly with the Officers of the Dock Yarde [I would ask you] to direct two, three, or more of those who can speak and understand English well to be constantly here whilst the ships may be refitting.[7]

On 12 April Khanikov wrote to thank Charles for his letters. His letter was a model of diplomacy: 'I am extremely obliged to you for the information they contain, as it is the only method of avoiding mistakes in the future and shall give Orders for their being punctually observed.'[8]

Whatever his personal reservations may have been, however, Charles continued to act completely correctly and to carry out his instructions from the Admiralty vis-à-vis the Russian squadron to the letter. By the end of April, the repairs had been largely accomplished and the ships resupplied from British naval stores, which were greatly prized by the Russians. On 25 April, Khanikov wrote a grateful letter to Charles: '. . . accept my sincere thanks for the polite and kind attentions you are so good to shew us on many occasions, and for the trouble you have been pleased to take, in procuring, for our benefit and ease, the British Establishment of Naval Stores, in doing which you have conferred a favour on me and every commander in the Squadron.'[9]

None of these tensions affected the growing relationship between

Pavel and Elizabeth. Despite the restrictions that were usually placed at this time on unchaperoned encounters between young people of the opposite sex, Elizabeth and Pavel could have passed many hours together with only the mildest supervision from Charlotte. The end of winter would have lent itself to expeditions into the surrounding countryside. In springtime, the gently rolling hills above Chatham were covered with wild flowers; and away from the busy coach road to London, the placid villages and orchards of rural Kent were linked by winding lanes that had been trodden for generations. Downstream, along the river bank, lay the network of paths that followed the slow-moving waters of the Medway to the sea, while upstream was Rochester, with its elegant High Street and shops.

Charlotte's vigilance may well have been diverted by another romance in the family. We do not know exactly when Beatrice met Captain Charles Cunningham, but judging by the date of the wedding, it must also have been during 1796. In April 1796 Cunningham, who was a 40-year-old widower with two daughters, received the command of the 46-gun frigate, the *Clyde*, attached to the North Sea Fleet. He had already enjoyed a varied and interesting naval career and had even served briefly in the West Indies with Nelson, whose reputation was beginning to attract attention in naval circles. In 1794 Cunningham had seen action in the Mediterranean and had taken part in the attack on the Corsican fortress of Calvi, where Nelson lost his eye, after which he had been entrusted by the Admiral, Lord Hood, to carry the news of the subjugation of Corsica overland to England. Despite the long detours that he had been obliged to make to avoid the French army, he made the journey at top speed and arrived in London in only three weeks. The dispatches contained some flattering lines about the bearer and, in consequence, he was assured of receiving a good command in the future.

Like many captains of British ships blockading the coasts of Holland and France, Cunningham probably took advantage of the decreased activity of the winter season to put into Chatham for repairs where, like Pavel, he was invited to the hospitable house of the Commissioner and fell in love with one of his daughters. Cunningham did not delay his declaration, and if, as was his custom, Charles Proby had already initiated discreet enquiries into the character and finances of his latest prospective son-in-law, the results would have more than satisfied him. He may even have been told of Lord Hood's glowing testimonial to the Admiralty: 'Captain Cunningham, who has cruised with infinite diligence, zeal and perseverance, under many difficulties, for three months past, off Calvi, is charged with my despatches. . . . I beg to recommend him as an officer of great merit, and highly deserving any favour that can be shewn him.'[10] Furthermore, there was a Cunningham property in Suffolk, to which Charles was the heir. His proposal would, therefore, have been awaited with pleasure and the wedding, which took place on 7 February 1797 at St Mary's, Chatham, was a joyful occasion.

In contrast, the passions that were inflaming Elizabeth and Pavel seem to have taken Charles Proby completely by surprise. He cannot have failed to observe Pavel's frequent appearances at his house and on one occasion, he reprimanded Elizabeth for sitting with Pavel 'so generally and so pointedly at the Harpsichord'.[11] On another evening, he was startled by the expression on Elizabeth's face as Pavel sang her praises before a group of fellow officers from the Russian squadron whom he had brought with him to the soirée. Charles, however, was accustomed by now to Pavel's court manners and, at the time, gave this incident no further thought. Charlotte and Beatrice, on the other hand, must have been more aware of Elizabeth's emotions and perhaps wondered where they would lead to.

Pavel's memoirs draw a discreet veil over the details of his declaration. We can only surmise that one day in early spring Pavel managed to find Elizabeth alone. Perhaps they stood on the long balcony beside the drawing-room or perhaps they strolled in the garden and pretended to look at the flowers. At some moment Pavel must have told Elizabeth that he loved her passionately and that he could not live without her. Then he asked her the question which she had been expecting for quite some time, to which Elizabeth said yes.

Pavel's declaration had been carefully timed. He knew that his sojourn in Chatham was drawing to a close and that he had sufficiently engaged Elizabeth's affections to lead her to expect a proposal before he departed. He had spent many nights wrestling with the problem. He adored her, but how would she ever survive in St Petersburg? For all her intelligence, she had no conception of what life in Russia was like. He loved her enough not to want to inflict an existence on her that would be insupportable. Then there was the problem of her father: he was far more hard-headed than she was. Would he ever permit his daughter to marry a Russian? In the end, Pavel decided to make his proposal just before his departure and if it were refused, he could leave with dignity.

Elizabeth was happier than she had thought it was possible to be. She and Pavel exchanged endearments in Russian and he called her his 'Lizinka'. In the euphoria of the moment Elizabeth was sure that her father would not create any obstacles to their union. After all, it was he who had originally invited Pavel to the house and had consistently shown him marks of favour. Her sisters would be overjoyed. Pavel left to compose a letter to the Commissioner and Elizabeth impatiently awaited the return of her sisters to share the news with them. Despite her professed confidence, however, Elizabeth may have been nervous about her father's reactions. Charles was a very proud man who had often resented what he considered to be the indignities of his position at the dockyard. Once he had taken a decision, his stubborn pride would prevent him from ever changing his mind.

When Elizabeth heard that her father wished to see her downstairs, alone, she composed herself and descended, but even as she entered the room, she knew the worst. Charles's face was flushed with anger. He held a letter in his hand with writing that she knew well and he asked her to explain herself. A very painful scene followed, in which Charles expressed his disgust and anger that any daughter of his should have entered into a romantic relationship with a foreigner, let alone a Russian, who did not even share the same faith and whom Charles did not want to see 'in any other light than as a foreign Acquaintance, or as a foreign Friend, but not as a son in law'.[12] Elizabeth's carefully prepared phrases fell on deaf ears and before he dismissed her, Charles told her that he would write to Captain Chichagov that very evening to tell him that any union between a member of his family and a Russian was unthinkable. Elizabeth had managed to control herself throughout the interview, but the moment she reached her own room, she flung herself on her bed, racked with sobs. Charlotte and Beatrice tried to comfort her and both in turn tried to plead her case with their father, but Charles was adamant and confined Elizabeth to the house.

Pavel received Charles's refusal the next morning. Charles had written Pavel a very fair letter, in which he acknowledged that, notwithstanding his friendship and esteem for Pavel personally, he could not give his consent to the marriage of his daughter with a foreigner. Pavel was stunned. He thought that he had prepared himself for the possibility of rejection and he tried to rationalize his feelings by pouring out his anger against his own country. Of course, no freedom-loving Englishman would send his beloved, youngest daughter to live in a country which did not even have a parliament. Such reasoning, however, did nothing to diminish his intense disappointment. He wrote a careful and dignified reply, in which he accepted Charles's decision and, in a state of numbed despair, began to make his preparations for departure. Suddenly Chatham held no more charms for him and he longed to leave.

During the few days that followed, Pavel gave the Commissioner's house a wide berth and spent the evenings alone at his lodgings. One evening, shortly before he was due to leave, he was surprised to be disturbed by his landlady, Mrs Didham. She looked flustered and asked if she might have a few words with him. Mystified and possibly slightly irritated, Pavel agreed. Then it all poured out. She knew everything because she had, for many years, been the nurse of the Commissioner's daughters and had remained their close confidante. That day she had been up at the Commissioner's house and had found the place in an uproar. Elizabeth was shut in her room and the Commissioner was in a fury. Charlotte and Beatrice had spent hours with their father, begging him to relent, but the more they pleaded the more entrenched his position became. For her part, Elizabeth was every bit as determined as her father and had told her sisters that she would never give in. Pavel was deeply moved by Mrs Didham's account and was about to dismiss her when she handed him a sheet of music. For a moment, Pavel did not understand its significance and then he recognized it as the music and words of a favourite Italian song which Elizabeth had often sung for him. There was no message on the sheet, but throughout Elizabeth had firmly underlined every repetition of the word 'constancy'.

Looking at Elizabeth's message, Pavel suddenly felt the black despair that had paralysed his mind and senses throughout the previous days begin to clear. He turned at once to Mrs Didham and asked her if she would be prepared to act as an intermediary, to which she readily agreed. Pavel sat down and wrote a passionate love letter to Elizabeth. If she loved him as much as he loved her, then he too would be constant and with perseverance they would, one day, succeed. The letter was safely delivered by Mrs Didham and for his remaining time in Chatham, she or Elizabeth's sisters carried messages between the lovers. In the solitude of his room, despite his stated sympathy for Charles Proby's attitude, Pavel could not prevent himself from speculating on how simply all could be resolved if the elderly Commissioner were to succumb to one of his frequent asthma attacks.

The *Retvisan* was rigged and ready to depart. Her captain came aboard and gave the order to raise the anchor. From the deck, he could see the great curve of the River Medway as it snaked its way lazily to the sea and the windmills of Chatham clustered on the hills above the town. There was the lightest possible breeze, but the *Retvisan* instantly responded to the helmsman's touch and as the wind filled her sails, she slipped away from her anchorage with gathering speed. Every inch of her hull and rigging had been overhauled. Her decks were immaculate. She had a new set of sails and with her copper bottom, she was the fastest and most manoeuvrable ship in the Russian fleet, but to her captain, none of this mattered any more. Night and day, his only thoughts were for the slim, pale girl weeping alone in her room while her father paced angrily below.

Pavel completed a second season on the blockade of the Texel, but as soon as an opportunity to return to St Petersburg presented itself, he applied to Vice-Admiral Khanikov for permission to leave. The memories of his time at Chatham and of Elizabeth made his proximity to her unbearable. While at sea, a letter from her had reached him, in which she confirmed her devotion to him and her longing to have news of him. During this time, Pavel corresponded intermittently with Vorontsov in the deeply respectful tone that he considered appropriate for someone as influential as an ambassador. In a letter of 14 May, he mentions the continuing poor professional reputation of the Russian squadron and its captains, and he also tells Vorontsov of his meeting and friendship with the famed Captain Bligh of the *Bounty*, who was sailing with the fleet.[13] It is probable that Pavel also confided his personal sorrows to Vorontsov before he left English waters and begged him to exert what influence he could to bring about the match. With his intimate knowledge of the English political and social scene, it would not have taken Vorontsov long to make the link between Pavel's 'Lizinka' and her cousin Lord Carysfort, with his powerful Grenville connections. But even if Elizabeth had not been closely linked to some of the most influential figures in British public life, Vorontsov would have helped the lovers. He had lost his own wife tragically and he was deeply sympathetic to the sufferings of the human heart. As winter approached, Pavel returned to St Petersburg to grieve for his lost happiness and shortly afterwards, on 6 November 1796, the death of the Empress plunged all Russia into mourning.

# CHAPTER FOUR

## *Mutiny*
### *1796–1799*

The Commissioner's house at Chatham had become an inferno. The serenity and affection that had always reigned within the family had vanished and its members were torn apart by the battle raging between two of its most powerful personalities. Charles was convinced that Elizabeth's passion for Captain Chichagov would pass if she could be made to understand the error of her ways. In the meantime, as his rage and frustration at the stubbornness of his daughter mounted, he stopped at nothing to bring about a change of heart. The terms that Charles employs in his later letters to Elizabeth readily convey the mood that must have prevailed. Captain Chichagov was a 'Breacher of Hospitality' and, as a father, he was sickened by Elizabeth's willingness to 'wallow [in] such fulsome Flattery with avidity . . .which your Mother would have turned her back on and never have uttered another word to them'. Furthermore, Captain Chichagov was politically unsound, 'a Disciple of Rousseau's whose principles he took pains to introduce into my family'. Elizabeth's desire to ally herself, at such a time, with a Russian 'bitten with the french Manner . . . whom you did not neither can you now know' was both unpatriotic and unchristian. She was a disgrace to the family.[1]

None of Charles's harangues had any effect on Elizabeth's resolve. She had always had a mind of her own and she knew that Pavel's devotion to her was sincere and profound. Behind her father's patriotic stance, she perceived an angry, jealous man, whose personal and political outlook differed greatly from hers. However, Charles now took a step which affected Elizabeth deeply. He extracted a promise from her that she would leave things in abeyance for twelve months, and powerless in the face of paternal authority, Elizabeth finally agreed. This concession was intended to mollify Charles. Elizabeth may have hoped that it might even lead him eventually to modify his position. Furthermore, in his letter, Pavel had promised her that nothing would ever change his feelings for her and that he would wait for as long as was necessary until she was free to marry him.

The nature of Charles's announcement in the *Gentleman's Magazine* on the death of his wife, Sarah, and the wording of his memorial to her in the parish church suggest that even after years of happy marriage, her most important attributes, in his eyes, remained her relationship to his friend 'the brave Capt. Pownall' and her sense of duty. It seems probable, therefore, that Charles's choice of bride was made with his head rather than his heart and that he had no comprehension of what it was like to be in love. Once he had gained Elizabeth's agreement to a twelve-month break in the relationship, he doubtless imagined that she would soon recover from her folly and become, once more, the tender and devoted daughter who cheered his old age and infirmity. Racked with constant asthma attacks, Charles looked and seemed far older than his 70 years – at their first meeting, Pavel had judged him to be at least 80. Charles, however, had completely misunderstood his daughter. In her eyes, her relationship with Pavel was as solemn and as binding as an official engagement. She would not and could not renounce it.

The mood of the country was grim. In 1796, stones were thrown at George III's carriage as he went to open Parliament and the coalition of allies that Pitt had established in 1793 was about to disintegrate. The war with France was continuing to go badly, as during the campaign of 1796, the French army, under the command of the 27-year-old General Bonaparte, marched into Italy, conquered the Kingdom of Savoy and expelled the Austrians from Lombardy. Bonaparte went on to invade Austria and in the Treaty of Campo Formio obliged the Austrians to cede to France their rights over the Netherlands. In October 1796, the Spanish declared war on England and the British fleet had to be withdrawn from Gibraltar and the Mediterranean. Naval morale was at rock bottom and even the victory of the fleet at Cadiz over the Spaniards at Cape Vincent in February 1797 did little to improve the growing discontent in the Channel and North Sea fleets. Early in 1797, the sailors of the Channel Fleet, whose task was to blockade Brest, demanded better pay and conditions from their commander, Lord Howe, and refused to work until their demands were met. The Admiralty managed to settle this dispute fairly rapidly, but the mutiny of the North Sea Fleet was far more serious.

The lot of British naval seamen during the eighteenth century gave ample grounds for discontent. Many of them were the victims of press-gangs and had been kidnapped off the streets of towns like Chatham and Rochester and forced into naval service. Their living conditions and food were appalling and their pay, which was 4d a day, was often denied them in cash and was given instead in tickets which they could only convert into goods at the dockyard.[2] Such circumstances created a large number of men who were particularly susceptible to the ideas of equality that fuelled the French Revolution. It has been suggested, also, that there was a link between the visits of members of the London Corresponding Society to Portsmouth and the Chatham area in 1796 and the subsequent mutinies.[3]

In May 1797, twenty-one ships of the North Sea Fleet were stationed at Sheerness to guard two areas of crucial strategic importance, the mouth of the Medway and the entrance to the Thames. Among them were ten of sixty-four guns, one of seventy-four guns and another, the *Sandwich*, of ninety guns. Together with their crews of fifteen thousand men these ships represented a formidable array of force. On 22 May, an uprising was led by a sailor called Richard Parker, who had organized a general mutiny against the ships' officers by their crews. The ships were taken over by the crews and moved from Sheerness harbour to the nearby Nore anchorage in the Thames estuary. From this commanding position, they could dominate the Isle of Sheppey and threaten shipping to London. Some officers were put ashore at Sheerness and others were held hostage on board, while Parker and his supporters paraded the streets in revolutionary style with a red flag. Like the crewmen of the Channel Fleet, the mutineers had a list of demands, but their intransigence with the Admiralty suggests that they may also have had a revolutionary agenda of their own. With such an assembled firepower they could easily have bombarded British ports and brought the Government to its knees. They also threatened to surrender the fleet to the Dutch. The Isle of Sheppey was in a state of siege, acts of piracy and plunder took place and the inhabitants of the area, including Chatham, lived in daily fear of violence. The Government retaliated by placing soldiers on both sides of the Thames in an attempt to starve out the mutineers. Meanwhile, the Resident Commissioner at Chatham, who was closely associated with Sheerness, and his family may well have prepared themselves to face the tumbrels.

The situation was particularly tense for Beatrice, whose husband of less than four months was on board the *Clyde* at Sheerness. Charles Cunningham, however, was one of the very few officers in the fleet who had not lost his authority. He had also had a moral victory over Parker, who had come aboard the *Clyde* and tried to persuade the crew to mount

1. Captain Charles Proby (1725–99) by Reynolds, *c.*1765. Splendidly attired in the newly introduced official naval uniform, he is shown at the height of his period of active naval service, six years before taking up the post of Commissioner of the Chatham Dockyard.

2, Sarah Proby (1741–83). Copy of a miniature
after a portrait by Reynolds of *c*.1759, when she
was aged 18 and recently married to Charles Proby.

3. Charlotte Proby (b. 1770). Miniature of
Elizabeth's second sister, possibly painted
in 1789 at the time of her first marriage.

4. Elizabeth Proby (1774–1811). Miniature
by an unknown artist, possibly dating from
before her marriage to Pavel in 1799.

5. Vasilii Chichagov (1726–1899). A successful admiral, much esteemed for his modesty and gentleness.

6. Catherine the Great (1729–96). An obscure German princess, who became one of Russia's outstanding rulers.

7. Paul I (1754–1801) by Shchukin. He had an uncontrollable temper and imprisoned Pavel for wanting to marry an Englishwoman.

8. Alexander I (1777–1825) by Gérard. He tolerated Pavel's outspokenness because he valued his honesty and ability.

9. Elizabeth Chichagova (1774–1811). Portrait by an unknown artist, *c.*1806. Probably painted in St Petersburg, when Pavel's star was in the ascendant. Elizabeth's air of serenity is in marked contrast to her demeanour in the earlier miniature.

10. Pavel Chichagov (1767–1849). Portrait by an unknown artist, early 19th century, which admirably captures Pavel's liveliness and sense of humour. Even today, his portrait is banished from its rightful place in the 1812 Gallery of the Hermitage.

11. Count Joseph de Maistre. One of Pavel and Elizabeth's closest friends, he probably understood their relationship better than anyone else.

12. The Marquis de Caulaincourt, after a portrait by Gérard. As French Ambassador, he frequently attended the soirées at the Chichagovs.

13. John Joshua Proby, Earl of Carysfort, by Reynolds, c.1784. The portrait is contemporary with his visit to Russia.

14. Count Simon Vorontsov by Lawrence, c.1805. A passionate Anglophile, he was a father figure to Pavel and Elizabeth.

15. Military Parade led by the Emperor Alexander I in the Palace Square, St Petersburg. Etching by Benjamin Paterssen, *c.*1803. The high spire of the Admiralty is visible beyond the façade of the palace.

16. *View of the centre of the Great Bridge of the Neva.* Etching by John H. Clark after Mornay. Published 1815. Taken a short distance upstream of the Chichagov mansion, Elizabeth would have known this view well. Vasilevskii Island is on the left.

17. *The Snake in the Grass* by Reynolds, *c.*1788. There are five versions of this picture. This one is at Elton Hall. The one purchased by Carysfort for Potemkin is in the Hermitage.

18. The Crossing of the Berezina in 1812. Gouache by an unknown artist, who was evidently an eyewitness. There is no sign of any Russian troops on the opposite bank.

an action against the fort at Tilbury. Cunnungham had prevented this and on 29 May he ordered his crew to disregard a signal from Parker and instead, under cover of darkness, the *Clyde* and one other ship, the *St Fiorenzo*, managed to work their away into Sheerness harbour and the protection of the shore batteries. The *St Fiorenzo* was damaged by fire from the mutinous fleet, but the *Clyde* escaped unscathed.

Within two weeks, disunity was tearing the mutineers apart and other ships tried to follow Cunningham's courageous example. The *Repulse* ran aground in her headlong flight to the shelter of Sheerness harbour and was callously bombarded by Parker's vessel, the *Monmouth*. The *Ardent*, which was also intent on escape, passed close to the *Monmouth* and opened fire in support of the *Repulse*. Meanwhile, in the atmosphere of general mistrust, fighting had broken out between the other ships of the fleet and all eventually decided that their only hope lay in surrender to the authorities at Sheerness. The final ship to surrender was the *Monmouth*. Parker gave himself up and was tried and sentenced to death. He was executed at Sheerness aboard the *Sandwich*, dressed in 'a neat suit of mourning (waistcoat excepted) wearing his half-boots over a pair of black silk stockings'.[4] As a last request he was permitted to drink a glass of white wine.

During the mutiny, the mouth of the Texel would have remained unguarded, if it had not been for the ingenuity of Admiral Duncan, who remained alone off the Dutch coast with his loyal crew. His ploy of sailing up and down the coastline sending signals to an imaginary fleet was completely successful and the enemy was not aware of the deception until the mutiny was over.

Within days of his escape, Cunningham received a letter of thanks from the merchants of London:

London Marine Society's Offices, June 8, 1797

Sir. – I have the honour to convey the unanimous thanks of a very numerous and respectable meeting of merchants, ship-owners, insurers and others, held on the Royal Exchange of London, to you, as commander, and to the officers and crew of H.M.S. the Clyde, for their spirited conduct in carrying your ship through the mutinous fleet.[5]

Later, Cunningham's defiance of Parker and the escape of the *Clyde* were regarded as the turning point of the mutiny. For the family at Chatham, the deliverance of Beatrice's husband must have been a great relief, but there were other concerns. The health of Thomas Pitcairn was deteriorating and on 27 October he died at the Commissioner's house after many months of illness. Nor was Thomas's death the only sorrow to afflict this already unhappy family. The younger of Sarah and James Pigott's twin sons, who had been christened Charles and William respectively, had been born blind and would require constant attention for the rest of his life. In addition to all these woes at both national and personal levels, the deadly conflict between Elizabeth and her father continued. With Beatrice married and Charlotte deeply involved in caring for her dying husband, more and more domestic tasks fell on Elizabeth's shoulders. Her brother Francis Henry was also periodically at home and both he and Charles counted on Elizabeth's availability to run the household. Since the departure of Pavel and the cessation of all communication between them at the behest of her father, Elizabeth had fallen into a deep depression and her health had seriously declined. She lived mechanically from day to day, unable to see any way out of the deadlock, but her commitment to Pavel never wavered.

Charles was baffled and increasingly disturbed by a situation which he had thought would blow over. He sensed Elizabeth's implacable resolution and mistook it for enmity. His complaints grew increasingly querulous. He firmly believed that he was only acting from parental duty and that he was saving her from a disastrous marriage. He was incensed that

you thought proper some time past when I was endeavouring to obstruct your progress (which I could not approve of, into the extreme of Dissipation) to tell me that I had forfeited your esteem by my disapproving of your Marriage to the Russian Captain Chichagoff . . . and as you thought proper to whisper (when I observed to you that you seemed inclined to use every method to make me unhappy in my mind) that your Conduct towards me would have been very different if I had not disapproved of the said Marriage.[6]

In reality, Elizabeth's suffering was quite as great, if not greater, than her father's. She was torn between the lifelong bonds of filial love and obedience and the sure knowledge that she was in danger of losing her greatest chance of earthly happiness through her father's inability to see beyond the limitations of his own prejudices. An undated miniature shows her as a very pale young woman in a simple muslin dress with a wide yellow sash. Her face is framed in soft dark curls and her large blue eyes gaze steadily ahead (Plate 4). The blend of resolution and unhappiness that characterizes Elizabeth's expression reflects so perfectly what must have been her state of mind at this period of her life that one is tempted to attribute the miniature to this time. True to her promise to her father, she had broken off all contact with Pavel for twelve months, but she could not continue to live like this indefinitely. She had to contact Pavel.

There is no indication of how Pavel became aware of how seriously Elizabeth was pining for him. An obvious conduit for correspondence would have been Vorontsov, although Pavel does not mention this in his memoirs. Similarly, although the Russian squadron was officially withdrawn from the North Sea Fleet in the early summer of 1797, Vorontsov managed to maintain a few Russian ships in British waters under Rear-Admiral Makarov. The rest of the squadron returned to England in 1798, when Pavel received letters from Vorontsov through Makarov. Charles was also able to learn from Pavel's fellow officers that he had left the navy, which suggests that members of the Russian squadron continued to use the dockyard throughout this period and could also have carried letters for Elizabeth.

For many months Pavel and Elizabeth had been cut off from each other, but while Elizabeth was enduring the trials of separation and paternal fury, Pavel was undergoing an equally painful ordeal of his own. The ascent to the Russian throne in 1796 of the Emperor Paul, the unstable eldest son of Catherine the Great and her lover Sergei Saltykov,* brought many changes to the lives of those close to the court. Paul probably suspected that he was not the son of the murdered Peter III, but he nevertheless revered the memory of his supposed father and never forgave his mother for Peter's unexplained death. Their dislike was mutual and throughout her reign, the Empress kept him at a distance, giving him palaces and estates outside St Petersburg at Pavlovsk and at Gatchina, where he indulged his obsession with military uniforms and drill with a small private army. His first wife died in childbirth, but he then married a German princess, Sophia Dorothea of Württemberg, who took the name of Maria Feodorovna and bore the Emperor a large family. Maria Feodorovna was a formidable personality, who was to remain a power in the Russian court for many decades.

The Emperor Paul threw the established order of St Petersburg into chaos. Waliszewski writes: 'Even when he was calm his mind was quite

---

* The identity of Paul's father has never been fully resolved. Paul was also said to bear a strong resemblance to Peter III, his mother's husband.

unequal to the task of controlling, as he wished to do, the whole complicated machinery of government in its smallest details.'[7] A flood of imperial orders issued daily from the palace on the most extraordinary subjects, many of which reflected the Emperor's eccentric preoccupation with uniform and dress. Certain hats were banned and their banishment was enforced by the police. It was forbidden to wear shoes with ribbons or laces, or high cravats, and military tailors who did not follow his orders minutely were arrested. Those who had been favoured during the reign of his mother were robbed of their influence, although initially, at least, they were not persecuted. The remains of the Emperor Peter III were disinterred and reburied with great pomp beside those of the Empress in the Cathedral within the Peter and Paul Fortress. The navy was put into Prussian-style green uniforms and the imperial orders of St George and St Vladimir were abolished. The Emperor's foreign policy was muddled. Although he had a horror of the regicidal aspects of the French Revolution and the ideas of the 'Jacobins', his primary objective was to keep Russia out of the conflict in Europe. With this end in mind, therefore, in 1797 he postponed the annual departure of the Russian squadron to the Texel. Pavel found himself confined to Kronstadt and he wrote to Vorontsov lamenting the fact that he would not be coming to England that season.[8]

For the Chichagov family, one of the worst aspects of the new reign was the promotion of a junior naval officer, Grigorii Kushelev, whom Pavel refers to disparagingly as the 'one-time ensign'. Since early days, there had been no love lost between Pavel and Kushelev, and he was one of the fellow officers who had objected to what was considered by some to be Pavel's favoured treatment as the son of the Commander-in-Chief. Now Kushelev occupied, as a close favourite of the new Emperor's, the powerful position of Vice-President of the College of the Admiralty and could command the Russian fleet at will. Pavel ridiculed Kushelev's book, *A Study of the Maritime Signals now in use*, which won the approbation of the Emperor and which the navy was obliged to use.

Vasilii retained his position as Commander-in-Chief of the Fleet, but he found the new regime as trying as Pavel did. In July 1797, the Emperor decided that he wished, as High Admiral, to assist personally at naval manoeuvres which were to take place in the Baltic at his command. A special yacht was prepared for the Emperor and Empress, who were to be accompanied by the Grand Dukes Alexander and Constantine and the Emperor's mistress, the plain and middle-aged Catherine Nelidova.

Sixty-eight ships were involved in the occasion and for days beforehand, Kushelev bombarded his erstwhile superior with instructions that Vasilii found both impertinent and absurd. Vasilii's irritation mounted and shortly before the manoeuvres were due to begin, he wrote to the Emperor pleading his age and his health and offered his resignation. His resignation was accepted and his dismissal from the navy was published the next day.

Pavel bristled with indignation at the peremptory dismissal of his father, but having no pretext to resign himself, he was obliged to continue as commander of the *Retvisan*. The naval manoeuvres were bedevilled with bad weather and the imperial party suffered from severe seasickness. The Emperor, who had no knowledge of naval matters, attempted to direct operations from his yacht and spent a night on deck in full uniform, seated on a coil of rope, before being compelled by the stormy weather to return to Kronstadt.[9] As soon as he could, Pavel wrote to his father's successor as Commander-in-Chief and asked for leave on the grounds of ill health, before retiring from Kronstadt to the nearby country house of a friend. It was apparent to everyone that this was an act of family solidarity and the Emperor, enraged, insisted on a medical check by the chief naval physician. A medical certificate was somehow produced and Pavel promptly offered his resignation. Both his brothers, Peter and Vasilii, followed suit. On his return to St Petersburg, Pavel was incensed to be told that he was too young to be entitled to a pension, despite his fifteen years of naval service. He took advantage of the voyage of three friends to England to write a bitter letter to Vorontsov, in which he recounted his recent experiences. Now that he no longer basked in the reflected glory of his father's imperial favour, Pavel's enemies multiplied. Contemporaries who had long envied him and perhaps objected to his haughty manner took advantage of his fall from grace to avenge themselves. He mentions, with irritation, the promotion of two officers, Shishkov and Baratynskii, and adds that Baratynskii had become his sworn enemy and spoke maliciously of him on all possible occasions.[10]

The three eldest Chichagov sons, reunited in St Petersburg, rallied round their elderly father. He was now 71 years old and his eyesight was failing. They decided that their only option was to retire to the property at Shklov in the White Russian province of Mogilev, which the Empress Catherine had given to Vasilii. It was at this time that Pavel and Elizabeth's correspondence revived and Pavel's mind revolved continually around the problem of how to return to England.

Even a retired naval officer required the permission of the Emperor to leave the country. The dramatic decline in the fortunes of his family accentuated his concern for Elizabeth's complete incomprehension of Russia's despotic form of government. He was afraid that this trusting, sheltered English girl would never survive the hardships and injustices that the Emperor might at any time inflict on them. When he had made his declaration, he had been a successful naval officer with a bright future ahead of him. Now he had few friends at court and was buried in the countryside with no prospects except to devote himself to the agricultural improvement of the family property. One small consolation was that they had many congenial neighbours who were also the beneficiaries of the late Empress and were in similar circumstances.

Against this background, Pavel decided that he must try and warn Elizabeth of the situation to which she would be committing herself if they married. He wrote her a long letter, in which he described the behaviour of the new Emperor and the uncertainties of life in Russia. He also wrote again to Vorontsov to tell him that he had applied for five months leave in England to study agriculture, so that he might occupy himself as a farmer.[11] Elizabeth was bewildered and distressed by Pavel's letter. She found his representation of the new Emperor incredible. She had spent her life in the orderly world of provincial England and what Pavel was describing defied her powers of imagination and of belief. It could only mean that he wanted to break off the engagement. Her worst fears of the past year had been realized. Pavel had returned to Russia and fallen in love with someone else. Elizabeth replied to Pavel with as much courage as she could muster. She explained that she could not bring herself to believe what he had told her and that she had therefore concluded that he wished to terminate their engagement. With a heavy heart, she assured him that he was free to become engaged to someone else, if he so wished. For Elizabeth these must have been her darkest days, and the forebodings of her father must suddenly have taken on the threatening appearance of reality.

The politics of Europe were becoming increasingly complex as the army of General Bonaparte continued its victorious progress. In June 1798, on his way to Egypt, Napoleon occupied Malta, and the Order of the Knights of Malta turned to the Emperor Paul for protection and offered him the Grand Mastership of the Order. The Emperor had already extended a cordial welcome in St Petersburg to the emissary of the Order, because there was a priory in the previously Polish province of Volhynia, recently annexed by Russia. He therefore accepted the Grand Mastership with enthusiasm and requested Napoleon to relinquish the island. When Napoleon refused to co-operate, the Emperor decided to abandon his pacific position in respect of the war between Britain and France and to support the enemies of France. The Emperor presided over an elaborate ceremony in St Petersburg to celebrate his Grand Mastership, for which he donned an outfit of his own invention. This was a combination of a Maltese costume and a Prussian uniform, over which he wore a knee-length Dalmation coat and a sword.

Napoleon's advance on Egypt produced yet another twist in Russia's foreign policy. Egypt was part of the Ottoman Empire, and in 1798 the Sultan of Turkey approached Russia to form an alliance against the French. In October, a joint Russo-Turkish fleet attacked the Ionian Islands off the west coast of Greece in order to expel the French, who had acquired them as part of the Treaty of Campo Formio. The inhabitants welcomed the Russians and an independent Greek republic was set up under Russo-Turkish auspices. In the meantime, in August 1798, Nelson had inflicted a crushing defeat on the French navy at Aboukir Bay in Egypt and in 1799 a new coalition was formed against France, comprising Britain, Russia, Austria, Turkey and Naples. While Napoleon was isolated in Egypt without a fleet, the Russian general, Suvorov, successfully invaded Lombardy with an Austro-Russian army and Britain and Russia agreed to the secondment of two Russian divisions for a combined landing in Holland.

This maelstrom of shifting alliances, which affected the lives of millions, was also to decide the future of Elizabeth and Pavel. Their temporary misunderstanding was soon clarified and Pavel deferred any further attempt to describe Russia to her until they were once again together. Their letters reassumed their loving tenor and they agreed that in the face of Charles's continuing opposition, they had no choice but to defy his authority and marry without his blessing. Elizabeth was now 24 years old and the realization that parental permission to her marriage was not a legal requirement, but rather a courtesy, caused a dramatic reversal of roles in her relationship with her father. When she told her father of their decision, he was as stunned and dumbfounded as she and Pavel had been by his refusal to countenance their engagement over two years previously. It had never occurred to him that his dutiful daughter Elizabeth would ever dare to disobey him. His fury against Chichagov knew no bounds and in a last-ditch effort to exert his authority, he let it be understood that

Elizabeth would no longer be welcome under his roof if she persisted in this decision. He also cut her out of his will.

To Charles's great chagrin, Elizabeth welcomed his suggestion that they should live separately and she suggested that she should make a visit to some friends in London for a while. The day before she left Chatham, in a spirit of reconciliation, Elizabeth wrote him the following letter:

My dear Pa,

I am sorry you do not believe my assertions which I solemnly repeat are strictly true – of having given up the point for one twelvemonth – when, in consequence of my lost health and miserable state of my mind, which he [Pavel] became acquainted with, our correspondence first began; which has evidently restored it. As I am persuaded he will either live in England, or remain for a length of time, I shall, after having paid a few visits, with great pleasure return here according to your kind permission.

With regard to pecuniary affairs, as you had frequently informed me that I was to expect nothing from you if I married a Foreigner, I could not but acquiese in it; knowing that Chechagoff's fortune was sufficient to enable us to live comfortably; the consideration of receiving nothing with me, made no alteration in his wishes with regard to our union, therefore I wished to convince you that in seeking a reconciliation with you, I was not activated by any interested motive, but from affection alone. With respect to settlements I am sure he will agree to any thing that may be thought proper for him to do, at the time.

Finding from Mrs Pigott that you are displeased from suspecting Mrs Lutwidge to have been concerned, I must positively assure you that she *never* has been, or is now acquainted with the circumstances of my ever having heard from him.

I most gratefully receive the expressions of your good wishes, which I trust you will one day see realized – and which I have no doubt of from his universally esteemed character – and I beg you to believe me very sincerely, yr affecte Elizth Proby

I shall be obliged to you for what money you propose giving me for the present, as perhaps it may not be convenient to get it tomorrow morning.[12]

In February 1799 Charles added the following codicil to his will:

As my Daughter, Elizabeth Proby, hath declared (two years apparently after she having given this point up) that she is determined at all events to marry the Russian Captain Chichagoff for which purpose she expects him to arrive in this country in a short time; as I could not at first (about two years since) and cannot now either, as her parent, as her friend, or as a Briton, approve of it, my will and desire is that she be allowed at the rate of 100£ per annum to be paid quarterly until the said marriage takes place and then it is to cease for ever. . . . But if the Marriage should not take place between her and the said Captain Chichagoff or between her and any other foreigner then in that case my will and desire is that my said will and Testament remain in its full force except the harpsichord and its music which I now bequeath to my daughter Pigott and her heirs for ever.[13]

Elizabeth being the most musical of the sisters, Charles had always intended to leave her all the musical instruments, but he was determined to punish her – even if she did not marry Pavel. Furthermore, the harpsichord had been the most frequent scene of her 'dissipation'.

Elizabeth probably visited her sister Sarah at Beddington, but by March she was living in London, at Gower Street, with some friends called Campbell. Now that she had left home, she no longer saw her father as the tyrant who had tried to rob her of her happiness, but rather as an increasingly frail old man with whom she longed to make her peace. She tried to maintain some semblance of normality in their relations through regular correspondence:

Gower Street, Saturday<br>9<sup>th</sup> March

My dear Pa,

I was so sorry to have missed seeing Admiral Pigott the other evening, however I heard from Mrs Hargrave . . . that all were well at Chatham. I am afraid this third winter will not agree quite so well with you as the Summer weather we have had; however we may reasonably expect it to be of shorter duration than the last cold weather – Lately we really have not only been without fires during the Morning, but also have sat with the windows open – It was the more unlucky not seeing the Admiral as it was the first evening we had been out for sometime, then we were at the Oratorio, a thing I never was at before, nor do I desire ever to go again –

Madame Mara, who I have never heard since we were at the Abbey, has the finest voice I ever heard and the most warbling [illegible], therefore to hear her was delightful, tho' at the same time I regretted that the musick was not Italian – The rest of the performers were moderate as well as the instrumental part and altogether I never was so little pleased with *musick*, which I attributed partly to its want of excellence and partly to my having no great partiality to Handels musick – If Fanny Burslem should *hear this*, I conclude she will have the greatest *contempt for my taste*.

Mrs Pitcairn has sent these *young Ladies* a great quantity of Portuguese vocal musick – it seems very pretty and like the Italian, but the greatest part of it being written in the tenor clef, it is very tiresome to pick out and they have not tried a quarter of it yet. . . .

I have not been yet to get Mrs Proby's print, as it has not been convenient for Mrs Campbell to walk so far and she and the girls wish to go with me as those shops afford the sight of many fine prints – John Campbell goes every morning at ten o'clock to a Lawyer in Lincoln's Inn and studies there the whole morning, so that we have only his company in the Evening. William is not very fond of attending the Ladies, so I never go out but with them – they are all fond of walking, therefore the first fine morning we mean to go. We generally work and read before we walk out as Gower Street is such a distance from every place they are not much tormented with morning visitors. I have not heard from Charlotte since I wrote to you last and probably she has been equally silent to the Dock Yard as the productions of her pen are not very numerous. . . .

Love to all and kind regards from the Campbells and I remain my dear Pa's affecte Elizth Proby.[14]

But Charles was in no mood for forgiveness or reconciliation and after a brief respite, he began once again to pressurize Elizabeth, accusing her of having thrown 'all Domestic concerns aside and left your Father whether you could or not get any other person to attend him, to run after every Captain you could which did not pass unobserved in the Eye of the World for gossips whether Male or Female will ever amuse themselves with censuring then – this kind of conduct.'[15]

The last letters between him and Elizabeth make painful reading. Charles's letters are rambling, repetitive screeds that cover many pages. He wrote draft after draft of the same arguments in a hopeless attempt to convince himself of his rectitude. Worn out in mind and body by ill-health and the two-year battle for the heart of his favourite daughter, his thoughts revert constantly to her childhood, when the education of his children had seemed such a simple thing:

Some years previous to your Birth in 1774 your Mother and I settled our plan for the Education of all our Children, and for giving them a proper and requisite introduction into the World. . . .

In your youthful days to assist in bringing you on into the knowledge of the world . . . I made it a Rule, I believe first with your Mother, to communicate to you all private letters whatever their nature might have been, I have continued nearly the same to this Day, another assistance to the knowledge of the World and this was done with a view to lead you into an opinion that

74

Parents were the best Friends, Advisers, on all points, even in the most secret, as you advanced in years, it was a general remark that I appeared more your Admirer than your parent. . . .

*In great deference to your superior judgment to mine in all Matters* I must humbly presume to give mine viz That all Parents are in duty bound to watch carefully over every affection which their children may be liable to either from the State of their Nature or from their ignorance of Mankind; this is to continue to encourage them in a good path but reprobate and condemn their conduct in a bad Path – under these ideas, I presumed, that, as a Parent as a Christian as a friend and as an Englishman to disapprove of your marrying a Foreigner. . . .

I received a different character than you entertain of him. His quitting his Profession when he was in not very favourable circumstance; His friends say because younger officers were promoted before him, which must and do happen in all Government. . . .

I have already in this letter told you chiefly the real motives for my disapprobation of your marriage with C.C. he himself brought on another viz that a parent had no right to prevent his daughter from marrying the man of her affections and was apparently offended at my thinking to enquire after his Character Finances etc which if I had not objected to [his] being a Foreigner etc. I might have done through Ld Carysfort who has been some time in Russia or thro the Russian Ambassador here and then I should have taken the same precautions for my approbations as I did on your sisters and brothers marriages – but C.C. was to have my immediate approbation on demand. . . .

I am quite conscientially satisfied that, in my disapprobation of your marriage, I did my Duty as a Parent, as a Friend and as a Native of this Country, not willing to consent to his Daughters marrying a Foreigner of a different Religion, of whom I had no knowledge or a possibility of acquiring except from a few of his Acquaintances he introduced into my house, to extoll your Talents for Music and learning of the Russian Language. . . .

With these ideas of a Parents duty I could not, altho I might have thought it unavailing, avoid using my endeavour to break the match entirely off. I have failed and have experienced the same conduct from you as I have heretofore, viz treated undutifully, ungratefully and very wickedly. . . .[16]

Elizabeth's responses, in contrast, are a model of clarity and reason:

Saturday 23rd March

My dear Pa,

I cannot help being extremely sorry and very much surprised that you should have the least expectations of my making any alteration in my intention of marrying, as I have before seriously and truly declared to you that it is not in my power. My promise as well as affections being *solemnly engaged*, it becomes of course, impossible to make any change, and in every way is impracticable.

When I was on the point of leaving Chatham believing (according to your declaration) that I was going to be dismissed your house forever, I even wrote to Chichagoff to repeat my assurances, and promised to receive him at any time that he could now come and therefore believe that he may by this time be making some of the necessary preparations for his voyage here during the ensuing summer. I was the more easily induced to this from having observed that you have always appeared to dislike any person whom you suspected of attachment to me, altho English, therefore I really believed that whoever I married would be equally disagreeable to you.

I cannot confine my ideas so much as to think that happiness exists only in one Country in the world, believing that the same Providence extends to all, and that whoever is virtuous and good in any Nation will be equally acceptable to God. The exalted character [which] my dear C.— bears from all his own countrymen and invariably from all who have served with or known him here, together with his disinterested and continued affection, would compensate in my mind for many disadvantages, if any existed.

I much lament the extremes you have determined with regard to me . . . because it will oblige me to repair to the house of some friend for my union with him, assuring you that if anything could add to the happiness of seeing him again, it would be to have him received by you, with some degree of the very great partiality, you formerly expressed and testified towards him and which everybody felt as well as yourself – But, as you have resolved to the contrary, and likewise to deprive me of all fortune, I have nothing to do but patiently to submit.

I cannot believe you serious in supposing I should live with him without being married, being conscious that nobody can have the least foundation for forming such an opinion of me. I fancy all my friends and relations have pretty well guessed that I must have renewed the business, but as everybody must know how impossible it is to *assure* happiness to any one, most people are afraid of the dangerous undertaking of either breaking or making any Match. . . . I was in hopes after our comfortable reconciliation that nothing more would pass on the subject – However as I have only repeated my former assertions, I feel comfortably persuaded that this can be no interruption to it, as I shall ever remain, notwithstanding your resolutions, y$^r$ aff$^{te}$ Daughter Elizth Proby. [17]

Elizabeth's repeated efforts to bring about a rapprochement fell on deaf ears. In his reply to the above letter Charles tries to justify his blanket opposition to marriage with a foreigner by stating that 'Happiness, no doubt exists in all countries, but from what I know of foreigners or their Country, I am satisfied from our Religious laws and Liberties, that it exists in the greatest perfection in this Country.' He defends his act of disinheritance in much the same vein, adding that he was 'not willing to have any part of my Finances, due to my own country, sent to be spent in a Foreign Country and this by a Man apparently a Free Thinker of Rousseau's Sect and consequently might have thrown you off at will. . . .'[18]

Charles Proby died on 31 March 1799, only a few days after this exchange of letters, and on 6 April his funeral took place at St Mary's, Chatham. It was a solemn affair, for although he had specified in his will that he wished to be buried 'at as little expence and with as little pomp as possible,' he had also left careful instructions to his children: 'If I should be buried at Chatham in the same Vault with your Mother let it be in a leaden coffin carried to the Church in a hearse with one Mourning Coach to attend it as your Mother was carried to the Church by the Boat's Crew and possibly by some of the Yacht's Crew – let them be paid the same as at that time, that is to be properly considered.'[19]

The hearse was drawn to the church by four horses, and the coffin – covered with a fine black cloth – was carried in by eight pallbearers. The undertakers supplied three coachmen's cloaks and numerous mourning hatbands, scarves and black gloves for the large number of people who assisted with the ceremony. The boatmen were handsomely paid. After the service, Charles's body was carried out to the churchyard and placed in the stone vault with that of his wife, Sarah. His children had fulfilled his last wishes to the letter. In addition, the existing memorial to Sarah and Baptist was extended to include Charles and his descendants, listing the dates of their births and marriages.

Now that the Commissioner had died, Pavel urgently needed to obtain permission to go to England. One of the few allies that the Chichagovs possessed in the court of the Emperor was Bezborodko, who had survived into the new regime. Pavel therefore wrote to him requesting him to intercede with the Emperor on his behalf to obtain authority for his journey to England to get married. Pavel's request prompted an immediate and angry reaction from the Emperor and was instantly turned down with the comment that 'there were enough brides in Russia without having to go to England to find them.'[20] In despair, Pavel turned to the only other person he knew who still wielded some influence, Vorontsov. By this time, Vorontsov was fully aware of Pavel's involvement with Elizabeth and he exerted his considerable diplomatic talents on their behalf. Here also, the convolutions of Anglo-Russian relations played a vital role.

Under the terms of the new European coalition against the French, Russia had agreed to send two divisions of soldiers to participate in an Anglo-Russian landing in Holland under the overall command of the Duke of York. The troops were to travel to Holland on British and Russian ships, which would assist in the landing. Vorontsov, who was intimately concerned with the arrangements and was in close contact with all the key players in Britain, made use of this political development to further Pavel's romantic interests. He wrote pressing letters to Prince Lopukhin, the current Procurator-General, and to Count Rostopchin, the President of the College of Foreign Affairs, in which he suggested that the British government would be especially pleased to see Captain Chichagov as a member of the Russian squadron, because of his excellent naval reputation in Britain. Then, with a touch of genius, he added that Lord Spencer, the First Lord of the Admiralty, whom Pavel had met only briefly, held him in particularly high regard. The letters achieved their objective and some of their content must have reached the ears of the Emperor, but the slightly exasperated tone of Rostopchin's letter to Vorontsov of 10 May suggests that the task may not have been straightforward:

> Your commission or rather your orders on the subject of Mr Tshitshagow have been executed. He has been taken back into the service as a rear-admiral, which will give him back his seniority, and he has been given a place in Mr Macarow's squadron. He will arrive with you and then he can marry and go and kill himself. What could be more natural? Count Kushelev has taken enormous pains to fulfil your wishes; he confesses that Mr Tshitshagow is an officer of the highest merit and that he is only a bit arrogant, having obtained his employment through being the son of an admiral.[21]

The Emperor's approval was obtained to the marriage and a summons was sent to Pavel to present himself as soon as possible at the palace of Pavlovsk, with the assurance that he would be taken back into the navy with the rank of rear-admiral.

Two weeks later, late in the evening of 20 June, Pavel arrived at the Emperor's country residence outside St Petersburg. To his great discomfiture, he found himself obliged to wait for a considerable period with Kushelev, who quizzed him on his reappointment. The sight of Kushelev, already an admiral, made Pavel's blood boil. By rights, according to his years of service, Pavel's rank was well ahead of Kushelev's. He could hardly contain his irritation. The rank of rear-admiral that he had just received was no compensation for his outraged professional dignity, as it would nevertheless place him behind many others who were junior to him in terms of service. Kushelev was enjoying the situation. At last he had this arrogant admiral's son where he wanted him. With infinite slyness, Kushelev then asked Pavel whether he would prefer to serve in the Baltic or go to England and Pavel, still smarting over his lost rank, replied that he would prefer the Baltic, since there he would not be obliged to serve under Baratynskii, who had been nothing but an ensign when he was already a captain.

Pavel did not receive an audience that evening and left the palace with instructions to appear early the next morning. The next day, at the early morning parade, Pavel was presented to the Emperor, who greeted him warmly and invited him to come to his office afterwards. As Pavel was waiting in an ante-room, where a courtier had informed him that the Emperor was very favourably disposed towards him and was looking forward to their meeting, Kushelev appeared. On hearing that Pavel had yet to have his meeting, Kushelev vanished briefly into the Emperor's office and when he re-emerged he signalled Pavel to accompany him back to his office. Mystified, Pavel followed, only to be told that, regretfully, Kushelev had felt obliged to inform the Emperor of Pavel's disinclination to serve under Baratynskii in the squadron destined for England. Consequently, said Kushelev, the Emperor had instructed him to dismiss Pavel, once again, from the service. At this point, Pavel's famous temper was barely under control. With icy calm, he thanked Kushelev for his attentions and remarked that he would like nothing better than to retire to the country. As Pavel was waiting for Kushelev to write the instruction for his dismissal, he received an order to return at once to the office of the Emperor. The Emperor Paul was in a towering rage.

During the reign of Paul I, thousands of innocent people received his sentence to be 'flogged without mercy', which Waliszewski describes as being 'in the majority of cases equivalent to a capital sentence aggravated by torture.'[22] Many more were condemned in hideous suffering to exile in Siberia, often for crimes as absurd as failing to pronounce a word of command in accordance with some newly issued imperial ukase. Not for nothing was the word 'terror' in common currency. In a contemporary letter, the Vice-President of the College of Foreign Affairs, Prince

Kochubei, wrote: 'The terror in which we live here cannot be described. We tremble. . . . True or false, an accusation is always listened to. The fortress is full of victims. Black melancholy has settled on everybody.'[23]

Pavel stood before the Emperor in his full uniform and wearing his order of St George. The Emperor was surrounded by aides who stood, mute, beside their master and watched the ensuing scene with ghoulish fascination. 'So you do not wish to serve me? You wish to serve a foreign King?' Pavel prepared himself to reply, but the Emperor silenced him. 'I know that you are a Jacobin, but I shall destroy all those ideas.' The Emperor's voice rose and he turned to his aides. 'Dismiss him from the service and put him under arrest. Take his sword and remove his decorations.' Without a word, Pavel removed his order himself and handed over his sword. He felt absolutely no fear; the whole episode seemed to him like a sequence from some insane comedy; he was tempted to laugh. 'Remove his uniform – now.' A dozen willing hands obeyed the royal command, and Pavel, reflecting that he might be on his way to Siberia, murmured to one of the aides that he might need the purse that was in the pocket of his uniform and would he please bring it to him later. Pavel walked back through the palace, stripped to his shirtsleeves, to Kushelev's office, from whence, having retrieved his purse, he was conducted to be confined in the citadel of the Peter and Paul Fortress.[24]

This incident has been recounted many times and became one of the best-known episodes in the life of Pavel Chichagov. There are differing accounts and interpretations of the behaviour of both Pavel and the Emperor, but the general story remains the same. In his memoirs Pavel suggests that Kushelev, out of spite, had told the Emperor that his request to marry in England was simply a pretext to defect to the British navy and that the accusations of Jacobinism came from the same source. The Emperor was unbalanced and had been terrified since early childhood of meeting the same gruesome fate as his supposed father, Peter III. Therefore the mildest hint of conspiracy or treachery was enough to spark off his unbridled temper.

The Peter and Paul Fortress contained the state prison of St Petersburg and had witnessed some of Russia's most hideous executions. It was here that Peter the Great had his son tortured to death before his eyes, and it was in one of its many dank and murky dungeons that the hapless Princess Tarakanova died of tuberculosis after daring to lay claim to the throne of Catherine the Great. Few escaped from its clutches. Pavel, however, did not lose heart. He was met at the fortress by Count Pahlen, the Military Governor of St Petersburg, whom he knew and who consoled him that in these crazy days it was Pavel's turn today, but it might well be his tomorrow. Pavel was then conducted to the citadel and the prison in which he was to be detained. There he met another acquaintance, Prince Dolgorukov, who was the Commandant. Within a few hours, thanks to the offices of various influential contacts, Pavel found himself not in a subterranean vault with a few straw-covered planks, but rather in a small, well-furnished apartment, recently renovated and well supplied with books and even newspapers.

After eight days Pavel, who already had an inch of stubble and was suffering from a bout of fever, was abruptly moved from his lodgings. As he contemplated his new accommodation – a poorly lit cell containing nothing but a bed with a sentry at the end of it – Count Pahlen arrived and began to question him. Pavel retorted that he was extremely angry and did not see how he could have displeased the Emperor since he had never spoken a word to him. At this, Pahlen merely smiled and said that he hoped to have better news soon. Once Pahlen departed, Pavel was returned to his previous apartment, from which he had been removed because his captors feared that Pahlen would report to the Emperor that he was too comfortably lodged. Pahlen, however, was an ally and thanks to his efforts, Pavel was released two days later. The drama was not yet completely over, but when Pavel was readmitted to the imperial presence, the Emperor suggested that they should forget what had passed and appointed him the commander of the Russian squadron destined for England.

On 3 July, Rostopchin wrote another letter to Vorontsov:

I must give you the latest news of your protégé, Chichagov. He created a scandal on arrival, partly through his ignorance of the court and partly through his own sharp tongue. He said some things to the Emperor that were a bit strong, and between ourselves, quite inappropriate, above all at the present time. But now everything is arranged: he is going to command the first division of the squadron that will take the troops to Holland, and afterwards he will go to England to get married and to serve with Macarow.[25]

For all his bravado, his confinement in the fortress and the tensions of his recent experiences took their toll of Pavel. On arriving at Revel to supervise the embarkation of the troops, his health deteriorated and he was once again brought low by fever. The local doctors warned him to stay ashore for as long as possible and put him on a light diet with numerous drugs, but Pavel showed no improvement and grew weaker daily. The British ships had been at Revel for some time and their officers were anxious to set sail. As the days passed, one of them eventually arranged for Pavel to be seen by an English doctor, who appears to have diagnosed the nervous origins of his illness very quickly. The doctor directed him to be put on his ship immediately and fed with roast beef and port. On this cheering diet, Pavel rapidly recovered and professed to a great faith in British medicine for the rest of his life.

# CHAPTER FIVE

# *Marriage*
## *1799–1801*

The wind blew fair and Pavel, restored to health and vigour, and on board the fastest ship in the squadron, the *Venus*, could not bear to delay his reunion with Elizabeth any longer. He delegated the command of the squadron to a colleague and sailed full speed for England. He arrived at Yarmouth alone and there he found the rest of the Russian squadron under Rear-Admiral Makarov. In his memoirs, he notes cryptically that his early arrival permitted him 'to take such measures as were necessary and to receive instructions from the British Admiralty,'[1] but it seems far more probable that he wished to have some time with Elizabeth alone, before setting out for the coast of Holland. The Russian troops landed in Holland in mid-September 1799, which suggests that the emotional letter that Pavel wrote from Yarmouth to Vorontsov on 12 September was written during the precious few days that he had set aside to spend with his future wife.

Pavel's letter to Vorontsov overflows with gratitude, but it also reveals the extent of his hatred of the current regime and the frankness on political matters that now existed between the two men. He addresses Vorontsov as his 'adored benefactor', for whom he vows to do his very best in the forthcoming expedition. In hyperbolic terms he describes how he longs to come to London 'to prove to you by my ecstasy how great are my feelings of admiration and gratitude to you for your kindness; how much my heart is filled with respect, with veneration and affection for you, and how much horror I have for those who have succeeded, by their extreme barbarity, in awakening in me the greatest possible aversion and repugnance for that country where these monsters live'.[2]

The expedition to Holland was a fiasco. Pavel almost immediately found himself in conflict with General Essen, the German commander of the troops aboard his squadron, who had been appointed by the Emperor Paul. The wind was favourable and they were fortunate in finding a good anchorage off the Dutch coast, close to the port of Den Helder, where Pavel had been instructed by the Admiralty to make the disembarkation. The boats were lowered, but Essen, on failing to see a reception party on the coast worthy of the imperial troops, halted proceedings. In vain Pavel argued with him that this was the best place, that the shore batteries had been cleared and that, after all, they had not come there for a party. The general refused to land. The wind increased and Pavel was obliged to put into the treacherous waters of the Texel, by which time the news was coming through that the Duke of York had suffered a defeat and General Hermann, the commander of the Russian troops already ashore, had been taken prisoner.

The expedition went from bad to worse. Casualties among the Russian troops, in particular, were high, and demoralized by their inept leadership, they behaved badly and abused the local population. On 18 October, the Duke of York was obliged to sign a capitulation to the French and was given until 30 October to withdraw the Anglo-Russian army and the Russian squadron with it. Vorontsov cringed with humiliation at the role played by the Russian troops, although he lays the greatest blame on their commanders. Recalling the recent Russian victories under Suvorov, he wrote to his brother, Alexander: 'Soldiers of the same nation behave like heroes in Italy and in Switzerland; but in Holland they are bandits and cowards. Such is the powerful influence of those who command. General Essen has discovered the secret of destroying the honour of the troops he commands. . . . But as a Russian I groan at the shame that reflects on my nation. . . . All this makes me ill and unhappy.'[3]

Pavel, however, had no desire to dwell at length on this national disgrace, and after so many vicissitudes, his only thought was to return to England and to Elizabeth by the quickest possible means. He remained in Holland only as long as duty required and then, leaving the squadron under the command of a subordinate, he returned with a Russian brig to Yarmouth. The squadron, trapped by contrary winds, remained in the Texel – from which the Dutch had removed all the markers and buoys – until the last day of the armistice and narrowly escaped falling into French hands.

Once Pavel had returned to England, he and Elizabeth were together constantly. There is no record of their movements, but their feelings can easily be imagined. Their love, which had withstood the test of over three years of waiting, intense parental opposition and even imprisonment, was stronger than ever and they longed to be married without delay. Vorontsov, who increasingly saw himself as the architect of their union and as the protector of the fatherless Elizabeth, proposed that they should marry at the Embassy, but Elizabeth also wanted an

Anglican ceremony. In the end, they decided to have two services, one in the parish church at Beddington followed by another in the Russian Embassy chapel in London.

When Charles Proby died, the house at Chatham had to be handed over to the new Commissioner. This left Elizabeth without a home, but Sarah Pigott, in common with her other sisters, had always been sympathetic to Elizabeth's unhappy plight. In addition, Sarah was the eldest of the girls and she may have felt a kind of maternal responsibility for Elizabeth as well as for the widowed Charlotte. Sarah's husband, James, was already a very senior naval officer, a vice-admiral of the Red, and they owned an attractive and comfortable house not far from London, in the village of Beddington in Surrey. The fact that Elizabeth chose to marry there and that in 1800 Charlotte became the wife of the Rector suggests that both Elizabeth and Charlotte used the Pigotts' house as their home base after their father's death.

Elizabeth and Pavel left London for Beddington on Sunday 3 November 1799. Just before they left, Pavel wrote a letter to Vorontsov to let him know that the Carysforts had accepted his invitation to dinner at the Embassy to celebrate the wedding. Wisely, Vorontsov had not let this opportunity of consolidating his position with Elizabeth's excellent political connections slip through his fingers, but for Pavel, who was in a state of prenuptial euphoria, Vorontsov's approach to the Carysforts was simply another example of his overwhelming kindness and generosity. He begs Vorontsov to honour them with his presence at the Embassy chapel.[4]

On Tuesday 5 November, Elizabeth and Pavel were married at the fifteenth-century church of St Mary the Virgin at Beddington. The grey, flint church, with a tall tower at its west end, stands close to Beddington Hall, on the edge of a large park planted with chestnut trees. The dark and solemn interior is typical of old country churches throughout the length and breadth of England. The long nave has a high, hammerbeam roof and at the time of Elizabeth and Pavel's marriage there were wooden galleries on either side above the aisles. The choir stalls are richly carved and their dark, highly polished wood gleams in the light that floods into the chancel through the window at the east end. Elizabeth would have entered through the south porch, probably on the arm of her brother-in-law, and as they processed up the aisle, she would have felt that benign Providence, in which she had placed so many of her hopes, had finally smiled upon them.

It was not a grand affair. The service was taken by the curate and the register was signed by Sarah and James Pigott, two Chatham friends (Diana and Fanny Hargrave), Elizabeth Whitehouse (the family housekeeper from Chatham), J. Green and John Ansell (the clerk). No other members of the family are recorded. The next day, Pavel and Elizabeth returned to London, in order to prepare for the Orthodox ceremony which was to be held at 7 p.m. in the Russian Embassy chapel in Great Portland Street. Here the arrangements were far more elaborate and according to the marriage certificate, quite a number of people were in attendance. Only Vorontsov is named, but the certificate refers to 'others' who were present – most probably the members of the Embassy – and there is also specific mention of 'the relations of the bride', which certainly included the Carysforts and Sarah Pigott and maybe several others from the family as well. The officiating priest was Father Iakov Smirnov, a long-established figure in the Russian community in London, with whom Elizabeth and Pavel were well acquainted. For Elizabeth, the Orthodox ceremony of marriage, with its repeated exchanges of rings and its ritualistic nuptial crowns, was her first real taste of Russia. The elaborate vestments of the clergy, the solemn chanting of the all-male choir and the mysterious language of the Slavonic liturgy transported Elizabeth to the exotic Russian world of which she had so often dreamed, as the bridal couple, bathed in the heavy scent of incense, were led three times round the altar and drank together from the communion chalice to symbolize their future sharing of the joys and sorrows that life might bring them.

The chapel was a short distance from Vorontsov's house in Harley Street, where the dinner was held. Vorontsov was a perfect diplomat and those of his guests who were unaccustomed to official life would soon have felt at ease. His 16-year-old daughter, Catherine, who was always known to her friends as Katinka, and his son, Mikhail, had both become close friends of Elizabeth and Pavel's. The intimacy between Elizabeth and Katinka was such that Pavel often refers to her as Elizabeth's 'dear sister'. Indeed Pavel was coming more and more to regard Vorontsov as a second father and began to address him as 'my adored father' and to sign his letters 'your very humble, devoted and obedient son'. Later, Elizabeth became 'your daughter-in-law'.

For his part, Vorontsov would have been particularly interested to meet Lady Carysfort, the sister of Pitt's Foreign Secretary, Lord Grenville, who was one of the most powerful men in England, and to have talked with her husband, John Joshua, who was about to take up an important diplomatic post as British Minister in Berlin. The presence of the Carysforts at the wedding is a clear indication that the family did not share Charles Proby's hostile attitude to Pavel. John Joshua, who spent much of his time in London's highest political circles, may well have known Vorontsov for some time and Vorontsov's championship of Pavel would have demonstrated to him that a member of the Chichagov family was not an entirely unsuitable match for his cousin Elizabeth. With so many of her family around her on this happy day, Elizabeth must have felt, finally, that the nightmare of the past three years had passed and that her fidelity to Pavel had been more than justified.

Politics would not have been the only topic of conversation. With the strong naval connections of the families of both bride and groom, there would also have been talk of the navy. John Joshua's third son, Granville, had recently served as a midshipman on Nelson's flagship, the *Vanguard*, at the Battle of the Nile on 1 August 1798. After barely four months of naval service, the face of the 17-year-old Granville may well have betrayed some apprehension before his first taste of action and, according to family papers, as the engagement was about to begin Nelson observed to him cheeringly: 'well, my boy, this is better than being in Grosvenor Square.'[5] The reference was to the Carysforts' London house, in which Granville's stepmother received many eminent political figures. From the same source also comes the anecdote, perhaps fanciful, that it was young Granville Proby who was sent on the boat which tried unsuccessfully to persuade the heroic Captain Casabianca and his 10-year-old son to leave 'the burning deck' of the French flagship, *L'Orient*, the last of the French ships to surrender.

Charles Cunningham had similarly distinguished himself recently. During the summer, the *Clyde* had been engaged in a fierce battle with two French frigates in the Channel and had captured one of them. The news was brought to King George, who was at the Weymouth Theatre. 'He immediately stood up in his box, and commanded the news to be communicated to the audience; when "Rule Britannia" was loudly called for from every part of the house, and performed with reiterated applause.'[6]

We do not know where the honeymoon was spent: perhaps the wedding night was passed beneath Vorontsov's hospitable roof in Harley Street. The union, however, was clearly a success and by Christmas Day 1799, Elizabeth was expecting her first child. Meanwhile, the relations between England and Russia were cooling fast. The Emperor had been very disappointed by the failure of the joint Anglo-Russian expedition to Holland and he was angry about the Russian casualties. During the winter, the Russian troops were poorly housed on the islands of Jersey and Guernsey. A local English girl was abducted and raped and General Essen refused to give up the suspects, which had led to a riot on the islands.[7] Other aspects of the newly formed coalition were equally unsatisfactory. Neither the Austrians nor the British had treated their Russian allies well. The Austrians had abandoned Suvorov and the Russian army in Switzerland, where they suffered a defeat at the hands of the French and had been forced to retreat back through the Alps to Russian territory. In the Mediterranean, a Russian naval squadron suffered various indignities, including being prevented, by the British, from following instructions from St Petersburg to attack the French-held garrison on Malta, a distinction which the British then claimed for themselves.

In the early 1800s, the coalition began to fall apart and the French began making overtures to the Russian Emperor. Vorontsov soon became a victim of the deterioration of relations between Britain and Russia and in April he received the following instructions from St Petersburg: 'His Majesty, finding in your reports propositions contrary to his wishes, directs me to say that if you find it irksome to carry out these wishes it is open to you to resign.'[8] However, he did not leave Britain but obtained the right of residency and retired privately to a house in Southampton, leaving the Embassy in the charge of his counsellor, Lizakevich.

The Emperor had decided that both the squadron and the troops should be withdrawn from England, and as soon as the Baltic became navigable, Pavel was instructed to return to his ship to oversee the embarkation of the troops and to command a detachment of six ships that would sail with them back to Russia. By this time Pavel had reassumed the command of his old ship, the *Retvisan*, and he was aboard her at Spithead when he wrote a long letter to Vorontsov. From his letter, it is clear that Elizabeth was with him on board. The new captain's quarters that had been fitted in Chatham would have been quite large and comfortable enough for a couple to live in and Elizabeth would have felt completely at home in the familiar, naval surroundings. In his letters to Vorontsov at this period, Pavel's epistolary style becomes more diffuse than ever, but it is possible that there was a security reason for his circumlocution. From Pavel's reply, it is evident that Vorontsov had instructed him to memorize the contents of his letter and then burn it. It was not to be shown to Elizabeth, for whom Vorontsov had enclosed an introduction to the wife of Rostopchin. Pavel assures Vorontsov that 'it will be with the greatest application that I shall try to follow precisely, and to the letter, all that you order me to do.'[9] Amongst other things, Vorontsov had asked Pavel to pass on a message to Count Panin.

At the end of 1799, Panin, who at 29 years old had replaced Kochubei as Vice-President of the College of Foreign Affairs, had begun to consider the possibility of setting up a regency, citing the mental state of the Emperor, in favour of the Grand Duke Alexander. He had even aired this idea with Alexander, who had not shown himself completely opposed to it. By the summer of 1800, Panin, who was rapidly losing the struggle for power to the President of the College, Rostopchin, was utterly disenchanted with his royal master and convinced of his growing insanity. He appended a note to the Emperor's instruction to Vorontsov which prompted his resignation, in which he says 'You see what I am obliged to sign. . . . I wet your hands with my tears. . . . There is no help for it!'[10] Vorontsov, recently disgraced and a witness to the total destruction of his years of diplomatic work in the Emperor's expulsion of the British Ambassador and his staff from St Petersburg, certainly shared Panin's sentiments.

The frankness of Pavel's comments on the regime in his letters to Vorontsov suggests that Vorontsov had also taken Pavel into his confidence. Reading between the lines, it becomes apparent that Vorontsov was very uneasy about Pavel's return to Russia with Elizabeth at a time of such political uncertainty. The decision to accompany him, however, was probably hers. She was, after all, passionately in love and would have dreaded another separation. Pavel writes: 'I know very well that no one could judge better than you the sacrifice that my wife is making in following me.'[11] Later in the letter, in an attempt to convince Vorontsov that he is fully aware of his uxorial responsibilities, he writes: 'My wife has become not only the object of my most tender love but a treasure who has been confided to my keeping by him to whom I owe all my happiness.'[12]

A week later, still awaiting the arrival of the transport ships with the troops from Jersey, Pavel replies to another anxious letter from Vorontsov. Vorontsov had good reason to be concerned, having already seen the near-disaster that Pavel's refusal to pay lip-service to imperial favourites had brought upon himself. He gave Pavel minute instructions on his behaviour at the court and with those in positions of power, but he cannot have found Pavel's reply very reassuring: 'To conform with your instructions, I will go without fail and pay court, as a novice, to all those villainous idiots who do nothing but evil in the world.'[13] On the other hand, Vorontsov may have had more faith in Elizabeth's good judgement and Pavel's admission that he had shared the confidential contents of the letter with her may not have displeased him. He probably endorsed Pavel's comment that 'she is far more discreet and prudent than I am.'[14] Like its predecessor, Vorontsov's letter was memorized and destroyed.

As their departure approached, Pavel was hit by the full realization of the uncertainties and dangers that awaited them in Russia. On 28 June he wrote Vorontsov an emotional farewell letter in his inimitable, hyperbolic style:

> If only I could be with you now, my adored father, to pour out before you the sweet feelings that your last letter produced in my soul. . . . I congratulate you from the depths of my soul, my only benefactor, for the event which leaves you in precisely the place that must have been destined for you from the moment that the abyss, which will engulf our country, opened, and from which neither you nor the very small number of people like you, would have known how to escape. If I fall in it, it is a very great satisfaction to see the man whom I love more than myself, enjoying the peaceful happiness that is his due, and [to know] that he will be there as a consolation for the one, who having sacrificed herself for me – if she escapes the misfortune which menaces our country – will find in you and all those who belong to you, a support, a father, a benefactor, wise, powerful and sensitive. . . . Farewell, my very dear, much adored father; if only I could touch you one more time before parting from you without knowing if I shall ever see you again.[15]

The *Retvisan* finally set sail from England on 6 July 1800. Elizabeth was nearly seven months pregnant and this was probably the first time that she had been at sea for any period. The initial gentle breezes soon gave way to strong winds and rough seas and she struggled stoically with seasickness. They reached Copenhagen within ten days, having dropped anchor briefly in the harbour of Helsingør. Helsingør, or Elsinore, with its Shakespearean associations, was a favourite destination for eighteenth-century tourists, but with responsibility for a large number of troops, Pavel did not delay and pressed on to Revel. He and Elizabeth were blissfully happy throughout the voyage and once she had recovered from her seasickness, she revelled in the element in which generations of her forbears had passed their lives. It was a fantastic adventure and she had complete confidence in Pavel's assurances that on arrival, they would go straight to his father's house in St Petersburg, where his brother was in residence and where they would be in reach of all the assistance that she would need for her approaching delivery.

Nothing in her experience had prepared Elizabeth for the pitiful and barbaric appearance of Revel. The desolate coastline, the half-constructed batteries and the wretched housing shocked her to the core. She had never imagined that Russia could possibly be like this and her peace of mind was further troubled by the news, which Pavel received on arrival, that his brother had been dismissed from his position as chamberlain at the court for some trifling dispute and exiled to the family estate at Shklov. Thankfully, within a few days, they were able to proceed to Kronstadt, which Elizabeth found a great deal better than Revel. There the most pressing task was to find lodgings and they were fortunate in finding that Pavel's erstwhile commander, Khanikov, was the commander of Kronstadt. Khanikov knew Elizabeth from Chatham – he may even have been a guest at her father's house – and he busied himself with providing the newly-weds with the best accommodation available. Many of the returning soldiers, however, were forced to sleep under the stars.

In some ways Kronstadt may have reminded Elizabeth of Chatham and its dockyard. Situated on Kotlin Island, it too was a busy naval establishment and it overlooked the placid waters of the Gulf of Finland, whose many shoals and sandbanks were not unlike those of the Medway. The island was nearly five miles in length and about a mile wide and while it was some twenty miles by sea from St Petersburg, it was only a short distance from the southern coast of the Gulf and the town of Oranienbaum. In summer the journey had to be made by boat, but as soon as winter came, Kronstadt was linked to the mainland by a well-marked road across the ice. The island had been captured from the Swedes by Peter the Great, who placed batteries on it and later built a fortress, a town and a port, but because of Russia's traditional reliance on British naval expertise, it also had a long history of links with Britain.

Much of the early construction of the port was supervised by a Welshman, Edward Lane, who built two harbours, one naval and one commercial, and dug a canal, which enabled ships to pass into dry docks for repairs.[16] Although most of the warships were built and launched at the Admiralty dockyard in St Petersburg and were only brought to Kronstadt to be rigged and armed, there was still much of the usual dockyard paraphernalia of sawmills, slips and sailmakers' lofts. Many of the businesses were in the hands of British merchants. For example, the foundry was under the control of a Scotsman, Charles Gascoigne, and the rope-walk had also been established by a Scot.[17] In 1775 Admiral Greig had taken over as the commander of Kronstadt from Pavel's father and had made extensive repairs and improvements to its facilities and fortifications. Its appearance, therefore, would have had much in common with contemporary British naval installations.

There had been established British communities at Kronstadt and St Petersburg for generations. In England all trade with Russia was controlled by the Russia Company, which had its origins in the epic journey of the English merchant Richard Chancellor to the court of Ivan IV in the sixteenth century. The British merchants who lived in Russia were the employees or 'factors' of the company and thus the Russian end of the operation came to be known as the British 'factory'. During the eighteenth century, Anglo-Russian trade flourished and was further enhanced by the signing of a series of commercial treaties which ensured 'favoured nation' status for British merchants and ready British access to the vital raw materials, such as hemp and timber, that Russia was able to provide to British dockyards. It was the third of these treaties that was negotiated by Vorontsov in 1793 and it was to the members of the Russia Company – who represented a powerful lobby – that Vorontsov addressed his arguments in 1791 to prevent a rupture between Britain and Russia over the so-called Ochakov Crisis.*

In St Petersburg a palace on the banks of the Neva, which had belonged to Count Sheremetev, was purchased by the members of the British Factory and converted into an English church. Similarly, many of the elegant houses on the quay to the west of the church became the property of wealthy British merchants who had made their fortunes in Russia. This quay came to be known as the English Embankment and was soon considered to be one of the best addresses in St Petersburg. In Kronstadt, the British population was also sufficiently large to justify the existence of an English church with a resident chaplain, who was paid for by the Factory. The British presence in Russia, therefore, especially in St Petersburg and Kronstadt, was not limited to its considerable

* For the Ochakov Crisis, see note on p. 19.

naval ramifications: it also existed in many areas of civilian life. For example, there was a strong British medical tradition. Catherine the Great invited an English doctor, Thomas Dimsdale, to travel to Russia to inoculate herself and the Grand Duke Paul against smallpox. The inoculations were such a success that Dimsdale returned a second time to inoculate the Empress's grandsons, Alexander and Constantine. Scottish doctors, in particular, enjoyed imperial patronage and the celebrated John Rogerson, who according to some sources was required to 'vet' the favourites of Catherine the Great, became intimate with many influential political figures.

In August 1800, however, the large and prosperous British community, which had thrived in Russia for so many years, was in a state of turmoil. The Emperor's hostility to England was increasing. In London the counsellor, Lizakevich, was soon to be transferred to Copenhagen and Father Smirnov appointed chargé d'affaires of the skeleton Russian Embassy, providing what Waliszweski describes as 'the only example in the history of Russian diplomacy of an ecclesiastic having been entrusted with such functions'.[18] In St Petersburg British subjects no longer had the protection of diplomatic representation, for in June the Ambassador, Sir Charles Whitworth, together with his staff, had been withdrawn. Their Consul-General, Stephen Shairp, who had been recalled to London for consultations with the Russia Company, was marooned at Kronstadt on his return and unable to obtain a passport to return to St Petersburg. In London he had received instructions to advise all British ships to leave Kronstadt at the earliest opportunity.[19] Whitworth was now the British Minister in Copenhagen and the British detention of some Russian merchant ships, under the escort of a Danish frigate, further enraged the Emperor and he seized on this pretext to begin confiscating funds and property belonging to British subjects resident in Russia. On 7 September, relations deteriorated still further when the island of Malta fell into British hands and yet more reprisals were taken against the British in Russia. British ships were impounded and hundreds of sailors were imprisoned and sent, in freezing conditions, many miles into the interior. There could hardly have been a worse moment for an Englishwoman to take up residence in Kronstadt.

Despite the many features that the town may have had in common with Chatham, there must also have been much about the environment, especially in this threatening atmosphere, that Elizabeth found strange – the sensation of being confined to a small island, the long low featureless coastline and above all the complete absence of anyone from home. Many English women who travelled to Russia were accompanied by their English maids, but it would appear that Elizabeth was entirely alone. To add to her isolation, correspondence with England was growing more difficult and there was a strong possibility that the contents of letters were no longer secure. A contemporary British traveller, the painter Robert Ker Porter, aptly describes his first impressions of Kronstadt:

> On the night of the twelfth of September we arrived at Cronstadt. We landed next morning; when I was amazingly struck by the extraordinary appearance of almost every individual I met. Men with long beards, brown and sunburnt skins, strangely shaped caps, and greasy skin habits of all possible forms; were mingled with a few, dressed in the fashion of our nation; and numberless others in the dapper-cut uniforms of their own military, naval, and civil departments. This widely-contrasted crowd, meeting my eyes at the moment my ears were first saluted with a language I had never before heard, made altogether so strange an impression on my mind as is not to be described.[20]

In her vulnerable state of advanced pregnancy, Elizabeth was completely dependent upon Pavel and his family, and the sudden banishment of Pavel's brother from St Petersburg created an unexpected problem. The squadron had received orders to winter at Kronstadt and Pavel knew that even if he did obtain permission to spend time in St Petersburg, in the present unpredictable political climate he might be required at any time to return to Kronstadt. He had counted on his brother's presence in the house in St Petersburg to enable him to leave Elizabeth there for her delivery, where she would have access to the best possible medical attention. Pavel was unwilling for her to give birth in Kronstadt, where the medical facilities were very inferior to those in the capital. As Pavel and Elizabeth were wrestling with this problem, they received a message from Vasilii which seemed to solve everything. Despite his age and failing eyesight, Vasilii had made the 800-verst journey* from Shklov to welcome Elizabeth. The message was from St Petersburg and requested Pavel and Elizabeth to come and join him as soon as they could. Pavel was overjoyed knowing that his father's presence would enable Elizabeth to give birth at St Petersburg, but scarcely had they obtained a permit to travel, than another letter arrived from Vasilii announcing that he had been forbidden,

* A verst = approx 1.07 km, or 0.66 miles.

by imperial decree, from remaining in his house at St Petersburg and he was therefore obliged to return to Shklov.

Although Pavel had thought himself inured to the vindictiveness of the Emperor, he was outraged by this act of petty tyranny. The aged Vasilii had no quarrel with the Emperor, but the name of Chichagov had been sufficient to arouse his displeasure. Elizabeth too, was deeply distressed. It was not only the practical implications that upset her, but also the shocking realization that her life was now subject to the whims of a crazed despot. She remembered, with grief, how naive she had been in dismissing as unbelievable the letters in which Pavel had attempted to prepare her for this. In a state of intense unhappiness, they made their way to St Petersburg to try at least to obtain some basic necessities for the arrival of their first child. Elizabeth was feeling desperately homesick, exhausted by emotion and by the last days of her pregnancy. For the first time, she was assailed with doubts and she barely noticed the beauties of St Petersburg, which had left so many travellers open-mouthed in admiration, but looked about her at the abandoned family house of the Chichagovs and wept.

Despite his love, Pavel was little support to her. He was struggling with his own barely controlled emotions. What Elizabeth most needed was the support of another woman. But there was nobody. The old family servants gazed uncomprehendingly at the new Madame Chichagov, who spoke only a few words of broken Russian and who cried and cried. After three miserable days, their leave in St Petersburg expired and they returned to Kronstadt, where Pavel engaged the best doctor on the island for Elizabeth. On the 24 September 1800, Elizabeth went into labour and was delivered of a little girl, whom they called Adelaide. The baby flourished, but as Pavel had feared, the doctor was careless and Elizabeth fell ill. For eight weeks she lay, a pale shadow of herself, in their Kronstadt lodgings, while the days shortened and the island became encircled with ice. Pavel was frantic with worry and was in constant correspondence with Dr Rogerson in St Petersburg. As an old friend of Vorontsov's, Rogerson was assiduous in his attentions and sent his assistant, a Dr Galloway, to attend her. In her weakened condition, Elizabeth was unable to feed Adelaide – although she would dearly have loved to. Fortunately, however, they found an excellent wet-nurse, to whom Elizabeth was able to hand over her baby with confidence. In a nation that has always idolized children, loving and dependable nurses were not hard to find and Adelaide's nurse may well have been selected from the Chichagov serfs in White Russia. Finally, in mid-November, Elizabeth rallied and Pavel began at last to believe in her recovery.

Throughout this period, Pavel conducted himself with a new-found prudence and discretion. Some of this may be attributed to the guidance of Vorontsov, but Elizabeth may also have played a role – if only by her presence. Pavel felt completely responsible for the unhappy situation in which she now found herself : 'Oh my poor wife . . . who has been so mis-led by a love that is both unpardonable and insane, because it is disastrous for her.'[21] Judging from his earlier letters to Vorontsov, however, it seems likely that Elizabeth enjoyed Pavel's full confidence on all matters and that he found himself beginning to rely on her steady temperament and good judgement in a situation that was growing daily more dangerous. On his return to Russia, Pavel had struck up a friendship with an intimate of the Grand Duke Alexander's, Count Stroganov, with whom Vorontsov had put him in touch, and he had also seen Panin on several occasions. Panin had tried to have Pavel transferred to St Petersburg so that they could communicate more regularly and to this end he engaged another member of the embryo conspiracy against the Emperor, the sinister Admiral Ribas, to propose Pavel as a member of the College of the Admiralty. Neapolitan-born Ribas was 'an adventurer with the soul of a bandit',[22] who owed his position to a shady role in the kidnapping of Princess Tarakanova in Leghorn in 1774. Pavel's appointment, however, was turned down by the Emperor and in November Panin was removed from office and later banished to his estates. Shortly afterwards the death of Ribas put any plots for the removal of the Emperor into abeyance.

At the beginning of November, just before the exile of Panin, there was a temporary respite from the threatening atmosphere of fear and intrigue which seemed to pervade every aspect of Russian life. The Emperor announced an amnesty for public servants and officers who had been ban-ished during his reign and hundreds of them streamed back into the cap-ital in the hope of regaining their previous positions. Although the Emperor soon tired of the petitioners and many were disappointed, Pavel's letter to Vorontsov at this time reflects, after weeks of unrelieved gloom, a short-lived break in the gathering storm clouds. Pavel and Elizabeth were besotted with their baby and now the proud parents were considering who should be the godparents. Vorontsov had already agreed to be the godfather, and for godmothers they settled on Lady Carysfort and Katinka, with whom, despite the political problems, Elizabeth was in regular correspondence. Pavel tells Vorontsov that they are hoping to have Adelaide baptized into the Protestant faith and that they plan to visit Vasilii at Shklov as soon as the sledging season begins.[23] Pavel had done the journey many times and knew that it was far more easily accomplished once the snow had fallen. Then he and Elizabeth could travel by 'kibitka' – a horse-drawn wooden cradle on runners, in which the passengers lay snugly side by side on a bed of mattresses and pillows, enveloped in rugs and furs. In this conveyance it was possible to cover huge distances at high speed and many travellers continued their journeys through the star-lit winter nights.

The Emperor's antagonism to Britain continued unabated. Finally, in December, matters came to a head, when Russia once again entered into an alliance of armed neutrality against British shipping with Prussia, Sweden and Denmark. Furthermore, at Hohenlinden the Austrians suffered their second defeat in a year at the hands of the First Consul, and were obliged to sign a peace treaty with the French. At this point, any hopes that Britain may have had of preserving the coalition were abandoned and the sights of the British fleet were set on the Baltic. Pavel's presence at Kronstadt was not overlooked by the Emperor. Despite his rebellious reputation, his energy and ability inspired confidence and in early spring 1801, Pavel received a summons to St Petersburg. Pavel and Elizabeth were filled with apprehension, but Pavel did his best to reassure his wife that there was no reason for concern. As Pavel left in his sledge, he observed with disquiet that he was being followed by two *Feldjäger* – members of the Emperor's personal police.

On his arrival at the palace, Pavel found himself once more with Kushelev, who ushered him without delay into the presence of the Emperor. They sat face to face at a small table, while Pavel endeavoured to reply non-committally to the Emperor's remarks on the drunkenness of Pitt. Pavel left the meeting, having been entrusted with the defence of Kronstadt in the event of an attack by the British and with instructions to attend a further meeting the next day. The following day Pavel found himself at a council of war. The Emperor unveiled a series of ill-conceived plans for the defence of the capital, to which Pahlen, who was present, invariably replied in his clipped Baltic German 'Very military, Your Majesty.'[24] The Emperor then turned to the naval aspects of the defence, which were equally ill-conceived, and Pavel's opinion was solicited on the state of the fortifications at Kronstadt – which he knew to be deplorable. As Pavel began to reply with his customary honesty, the Emperor momentarily left the room, and Pahlen hissed to him in an undertone that the only possible response to the Emperor was either 'yes' or 'very good'. Disgusted by this deception, Pavel nevertheless heeded Pahlen's advice and informed the Emperor that his proposals were more than adequate to repel the British. The Emperor was delighted with this reply and declared loudly that Pavel was greatly improved thanks to his time in prison. Pavel had no further contact with the palace and he returned to Kronstadt to tell his wife that he was charged with the defence of his country against hers. In this nightmare scenario, Pavel was, at least, able to offer Elizabeth the consolation that the dilapidated guns of Kronstadt would do very little damage to her countrymen.

St Petersburg had become a city of conspirators. Strange rumours circulated around the town. The Emperor had enclosed himself in a hideous fortress of granite and plastered masonry, every entrance of which was guarded. Twice a day, the drawbridges were lowered to permit official access to the town, but otherwise the Emperor remained incarcerated behind the ditches and high walls, which, to his fevered imagination, finally represented an escape from the spectre of assassination that had haunted him since childhood. The Emperor named his new residence the Mikhailovskii Castle* after the Archangel Michael, whose role as the warrior angel may have struck him as appropriate. There was also a legend that a soldier on duty at the Summer Palace, which had formerly occupied the site, had had a vision of St Michael shortly after the Emperor's birth there.

The Emperor moved to the castle in November 1800, despite the fact that it was barely finished, and dragged his unwilling entourage with him. His current mistress, Princess Gagarina, was installed in a suite of apartments which were joined to those of the Emperor by a secret staircase. His favourite, the ex-barber and valet Kutaisov, was accommodated nearby. The apartments of the Empress, however, were separated from his by a large room. The Emperor's behaviour was becoming daily more deranged and his suspicions of his family increased. His two eldest sons, Alexander and Constantine, had been removed from their parents at an early age by their grandmother, Catherine the Great, who wished to control their education. Consequently there was little family feeling or affection between the Emperor and his immediate heirs, who lived in terror of him. The Emperor's relations with his wife were little better. After their first ten years of marriage, which had been very happy, the

---

* Since 1823 this building has been known as the Engineers' Castle (Inzhenernyi Zamok).

Emperor's physical affections had been claimed by a series of mistresses and there were even rumours that he planned to divorce the Empress in favour of Princess Gagarina. Furthermore, the childhood separation which had alienated the two elder boys from their father to a certain extent also created a distance between them and their mother. Understandably Maria Feodorovna was much closer to her younger children, whose education had not been interfered with by their grandmother.

Yet despite the animosity and rivalries that existed within the imperial family, none of them would have agreed to the murder of the Emperor. When Panin had first approached Alexander, whose consent was obligatory if the plot to place him on the throne in his father's stead was to succeed, Alexander did not give him an answer, but most historians believe that by the time the plot had passed under the control of Pahlen, Alexander had given his agreement. At the age of 56, Pahlen was a tall and impressive figure and during February and March 1801, he successfully recruited around sixty people into the conspiracy. Among their number were the three Zubov brothers, who had paid heavily at the hands of Paul for the favours obtained by Platon Zubov during the reign of Catherine the Great and had only returned to St Petersburg during the recent amnesty. There was also General Bennigsen, a serious military man, who had been sufficiently ill-treated by Paul to wish his removal.

Elaborate arrangements were made to ensure that on the night of 23 March there were supporters of the conspiracy among the officers on guard at the Mikhailovskii Castle. At 11 p.m. the conspirators gathered in an annexe to the Winter Palace. Many of them were already drunk and they continued to drink champagne while they awaited the arrival of Pahlen. At 11.30 Pahlen arrived. He and Bennigsen were among the few sober members of the group. According to tradition, it was at this point, in response to some last-minute reservations of Platon Zubov, that Pahlen made his famous comment that 'you cannot make an omelette without breaking eggs.'[25] Then the party divided into two groups, one led by Zubov and Bennigsen and the other by Pahlen, and made their way to the imperial apartments in the Mikhailovskii Castle, which they approached by separate routes. Earlier in the evening, the Emperor had been tricked into dismissing his usual guards and replacing them with two unarmed servants, one of whom was persuaded to open the door to the conspirators. Zubov and Bennigsen's group arrived first and their noise awakened the Emperor, who fled in his nightgown to hide behind a screen. The party, armed, drunken and disorderly, advanced upon him and after a short scuffle, the Emperor was thrown to the ground and strangled. Many gruesome details have been added to the account. Some say that his body was beaten and kicked, others that he was felled by one of the Zubovs with a golden snuff-box. There is also a version which suggests that the conspirators attempted, unsuccessfully, to force him to sign a manifesto and that the scuffle developed from this. Predictably, all the key members of the conspiracy later claimed to have taken no part in the murder.

Alexander, who also had apartments in the castle, was awoken and told the news, to which he reacted with intense shock. It was only with difficulty that Pahlen persuaded him to appear before the soldiers of the guard, who were becoming increasingly restless and suspicious, and to announce that his father had died of an attack of apoplexy. The new Emperor was greeted with enthusiastic applause, after which he fled by carriage to the Winter Palace. Maria Feodorovna's reactions were very different. On hearing the news, she rushed in her night-clothes to see the body, but she was prevented by the commander on guard and had to content herself with marching around the castle proclaiming to all and sundry that it was she who was the rightful sovereign. At seven in the morning, the family were finally permitted to see the corpse, which had, in the meantime, been tidied up. It is said that Maria Feodorovna grieved noisily before departing to join her eldest son at the Winter Palace.

In ice-bound Kronstadt, the death of the Emperor was first announced in whispers, but as the news spread, the country erupted into a state of national celebration, in which Elizabeth and Pavel participated fully.

# CHAPTER SIX

## *St Petersburg*

### *1801–1802*

The new Emperor did not immediately change the circle of advisers who had surrounded his father. Panin was recalled from exile and for a time Pahlen continued to wield considerable power – it was he who announced to Vorontsov that he could reassume his position as Ambassador in London. Pavel and Elizabeth were deeply disappointed to find that Kushelev still occupied his influential position in the Admiralty, but Pavel had by now fully mastered some of the subtleties of life at court and put into action a daring strategy to try and improve his prospects and those of his family. He sent Kushelev a letter of resignation, citing as grounds the insults and injuries that he had received at the hands of the previous Emperor, but simultaneously he sent a message to the Emperor, through the mediation of Panin and Stroganov, in which he stated that he would be honoured to serve his country if he were not made subordinate to those who were technically his juniors. The response was instant and positive. The Emperor wished to attach Pavel to his personal suite but in the meantime would like him to continue in his duties at Kronstadt until the threat of British invasion was completely dispelled.

This news caused almost as great rejoicing in Pavel and Elizabeth's modest household as the accession of the new Emperor had in St Petersburg. While Pavel enthusiastically applied all his considerable abilities to the fortifications of Kronstadt, Elizabeth, restored to health, was enjoying her first Russian winter. Indoors, Elizabeth found the houses admirably heated – their wood-burning stoves were far more effective than the open fires in England – and outside, well wrapped in her new Russian clothes, she felt deliciously warm. The sea around Kronstadt had become a vast expanse of white, criss-crossed with roads and tracks created by the constant passage of sledges and carriages between the island and Oranienbaum. St Petersburg was within easy reach. A foreign wife always arouses curiosity and amongst the local ladies of Kronstadt, Elizabeth had become the object of considerable interest. The haughty bearing of her husband and her own refinement may also have led them to believe that the Chichagovs were possessed of a large fortune. When, therefore, Elizabeth expressed a wish to travel to St Petersburg, one of the leading local ladies offered, with alacrity, to accompany her. Adelaide, whom they always called Adèle, was left in the care of her nurse and the two ladies sped off across the ice. Elizabeth was wrapped in furs and her cheeks, pale after weeks of illness, turned to a soft pink in the cold air. Her large blue eyes sparkled with enjoyment as she conversed in her improving Russian with her companion. In no time they reached the city, where the two ladies were to go their separate ways, but to Elizabeth's considerable consternation, her new friend then announced that she had forgotten her money in Kronstadt and 'borrowed' a hundred roubles.

Pavel and Elizabeth had very little money. The system of 'prize money' from captured ships, which enriched so many English naval officers at this time, was unknown in Russia, and under the Emperor Paul the pitiful salaries of naval officers were no longer augmented by material benefits. Things had been far easier during the reign of Catherine the Great, when Vasilii, as Commander-in-Chief of the fleet, became by Russian standards quite comfortably off. Apart from the provision of rations and other privileges that went with his position, Pavel tells us in his memoirs that his father received three thousand roubles as a reward after the Swedish wars. Parkinson, however, suggests that Vasilii's reward was an 'estate of 300,000 roubles a year', which is clarified in the notes as a reward of '3,805 serfs'.[1] Since the Empress usually recompensed services with gifts of property and Pavel twice mentions that his father received an estate from the Empress, it seems most likely that the sum of three thousand roubles to which he refers was the value of the income generated by the 'souls' or serfs on the property given to Vasilii at Shklov in White Russia. This land was in an area with a large Jewish population which had recently been acquired from the Poles, and it would have had resident peasants who, if they were not already serfs, would have been automatically transferred into serfdom by the Empress's gift. According to Seton-Watson, Catherine transferred 800,000 state peasants in this manner into serfdom, and her son, Paul, a further 600,000.[2] There were two main categories of service by the serfs, money payment or labour, which varied from area to area. If, as seems probable, the serfs on Vasilii's property at Shklov rendered their service in money, this would have produced an annual income for the family even after Vasilii's retirement. Both Pavel and Parkinson suggest that the value of the rouble at this time was somewhere between eight and ten to the pound, which makes the family income of the

Chichagovs in 1792 between £300 and £350 per annum. Even if the income from Vasilii's estate had increased over the years, and Seton-Watson suggests that by the end of Catherine's reign the average annual contribution of a serf was five roubles,[3] costs of living had also risen, and split between Vasilii and his four sons, and without the additional privileges of a commander-in-chief, this sum would not have permitted the Chichagovs to live extravagantly. Their position was very different from that of hugely rich landowners like Count Stroganov, the father of the Emperor Alexander's close friend Pavel Stroganov, who owned 23,000 serfs, or Count Sheremetev, who had 60,000.

Under the codicil to her father's will, Elizabeth was disinherited when she married Pavel and her portion was divided between her siblings. However, two of her sisters, Charlotte and Beatrice, gave up their share of her inheritance and this was used to provide Elizabeth's part of their marriage settlement, one of the trustees for which was Lord Carysfort. Pavel comments in his memoirs that the siblings who withheld the money were not motivated by cupidity but rather by respect for their father's wishes.[4] Charles Proby's original will stipulated that Elizabeth, who was unmarried at that time, should inherit: 'One thousand pounds stock of four pounds per cent per annum consolidated Bank Annuities and two thousand pounds stock of three pounds per cent per annum Bank Annuities.'[5] Presumably, therefore, her eventual marriage settlement contained only the portion of this amount inherited by her two sisters. Pavel was required to produce 10,000 roubles as his part of the settlement, which he refers to in a letter to Vorontsov as 'a small sum . . . which my father had the goodness to draw from our bank'.[6] This reference, however, should be taken with a grain of salt. Pavel was later delighted to receive an annuity of 10,000 roubles from the Emperor. His reference, therefore, to 10,000 roubles as 'a small sum' was probably a face-saving ploy in correspondence with a member of the hugely rich Vorontsov clan. While Pavel and Elizabeth were living at Kronstadt, their outgoings were modest. Life in St Petersburg, however, was to prove more costly.

Many visitors commented on the high cost of living in St Petersburg, but as Robert Ker Porter remarks, this had more to do with the extravagant lifestyle of the Russian nobility than with local prices:

> Before I reached this city, I had been told by many of its great expence. As a single man I did not find it so: but were I to pass a judgement on it from what I have seen, I should say that for a family it would be dear enough. And yet this would not arise from the high charges of any particular articles, but from the customs

of society, and the splendour which is here considered as a necessary of life. Under this view it is expensive. But were it fashionable to live here in the simple style which most genteel families do in England, the calculation would be in the opposite scale. . . . Provisions are cheap; and so are some other indispensable necessaries: £120 annually, will provide a good carriage, two horses, a coachman, and every requisite both for it and the sledge. Fifteen rubles a month (£25 per annum),* is the common wages for men servants; out of which they board themselves. House-rent is the most chargeable thing here.[7]

The Emperor's rapid response to Pavel's overtures was not as unpremeditated as it may have appeared. At 24 years old and having had a liberal education at the hands of a Swiss tutor named Frédéric-César de La Harpe, the new Emperor was anxious to find new and like-minded men to carry out the many reforms that he wished to initiate. For the first three years of his reign, his closest advisers were four friends of his youth, Prince Adam Czartoryski, Viktor Kochubei, Nikolai Novosil'tsev and Pavel Stroganov. They formed an 'unofficial committee', in which the Emperor discussed his policies. At a very early stage in his reign, the new Emperor became familiar with the story of Pavel's imprisonment and with his reputation for honesty. In addition, Pavel had the strong recommendation of both Stroganov and Panin. Thus, the Emperor was well briefed to respond unequivocally to an approach by Pavel, who embodied so many of the qualities that he was seeking for his new government.

The Emperor's approval was the only incentive that Pavel needed to set about drawing up a meticulous memorandum on the state of the fortifications at Kronstadt, which he promptly submitted to Panin. In the meantime, however, the Emperor had a delicate diplomatic mission, for which Pavel seemed the obvious candidate. On 2 April 1801, only a few days after the murder of the Emperor Paul, the British fleet had made an unprovoked attack on the Danes at Copenhagen. It was on this occasion that Nelson, as second in command, justified ignoring a signal from his superior to leave off action by placing his telescope to his blind eye and went on to win the day. This victory over the strategic entrance to the Baltic gave the British fleet control of the whole area and placed the Russians in a vulnerable position.

During the hiatus which followed the murder of the Emperor, a handpicked British squadron under Nelson, who had by now been appointed

---

* Ker Porter, who was writing in 1805, calculates the exchange rate at 7.2 roubles to the pound.

Commander-in-Chief, sailed up the Baltic as far as Revel. It is clear from Nelson's dispatches that this mission had several objectives. Firstly, he wished to make a show of British naval force to the Russians with a view to discouraging any hostile intentions, but more importantly, he was outraged by the Emperor Paul's treatment of British merchant ships and seamen and was determined to secure their release. As a bargaining card, he calculated on catching the Russian naval squadron that wintered at Revel while it was still icebound and before it could join up with the force from Kronstadt. On 5 May 1801 Nelson wrote to Lord St Vincent at the Admiralty as follows: 'I will have all the English Shipping and property restored; but I will do nothing violently; neither commit my Country, nor suffer Russia to mix the affairs of Denmark or Sweden with the detention of our Ships. Should I meet the Revel Squadron, I shall make them stay with me until all our English ships join; for we must not joke.'[8]

The news of the Emperor Paul's murder did nothing to deter Nelson from his intentions, although in a letter to Pahlen he gave his unsolicited visit to Revel a diplomatic gloss:

I am happy in this opportunity of assuring your Excellency, that my orders towards Russia from England are of the most pacific and friendly nature; and I have to request, that you will assure his Imperial Majesty, that my inclination so perfectly accords with my orders, that I had determined to show myself with a Squadron in the Bay of Revel, (or at Cronstadt, if the Emperor would rather wish me to go there,) to mark the friendship which, I trust in God, will ever subsist between our two gracious Sovereigns; and it will likewise be of great service, in assisting to navigate to England many of the English Merchant-vessels, who have remained all the winter in Russia.[9]

The ice, however, had melted early and when Nelson arrived at Revel on 12 May, he was disappointed to find that the Russian squadron had already sailed to the safety of Kronstadt. Furthermore, his disingenuous letter to Pahlen was soon to receive an unequivocal response, in which he was requested to remove his squadron immediately from Russian waters. The tone of Pahlen's letter was far from warm and Nelson deemed it wiser to retire from Revel at once, in order to avoid jeopardizing the negotiations for the release of the British ships. Meanwhile, the presence of a formidable British force within easy striking distance of the capital was causing considerable concern to the new Emperor and his advisers. The belligerence of Nelson's stance was very much at odds with the professed goodwill of his letter, and they were reluctant to rely on a message from an envoy in a matter of such crucial national importance. Pavel was therefore instructed to obtain a formal declaration, from Nelson in person, of the British government's desire to make peace in exchange for a similar document from the government of Russia. He was also authorized to discuss the question of the release of the British merchant ships.

Pavel was in his element. He was always at his best in the company of British naval officers and the exploits of Nelson had aroused his sincere admiration. In his memoirs, Pavel claims that it was more by luck than skill that his ship the *Venus* outsailed the frigate of the British envoy and discovered the British fleet cruising off Gotland, where he went aboard Nelson's flagship. The two men dined together in the greatest camaraderie, after which Nelson wrote out the requested declaration:

## MANIFESTO

Admiral Tchitchagoff having declared to me this day, that His Imperial Majesty The Emperor of all the Russias, has the greatest desire to return to his amicable Alliance with the King of the United Kingdom of Great Britain and Ireland, my most gracious Sovereign, I have, therefore, the pleasure to say, that I can declare the wishes of my Sovereign to return to His ancient friendly Alliance with the Court of Russia, and that my orders, on such a Declaration being given on the part of His Imperial Majesty, are clear and decisive to commit no act of hostility against anything appertaining to the Emperor of Russia. And I likewise declare, that the wishes of His Imperial Majesty respecting the freedom of the trade, both of Denmark and Sweden, in the Baltic, have been fully complied with.

Given on board His Britannic Majesty's Ship, St. George, in the Baltic, May 20th, 1801. Nelson and Bronte.[10]

Pavel stayed aboard for another hour, walking and talking with Nelson in full view of the portrait of Lady Hamilton that hung in the admiral's quarters, while Nelson showed him his numerous trophies and decorations. He was presented with a medallion which had been struck in Nelson's honour and they parted, according to Nelson, 'the best possible friends'.[11] Pavel had also assured Nelson that 'his Emperor would order the immediate restitution of the British shipping.'[12] The content of their personal conversation is not recorded, but Nelson would have been interested to learn that Pavel's wife was not only English, but also the first cousin of Lord Carysfort, now Ambassador in Berlin, with whom Nelson had been in regular correspondence since his negotiations with the Russians had begun. On his return to Kronstadt Pavel delivered Nelson's declaration, together with his copy of the Russian equivalent, to Panin. The mission had been entirely successful and further endorsed the Emperor's confidence in Pavel.

On 17 June 1801, a peace agreement was signed between Russia and Britain and with the evaporation of the British threat, Pavel was no longer required to reside at Kronstadt. Shortly before the signing of the treaty, he and Elizabeth and Adèle moved to the Chichagov family house on Vasilevskii Island in St Petersburg. In a letter to Vorontsov of 9 June, Pavel makes ironic reference to Elizabeth's reactions to the change: 'Since you are always interested in my little family, I have the honour to inform you that your daughter-in-law finds her stay in St Petersburg rather different to that in Kronstadt. I am even persuaded that if the first impressions, which are always the strongest, had not been so diametrically opposed to the possibility of imagining oneself happy in this country, she would be even better reconciled to her separation from her homeland.'[13]

Vorontsov had been worried about Elizabeth and in May he had sent a message to her with his son, Mikhail, when he sailed for Russia: 'Give my very best wishes to [Chichagov] and to his wife and say to her how much my daughter and I and all our friends have worried about her during the appalling period that she has lived through from the time of her departure from England up to the accession of the Emperor.'[14] He would soon have received Pavel's letter and another one from the informative Dr Rogerson, who enjoyed sharing all the St Petersburg gossip, intimate and otherwise, with the Ambassador of Russia at the Court of St James. Rogerson writes: 'Our friend Tchitchagow is established here at present being *à la suite* of the Emperor. I have no idea what the result of this distinction will be for him. Meanwhile his wife has gained greatly from the pleasantness of the situation.'[15]

It is evident from a letter written early in 1802 that Elizabeth was delighted with the location of her new home: 'Indeed the situation of our house is remarkably good – it is situated on the Neva and almost out of Town, so that the air is always pure and the water from the River is like the most beautiful spring water.'[16] At the beginning of the nineteenth century St Petersburg, which had a population of 220,000 people, was clustered around the three diverging arms of the river Neva. At the heart of the city, on the south bank of the main arm of the river, stood the Winter Palace and a short distance away was the Admiralty, from which ran the famous boulevard, Nevskii Prospekt. Opposite the Winter Palace, on the north bank of the river, lay St Petersburg Island, where Peter the Great had established the earliest settlement of the city in 1703 and had built the great fortress of Peter and Paul. To the west of this, joined by a bridge, lay Vasilevskii Island, which was in turn linked to the mainland, just west of the Admiralty, by a pontoon bridge across the main arm of the Neva. In winter, it was possible to cross the river at any point on the ice, but in spring, Vasilevskii Island was often cut off for days at a time, when the thaw filled the river with fast-moving ice floes and the pontoon bridge was removed to prevent it from being battered to pieces.

The most important buildings on Vasilevskii Island, several of which were associated with the busy commercial life of St Petersburg, were concentrated at its pointed eastern tip, where it jutted out into the widest part of the river and formed the main port of the city. The Customs House, the Exchange and various warehouses were all located here. On the south side, however, facing the Admiralty and the English Embankment, stood buildings of a more prestigious nature: the imposing 'Kunstkamera', built to house Peter the Great's collection of curiosities, and the Academy of Sciences. Close to these were the twelve 'Colleges' – some of the oldest buildings in the city – in which Peter the Great had originally housed the different administrative sections of government. Further on was the stately Dutch-style palace built by Peter the Great for his favourite, Prince Menshikov, which now housed the Cadet Corps, and beyond that stood the majestic Academy of Arts.

The Chichagovs lived only a few blocks to the west of these public buildings, where a grid of residential housing – composed of quiet, well-ordered streets and a number of large and beautiful churches – covered about a third of the island. For decades this area had been favoured not only by well-to-do Russians but also by foreign residents who had built many handsome houses there. This foreign presence probably accounted for the establishment of a cemetery for non-orthodox Christians just outside the residential limits. The island boasted many agreeable houses, but the Chichagov house on the southern embankment was indisputably in a prime location – despite being on the very edge of the city. It was one of a short block of large, free-standing houses built on the quay where it overlooks a southward bend in the river. Directly opposite, on the mainland, lay the galley wharves and storehouses belonging to the

Admiralty, but just upstream was a breathtaking view of the façades of the English Embankment and of the distant Admiralty beyond. On one side of the house was a quiet street leading into the still rural heart of Vasilevskii Island and on the other was an impressive brick mansion, dating from early in the reign of Peter the Great, which housed a large ecclesiastical establishment belonging to the Bishopric of Yaroslav and contained a church. Beyond this lay two more houses of similar quality, the further one of which – according to the records of the church – was for a time the residence of General Saltykov, to whom, with La Harpe, Catherine the Great had entrusted the education of her grandson, Alexander. As Elizabeth indicates in her letter, the area was quiet and clean and must have presented a stark contrast to their lodgings in the grimy town of Kronstadt.

Elizabeth now found herself living in a typically Russian household, which was shared by the whole family. Pavel's father, who divided his time between his residences at St Petersburg and Shklov, was very infirm and virtually blind, but his gentleness and his courtesy soon won Elizabeth's affection. She, too, must have gained his approval, for he presented her with a delicate cameo necklace with matching earrings which he had received as a gift from the Empress Catherine. Pavel's brother Vasilii – his junior by four years – was a shy and sensitive bachelor, to whom Pavel was devoted and with whom Elizabeth also felt completely at ease. His large dark eyes were full of expression and an engaging smile seemed to lurk in the upturned corners of his mouth. Despite his timidity, it was rumoured that Vasilii was quite a ladies' man, and although he never married, he later fathered a daughter. Pavel's youngest brother, aged 24, was equally congenial and is described by Pavel as 'gentle and full of tenderness and friendship for us all'.[17] The only brother who is never mentioned is Peter, who was closest to Pavel in age. He was already married in 1798, but Bezborodko notes in a letter to Simon Vorontsov that 'things are not going well at home. He is tired of his home atmosphere. His wife behaves in such a way, that it is hard to see how he puts up with it.'[18] The absence of any other references to the couple suggests that they did not live under the paternal roof.

By all accounts Elizabeth adjusted happily into her new family. Its largely male composition and the absence of a mother-in-law can only have eased the process, but she would have found many of the domestic aspects of Russian life very different from those in England – starting with the number of servants. The hymn writer Reginald Heber, who later became Bishop of Calcutta, visited St Petersburg as a young man in 1805 and commented as follows: '. . . every person keeps exactly ten times the number of servants which we do in England, which could not be the case were labour so dear as we are sometimes told it is. Mr. Dimidof, with whom we have dined today, said that he had 125 servants in his town-house, and many persons had twice that number, all of them peasants and all their own property.'[19]

The Demidovs were a hugely rich family of Ural ironmasters and landowners and the Chichagovs would not have lived on the same scale. Nevertheless, by English standards, they kept a large household. As the wife of the eldest and most prominent of the Chichagov sons, Elizabeth was the senior lady in the family, but this did not automatically confer on her the responsibility of running the house. On the contrary, in many Russian establishments, where the shadow of pre-Petrine female subordination still lurked, the domestic servants still looked to the master of the house for orders. It is, therefore, far more likely that as a foreigner with limited Russian, she left the mysteries of Russian housekeeping to the long-established staff. Pavel later complains that his shortage of money led to constant interruptions at his office by his domestic servants, which suggests that it was to him, not Elizabeth, that they came for money and directions.

Even if she had little hand in the housekeeping, Elizabeth cannot have failed to visit the frozen food market, which took place at the outset of winter and was a fashionable venue for Russians and foreigners alike. Lord Carysfort considered it sufficiently curious to merit a sketch. Large numbers of animals were killed with the first frost to supply the winter meat supply for the capital. The meat was cut into joints and frozen solid. Fish, chicken, butter and eggs were treated in the same way and purchasers were able to store these frozen provisions in the cellars of their houses for as long as the cold weather lasted. This custom sometimes brought surprises and on one occasion, a gift of frozen eels is said to have alarmed the cook by returning to life on being thawed!

At this time the main meal of the day in both Russia and England, taken at midday, was called dinner, but Elizabeth would have found it rather different from dinner at Chatham. A lively account of a dinner party in St Petersburg comes from the pen of Martha Wilmot, from County Cork, who in 1803 was on her way to visit Vorontsov's sister, Princess Dashkova, on her estate outside Moscow:

I have nearly exhausted my Gossip unless I was to write about the difference of Cooking . . . two Soups are always brought to Table and distributed by a servant, one compos'd of Herbs, I believe some odious essence of Rosemary or some such thing, ornamented and enrich'd by lumps of fat – the other is neither more nor less than offer'd *petits patées* of bad paste and much worse chop'd Veal, hard Eggs and Herbs. If you don't chuse any, you may let it alone and sit looking at those that do till they have done. You are then presented with a Fowl smother'd in butter and boil'd to rags, and the same ceremony goes forward. Next is offer'd vegetables of various kinds and so disguis'd that it requires some Wit to find them out. Next roast Meat, then Wild Boar Ham, and in short such a train of dishes after the same fashion as keeps one hours at table. At length comes the dessert, and tho' the fruits are handed about and you must eat according to the servants' taste not your own, yet all their fruit being good this does not signify. The Water Melon is a very fine fruit and grateful in warm Weather as it [is] Cold as Ice and so juicy that 'tis like a pleasant draught of some agreeable liquid. Coffee follows. . . .[20]

Like Martha Wilmot, Elizabeth was probably disconcerted by the Russian habit of having dishes offered to each guest individually by a servant instead of the usual English practice of placing everything on the table at once. In France 'le service à la russe' was introduced for official occasions by the two Princes Kurakin, who followed each other as ambassadors to Paris in the early eighteenth century and had an army of domestic servants. Martha's sister, Catherine, who followed her to Russia, was also struck by the elaborate and lengthy nature of the meals:

Have you a fancy to eat your dinner? . . . Run down stairs then & take your seat at the great square board. You must first eat Egg patés with your Soup and then drink Hydromel to wash them down or else Quass. With your roasted meat you must eat Salt Cucumbers, & then Caviare made of the roe of the Sturgeon. Young Pig & Curdled Cream is at Your service next, & lachat which is the general name for all grain baked with Cream. Fish soup do you chuse? Fowls? Game? Vegetables? or Apple bread? or raw Apples from the Crimea? or the Siberian Apples? or the transparent Apples? or the Kieff sweetmeat? or Honey comb? or preserved rose leaves, or pickled plums?

In the name of goodness eat no more, for in six or seven hours you will have to sit down to just such another dinner under the name of Supper![21]

Baroness Dimsdale, the third wife of Thomas Dimsdale, who accompanied her husband on his second visit to Russia, took particular care to note the fare that she and her husband were offered as guests of the Empress at Tsarskoe Selo:

111

The Empress dines at one o'clock . . . our Dinner came next. . . . We used to have a Dinner not inferior to the following every day.

> Soup, Fish, Boiled Chicken & Cauliflower,
> Roast Leg of Mutton or Beef with Potatoes over it,
> A small Dish with a ForeQuarter of Lamb roasted
> Duck, Fowl, and two Snipes (all in one Dish)
> Fine piece of Hamburgh Beef
> Cutlets and Sausages,
> Hash Duck and stewed Mushrooms
> Cray Fish.        Apple Puffs
> Seven dishes in the Desert.   Oranges, Apples, Pears,
> Cherries, Macaroons, Biscuits, Stewed Pippens, and
> Parmesan Cheese.

And always a hot Supper with seven or nine Dishes.[22]

Even such a mundane task as laundry took on a new and exotic aspect in St Petersburg and is described in Reginald Heber's journal:

> The washing of clothes at Petersburg is very remarkable; it is done by women, who stand for hours on the ice, plunging their bare arms into the freezing water, in, perhaps eighteen or twenty degrees of frost. They shelter themselves from the wind, which is the most bitter part of winter – fifteen degrees of frost, with wind, being more severe than twenty-five or thirty without – by means of large fir branches stuck in the ice, on which they hang mats. In general the women seem to be more regardless of cold than the men; they seldom, even in the most intense cold, wear anything on their heads but a silk handkerchief.[23]

Heber notes luridly that 'the river, while frozen, is sometimes considered dangerous to cross by night, being far removed from houses or lamps; and the different holes which are made to wash linen, afford a convenient hiding place for murdered bodies.'[24]

Much was strange, but Elizabeth would also have been struck by the extent of British influence on life in St Petersburg. In his book *By the Banks of the Neva* Anthony Cross writes that 'by 1791 there seem to have been no fewer than four establishments known as "The English Shop" in various parts of St Petersburg.'[25] One of the shops, at the eastern end of Vasilevskii Island, was owned by a Mrs Sarah Snow, who sold 'at most reasonable prices: the latest editions of English books, hats, stockings'[26] and a quantity of other goods imported from England. Elizabeth may well have found that it was easier to obtain fashionable English clothes in St Petersburg than in Chatham.

A key to the continuing prosperity of the British merchants of St Petersburg was the Russian demand for imported luxury goods from Britain. These goods were also, of course, available to the resident British population. It is difficult to obtain an exact figure for the number of British people in St Petersburg at this time. Once again, Anthony Cross provides the most useful information and suggests that:

> Although the figure of 1,500 may be taken to represent the upper limit of the British community in Russia in the last years of Catherine's reign, the composition of the population was constantly changing. Great family dynasties were begun in the eighteenth century and continued for generations. . . . There was also a constant flow of men and women, staying for periods of a few months or a few years, an increasing number of tourists (particularly in the last decades of the century), large numbers of naval officers, craftsmen and workmen of all kinds, to say nothing of the crews of the hundreds of British ships.[27]

Social life followed much the same pattern as it did in the rest of Europe and once she was living in the capital, Elizabeth was occupied with the same round of daily walks and social calls that filled the days of her counterparts in England. She soon made some women friends in the British community, of whom one of the most attentive was Catherine Cameron, the wife of the Scottish architect Charles Cameron. Catherine the Great employed Cameron extensively at Tsarskoe Selo, but he was also the original architect of the palace and the park at Pavlovsk. He had, however, enjoyed mixed fortunes during the reign of the Emperor Paul and may well have been looking for official employment at about the time when his wife and Elizabeth met. In early 1802, when Pavel already had considerable influence in naval affairs, Cameron was appointed as the chief architect to the Admiralty, but since there is no record of the date of Catherine's and Elizabeth's first meeting, it is impossible to judge whether or not Catherine's attentions to Elizabeth had a measure of self interest. In any case, she provided exactly the sort of female support that Elizabeth had lacked at the time of Adèle's birth. She was about ten years older than Elizabeth and had a single daughter, who by 1801 was already married and living outside Russia. More importantly, Catherine herself had lived in Russia since 1771, when her father, John Bush, had taken up employment as a gardener to Catherine the Great and had moved with his family to live in a house adjoining the Orangery at Tsarskoe Selo. Thus she was ideally equipped to initiate the newly arrived Elizabeth into the art of living in Russia as a foreign woman.

113

The Bush ladies had a good track record of helping new arrivals to settle in. In 1781 the Baroness Dimsdale was very kindly treated by Mrs Bush and her four daughters during her time at Tsarskoe Selo and was relieved to discover that in the expatriate community of St Petersburg, the family of the royal gardener was quite socially acceptable.[28] She describes them as 'very agreeable good sort of People'[29] and they took her to visit a Russian village and even to a Russian bathhouse. It is quite possible that Catherine Cameron also accompanied Elizabeth on similarly ethnic expeditions, but as the wife of a Russian nobleman, Elizabeth may have felt it was inappropriate for her to indulge in quite such blatant 'tourism'. Most probably, the Chichagovs already had suitable bathing arrangements at home, which meant that they could avoid the notorious public 'bagnias', where the sexes were reputed to mix freely in complete nudity – although by the time Elizabeth arrived this practice had been banned by ukase in St Petersburg. Martha Wilmot and her sister made regular use of the private 'bagnia' in the garden of the estate at Troitskoe belonging to Princess Dashkova. Catherine describes it in a letter:

> . . . this reminds me of the Bath Establishment in the Shrubbery here which is lovely & most perfectly arranged. The Women have nothing else to do but to heat the Furnace & keep everything in order, and you know Bathing is with the Russians as with the Turks a religious observance as not one of the lower order would or could profane the Church without having been in the Hot Bath the Night before. This secures a universal ablution every Saturday regularly. The Bath here has three seperate Chambers. In one is a gradation of stairs to increase the heat of a Vapour Bath if you like it. There is also a great Tub in which ones sits up to the Chin & the Ceremony is to scour oneself with Horsereddish till you smart & then with Soap. You should first sit up to your knees in a composition of wormwood Nettles, Grass-seed, Mint, & Horsereddish! I have gone through this operation frequently. The Pss [Princess] always goes to bed after bathing. One is prepared in an adjoining Chamber, but I go walk about and only feel the stronger.[30]

When she arrived in St Petersburg in August, Catherine took a cold bath every morning and at Troitskoe, Martha went swimming during the summer months. As there was no longer mixed bathing in St Petersburg, many male visitors to Moscow and other Russian cities succumbed to the temptation to observe the 'bagnias' elsewhere, but they were usually sadly disillusioned by the standard of female beauty. Robert Ker Porter gives the following description:

From motives of gallantry we posted ourselves opposite the ladies . . . .
Picture to yourself nearly a hundred naked naiads, flapping, splashing, and
sporting in the wave with all the grace of a shoal of porpoises! No idea of
exposure ever crossed their minds, no thought of shame ever flushed their
cheeks; but floundering about they enjoyed themselves with as much indif-
ference as when standing in all their trim array staring at the gay groupes in
the Summer-garden. Even on the confines of their bath, nay, in the very midst
of it, lusty boors were seen filling their casks for the use of the city. So many
masses of granite would have been regarded with equal attention by either
party. With the women bathed many men; all mingled together, just as they do
in the hot springs at Bath, where both sexes boil in one cistern, looking more
like sodden beef-steaks than human beings. Bad as they are in Bladud's pool,
they are ten thousand times more hideous in that of the Summer-garden: for
the men are almost all bearded, or grinning grimly through horrible whiskers
and fierce mustachios. The bathers are of every age, form and size; Don
Quixotes, Sanchos, Sampsons, etc. as well as all the misshapen figures that ever
came from the hand of nature, or suffered the ill effects of maims, bandy, or
other foe to the beauty of man. And as to the gentler sex, I can witness they
were more like the real than the fancied Dulcinea; more like the buxom
Maritornes, than either the agile Diana, or the beauteous Susannah . . . in my
life I never beheld any thing so disgusting. Women of twenty years old . . . possessed a bosom which a painter would have given to the haggard attendants of
Hecate. I will not proceed farther in my observations on this delicate part of
creation.[31]

One touristic visit which would not have eluded Elizabeth, however, was
the gruesome Kunstkammer of Peter the Great, which was housed in the
Museum of the Academy of Sciences and was a requirement for every visitor to St Petersburg. Elizabeth's reactions to the pickled babies and other
deformities that Peter the Great had purchased from a Dutch collector to
embellish his new capital are not recorded.

During Elizabeth's absence in Russia, several events of note had
occurred in her family in England. Sarah Pigott had had another child,
a little girl called Frances, who was born on 29 August 1800, but the
most exciting news was the remarriage in the same year of Charlotte to
the Revd John Bromfield Ferrers, the rector of the parish church at
Beddington, in which Elizabeth and Pavel had been married. Ferrers
was 42 years old at the time of their marriage and had already been at
Beddington for seventeen years. It seems most probable, therefore, that
he knew the Pigotts and that it was through them that he and Charlotte
met. A portrait of Ferrers in Thomas Bentham's *History of Beddington*

shows him as a stern and impressive figure, with a severity of gaze that would have put the fear of God into his parishioners, but an anecdote in the same volume shows him in a rather more endearing light. It would seem that he enjoyed his food and had taken the trouble to obtain a copy of the recipe of a soup that he had particularly appreciated at the house of a friend. To his great disappointment, the recipe was mislaid and thus it was with great delight that he discovered it, in the middle of a service, amongst his notes for the sermon. Such was his excitement that, according to Bentham, he quite forgot himself and to the intense amusement of his parishioners, waved the recipe at Charlotte from the pulpit with a cry of 'Here is the recipe for the soup!'[32] Ferrers was comfortably off and lived close to the church in a spacious house called Riverside, where he and Charlotte rapidly started a family. As was the case with Pavel and Elizabeth, their first child was a girl and they invited Elizabeth to be her godmother. It is partly on the subject of the common experience of parenthood that Pavel, around this time, addresses a warm letter in English to Charlotte, in which his Rousseau-style advocacy of maternal breast-feeding would have infuriated his late father-in-law:*

Among the agreeable succession of happy events, that have lately taken place here, the free correspondence with our friends in England is one of those that we felt the most . . . you will have no difficulty, to believe, my dear Mrs. Ferrers if I say that your agreeable letter to me is classed at the head of this friendly intercourse and that every thing you sayd in it has given me the greatest pleasure. I must begin as a tender father by shewing what share I take in the happy feminine propagation of our families. I certainly agree with you that your daughter is the finest girl in England, but that mine is the finest in Russia, now we must compare them before we conclude which is the best of them two – perhaps yours will be the prittiest *brunettina* and mine a beautiful *biondina*. As there is allways very little of what is really good, so she has a very precious and valuable nose, for it is as small as can be, exactly what they call *un petit nez retroussé* which besides the addition it makes to the beauty denotes a very intelligent being. Fortunately for us we found a very healthy nurse which has greatly contributed to her strength and fresh colour and was the only mean that could reconcile me to that most unnatural and cruel way of bringing up children. I am extremely happy to find that your daughter is much better off and that she has Mama for her nurse. The consolation I have is that if such a thing is happened to us it was not for want of

---

* Jean-Jacques Rousseau devotes several pages of Book 1 of *Émile ou de l'éducation* to the merits of mothers feeding their babies themselves as opposed to wet-nursing.

Lizinka's wish, but because she could not do it, poor thing. It is likewise a great advantage for you to have inoculated her with the cowpox, we were willing to have inoculated the smallpox to ours but it happened very unfortunately that the nurse had not had it, and this obliges us to wait till she is weaned. . . .

I never doubted of the steadiness and firmness of the character of the dear Charlotte the more so as I had a great example of patience and resignation in one of the family which is most like Charlotte, viz. my wife – every mortal would be surprised to see how she bore all sorts of uneasiness spread over the whole nation in the time she arrived in Russia and you will surely agree that to live ten months under Paul the Ist's reign is at least equal to 60 hours of the most painful labour. I suppose you will conclude from all this that you have to deal with a man who won't easily give up the preeminence in the good qualities of his child or his wife, but believe me that for all that I neither boast of my things nor do I less admire for it yours. . . .

At last I arrive to the period where it may be allowed to say something of myself, for I have almost sayd everything else. Since the death of Great Paul when I came to Petersburg I met with a very good reception by the Emperor Alexander, he sent me soon after in a frigate to the English fleet for some explanation with your chief commander, which happend to be Lord Nelson, my mission became so much more agreeable to me as I made the acquaintance of that so deservedly renowned seaman, and I found him as modest as a real great man and as polite and amiable as *some of you are sometimes*. When I returned from this expedition the Emperor was so kind as to attach me to his person, permitting me by that to live quietly in Petersburg without doing anything, and so I am become a little bit of a courtier, and this must be very little indeed as I mean to be so without intrigue, adulation, etc. . . .

I have hardly a doubt at all of our meeting again and I hope that you will pay us a visit first, we enjoy all possible freedom now, the Emperor has declared that any body who chooses to come in the country or go out of it is perfectly master of themselves, this is a reason for which I advise you to wait a little for the increasing of your family as it may not be very convenient to travel with many small children, but before we meet again I wish to hear of you all as often as possible and such intercourse will no doubt improve my style which is bad enough now. My best and sincerest wishes for everything yours. Adieu my dear Mrs. Ferrers, I am very truly your most affectionate

P. Chichagoff.[33]

After the northern winter, when for seemingly endless months the ground is frozen solid and covered with snow, Elizabeth found herself craving for a glimpse of greenery. All her life she had lived within the sight of woods and fields and the sterility of her snowbound environment had grown oppressive. When at last the snow melted and the temperature began to soar, Pavel and Elizabeth took advantage of the long summer days to make some social visits into the surrounding countryside, where many of the wealthier residents of St Petersburg passed the summer to escape the stifling heat of the city. After his meeting with Nelson, Pavel had several weeks of enforced leisure as he waited in vain for some instructions from the Emperor, but the arrival of his father from Shklov soon brought this period of idleness to an end. This was Vasilii's first visit to the capital since the accession of Alexander and he was anxious to pay his respects to the new sovereign. Pavel was puzzled by the Emperor's lack of reaction to the memorandum which he had earlier submitted to him on the state of the fortifications at Kronstadt. He may even have used the pretext of his father's visit to request an audience. During their audience, however, the Emperor expressed his displeasure at Pavel's absence during his recent tour of inspection of Kronstadt and he proposed that Pavel should accompany him on a second visit.

The Emperor's second visit to Kronstadt was the turning point in Pavel's career. The day started at the Emperor's summer residence at Peterhof, which was a few miles west of Oranienbaum, on the coast of the Gulf of Finland. As the imperial party embarked for Kronstadt, Pavel asked the Emperor whether he had been shown the naval port and was astonished to learn that this had been omitted from his previous visit. On landing, to the intense embarrassment of Kushelev, Pavel gave the Emperor a brilliant and detailed tour of the crumbling naval port, whose dilapidation had long been concealed from the crown by the Admiralty. The Emperor was appalled by the state of neglect and disorder. The piers were rotting and heaps of anchors and cannons lay abandoned to the elements; furthermore, there was not a single ship, because the port no longer had sufficient depth. Warming to his task, Pavel then took the Emperor to see the naval barracks, which were overcrowded, in ruins and located in a chronically fever-ridden area. He cited the mortality rate among the sailors – that year two thousand had died of illness between January and May – and the Emperor's agitation increased. Finally they went aboard the imperial yacht to watch the manoeuvres of the squadron which was anchored in the harbour, but the Emperor's attention was only for Pavel, who gave him a precise and devastatingly frank commentary on the state of the assembled ships. By the end of the visit, Pavel's mastery of his subject and his complete honesty had made a profound impression on the Emperor and on his return, the Emperor directed his full attention to the memorandum and instructed the College of the Admiralty to follow up on many of its recommendations. Furthermore, he gave Pavel a special status as his independent adviser on all matters concerning the navy, with instructions to report direct to him on a weekly basis.

Throughout the first months of his reign, the Emperor devoted himself to discussions with his 'unofficial committee' on many aspects of governmental reform. The outcome of these discussions was, in broad terms, a decision to bring the system of government more into line with its European counterparts, without diminishing the autocratic powers of the Emperor. In September 1802, a system of ministries was introduced, headed by ministers who, although theoretically subject to Senate scrutiny, in fact reported direct to the Emperor. There were eight new ministries, Foreign Affairs, War, Navy, Finance, Interior, Justice, Commerce and Education, but only the last two were genuine innovations. The first three had always existed under the name of Colleges and the second three had been the domain of the Procurator-General. In an attempt to co-ordinate the work of the ministries, it was also agreed that there should be a Council of Ministers, but in practice all matters of real political importance were discussed by another body entitled the Committee of Ministers.

Pavel's personal bureau, which was not answerable to the College of the Admiralty, came into existence a year before the creation of the ministries. With Kushelev still entrenched as Vice-President of the Admiralty, the scope of Pavel's activities was still fairly restricted and he initially busied himself with drawing up a new prospectus for the education of naval cadets. His proposals were immediately approved by the Emperor, who authorized their implementation. To assist him with the expanding workload, Pavel chose the most talented men of his acquaintance, including his erstwhile tutor, Gur'ev. In September 1801 many members of the court accompanied the Emperor to Moscow for his coronation, but Pavel was beginning to feel the shortage of money and was granted permission to remain in St Petersburg to pursue his labours. The Emperor was delighted with the energy and abilities of Rear-Admiral Chichagov and shortly after the ceremony, Pavel received a diamond plaque in recognition of his services.

By October France and Russia were already at peace and Britain and

France were in the process of negotiating the Treaty of Amiens. The cessation of hostilities in Europe enabled the Emperor to open up another attractive vista for Pavel and Elizabeth by proposing to Pavel that he should gain further naval expertise by making a tour of Europe, accompanied by Elizabeth. Pavel was in regular correspondence with Vorontsov throughout this time and told him of the Emperor's latest plan in a letter written just before Christmas: 'The Emperor has another project which is to send me on a tour of the best ports in Europe, from which I can learn and then communicate my observations to him. This is to start in Sweden to see the celebrated Chapman, from there to Copenhagen, then to Holland, France and finally England. I am very pleased about all this and above all because my wife can come with me and the Emperor will cover the costs of our journey.'[34]

Since the death of the Emperor Paul, the political influence of the Vorontsovs had increased. After a short period, the new Emperor had dismissed first Pahlen and then Panin as the main conspirators against his father, and Vorontsov's brother, Alexander, was becoming increasingly prominent. The protection which the Vorontsovs extended to both Pavel and Elizabeth can only have helped Pavel's rapid rise. It is difficult to assess how important Vorontsov regarded Elizabeth's family connections. As early as May 1801, the names of Lord Carysfort and his brother-in-law, Thomas Grenville, were mentioned in a letter from Panin to Vorontsov as the Emperor's preferred candidates for the position of British Ambassador to Russia.[35] Since the re-establishment of diplomatic relations, Lord St Helens had been temporarily in residence as the British envoy in St Petersburg, but the Russian government was anxious to have a more permanent appointment. In the meantime, however, Vorontsov and Panin had a violent quarrel and in a cutting reply to the banished Panin, with a sly reference to Panin's notorious 'Prussomania', Vorontsov writes:

When it was a matter of your own opinions, you found the time to write to me, for example, to tell me that it was the Emperor's wish that either Mr Thomas Grenville or Lord Carysfort should be sent to us. I know very well that the Emperor never even considered this, not having known either of them; he has never met the first one, and when the other left Russia, where he was as a traveller, the Emperor was a child of ten or eleven years old. The truth of the matter is that you knew the first one and the other one was pleasant in Berlin, which is of course a great merit in your eyes, Monsieur le Comte, in view of your predilection for Count Haugwitz. . . .[36]

From his correspondence, it is clear that Lord Carysfort was tempted by the prospect of returning to St Petersburg and he delayed giving an answer as he weighed up the merits of the appointment. Particularly while Carysfort was a candidate for the post of ambassador, Vorontsov must have regarded Elizabeth's safety and happiness as a diplomatic responsibility. Despite his many years in Britain, Vorontsov remained very Russian in his way of thinking and he could well have held the mistaken, but typically Russian, belief that any mishap that befell Elizabeth could bring the wrath of the entire British cabinet on his head. The only person who makes even an oblique reference to this is Dr Rogerson, who made a point of keeping Vorontsov regularly informed on Elizabeth's health and knew a great deal of what went on behind the scenes. After Elizabeth had been dangerously ill, he wrote the following to Vorontsov: 'Her husband was more dead than alive and had completely lost his head, and in truth, if he did lose her, he would lose everything for the interest that is taken in her is a great safeguard for him and has done a lot of good.'[37] Vorontsov, however, did not need to rely on Rogerson for news of Elizabeth, because she was in constant contact with Katinka, with whom she shared all her impressions of Russia.

Elizabeth had by now met the Emperor. Pavel was already a frequent guest at the palace, but the court journal shows that Elizabeth did not make an appearance at court until November 1801, when she accompanied Pavel to the Winter Palace. The one-thousand-room Winter Palace was designed in an opulent baroque style for the Empress Elizabeth by the Italian architect, Rastrelli. Ever since its completion in 1768, the Palace had been, as the winter residence of the rulers of the Russian Empire, the centre of imperial power. Catherine the Great did not share the baroque tastes of her predecessor – hence her patronage of the neo-classical Cameron – and she made several additions to the eastern end of the Winter Palace. These included a more intimate suite of rooms which became known as the Hermitage, a series of larger rooms in which to hang her collection of pictures and a neoclassical theatre. The State Apartments, in which the Emperor Alexander entertained, however, were on the first floor of the Winter Palace and guests would have arrived by the imposing Jordan Staircase, which is the embodiment of Rastrelli's baroque. The walls are entirely faced with white marble and heavily decorated with gold. The ceilings are covered with frescos and the upper balustrade is lined with forty-foot-high granite columns crowned with golden capitals. The effect is, as intended, both magnificent and overpowering.

After such an approach, Elizabeth would have found the 24-year-old Emperor refreshingly simple. He was three years her junior, blue-eyed, tall, slim and fair and, not surprisingly, very Germanic in appearance – his only real Russian blood being through the unproven paternity of his grandfather. Pavel describes him in the early years of his reign as follows: 'The Emperor Alexander had something so gentle and so considerate about his manners and his person, his way of talking was so attractively devoid of self-esteem and his desire to do good was so apparent from all he said and did, that he was initially adored and assiduously obeyed by all those who had the good fortune to meet him.'[38] Pavel was already well used to the atmosphere of the court, but for Elizabeth this must have been a memorable evening and in a letter written a few months later, she describes the Emperor as 'charming' and 'amiable'.

After her presentation at court, Elizabeth was fully launched in the highest society of St Petersburg, but on their limited budget, the Chichagovs seem to have opted for a life of cosy domesticity. They had neither the means nor the inclination to belong to the glittering world of the court and they preferred the company of an intimate circle of good friends, with whom Pavel could indulge his passion for debate and with whom Elizabeth could play her music. While, therefore, Pavel continued to dine at court regularly in order to conduct his business with the Emperor, it was to be some time before Elizabeth's name again featured in the court journal.

The Christmas season came and went in a whirl of festivities. The city was once again ice-bound, but at the height of the winter season, it presented a scene of the greatest gaiety. The streets were full of the sound of sledge bells as the wealthy of St Petersburg indulged in a very Russian love of display and drove around the city in a fantastic variety of ostentatious vehicles driven at maximum speed. Horse races were held on the river and there was skating on the ponds. Amongst the many contemporary descriptions of sledges and the winter scene in general, Robert Ker Porter's – with his artist's eye – is one of the best:

> The sledge-carriage of a prince, or a nobleman, is uncommonly handsome. All its appointments are magnificent; . . . and a picturesque effect, peculiarly its own, is produced by the vehicle itself, its furs, its horses, their trappings, and the streaming beards of the charioteers. The nobleman's sledge . . . is warmly lined with rich furs; and to prevent the lower extremities of the occupier from

being cold, has an apron (like those of our curricles) formed of green or crimson velvet, bordered with gold lace. On a step behind, stand the servants with appropriate holders. This place is often filled by gentlemen when accompanying ladies on a sledging party.

The horses attached to this conveyance are the pride of the opulent. Their beauty and value are more considered than the sledge itself. The excess of vanity amongst the young officers and nobility here, consists in driving about two animals whose exquisite elegance of form, and playfulness of action, attract the attention of every passenger. . . . Only one is placed in the shafts which never alters its pace from a rapid trot; the other is widely traced by its side; and is taught to pace, curvet, and prance, in the most perfect taste of a finished manège. Their tails and manes are always of an enormous length; a beauty so admired by the Russians that twenty horses out of thirty have false ones.

The harness of these creatures is curiously picturesque, being studded with polished brass or silver, hundreds of tassles, intermixed with embossed leather and scarlet cloth. These strange ornaments give the trappings an air of eastern *barbaric* splendour. . . .

The surrounding winter scenery; the picturesque sledges and their fine horses; the scattered groups of the observing multitude; the superb dresses of the nobility, their fur cloaks, caps and equipages adorned with coloured velvets and gold; with ten thousand other touches of exquisite nature, finished the scene, and made it seem like an Olympic game from the glowing pencil of Rembrandt.[39]

Great mountains were built from blocks of ice, down which the local population hurtled on wooden toboggans at breakneck speed, and the Emperor and the imperial family presided over the annual blessing of the water of the Neva, which was taken, in an elaborate religious ceremony, from a hole cut in the ice just in front of the Winter Palace. In the past, after the blessing was over and the magnificently attired throng of courtiers and clerics had retired from the biting cold, local women were said to have rushed to dip their newly born children naked into the opening in the ice in the belief that this would gain them additional spiritual protection for the rest of their lives. The Ambassador of Sardinia, Count Joseph de Maistre, repeats a well-known and probably apocryphal anecdote concerning this practice: 'Formerly great importance was attached to baptizing children in this water: in accordance with the Greek rite, they were plunged into the waters of the Neva; and some travellers have recounted in all seriousness that, when the archbishop, with his hands frozen, let one of these children slip from his hands, he said coolly "Give me another one."'[40]

In the midst of all this, Elizabeth and Pavel were idyllically happy, as they contemplated their forthcoming voyage and Pavel's excellent professional prospects. In March 1802 Elizabeth wrote a long letter to an unidentified friend which reveals much of her state of mind:

I have very often reproached myself, my dear Joey, for never having taken up my pen to you since I have been in the land of the *Bears*, as I am well convinced that few people have so sincere a regard for me; consequently nobody will be more glad to know from such good authority as my own hand, how perfectly happy and contented I am in *these barbarous climes*.

Strictly speaking, (were I to begin to criticise) the climate is what I find the least fault with; and the houses and clothing are so admirably suited to it, that there is no possibility of suffering from the cold. I have my health perfectly . . . Tho' I have been tolerating the climate so much, (for there really is a vast deal of fine weather) I do not at all admire the affects of it, and for anybody who likes the country and the beauties of nature, it is a sad deprivation to live where there is neither one nor the other for certainly nature may be said to be devoid here, her productions are so miserable. I am very sure that the first time I find myself in a beautiful and cultivated country, I shall go into an ecstasy that will not soon have an end.

This pleasure may not be very far distant – you may have heard a hint from some of my sisters that we are likely early this summer to set out on our travels, and if Pavel can finish everything he may find to do in Sweden, Denmark, and Holland, we shall probably winter in France. So extensive a plan cannot be followed with any exactness, as much will depend upon local circumstances but of course the bonne bouche will be to spend some time in England before our return to Russia. The scheme altogether enchants me, and I cannot but love the charming Alexander for procuring us the advantage of travelling and seeing our friends, the former of which being a thing our own pockets could not have compassed.

By this you will learn that the essential expenses of this undertaking will all be paid for by the Emperor, as it is his wish that my husband should visit every country where he may be likely to find something new and useful for this country. The only evil I see in all this is, that, the more intimate Pavel becomes with the Emperor the more difficult it will be to leave this country, which is certainly finally our wish. He is so amiable in himself that it would be impossible to refuse him, and yet it is hard to sacrifice yourself and do no good after all, for there is such a preponderance of bad people here that Pavel can do nothing, and he is really a pearl before so many swine. I believe the Emperor is convinced of it, for he shews him much confidence and regard, and by appointing him in his suite and giving him free access at all times, shews at least a wish of getting at the truth. He generally goes and dines with him once or twice a week and if he has any business with him can retire after dinner. He has no actual duty in the Navy, having refused to remain in it under the command of a set of ignorant F—ls that [the Emperor] Paul put over his head. By being about the Emperor's person he is free from every other persons command, and he employs him in various confidencial ways as occasion offers.

I dare say you are dying to know something about my little Adèle and indeed I believe she is exactly such a little creature as you formed an idea of even before she was born. Nevertheless I must proceed to a description of her. She is short, round, fat, white, and a *pretty* little thing, which perhaps you will with difficulty believe, when I say she is the image of Pavel; however as there is nothing bad in his face except the small nose and the small pox, the former is not bad in a child, and the latter I trust she never will have as she has already gone through the Cow pox. She has bright blue eyes with dark lashes and yellowish hair, and without any partiality a very intelligent open countenance. Pavel is convinced she is a *prodigy* notwithstanding she does not say a word at a year and a half old except Mama, but she understands everything and can make others understand everything by signs and acting. The best of all is that she is a very quiet good tempered child and I hope she will not lose her good character before I have the pleasure of introducing her to you. . . .

I am very sorry to be setting out just as the Woronsows are coming here to spend the summer and likewise upon the first arrival of the Carysforts, but we must profit by the summer to get thro' the Northern Countries.[41]

In the coming year Elizabeth's fears that Pavel's growing intimacy with the Emperor would limit their ability to travel were fully realized. They never made their journey to England.

# CHAPTER SEVEN

# The Rise of Pavel
### 1802–1805

Nobody had ever talked to the Emperor as Pavel did. Although much of what he had to say about the state of the navy was disagreeable, Pavel – in complete contrast to the Emperor's other advisers – hid nothing. The Emperor had witnessed the accuracy of Pavel's assessments during his visit to Kronstadt, where his withering comments on the state of the coastal fortifications and the ships had been more than justified, and he knew that Pavel had only told him the truth. During 1802, therefore, the Emperor came to regard Pavel as one of his most indispensable and trustworthy advisers and the voyage to Europe seems to have been indefinitely postponed. Instead, Pavel became the prime mover in a plan to reform the navy and spent many hours in his office or with the Emperor at court. The court journal for 1802 shows that Pavel attended the court on at least forty occasions and that he was frequently one of a small number of a dozen or so guests who dined with the Emperor. Elizabeth must have been bitterly disappointed by the postponement of the trip and also by the news that Carysfort had decided to refuse the appointment to St Petersburg. The arrival of Vorontsov on a summer visit must, however, have been a compensation, as well as the knowledge that she was expecting a second baby.

During the summer Pavel was in frequent attendance on the Emperor and Empress as they divided their time between the summer palaces of Peterhof and Kammenii Island, with occasional visits to the Dowager Empress, Maria Feodorovna, who held a summer court of her own at Pavlovsk. A portrait of the Dowager reveals her as a Junoesque figure with an ample bosom and an elaborate headdress sporting numerous ostrich feathers. Her facial expression is one of extreme determination. The dominance at court of Maria Feodorovna, at the expense of her daughter-in-law, the Empress Elizabeth, was remarked on by many visitors to St Petersburg. The future cleric, Reginald Heber, was impressed by the extent of the Dowager's good works:

> The great patron of these, and of every charitable institution, is the dowager empress, whose sound judgement, good sense and good character are

apparently very remarkable. She shows great fondness for every active employment; and even in her amusements, which are turning ivory and studying botany, she proves her hatred of idleness. She is the only person who keeps up any degree of state in the empire; the emperor, his brother and his wife, live more like private persons than princes.[1]

General Savary,* who was sent as Napoleon's ambassador to Russia in 1807, wrote the following report on the court shortly after his arrival:

## ABOUT THE COURT

It is divided in three

The Emperor
The Empress
The Dowager Empress and her children

The court of the Emperor is composed of his ministers and the important officials of the household, amongst whom the following are present on a daily basis. . . . All these people have the right of entry to the Salon of the Emperor at any time and dine regularly three times a week, and sometimes more, at the court. The conversation at dinner usually covers travel, war and administration. There is no circle with the Emperor, by 8 p.m. at the latest, he has retired. . . .

The Empress lives completely withdrawn from society. At least three times a week she eats in her own apartments, alone with her sister, Princess Amelia of Baden, The other days, when she dines with the Emperor, she appears in the Salon one moment before the dinner is served; she retires immediately after the coffee and goes back to her apartments, from which she dismisses even the maid of honour, or lady-in-waiting who is on duty with her. Thus she remains completely alone. . . . With her there is no kind of court representation or etiquette and very little gaiety. She is concerned with serious matters; she reads a great deal. . . talks little and appears in general to have a very cold nature. . . . She is almost continually on bad terms with the Dowager Empress, and has not been living with her husband for a long time. . . . I believe that the Empress Elizabeth is very shrewd and has a keen judgement. . . .

The Dowager Empress. It is with her that one finds all the representation of the Russian court. There one sees etiquette carried down to the last detail of private life. In this court there are maids of honour, ladies-in-waiting, chamberlains, equerries and pages. . . . She brings up her children in her palace. . . . A foreigner who arrives in Russia is struck by the difference which exists between the court of the Dowager Empress and that of the Emperor . . .

---

* Created Duc de Rovigo by Napoleon in 1808.

in fact it is at the court which is not of the *Sovereign* that one finds all the prestige which surrounds a throne! . . . During public ceremonies, the Dowager Empress most frequently takes the arm of the Emperor – the Empress walks behind her, alone – In the carriage, she always takes the back right-hand seat – the Empress is on her left and the Emperor in front.[2]

This curious division did not only stem from the authoritative personality of Maria Feodorovna; it was also a reflection of a widespread belief that the Empress might never produce an heir. Until she did, the Crown Prince remained the Emperor's brother, the Grand Duke Constantine, and therefore Maria Feodorovna's long-term prospects of power were far greater than those of the childless Empress. The position of the Empress was also further undermined by the behaviour of her husband.

As a 16-year-old youth, the Grand Duke Alexander had been the devoted admirer of Louise of Baden, who took the name of Elizabeth Alexievna on her marriage to him on 9 October 1793. The classical German beauty was selected by Catherine the Great as a bride for the heir to the Russian throne, but as the years passed and the longed-for heir failed to appear, their relationship cooled. Some said they had made a pact to tolerate each other's love affairs, although the close surveillance of her mother-in-law would not have made this easy for the Grand Duchess. Despite this, it was whispered that at one stage the Grand Duchess had been attracted to Prince Adam Czartoryski and that it was for this reason that he was sent by the Emperor Paul on a diplomatic posting to Sardinia. The Emperor Alexander's liaison with the Polish-born Madame Narishkina,* on the other hand, was public knowledge. The uxorious Pavel disapproved strongly of their relationship and suggests in his memoirs that Madame Narishkina did not return the Emperor's feelings:

> At this time, the Emperor took as his official mistress, Madame Narishkina, a Pole, born Princess Czetvertinska, the most beautiful woman in St Petersburg, but who was far from reciprocating the passion of the master and did nothing but observe the necessary outer appearances to maintain his illusions. The Empress Elizabeth thus found herself exposed to all the humiliations which a man who needed to appear more gallant than he was could pour on her. He insisted so much on paying court to his mistress in the presence of his wife that not content with his daily visits, he also met her in public places and was continually at the door of her carriage.[3]

Historians do not agree on the date that Marie Narishkina first became

---

* Née Marie-Antonova Chetvertinski (1782–1854).

the mistress of the Emperor. The Grand Duke Nicholas Mikhailovich, who as a member of the imperial family writes from authoritative sources, claims that 'the intimate relations' between the Emperor and Marie Narishkina did not begin until 1804, when she was 22.[4] She had, however, been the toast of St Petersburg for many years before this. At a very young age, she had married the hugely rich Dmitrii Narishkin and by 1800, the soirées at her sumptuous residence in St Petersburg and her dacha on nearby Krestovskii Island were sought out by the highest society of the capital – including the two elder Grand Dukes, Alexander and Constantine. The Emperor's infatuation probably dates from this time. Meanwhile, Constantine fell in love with Marie's younger sister, Jeannette, with whom he also had a long-standing affair.

Roxana Sturdza, later the Countess Edling, who as a maid of honour was closely acquainted with the imperial couple, blames the breakdown of their relationship on the coldness of the Grand Duchess towards her husband when he was deeply distressed by the murder of his father.[5] But other accounts suggest that the Grand Duchess was a pillar of strength on this occasion.[6] What seems more likely is that with the removal of his father, the newly crowned Emperor at last felt free to indulge his passions. By all accounts, Marie Narishkina was divinely beautiful. In the eyes of her contemporaries, her large dark eyes and luxuriant curls, combined with the curves of her voluptuous figure, invariably set off to perfect advantage by a clinging white gown in the style of Madame Recamier, were without rival in St Petersburg. Beside her, the slim, fairhaired Empress paled to insignificance and Marie Narishkina retained the favours of the Emperor for over a decade.

Despite General Savary's observations, it is clear from the court journal that during the daytime the Empress was frequently present at court with her husband and thus she would have met Pavel on many occasions. His excellent German and innate gallantry would have endeared him to her and, in a court where she had few supporters, she may even have regarded him as an ally. Certainly the tone of his comments on the Emperor's affair with Madame Narishkina suggest a sympathy for the Empress, and in one of the long letters which she spent much of her time writing to her mother in Baden she describes Pavel as 'a man of great wit and pleasant company'.[7] Many male visitors to the Russian court found the Empress Elizabeth's habitual air of sadness very attractive and the following comments of Lord Granville Leveson-Gower, who was British Ambassador to Russia between 1804 and 1807, are echoed by numerous others:

There is something extremely interesting in the young Empress; she has a beautiful expression of countenance, with withal an air of melancholy that is quite touching. I danced with her a Polonaise which is nothing more than a walk about the Room, handing the same Lady for about five minutes. I assure you I was quite moved by the Tristesse of her manner of talking. The Emperor treats her with respect, but there is great mutual coldness between them; it is doubtful on which side the coldness first began.[8]

Despite the scandalous rumours that circulated from time to time, there is no documentary evidence that the Empress had any extramarital attachments. Even if she was aware of the emotions she aroused, she had probably learnt from experience that Maria Feodorovna would prevent her from cultivating potential admirers. Instead, she cultivated her mind in the seclusion of her apartments, but to those who remembered the court of Catherine the Great, it must have seemed insufferably dull.

In the College of the Admiralty, Pavel's spectacular success with the Emperor was arousing universal jealousy. Pavel had become a member and the secretary of a special committee for the reorganization of the navy. The president of the committee was Vorontsov's brother, Alexander, who was by now the Chancellor. Admiral Mordvinov was also a member, but he objected to Pavel's role and rarely attended. In August Pavel escorted the Emperor on another tour of Kronstadt, where they spent an agreeable morning together looking at the fleet, returning to Oranienbaum to dine with the Empress, Maria Feodorovna and many other members of the court. After dinner everyone strolled in the garden, which would have given Pavel an ideal opportunity to air with the Emperor his plan of drawing up an expert report on the condition of all ships and buildings belonging to the navy with a view to carrying out repairs. The proposal was presented to the committee and gained the Emperor's enthusiastic support. One of those employed on this project was the architect Charles Cameron, who subsequently built a large naval hospital complex at Oranienbaum.[9] Meanwhile at the Admiralty, Mordvinov, Kushelev and Shishkov were incensed by all this independent activity and in a last-ditch effort to check Pavel's meteoric rise, Mordvinov refused on a point of protocol to approve Pavel's request, signed in the name of the Emperor, to set the latest project in motion.

In different circumstances, the Mordvinovs and the Chichagovs might have become friends. Mordvinov was a brilliant man, thirteen years older than Pavel, who had also met and married an English girl while on naval duty. Furthermore, he had met his wife while serving with the Russian squadron commanded by Vasilii at Leghorn.[10] However, unlike Pavel, his real passion in life was not the navy, but economics, and he found Pavel's reforming zeal intensely irritating. At this stage, Pavel was unstoppable; the Emperor would refuse him nothing, and despite Mordvinov's objections, the project went ahead and with it two others with even more far-reaching implications.

With his customary bluntness, Pavel had explained to the Emperor that the origin of many of the troubles of the Russian navy was dishonesty. Thousands of roubles were stolen annually from the coffers of the Admiralty by unscrupulous officials and dishonest suppliers. Pavel wished to set up an office of inspection, with branches in all the main Russian ports, which would investigate all naval purchases to try and stamp out the corruption at its root. The proposal was drawn up and presented by the committee to the Emperor, who approved its immediate implementation. The final, gargantuan task undertaken by the committee was to determine the ongoing requirements of the Russian navy in terms of numbers of ships, the frequency of replacement and the costs of maintenance and construction. In all this, Pavel was the driving force and he worked with the burning enthusiasm of a man who had at last found his true vocation. On 28 November 1802 Pavel went to the Winter Palace to thank the Emperor for his recent promotion to vice-admiral and within weeks, Mordvinov had resigned his position and Pavel, with the title of Deputy Minister of the Navy, was asked to take over his portfolio. Pavel was also decorated with the order of St Alexander Nevskii.

Pavel's conquest of the Emperor and his rapid rise to the very top of his profession would not in the least have surprised Elizabeth. She had, after all, been similarly taken by storm herself and she had also long ago made her own assessment of his qualities. She had complete confidence in his abilities and, more importantly, in his affections. In the intimacy of his home, the impatient and sometimes irascible admiral was transformed into a tender and adoring husband. Elizabeth was his greatest treasure and he worried continually about her slightest ailments. In the autumn of 1802 Elizabeth succumbed to St Petersburg's notoriously damp and unhealthy climate and was unwell for several weeks. Pavel watched over her in a state of frantic anxiety and even when the worst of her illness had passed, he listened with dread to the little cough that she seemed to have acquired which would not go away. Like many people of exceptional ability, Pavel did not mix easily with his fellow men, nor did he place his affections lightly, but his love and friendship, once given, were unshakeable. Amongst his male friends, Vorontsov held pride of place, and it is with Vorontsov that Pavel shares his deepest feelings about Elizabeth: 'You are the only person, my adored father, who seems really to know her; you yourself feel things deeply and you know what it is like to possess a wife who means everything to her husband and without whom everything is nothing.'[11]

The winter was a particularly hard one and as Elizabeth's pregnancy advanced, she found herself frequently housebound because of the intense cold. While Pavel passed his days in a frenzy of activity, Elizabeth was condemned to a sedentary existence at home, her hours punctuated only by the demands of Adèle and the regular chiming of the nearby church bells. On the last day of January, to Elizabeth's relief, the temperature rose and she managed to take a good walk outside in the morning and later visited some friends. That evening, around ten o'clock, she was assailed by stomach pains, which were followed within an hour by a violent haemorrhage. She had only just completed the seventh month of her pregnancy, but the baby was on the way. Complete pandemonium broke out in the household. Nothing was prepared for the birth and at such an hour, in midwinter, it was impossible to find either a doctor or a midwife. Eventually Pavel managed to summon to Elizabeth's aid what he calls 'some of her English female acquaintances',[12] without whom Elizabeth would have fared far worse. It is likely that Catherine Cameron, who according to Rogerson was assiduous in her attentions to Elizabeth,[13] was among those who helped to care for her. The Camerons were now living in a flat in the Mikhailovskii Castle, from which Catherine could easily have been summoned to Vasilevskii Island.[14] The next day a doctor was found and after forty-eight hours of labour, Elizabeth finally gave birth to a little girl who was so tiny and so pitifully frail that her early demise seemed inevitable. After a glance at the baby, Pavel thanked God that at least he had been spared Elizabeth.

Since both parents believed that she would die within a few days, the baby was baptized immediately. During her first few days, Julie's life hung in the balance. On three occasions, when her breathing had nearly stopped and her face was already growing cold, she was saved only by the skills of the doctor, who resuscitated her by wrapping her in a cloth soaked in hot wine. For the next two months Elizabeth watched over her baby night and day and by April, Julie was out of danger and growing fast. However, the ordeal of premature labour and her anxiety over Julie took its toll of Elizabeth's health, as did the icy winter fogs of St Petersburg. She often felt tired and breathless – symptoms that Pavel tried to persuade himself were caused by the rapid changes in the weather.

Now that Pavel was the head of the Admiralty, Elizabeth's social obligations increased considerably and, in common with other prominent figures in St Petersburg, the Admiral and his wife were expected to 'receive' regularly. In his anxiety to westernize Russian society, Peter the Great had been the first Russian monarch to insist that his more distinguished subjects followed the European custom of entertaining at home. In his *Memoirs of Peter the Great* (1836), Sir John Barrow describes how senators and generals were ordered to receive guests twice a week from eight to eleven o'clock for conversation, cards and dancing. These assemblies were open to all 'of the rank of gentleman, foreigners as well as natives,'[15] but at the time, the real innovation was the inclusion of wives and daughters. Over the years, this custom had changed little and in 1805 Robert Ker Porter describes the evening activities of the leisured classes of St Petersburg as follows:

> The evening produces the theatre, or assemblies at their own houses, when, either cards are again resorted to, or a light dance exhilarates the scene, to which the company who prefer sitting, play on the piano-forte and harp. Various little pastimes, such as forfeits, the magic music, etc, etc, are brought forward. And thus wit and innocent mirth carry on till supper is announced. This meal is generally too luxurious for the health and beauty of those who draw round the table. Soups, fish, roast and boiled meats, and savoury dishes, fill the groaning board. Good appetites are seldom wanting; and thus, both mentally and bodily recreated, or rather overburthened, do the parties betake themselves to rest; their stomachs fevered with the richest food, they lie down in bed-rooms where an artificial heat, like that of a hot-house, ferments their digestion, leaving them at waking, pale, languid, and spiritless.[16]

Porter also comments on the detrimental effects of this lifestyle on the looks and health of the women: 'Stoved rooms, fresh air excluded, no exercise, hot suppers; all tend to demolish the shape, destroy the complexion, and impair the health,'[17] but, he adds, 'there are several lovely Polish women here at present: and also a few from our little Island. Their gentle countenances, affable manners, and affectionate hearts are sweet remembrancers of home.'[18] It is tempting to think that Porter may have had Elizabeth in mind as one of the English women who reminded him of home. He certainly knew Pavel well and was engaged by him in 1806 to paint several grandiose pictures to decorate the Great Council

Chamber of the newly planned Admiralty. Through his sentimental life, however, he may also have come to know Elizabeth. Porter had a protracted love affair with one of Elizabeth's Russian friends, Princess Mary Shcherbatova, whom he eventually married in 1812, but not before the lovers had endured many difficulties and separations. Elizabeth would have understood their situation only too well.

Not all the foreigners in St Petersburg appreciated its busy social life. In 1804 the youthful, newly arrived British Ambassador, Lord Granville Leveson-Gower, complains about it bitterly: 'When I tell you that there are above a dozen or twenty persons who are at home and receive every evening, you will with difficulty understand the extreme tiresomeness of the Society, but the people who meet seem to be but little acquainted with each other, and the chairs are placed in a formal order, and out of respect to my ambassadorial Dignity I have been generally obliged to sit next and make the agreeable to the old Lady of the House.'[19]

Leveson-Gower also disapproved of the Russian habit of keeping late hours and of rising late in the mornings. A few years later his sentiments are echoed by the American envoy, John Quincy Adams, who writes from St Petersburg in midwinter: 'Nov. 28. – Day. We rise seldom before nine in the morning – often not before ten. Breakfast. Visits to receive, or visits to make, until three; soon after which the night comes on. At four we dine; and pass the evenings either abroad until very late, or at our lodgings with company until ten or eleven o'clock. The night parties abroad seldom break up until four or five in the morning. It is a life of such irregularity and dissipation as I cannot and will not continue to lead.'[20]

A year later, however, even the disciplined New Englander had been obliged to conform to the hours dictated by the climate and society of the host nation:

Nov. 30. – Day. The sun rises now about nine in the morning. It is scarcely daylight at eight, and I seldom rise from bed before ten. Read five chapters in the French Bible, with Ostervald's reflections. Breakfast. Noon has arrived . . . It darkens soon after two o'clock, even in the few days when the sun is seen, which is, upon the average, about once a week. The six others there is a gloomy half-darkness through the day, so that from ten until two I can just see to write . . . From nine or ten at night until one or two in the morning I pass in company abroad, or at home, or at cards with the ladies. The difficulty of writing anything, and the disgust at the occupation, grows upon me in a distressing manner, and I feel more and more every day the importunity of miscellaneous company.[21]

In April 1803 Pavel was still protesting to Vorontsov that 'we have virtually no contacts, but live apart from the tumult, with great reserve in our social relationships; we content ourselves with the pleasures that one finds in the bosom of the family, and it is on them alone that my happiness and my unhappiness depend.'[22] But this pleasant seclusion was soon to end. Before long the twice-weekly soirées at the Chichagov house were being sought out by foreign diplomats wishing to become more closely acquainted with the influential Minister of the Navy, who was such a favourite with the Emperor.

The diplomatic corps in St Petersburg contained several remarkable figures at this time. Its longest serving member was the Neapolitan Ambassador, the Duke of Sierra Capriola, whose first wife had so fascinated Lord Carysfort nearly twenty years earlier and who, through his second wife, a member of the aristocratic Viazemskii family, had further consolidated his influential position at the Russian court. Another prominent diplomat was the British Ambassador, Sir John Warren, who served in St Petersburg from 1802 to 1804, having been offered the post after it had been declined by Lord Carysfort. Sir John never enjoyed the same 'insider' status as the Duke of Sierra Capriola, but because of Britain's political importance to Russia and the significance of the British community in St Petersburg, he nevertheless occupied an eminent position. Pavel and Elizabeth were well acquainted with the Warrens, who were amongst the diplomats attending their soirées.

A sympathetic picture of Sir John emerges from contemporary sources of a bluff naval officer, whose linguistic and intellectual deficiencies were at least partially compensated for by his good nature. Martha Wilmot describes him as a 'sweet Good Man . . . So benevolent! . . . on whose amiable honest face I always dwell with delight . . .'[23] Lady Warren, however, is less charitably portrayed. Leveson-Gower, who succeeded the Warrens in 1804 and overlapped uncomfortably with them for some weeks, found her nauseating: 'I never was more disgusted than with the mean adulation that she has been paying to everybody connected here with the Imperial Family – her extravagant and Hyperbolic praises of even the youngest Brothers and Sisters of the Emperor (*ce sont des êtres tombés des cieux*) positively make me sick.'[24]

Pavel describes her as 'meddling' in the affairs of her husband, 'a distinguished sailor but a novice in diplomacy'.[25] In particular, Pavel never forgave Lady Warren for bringing the Corsican emigré, Count Charles Pozzo di Borgo, to one of his evening parties. Pozzo di Borgo was a sworn enemy of Napoleon's, who entered the service of Russia in 1803 and rapidly gained the confidence of the Emperor. Pavel distrusted him from the outset and saw the powers with which he was invested by Alexander as yet another example of the tendency of Russian rulers to give positions of national importance to foreigners. Not surprisingly, Elizabeth and Lady Warren do not seem to have become particular friends; on the other hand it was through the mediation of Lady Warren that the Chichagovs made the acquaintance of another diplomat, who was to become one of their closest and most faithful allies.

Count Joseph de Maistre was nominated in 1802 by the King of Sardinia as his diplomatic envoy to St Petersburg. During the latter part of the eighteenth century, the territories of the Kingdom of Sardinia, which included Savoy, Piedmont and the island of Sardinia, had been dramatically reduced. After the French Revolution, Savoy fell to French republican forces and became a province of France. The Piedmontese put up a greater resistance to the French, but in 1798, the King, Charles Emmanuel IV, abdicated and retired to the island of Sardinia after permitting French troops to occupy Turin. Subsequently the whole of Piedmont was occupied by the French. Since 1798, therefore, the position of the King of Sardinia had been extremely precarious and his predicament as a monarch threatened by revolutionary forces earned him the support of the Russian Emperor Paul. In 1799 Turin was briefly liberated by the Austro-Russian army commanded by Suvorov, and the King returned from Sardinia in the hope of regaining his mainland territories, but he was forced to flee again in 1800 after Napoleon's victory at Marengo. After the death of the Emperor Paul, Alexander's continuing support for the King of Sardinia was demonstrated by the inclusion in the Franco-Russian peace treaty of 1801 of a statement that both governments would try and reach agreement on the problems of the Kingdom of Sardinia. Napoleon's refusal to address this aspect of the treaty was soon to become a source of friction between France and Russia.

De Maistre arrived in St Petersburg without his family and with practically no financial resources. A Savoyard by birth and a passionate royalist by persuasion, he was no stranger to the vicissitudes of exile. His refusal to swear allegiance to the French republican government in Savoy had obliged him to abandon his possessions and flee from his native Chambéry to Switzerland, where he was later joined by his wife and two elder children. From there, they moved to Turin, only to be driven into exile once again when the city fell to the French. During the confusing period that followed, de Maistre and his family had their full share of the uncertainties and hardships that have always been the lot of war refugees, but his determination to serve his king never wavered and he embarked on his open-ended mission to St Petersburg with typical fortitude.

The lonely hours of de Maistre's bachelor existence, however, were turned to good account. Through copious reading, he expanded his already profound knowledge of philosophy and religion and embarked on the writing of a variety of philosophical works. John Quincy Adams, who was appointed Minister to Russia by the American government in 1809 and later became President of the United States, was quick to observe the quality of de Maistre's mind. In his diaries, he describes him as being one of the few members of the diplomatic corps in St Petersburg who had any interesting literary conversation and adds that he was 'always amusing.'[26] Adams's authoritative comments on de Maistre's manuscript translation of Plutarch's treatise on *The Delays of Divine Justice* aptly convey the learned flavour of their discussions. Despite his absorption in literary matters, however, de Maistre also enjoyed social life and the company of women. His personal charm soon gained him access to the highest society in St Petersburg, where in compliance with the wishes of his sovereign, he frequented, amongst others, the salon of the imperial mistress, Madame Narishkina. From his published correspondence, it is apparent that he also maintained a regular correspondence with several women on topics that ranged from philosophy to social gossip. He was such a favourite with Lady Warren that on her departure she left him all her books. He also won the trust and affection of Elizabeth.

De Maistre was undoubtedly initially interested in gaining the confidence of the Chichagovs for political reasons. He was concerned for the welfare of several of his countrymen from Piedmont who hoped to further the cause of their struggling kingdom by serving in the armed forces of her Russian ally. His first mention of Pavel, in a report to his own government, is strictly businesslike and is in connection with a Piedmontese officer whom he had managed to place under Pavel's protection: 'The Admiral is a Prussian and he has the wind behind him; there is no more determined protector; but he is quick-tempered and fiery which, in the first place, makes him a lot of enemies. Furthermore he has an insupportable love of ridicule: he does not steal, and he does not permit theft in his department which makes him hated. You must take what I tell you literally, as it is not intended to be a joke.'[27]

But their relations grew far closer when Pavel later extended his protection to de Maistre's younger brother, Xavier, an unconventional figure who had served under Suvorov in Italy and had then retired to Moscow, where he eked out an existence as a painter. Xavier also enjoyed a certain literary reputation, thanks to the overnight success of his charmingly written small volume entitled *Voyage autour de ma Chambre*. Through the influence of Pavel, Xavier acquired a secure position as the director of the naval library and museum. This act of kindness earned Pavel and Elizabeth the eternal gratitude of de Maistre. For his part, Joseph was astounded by the ease with which he entered into intimacy with the Chichagovs. Despite the social obligations incumbent on Pavel's position, he and Elizabeth jealously guarded their privacy. In a dispatch to the King, de Maistre describes their house as being 'perhaps, the most difficult house to penetrate in St Petersburg, [but] I entered it easily, without quite knowing how, like water entering a sponge, and I am there as a friend.'[28] 'I first went there, like all foreigners who go to places, in ignorance. Had I known anything about the house, I would have dreaded it, but somehow I found myself completely at ease there, without any preliminaries, a friend from the first moment we met.'[29] De Maistre was fascinated by Elizabeth's cool gaze and by Pavel's passionate attachment to her: 'She is English and she continually reminds me of the French notion which compares Englishwomen to Mount Vesuvius – covered with snow on the outside, but burning within.'[30] Their relationship never ceased to intrigue him and he was one of the very few who understood its intensity.

The writings of de Maistre evoke two contrasting pictures of the Chichagov household. The first is one of a cosy, hospitable house, in which he often passed the night asleep in an armchair after an evening of furious and invigorating debate with Pavel. He found in Pavel an intellectual equal and became a close friend: 'I have always remained loyal to him, while always being honest with him; and he, for his part, has given me great proofs of his affection.'[31] The debates ranged from philosophical topics to such everyday matters as the introduction of a paper currency, but the spirit was always the same. Years later, in a letter to Pavel, de Maistre recalls his evenings at their house: 'I could live for a thousand years and still never encounter anything which compares with our suppers. They were touched by lightning and, amongst the ranks of those tender memories which tear us apart and which one so cherishes, there are none which are more deeply engraved.'[32] Elizabeth was one of the party, and the tone of de Maistre's later letters to her suggests that his relationship with her was a mixture of playful tenderness and respect for the influence of her good sense over her hot-headed husband. He tells the King of teasing her about Pavel's mischievous habit of confusing his interlocutors as to his political affiliations: 'Sometimes I call him *the gentleman from the other camp*, to make his wife – who is English and whom he loves passionately – laugh,'[33] and he mentions Elizabeth's habit of recording their discussions in her journal[34] – undoubtedly the successor to the 'Tag-Rag letters' of her childhood.

The second picture is the one that the Chichagovs, in particular Pavel, projected in the society of which they were becoming increasingly prominent members. Pavel's delight in debate for its own sake misled many of his acquaintances. Even as close a friend as de Maistre was sometimes puzzled by Pavel's political stance and in a letter to the King of Sardinia he dedicates a long paragraph to a portrait of Pavel:

> I owe you a chapter on an outstanding minister at the moment, namely Admiral Tchitchagoff, the Minister of the Navy. . . . [He] is one of the most extraordinary minds in the country. He was educated in England, where he learnt, above all, to despise his own country and everything to do with it. His conversation is of a boldness that could be given another name. As he is very witty and original, his polished sallies are deeply penetrating. He passes for being extremely French, but this is less true than one might think, for it is certain that he contracted an admiration for England while he was in that country, which is very visible. I believe him to have quite a number of French ideas in his head, but it is hard to know what to believe, for he contradicts everything, just to amuse himself.[35]

De Maistre wrote this letter in 1808, after Russia and France had been united against England by the Treaty of Tilsit in 1807, but Pavel's apparently francophile leanings had been in evidence for many years. Early in 1804, the elderly and gossipy Rogerson, with whom Pavel was becoming increasingly impatient, broached the subject of Pavel's suspected disaffection for England in a damning letter to Vorontsov:

> Young Mr. Nicolaï [the bearer of the letter] will tell you many things that will make you anxious about everything to do with Pavel Vassilevitch. Despite his great zeal and activity, he has so many shortcomings that the very few friends that he has cannot see how he can last for long. Apart from the numerous blunders he has made in his department by his unconsidered actions, he makes himself conspicuous on all occasions by propagating an enraged anti-Britishness and in pleading (scarcely indirectly) the cause of Bonaparte. For example, on the latest occasion, by applauding the Consul and severely blaming

Markov.* I attribute this to a decided love of paradox. With all this, he is quarrelsome and unreasonable . . . he conceals a lot from me, but what I am telling you comes to me from everywhere. Even your brother knows about it, for dining alone with him, he revealed to him his devotion to the person of B[onaparte]; he believes him to be a demi-god. Judge for yourself, my dear Count, whether all this is calculated to topple him in the end. Mr. N[ovosil'tse]v and young Stroganov who (with you and your brother) have most contributed to make his fortune, have changed their attitude towards him, and see him now with the same sensations as you would look at a catch of ipecacuana. This does not come from a preference for somebody else, but rather it is the development of his personality that causes this aversion. His good wife is much to be pitied; for, notwithstanding all his tenderness for her (which is really extreme and which makes me pardon many of his faults), it is impossible that she does not suffer with intensity from these ungrateful blows, which she sees his unreasonableness inflicting all too often on those who hear him. [36]

Rogerson was probably conveying, fairly accurately, the mood in St Petersburg about Pavel. Pavel's honesty had won him many enemies in a society whose most senior members regarded the fruits of corruption as part of their rightful rewards. His fellow ministers loathed his ruthless attacks on dishonesty and theft and feared the eventual exposure of their own malpractices. (Count Zavadovskii, the Minister of Education, refers to Pavel sarcastically in a letter at this time as 'our Neptune' who has 'the cunning of a Jesuit'.[37]) Even a man as apparently upright as Admiral Mordvinov had obtained huge personal properties in the Crimea through political influence and continually exploited his position of power to serve his own interests. The 'unconsidered actions' to which Rogerson refers were most likely the numerous sackings that had taken place in Pavel's department, which had inevitably aroused a wave of antipathy against him.

But Vorontsov had already heard about all this from Pavel himself nearly a year earlier. Shortly after taking control of the navy in 1803, Pavel had written two long letters to Vorontsov full of family and political news and outlining his reforms:

I have caught a quantity of thieves, of whom the most notorious are a commissioner who had stolen one thousand sacks of flour, a marshal who had stolen five hundred axes which were found at his house, and a master carpenter who earned 370 roubles a month and a pood [36 lbs] of flour a day from those who worked under his direction. Finally, the squandering, the

* For the Markov incident, see p. 142.

wastage exceeds anything that one could have imagined and the confusion is at its height, and it seems to me that of all the countries in the world . . . our country has arrived at the limits of evil and of a nearly universal corruption . . . . I have therefore divided my men into three classes, as follows: the bad and lazy ones, the good people, but old or incompetent for reasons which do not depend on them, and the good ones. The first are dismissed without further ado, the second are given pensions and the third remain and are recompensed as well as is possible given our unsettled financial circumstances.[38]

A few weeks later, as his reforms began to be felt, Pavel wrote again to Vorontsov:

You will not be surprised to hear that I have made an infinity of malcontents and this is why. They are angry because of the means by which I am seeking to prevent theft, and because I require everyone to do their duty or at least to do something and be answerable for it; and because I insist that if someone has business to do, he should come and see me at an appointed time. This last is regarded as arrogance and the rest as wickedness and diabolical spitefulness. . . . You can see by this how difficult it is to bring about reforms; but if one does not weary of me, I do not despair of producing them.[39]

Pavel's reforms embraced every aspect of the Russian navy. He completely restructured its administration and reorganized the system of training naval recruits. He ordered the destruction of irreparably unseaworthy vessels and launched a programme of shipbuilding; he overhauled the navigational systems and purchased new beacons. On the architectural side, it was Pavel who pushed ahead with the ambitious alterations to the Admiralty, which became the most important building of its era in St Petersburg. Cameron was replaced by a dynamic Russian-born architect named Andreian Zakharov, who succeeded not only in meeting the expanding needs of the Admiralty's shipbuilding yards but also in creating a dignified building, which preserved the golden spire of the earlier structure and was in keeping with Pavel's exalted image of the Russian navy. Pavel also revived his father's plans for the rebuilding of the port of Revel. Similarly it was under Pavel's patronage that Xavier de Maistre was able to expand the naval library and to reorganize the naval museum.

In every aspect of these activities, Pavel had the unfailing support of the Emperor, but of practically no one else. Furthermore, he did little to disguise his feelings of disgust for much of what went on behind the scenes. His eye turned continually westwards to those European nations where the ideals in which he so profoundly believed seemed to be universally respected. 'I am convinced that the most humble individual in certain countries can be a thousand times happier that he could ever be – with all the means that grandeur and honours could give him – in this vast and uncomfortable empire where nature has refused everything and where the human mind has created nothing good.' [40]

In such a state of mind, it is hardly surprising that he was full of admiration for the extraordinary civic reforms that Napoleon, in this brief period of peace, was succeeding in implementing in France. In May 1803, Britain's backtracking over the evacuation of Malta led to a renewal of the war between Britain and France. This enraged the Emperor Alexander, who largely blamed the British, an opinion with which Pavel concurred. But Rogerson's concerns for Elizabeth's emotional and patriotic sensibilities were ill-founded. Elizabeth would never have taken the irrevocable decision to leave her family and her country to throw in her lot with Pavel if she had not believed in him completely. Compared to many of his compatriots, he was, in her view, 'a pearl before so many swine',[41] and while, as both Rogerson and de Maistre observe, she had to contend with his public tirades against her country, she knew him well enough not to take them seriously. Furthermore, at the time when Rogerson was writing, Elizabeth would have had little support for the policies of the British Prime Minister, Henry Addington, who had succeeded Pitt in 1801 and was considered by many people in Britain to be inept. Coming from a family closely allied with Pitt, she would undoubtedly have agreed with the contemporary jingle, written by Pitt's friend George Canning, that 'Pitt is to Addington as London is to Paddington.'

On the other hand, Rogerson's comments on Pavel's attitude to the Markov incident would have seriously alarmed Vorontsov. Count Markov was the Russian envoy to Paris, but was suspected, with reason, of intriguing against Napoleon with an anglophile faction which included Vorontsov. Napoleon insulted Markov at a diplomatic reception and in September 1803 Markov was recalled to St Petersburg, where he was publicly honoured by the Emperor. Vorontsov had also taken exception to Pavel's decision to send some young naval officers for training in France and for the first time in their close friendship, a coldness developed between the two men.

Apart from relaying gossip, however, Rogerson had a personal reason for wishing to tarnish Pavel's reputation with one of his few supporters. In February 1804, Elizabeth went into labour with her third child. It was her most agonizing experience to date and as the night progressed, she passed from excruciating pain to convulsions and eventually, when her frail body could take no more, to unconsciousness. Throughout the hours of convulsions, Pavel stood helplessly by, raging at the incompetence of the two Russian doctors he had called, one of whom prescribed rhubarb and the other fresh air. He was horrified by the sight of Elizabeth with leeches on her temples and covered with blood and sweat, as she writhed in torment before him. By 4 a.m. Pavel could stand it no longer and, despite the hour, sent for Rogerson, who was in no mood for courtesy by the time he arrived, in the middle of a freezing winter night, at Elizabeth's bedside. He stayed for a brief fifteen minutes, during which he gave Pavel little sympathy and remarked that in his view, Elizabeth was not in danger. He left and Pavel, who was now convinced that he was about to lose his wife, sent for yet another doctor – an Englishman recently arrived in St Petersburg called Leighton, who had been recommended to him by Father Smirnov. Leighton instantly grasped the seriousness of the situation and pronounced that only drastic bleeding would stop the convulsions and save the life of the mother and child. After the third bleeding, the convulsions finally stopped and shortly afterwards Pavel and Elizabeth's third daughter was born.*

Elizabeth lay in a darkened room, drifting in and out of consciousness. Periodically Pavel's anguished face swam before her eyes. She was far too weak to hold her baby and in her exhausted state, Leighton prescribed complete rest and quiet. But throughout the day, the silence was regularly shattered by the clamour of the church bells of the neighbouring mansion belonging to the Bishopric of Yaroslav and despairing for Elizabeth's recovery, Pavel decided to seek the intercession of the Emperor. The Emperor replied immediately:

> I have just received your letter. I cannot tell you how greatly it distressed me. I can enter into all the horror of your situation. But do not lose all hope.
>
> I have at once given the order that the bells should not be rung; but I am afraid that they may already have done so. Your letter was brought to me while I was at the Grand Parade. I have only returned now.
>
> Yours ever, Alexander.[42]

Pavel preserved this letter for the rest of his life.

---

* Pavel's descriptions suggest that Elizabeth suffered from the recurring condition of high blood pressure in late pregnancy (pre-eclampsia). If untreated, this can lead to high temperatures, convulsions and the eventual death of the baby. The blood pressure of the patient can be lowered by extensive bleeding, but during convalescence, further attacks can be triggered off by loud or sudden noises.

On 14 March, French agents kidnapped a member of the French royal family, the Duc d'Enghien. The Duke was accused of involvement in a conspiracy against Napoleon and summarily executed, throwing the royal families of Europe into an uproar. The Russian Emperor was particularly outraged, since the kidnapping violated the territory of Baden, which was ruled by his father-in-law. He ordered a note of protest to be sent to the French government and decreed court mourning. The rupture with France was exacerbated by Napoleon's reply, in which he made references to the murder of the Emperor Paul. When, therefore, on 18 May, Napoleon declared himself Emperor, Russia refused to acknowledge him and a break in diplomatic relations soon followed. At the same time, negotiations were opened with England which eventually resulted in the formation of a third coalition against France, composed of Britain, Russia, Austria and Sweden.

No one was more delighted with this turn of events than Vorontsov – although his position as ambassador had been weakened by the arrival in London of the Emperor's personal envoy, Novosil'tsev – but the contents of Rogerson's next letter increased the rift between him and Pavel:

> Paul Wassiliewitz is alone and unrivalled, having an astonishing credit, but absolutely no solid connections; because anyone of perspicacity soon sees the risks of approaching him too closely, since he is always immoderate, passing from one extreme to another, torn between hatreds and infatuations; but that which distances him from others gives him the ability, for the time being, to capture the Master by assault.
>
> Being on the road to see his wife, I learnt of the catastrophe of the duc d'Enghien. I decided to give him the news, as a *touchstone*, which he received without the slightest apparent reaction, and shortly afterwards he said: 'Who do you consider among the kings of Europe could be compared to Bonaparte?' In truth, my dear Count, I simply can't account for him, except by attributing to him some sort of *nuttiness*, because I am sure he wants to be an honest man.[43]

For his part, Pavel had not hesitated to give Vorontsov an account of Rogerson's lamentable medical performance, calling him 'the greatest of all charlatans',[44] but this did not prevent Vorontsov from rebuking Pavel severely for his admiration of Napoleon and from ceasing to correspond with him. Whatever his shortcomings as a doctor, Rogerson was a shrewd judge of human nature, and his observations on Pavel's isolation were very accurate. This made the withdrawal of Vorontsov's approval all the harder to bear.

At last the endless winter came to an end and Elizabeth emerged from her seclusion. The two little girls flourished, but the baby did not survive and the recovery of her mother was distressingly slow. The climate of St Petersburg, cold and damp in winter and stiflingly humid in summer, was continuously detrimental to someone of her constitution and the doctors suggested that, as a last resort, she should be taken on a voyage. The Emperor willingly gave Pavel leave and during the summer of 1804, Pavel and Elizabeth embarked on a five-week cruise of the Baltic.

From the moment she set foot on the immaculately scrubbed decks of the yacht which had been put at the disposal of the Minister of the Navy, Elizabeth felt better. A light breeze billowed the sails and the water lapped steadily against the hull as the yacht gathered way. The domes and spires of St Petersburg became more and more indistinct as the yacht moved out into the Gulf of Finland, until finally they mingled with the summer haze that hung over the mainland and vanished completely. The outlines of Kronstadt and of the summer palace of Peterhof were also soon left far behind and by the time the short summer night began to fall, Elizabeth could no longer see the long low coastline of her adopted country. After several hours on deck, she and Pavel eventually retired to the privacy of their cabin and for the first time in many months, they made love.

Pavel does not specify their route in his memoirs, but many parts of the Baltic are idyllically beautiful in summer and nowhere more so than the archipelago off the west coast of Finland, where dozens of tiny islands offer secluded anchorages and an atmosphere of total peace. In a letter Pavel does mention that they made a brief, unscheduled visit to the coast of Denmark, which is described by Robert Ker Porter just a year later:

> The shore, all along the Danish side, presents the most lovely stretch of landscape I ever beheld. Mount Edgecumbe is looked upon as the paradise of England: and what Mount Edgecumbe is in one spot only, so appears the whole of Denmark from Elsinor to Copenhagen. The land is high, and undulating in various romantic and sublime forms. Rich woods, broken by park-like openings and verdant pastures, and interspersed with country-houses and villages for an extent of twenty-three miles, form the clothing of these beautiful hills.[45]

On their unplanned arrival at Copenhagen, Pavel and Elizabeth received a warm welcome from the Russian Ambassador, Lizakevich, who had been a member of the Russian Embassy in London at the time of their marriage and who did everything to make their visits ashore enjoyable. But neither of them could persuade the elderly Lizakevich to set foot upon the yacht. As the days passed, Elizabeth felt the nightmarish memories of her recent ordeal fading. She always felt happy and well at sea and her looks reflected her contentment. Pavel, too, regained his *joie de vivre* and finally stopped worrying about Elizabeth. The five weeks passed all too quickly and only the thought of their two little girls in St Petersburg made the prospect of return palatable. For Elizabeth there was another welcome event, the arrival to stay of her long-standing Chatham friend, Fanny Burslem. Fanny arrived in St Petersburg just before the ice closed the gulf to navigation and her familiar presence did much to cheer Elizabeth's spirits during the months of winter. On her return, Elizabeth soon discovered that she was expecting another baby.

In St Petersburg Pavel found Vorontsov's letter of rebuke awaiting him and in a lengthy reply reassures him that his feelings towards Napoleon have altered: 'The recent actions of my hero have brought about this conversion . . . and at this very moment I believe I can say without exaggeration that the horror which he has inspired in me by his recent behaviour could equal that which his most inveterate enemies have for everything that he does.'[46] Pavel repeats his comments at the end of the letter: 'Please send my regards to Mlle la Comtesse [Katinka] and to Miss Jardine, and declare me to be the sworn enemy of the one whom they detest even more than me, of Bonaparte.'[47]

Given Pavel's passion for honesty and his reverential regard for Vorontsov, this declaration should be taken at face value. In the light of history, it is quite easy to understand how he could have been both disgusted by Napoleon's behaviour and a genuine admirer of his genius, but at a time when much of Europe had been devastated by Napoleonic troops, no one appreciated this distinction. Thus the rumours of Pavel's admiration for Napoleon were not easily dispelled and were to have very adverse repercussions on his reputation in the future. Another even more unfortunate rumour became firmly attached to Pavel at this time, namely that he disliked Russia. This was a direct result of his devastating frankness and his refusal to moderate his conversation in the hothouse atmosphere of St Petersburg society. Even a friend as loyal and as intimate as de Maistre believed that Pavel despised his own country; others less well disposed questioned his patriotism. But the truth was, as always, far more complicated. In some ways Pavel's relationship with his fatherland was as paradoxical as his feelings for Napoleon. His dearest wish was to improve and enhance his country; at the same time, he hated its corruption and above all its lack of personal freedom. In a small notebook, Pavel vented his frustrations on what he considered to be Russia's greatest defect:

> Russian slavery resembles no other. In all the countries mentioned in ancient and modern history, there have always been distinctions of state and condition. There have been free men, serfs and slaves. The Romans, the Greeks, the Gauls had them, but in Russia the whole population without exception is enslaved by the force of despotism. In other countries, slavery has been tempered by certain conditions favourable to their interests . . . there was a certain reciprocity of duties and obligations, but today every Russian is a slave, pure and simple. He is dispossessed of every privilege and right and is nothing but the property of the Emperor, who does with him as he wishes. [48]

In his first difficult months as minister, Pavel wrote to Vorontsov saying that he feared for nothing but the health of Elizabeth. A year and a half later the stress of his position and his growing isolation were beginning to take their toll of his physical and psychological health. He began to suffer from continual headaches, a buzzing in his ears and a conviction that everyone was against him. In private, Elizabeth and he began to dream of escaping with their children to England. There was also another problem – money. The practice in St Petersburg of ministers making money out of their positions was so universal that it had not occurred to the Emperor that Pavel needed a salary, and Pavel was too proud to ask for one. The style, however, that he was expected to maintain as minister had completely exhausted his resources and those of the family. Pavel tried to sell some of the family property, but no buyers were forthcoming. Retirement seemed to be the only honourable solution.

Late in 1804, a combination of professional and private problems finally brought matters to a head. To Pavel's intense indignation, the Russian naval squadron destined for Corfu, a Russian naval base since 1799, was placed under a military commander answerable not to Pavel, but to the Ministry of Foreign Affairs. Pavel had taken endless pains with the preparation of this squadron, which was to liaise with the British navy, and he was incensed by this latest slight to the authority of his department. His financial position was also becoming desperate and in a state of high agitation he asked to see the Emperor and he tendered his resignation.

To Pavel's extreme discomfiture, the Emperor pressed him to pour out his woes, which are also outlined in a letter to the Chancellor, Aleksandr Vorontsov:

> I have nothing with which to pay for my household; so I shall have to sell it and retire to the country: for here, given the ever-growing costs and the debts which I am incurring annually, I shall inevitably be ruined, especially as I have decided that I positively will not receive anything. Having told you of my poverty, nothing remains for me but to support it. I have never wanted to enrich myself; I must be given the means of existence, but I shall never tolerate the idea of being paid just because I asked for it.[49]

Pavel retired home to bed with a bad cold and in a state of emotional turmoil. He was alarmed by palpitations of the heart, which he attributed to worry. His ill health cast a cloud over the Christmas celebrations of the family and Elizabeth spent much of her time in her now familiar role of calming and reassuring her overwrought husband. Her steady confidence in him restored his equilibrium; moreover, she was the only person who fully understood his sense of frustration at the endless professional obstacles that were preventing him from achieving his objectives. He fretted continually over the rift that had occurred between him and Simon Vorontsov and he wrote pitifully to him, assuring him of his unchanging affections:

> I do not wish . . . to believe that you could doubt for a moment the inviolable and tender affection which I have for you. There is certainly no event that could possibly bring about the slightest alteration to it, not even your coldness towards me. . . . The good that you have done for me, which is always before my eyes, should be the greatest guarantee of this. It should not be difficult for you to guess that I am referring to my wife: she is the only good thing that I possess, who sweetens my life and consoles me about everything else, and I owe her largely to you.[50]

Brooding in his room, Pavel wrote several further letters to Aleksandr Vorontsov, complaining bitterly about the low status of the Russian navy and his own subsequent lack of authority.

During this difficult period, Elizabeth and Fanny busied themselves with the children. Fanny had always been a close friend of the Proby family at Chatham – it was she who verified Charles Proby's will. She had also managed to remain on close terms with both Elizabeth and her father throughout their last terrible quarrel. It is to Fanny's partiality for Handel that Elizabeth makes light-hearted reference in a letter to her father, when she was trying to restore some normality to their relationship.* Elizabeth corresponded regularly with her sisters and with Katinka, but the mail from St Petersburg was notoriously insecure. Thus she would have treasured this opportunity to talk intimately with a trusted friend, not only of many things in Chatham but also about her life with Pavel.

It was not until well into the new year that a ray of light finally pierced the aura of gloom surrounding the Chichagov household. Pavel's letters to the powerful Aleksandr Vorontsov had not been in vain and his plight had been fully explained to the Emperor, who in addition to awarding him a further decoration, refused to accept his resignation. In a lengthy audience, the Emperor managed to convince Pavel that he attached more importance to the navy than had any other Russian sovereign since Peter the Great. A short time later, he granted Pavel a life annuity of 10,000 roubles. Pavel was overwhelmed with gratitude to the Emperor and Aleksandr Vorontsov. In early January, Simon Vorontsov's son, Mikhail, was instructed by his father to visit the Chichagovs regularly and at the same time Vorontsov himself finally wrote to Pavel. It seemed that the episode over Napoleon, which had so nearly destroyed their friendship, had at last blown over. Their correspondence revived and with it Pavel's energies and spirits.

Pavel flung himself once more into a flurry of preparations for the dispatch of a second naval squadron to Corfu. His insistence on the highest standards set him on an inevitable collision course with an administration accustomed to a more easygoing regime, and there were endless bureaucratic wrangles with his colleagues. During the long hours of paperwork at his desk, the thought of escaping from the responsibilities of office to command the squadron himself became increasingly attractive. He longed to get away from it all, with Elizabeth and the children, to a milder and more ordered world. His dreams, however, were unfulfilled and the squadron – in impeccable order – was dispatched under the command of Vice-Admiral Seniavin, but not before Pavel and the Emperor had enjoyed a considerable altercation. Pavel, infuriated to discover yet again that naval decisions were being taken by the military without his knowledge, had stormed out of a committee meeting and had written a fuming letter of resignation to the Emperor. Alexander's reply, dated 27 July 1805, bears witness to the strength of their exchange:

* See p. 73.

After all that has happened between us, I did not expect you to make a new attempt to leave the service. I thought that the daily experience of my respect towards you would have aroused some kind of gratitude in you and that, especially at this time when you yourself know how many cares I have, you would not have tried to multiply them.

However, seeing how wrong I have been, I have no choice but to act in accordance with my conscience and the requirements of office. I therefore reject your request, nor will I tolerate anything of this kind in the future. I have no one to replace you and our country needs your services until things are properly organized. . . .

Consequently, I lay upon you the personal responsibility of accomplishing everything in the best possible manner. You may come to me at any time for further explanations. Meanwhile I am sure that your love of the Fatherland and your desire for its prosperity will be stronger than any of the personal motives which are so unworthy of a man of your talent and spirit.

Alexander [51]

For Elizabeth, the resolution of their financial worries was a great relief and with the departure of Fanny in May, she accepted Catherine Cameron's invitation to stay at Oranienbaum. After months in a barren winter landscape of white and brown, Elizabeth found the sudden lushness of the greenery along the road to Oranienbaum almost suffocating. The countryside seemed to have changed from winter to summer overnight, and she felt the frantic intensity with which everything around her was growing in these few precious weeks of warmth and sunshine before the ice returned. She passed the royal summer palace of Peterhof, built on a commanding hilltop overlooking a complex of fountains and cascades which were said to rival those of Versailles. Around the palace lay many miles of wooded parkland dotted with exotic pavilions built at the whim of successive rulers. Once a year, in the height of summer, Maria Feodorovna celebrated her name-day there. The park was thrown open to the public, who camped in their thousands in the vicinity to participate in the festivities that culminated in a magnificent nocturnal illumination of the park. As Elizabeth's carriage drew closer to Oranienbaum, the road passed between the walls of the secluded gardens concealing the country mansions to which the wealthy of St Petersburg retreated during the summer months. Amongst the summer population were many members of the English community, whose houses lay in English-style gardens full of flowers. Now that they had a regular income, Elizabeth and Pavel were determined to find a summer residence of their own.

Catherine Cameron welcomed Elizabeth warmly. Perhaps she already suspected that her husband's days as Architect-in-Chief to the Admiralty were numbered, but he was still, at this stage, engaged in admiralty-related projects. At Oranienbaum he had built a spacious naval hospital complex to replace the insalubrious arrangements at Kronstadt that had so disgusted Pavel, and he and Catherine spent much of the summer in the locality. Cameron, who was many years older than his wife, had few social skills, but he had enjoyed a charmed life under Catherine the Great, who had a taste for his neoclassical style. Cameron led the Empress to believe that he was a direct descendant of the Camerons of Lochiel, although his origins were considerably less glamorous. According to Anthony Cross, Cameron's father was a London builder, with whom he quarrelled violently and who was in prison for debt at the time that Cameron left for Russia.[52]

Despite the social limitations of her host, there was much to interest Elizabeth at Oranienbaum. It had been the private pleasure ground of Catherine the Great and she had built an extravagant Chinese palace there with sumptuous interior decorations. More fascinating still was the enormous wooden structure which had accommodated the Empress's private roller coaster – a summer version of the ice mountains which were built for similar entertainment in winter. Several roller coasters were also constructed in the park at Tsarskoe Selo during the reign of the Empress Elizabeth, and on one occasion Catherine nearly came to grief when her toboggan slipped out of its wooden groove at high speed. Only the superhuman efforts of her escort, the muscular Grigorii Orlov, saved them both from disaster.

After a week with the Camerons, Elizabeth went on to visit the Gascoignes, whose flamboyant lifestyle would have offered a striking contrast to the quiet household of the Camerons. Charles Gascoigne was yet another Scotsman who enjoyed a successful career in the service of the rulers of Russia. He had originally been employed by Catherine the Great in 1786 to direct and improve a cannon-making factory situated at Petrozavodsk, 185 miles north-east of St Petersburg, on Lake Onega. Like Cameron, he soon impressed his new employers and by 1805 he had far-ranging responsibilities for a variety of government factories and foundries, including the Admiralty works at Kolpino, about fifteen miles south-east of St Petersburg. Pavel was an enthusiastic admirer of Gascoigne's abilities and it was he who had persuaded the Emperor in 1804 to employ Gascoigne to re-establish the Kolpino factory, originally founded by Peter the Great. Within six months, Gascoigne had turned the ruined works into a flourishing concern to the great satisfaction of Pavel, who wrote to Vorontsov that 'Gascoigne is the only man in the world capable of bringing about such a change.'[53]

Gascoigne's labours did not go unrewarded. He became a millionaire and received imperial honours, together with the rank of state counsellor. It is presumably in deference to these that contemporary English travellers began to style him 'Sir Charles', for Gascoigne was certainly never honoured in his own country. On the contrary, he was for many years regarded askance by his compatriots for passing on to the Russians a system of cannon-making invented by his previous employer, the Scottish company Carron. Gascoigne built himself splendid mansions in Petrozavodsk and St Petersburg, where he lived, according to a former English acquaintance, 'in more splendour and has greater connections than he can ever have in this country'.[54]

We know from Rogerson that Elizabeth stayed with the Gascoignes at Kolpino, where she was most probably invited by Gascoigne's two daughters, Anne and Elizabeth. Anne was considerably older than Elizabeth and was the widow of the Earl of Haddington. In 1796 she had remarried and was now Mrs James Dalrymple. The younger sister, who was closer to Elizabeth in age, had in 1803 married a handsome Englishman called George Pollen after a whirlwind romance. Martha Wilmot describes Pollen as 'that brilliant fine Creature . . . brilliant with beauty & full of life, surrounded with a sort of atmosphere which excited & created gladness wherever he appear'd'.[55] Pollen had left considerable debts in England, but thanks to the fortune of his father-in-law, he and his new wife lived lavishly in St Petersburg and in summer took up residence at Petrozavodsk – 'they say the most romantick country possible'[56] – where there was riding, shooting and even salmon fishing. After the wedding, in order, perhaps, to impress his new son-in-law, Gascoigne brought an entire band from St Petersburg to provide music for his summer guests. No similar description has come to light of the Gascoignes' house at Kolpino, but it was doubtless as agreeable as their other dwellings.

Elizabeth returned to St Petersburg strengthened in mind and body. Apart from a miscarriage, she had been spared the rigours of childbirth for over a year and her health had improved accordingly. Furthermore, these independent visits to friends seem to mark a turning point in her attitude to life in Russia. The ever-observant Rogerson was quick to spot the change: 'Admiral Tchitchagow and his wife are quite different: he has softened and become milder, his relationships are all good and he is fulfilling the duties of his position well; and she is, in the end, naturalized here and so much in tune with the country that if some unforeseen accident were to take her back to live in England, she would regret it even more than Lady Warren. Her health is good and will remain so if she does not have any more children.'[57]

Meanwhile, on 21 October 1805, the British had inflicted a crushing naval defeat on the French at Trafalgar. But they had paid for it with the life of Nelson.

# CHAPTER EIGHT

# *War*

## *1805–1808*

In September 1805, the Emperor left St Petersburg to join the Russian army that was assembling against Napoleon. On his way, he stopped for several days of lavish entertainment at the Polish estate of his close friend, Prince Czartoryski, who was his chief adviser on foreign affairs. Czartoryski had never ceased to hope for the restoration of the Kingdom of Poland, so callously divided up during the reign of the Empress Catherine, and he believed – mistakenly – that the Emperor supported him. Meanwhile Napoleon's advances in Italy, of which he had proclaimed himself king, had finally roused the Austrians into action. His incursions into Prussian territory also appeared to have prompted the King of Prussia to abandon his procrastinations in favour of the anti-French coalition. By November, Napoleon had defeated the Austrian army at the Battle of Ulm and had entered Vienna. The Russian army, under its best-known general, Mikhail Kutuzov, had retreated north-east into Moravia.

The Emperor hastened to join Kutuzov and, overriding Kutuzov's objections, demanded that a stand should be made against Napoleon's advancing army by the joint Austro-Russian forces. On the night of 1 December a thick fog enveloped the countryside surrounding the village of Austerlitz and concealed the massive body of troops which Napoleon had positioned there. As the sun rose and the fog cleared, the French launched their attack and caught the Russians and the Austrians unprepared. The lines of communication between the allies were confused and Kutuzov, who believed the action to be an error, was apathetic. By evening the Austrian and Russian casualties numbered many thousands. It is on the field of Austerlitz that Tolstoy portrays Prince Andrei Volkonsky bleeding to death and describes his rescue at the command of Napoleon.[1] Many of the retreating Russians were drowned as Napoleon fired red-hot cannon balls on to the ice-covered lake over which they were fleeing. Kutuzov managed to lead the remnants of his army back to Russia, but it was another overwhelming victory for the French.

In St Petersburg the news of Austerlitz was received with dismay and disbelief. The Russians had always considered their army to be invincible. The Emperor attempted to mitigate the shock of defeat by giving a lavish ball at the Hermitage theatre and by the distribution of a large number of decorations, but to little avail. The population was stunned and Pavel's worst fears about the inefficiency and the ill-founded complacency of his country's armed forces were further confirmed. In this moment of national humiliation, a resentment that dated from his boyhood re-emerged and took the form of a long tirade against the Emperor's prac-tice of employing foreigners in positions of importance. In a letter to Simon Vorontsov, whose brother, Alexander, had recently died, he writes:

> Suppose we had a Westminster Abbey or a St Paul's Cathedral in which to place monuments to honour the memories of people who have been useful at this time. Wouldn't we see, first of all, the mausoleums of Czartorisky, of Winzingerode, of Richelieu, of Rosenkampf, of Campenhausen, of Michelson, of Bouxhoevden, etc. etc.? Those travellers who came to see this superb col-lection, wouldn't they be tempted to say: What a poor-spirited country, for all their great men are foreigners! And then I ask you, what do we feel, we Russians, for the same reasons? When one cannot be sure of preference over a foreigner in one's own country and one knows that one is better off any-where else than at home, what sort of attachment can one have for such a place? It makes the heart bleed and I prefer not to talk about it. To reflect is a misfortune in a country where there is neither security nor rights, nor any hope of obtaining them.[2]

Pavel casts an envious eye at England, still basking in the glory of Trafalgar. The death of Pitt in January 1806 had led to the appointment of a coalition ministry containing Tories and Liberals known as the 'Min-istry of all the Talents', of which Lord Carysfort's youngest brother-in-law, Lord Grenville, was the leader: 'When I compare our present state with that of England, who, victorious in her element, and possessing a mass of talents and merits from which her new cabinet will be made up . . . I cannot but deplore the wretched fate of those who have the misfortune to be born in a place so disastrous for a thinking being.'[3]

Vorontsov was soon to have reasons of his own for dissatisfaction with the Emperor. In April 1806 he was obliged to retire to make way for the Emperor's close friend, Pavel Stroganov, who briefly replaced him as Ambassador to Britain. Like the Emperor's previous special envoy to London, Novosil'tsev, Stroganov had been a member of the 'unofficial committee' with whom the Emperor had consulted during the early years of his reign and unlike Vorontsov – who was suspected of being too closely associated with his hosts – he enjoyed the Emperor's confidence. Vorontsov's decision to remain in England after his retirement encouraged the widespread belief in St Petersburg that he was no longer fully committed to the interests of Russia.

Vorontsov was well aware of the damage that rumours could do to a reputation. After their misunderstanding over Napoleon, he warned Pavel to keep his more extreme political views to himself to prevent his growing band of detractors from using them to his detriment. However, some of the Emperor's mistrust of Vorontsov may well have rubbed off on Pavel, whose letters to Vorontsov often contained detailed information on the state of the fleet. Consequently, during 1806, to Pavel's increasing irritation, the Emperor refused to tell him anything about the operation for which a further naval squadron was being prepared. Suppressing his annoyance, Pavel continued to direct his department with the greatest professionalism, while complaining to Vorontsov that his role consisted merely of 'the mechanism of administration, that is the building, launching, arming and provisioning and that is all. Then I deliver the ships to the Minister, who promptly gives them either to some army general or to some special envoy without my knowing what is going to happen to them.'[4] Driven by his desire to prove that with an honest and just administration, Russians could more than match foreigners, Pavel was determined to dispatch the squadron in immaculate order. When it transited through Portsmouth later in the year on its way to the Mediterranean, reports of its excellence reached the Embassy in London and the new Ambassador, Stroganov, went down to admire it.

It is possible that the Emperor's refusal to confide in Pavel at this stage was not only due to a lack of trust but also to the absence of any clear naval strategy. In November 1805, Russian troops in the Mediterranean had joined with British troops in support of the Kingdom of Naples and had managed, briefly, to expel the French. However, the retreat of the Austrians from Italy and the subsequent defeat of the allies at Austerlitz prevented any further progress. In January 1806, the French successfully invaded the Kingdom of Naples and Russian troops were withdrawn to the Ionian Islands. But Admiral Seniavin, who by now had a considerable and well-equipped fleet under his command composed of ships from the Black Sea fleet and the two squadrons sent by Pavel from St Petersburg, cruised the Adriatic with impunity. Seniavin's position was further strengthened by the forming of an alliance with the independent Slav Christian principality of Montenegro.

Meanwhile, Napoleon was becoming increasingly uneasy at the growing Russian naval presence in the Adriatic, which was facilitated by the renewal of the Russo-Turkish alliance in September 1805. This permitted Russian ships from the Black Sea to pass through the Dardanelles and the Bosporus to supply the Ionian garrisons. The defeat at Austerlitz, however, altered the delicate relations between Russia and her Turkish neighbours and the Sultan began to listen more readily to the diplomatic overtures of the French.

In this volatile situation, the Russian navy, which had for so long played a very subordinate role to the army, took on a new importance. This made the Emperor's lack of frankness all the more frustrating for Pavel and in an impulsive moment, he even asked to be allowed to conduct the new squadron to Corfu and take over the command of the Adriatic fleet from Seniavin. The Emperor was prepared to agree, but in the end nothing came of it. Furthermore, the atypically measured tone of Pavel's response to the Emperor suggests that someone – most probably the level-headed Elizabeth – had prevailed on him to reflect before throwing up a brilliant ministerial position, which he was admirably equipped to fill.

After nearly seven years of marriage, Elizabeth knew Pavel very well. For her, his devotion and his integrity more than compensated for the shortness of his temper and the swings of mood which transformed him from dazzling confidence to hopeless despair on a daily basis. At 31 years old, Elizabeth had acquired a maturity and poise that others admired, not least in her self-assurance in her relations with Pavel – who struck terror in many of his acquaintances. She was no more intimidated by him than she had been by her father and she did not hesitate to disagree with him if she thought he was wrong.

The only known full-size portrait of Elizabeth that survives (Plate 9) is believed to be of Russian origin and may date from around this time. In it she looks both in perfect health and desirable. Her pearl and fur-trimmed gown, with its elaborately slashed sleeves, suggests a social standing consistent with Pavel's prominent position – although she is wearing only simple jewellery of drop earrings and a long string of pearls. She undoubtedly bears a strong resemblance to the pale and pensive girl in the earlier miniature; her hair is still gathered up from behind with soft curls framing her face and her gaze is serious, but she radiates a new serenity.

One of the women who admired Elizabeth was Roxana Sturdza,

whose mother was a member of the princely Moldavian family, Morousi, and had emigrated to Russia with her parents during the reign of Catherine. In 1806, in her twentieth year, Roxana was trying to make her way in St Petersburg society without the support of her parents, who had been shattered by the recent suicide of her brother. Later she became a maid of honour to the Empress Elizabeth and wrote her memoirs under her married name of Countess Edling, in which she describes Elizabeth and Pavel at this time:

> For all that, I was very isolated, and I was looking for a way to attend the parties at the Court with another woman to support me. I had known Admiral Tchitchagoff since childhood; for during the stormy reign of Paul he was exiled in our province, and his estate bordered on ours. I became friends with his wife who had a perfect reputation. The extreme passion that she aroused in her husband, her delicate health and the originality of her turn of phrase made her interesting. Mr Tchitchagoff had a remarkable mind. The Emperor honoured him greatly and tried in vain to attach him to himself. A passionate admirer of the French Revolution and of Napoleon, Mr Tchitchagoff affected the greatest scorn for his compatriots. He did not even make allowances for the English in consideration of his wife who was English and whose opinions were always in contradiction with his. Convinced of the superiority of his talents, he indulged in all the peculiarities of an impetuous and inconsistent character. His witticisms were quoted; people feared them, and few had the courage to live in intimacy with him. Obliged by his position (he was the Minister of the Navy) to receive society, he gave a supper twice a week at which one met a lot of foreigners.[5]

That summer, during which it rained continuously with devastating effects on the harvest, Elizabeth and Pavel made several appearances at court together. Pavel had been constantly at court throughout the past five years, often dining in a small group with the Emperor followed by a committee meeting. In June, however, he and Elizabeth were both invited to the Emperor's summer palace at Kammenii Island, on the edge of the city, from where they drove by carriage to dine at Maria Feodorovna's summer residence about seventeen miles south of St Petersburg at Pavlovsk. The party, which numbered twenty-two people, including the Emperor, his mother and the Grand Duchess Catherine, sat down at 4 p.m. Elizabeth was honourably seated close to the imperial family, just three places to the right of the hostess, Maria Feodorovna. Further down the table, Dr Rogerson was also one of the party.

After dinner, the Emperor rode back to his palace at nearby Tsarskoe

Selo, but Elizabeth and Pavel stayed behind at Pavlovsk. The weather must have cleared for, before supper, the remaining members of the royal family and their guests went for a carriage drive. The extensive park at Pavlovsk had been designed, largely by Cameron, to suit the summer activities of a court. His aim was to create a landscape of idyllic beauty, in which the natural environment appeared to be unsullied by human intervention. In this task he was greatly facilitated by the existing features of the countryside, in which the steep banks of the Slavianka river and the deep woodland ravines combined with numerous streams to provide the raw material for the romantic scenery that Cameron had in mind. The level of the meandering river was raised by damming; the banks were cleared of their tangled undergrowth and in place of it, Cameron planted beautiful groves of trees that had been especially selected for their shape and colour. Beside the river, a lake was made with a wild cascade that tumbled over apparently authentic boulders and, to enhance these natural beauties, Cameron and his successors erected pavilions, temples, obelisks and bridges. In addition, a number of avenues were cut through the forest so that guests might drive through its coolness during the stifling summer days.

It seems likely that the Chichagovs were lodged either within the palace or nearby, for the court journal shows that Elizabeth and Pavel were also present at the large party given by Maria Feodorovna the following day. Before dinner a service was held in the palace chapel, after which Maria Feodorovna, accompanied by the Grand Duchesses Catherine and Anna and the Grand Dukes Nicholas and Mikhail, received the homage of a large crowd of nobles and admirers, who thronged the great gallery in the hope of being presented. In the evening, Pavel and Elizabeth went to a ball in the Greek Hall, the most splendid room at Pavlovsk, designed by Vincenzo Brenna, the favourite architect of the murdered Emperor Paul, and adorned with green fluted Corinthian columns. While her younger guests danced, the Dowager Empress played cards.

Three weeks later, Elizabeth and Pavel were once again invited to Pavlovsk. On this occasion the British Ambassador, Lord Granville Leveson-Gower, had come to make a farewell call on Maria Feodorovna. He had found life in St Petersburg irksome and had asked to be recalled to England; however, like many other male visitors to St Petersburg, he had fallen in love with a Russian. The object of his affections was the wife of Prince Serge Golitsyn, the beautiful Princess Eudoxie. According to Leveson-Gower's daughter-in-law, who edited his letters, the Princess had been abandoned by her husband at the church door and one of the objectives of Leveson-Gower's return to England was to consult his family on the subject of his marriage to her – if she could obtain a divorce.[6] In 1807 Leveson-Gower was briefly reappointed to St Petersburg, but by then his ardour for the Princess, whom he nick-named 'the little Barbarian', had cooled and any marriage plans were abandoned.

Leveson-Gower was distantly related to Elizabeth through her pater-nal grandmother, Jane Leveson-Gower, but this kinship (if either of them were aware of it) does not seem to have led to any particular closeness between them. Leveson-Gower, the ladykiller whom Catherine Wilmot describes as 'a *flaming* beauty',[7] belonged to a sophisticated, political world light years away from the grime of Chatham Dockyard. He had two children by his long-term mistress, Lady Bessborough, who was twelve years his senior and was the younger sister of the Duchess of Devonshire. It is to Lady Bessborough that most of his correspondence from St Petersburg is addressed.

The day at Pavlovsk followed the same pattern as the previous occasion, with a church service in the morning and a large crowd awaiting the Dowager Empress in the gallery. In the evening there was another ball and a supper for sixty-six guests in the Greek Hall, but according to the court journal, Leveson-Gower was obliged to pass his evening playing cards with the Dowager. The next day, a Monday, Elizabeth was once again at Pavlovsk, this time on her own. She attended a small party for the Emperor and when he departed at 8 p.m. for the capital, she joined the Dowager, the Grand Duchess Catherine and their suite for a walk in the gardens. The day ended with a supper party, consisting mostly of women, in one of the pavil-ions. From the scant evidence that remains, it would seem that Elizabeth had gained the approval of the formidable Maria Feodorovna, whose court she attended regularly in her own right. Two weeks later she was once again present without Pavel at a supper party, preceded by a concert of Russian songs, as the guest of Maria Feodorovna. The entertainment took place in the hall of the charming Dutch-style house known as Mon Plaisir, built by Peter the Great in the park of the imperial palace at Peterhof. Fifty-two guests attended, including the Emperor, the Crown Prince Constantine and the Grand Duchess Catherine. There is no further men-tion of Elizabeth in the Dowager's court journal for the rest of the year. A letter from Pavel to Vorontsov in July mentions that she was again in ill health and that what she most needed was a visit to her native land. The cold, damp summer was taking its toll.

Pavel was, as usual, immersed in naval business. The visit from England of the distinguished naval architect and engineer Samuel Bentham absorbed much of his energies. Bentham had earlier spent many years in Russia and had fitted out a Russian fleet against the Turks during the reign of the Empress Catherine. He later became Inspector-General of Naval Works in England and was visiting Russia in the hope of constructing ships for the British navy with Russian workmen and materials. Pavel immediately grasped the advantages to both parties of this proposal, but the political tide was turning against Britain and the Emperor rejected such close co-operation on defence matters with a foreign power. Instead, Pavel gained imperial approval for a building plan of a less sensitive nature, namely the construction of an all-embracing training school for naval workmen, which he refers to as a 'panopticon'. He had already successfully established a school for naval engineers, but the Panopticon was far more ambitious. Its design was startlingly modern, with a central cylinder from which radiated galleries containing the different workshops. The cylinder had transparent walls, through which the instructors, on moving chairs, could watch over their pupils at all times. It was to be heated by a system of Bentham's own invention. The building was soon completed, but as much of the machinery remained to be imported from England, subsequent political events interfered with its operation.

The political situation was becoming increasingly menacing. In the aftermath of Austerlitz, the King of Prussia had backtracked on his apparent support of the allies and had signed a treaty with the French. Furthermore, in January 1806, he had permitted his troops to occupy the British province of Hanover and attacked the Swedish troops that had gathered in northern Germany to form a base for the forces of Britain, Sweden and Russia against the French. Pavel shared the Emperor's concern at the growth of the influence of France 'which if it is not stopped, could make her the mistress of the continent in a few years'.[8] A Russian envoy, Baron d'Oubril, was sent to Paris to negotiate secretly with Napoleon and on 20 July a treaty was signed. Amidst an uproar of dissent and cries of dishonour in St Petersburg, the Emperor called a committee meeting, attended by all the ministers of the Russian government and their deputies, to discuss its ratification. D'Oubril had found the negotiations, conducted with Napoleon and Talleyrand, extremely tough and the treaty, while acceptable to Russia, failed to consider the interests of her allies – especially Britain. There was anger in London and the new Ambassador, Stroganov, cringed with humiliation. The committee as a body was against it, but Pavel, who as usual did not show any sense of self-preservation, isolated himself by taking a different line. His view was entirely pragmatic. He did not find the treaty dishonourable and after Austerlitz, Russia was in no position to dictate better terms to the French. One of the conditions was the withdrawal of the fleet and the troops from the Adriatic, which Pavel felt to be prudent in the circumstances. The essential advantage of the treaty was that it would avoid another clash with the French, for unlike his compatriots, Pavel did not have unquestioning faith in the ability of the Russian army to defeat a commander as brilliant as Napoleon.

Pavel's arguments fell on deaf ears, but he reiterated them to the Emperor, who asked him, during the meeting, if he really believed that Russian troops could not withstand Napoleon. Kutuzov, still licking his wounds, replied evasively to the same question, but the majority howled for the non-ratification of the treaty and the Emperor complied. After the meeting, news of Pavel's 'unpatriotic' stance spread far and wide. Vorontsov, who despite his retirement had remained in close touch with St Petersburg, was furious with Pavel and in August refers to him in a letter to his successor Stroganov as 'that madman Tchitchagov, who should never be listened to on anything except matters concerning the fleet'.[9] In September, Vorontsov received further details from the counsellor at the Embassy in London:

> I must give you some news, Monsieur le Comte, which will pain you. The Count Munster has asked me to communicate it to you in confidence. It has been pointed out to him from St Petersburg that when this unfortunate treaty was discussed in the council, *there were two voices for its ratification!* And who do you think they were? Admiral Tchitchagov and General Koutouzov! The latter, who was probably disgusted by all that he had seen at Austerlitz, may have said that he would prefer any sort of peace to the sort of war that had been made up till then. This is the only explanation that I can find for his voice. But as for Admiral T[chitchagov], one would not have expected this of him![10]

The only positive outcome for Pavel was that the Emperor ceased to suspect him of an indiscriminate Anglophilia and began to take him into his confidence on strategic matters.

Throughout the summer, relations with Turkey had been deteriorating, orchestrated by the French envoy to Constantinople, General Sebastiani. The situation was exacerbated by the Russians on the advice of the belligerent General Budberg, who had replaced Czartoryski as the Emperor's chief adviser on foreign affairs. In April 1806 the Turks began to renege on the terms of the Russo-Turkish treaty by raising objections to the Russian use of the Straits and in August, again in violation of the treaty, the Sultan replaced the pro-Russian rulers of the two Romanian principalities, Moldavia and Wallachia, with men who were pro-French. The Sultan, still vacillating between Russia and France, eventually agreed to withdraw his new appointments, but twenty-four hours before this diplomatic breakthrough by the Russian Ambassador in Constantinople, a Russian army had entered Turkish territory. On 24 December 1806, the Russians entered Bucharest and a few days later the Turks made a formal declaration of war.

The Russians now found themselves in the undesirable position of fighting on two fronts. Despite a number of secret negotiations between their countries, a war had broken out between the Prussians and the French and on 25 October Napoleon made his triumphal entry into Berlin. The French then advanced eastwards into the Prussian-ruled territories of Poland and were hailed by the Poles as liberators. Warsaw fell to the French on 28 November. French forces were now only a short distance from the borders of Russian territory and the two armies met for a hard, but inconclusive, encounter at Pultusk near Warsaw on 26 December. Less than two months later, another ferocious battle was fought at Eylau, with huge casualties on both sides. Neither side claimed victory, but after the action, the Russians, shaken, withdrew.

During this dark period, in the small hours of 15 November, the Empress Elizabeth gave birth to a child, which must have been conceived shortly after the Emperor's return from the disastrous battle of Austerlitz. Although his three brothers amply provided for the succession, it is possible that the Emperor's longings for an heir were reawakened by his close experience with the casualties of war, and this may have caused him briefly to revive his conjugal relations with the Empress. The delivery of a healthy child by the ruling Empress should have aroused hopes that the Emperor would now have a family of his own. In court circles, however, rumours about the child's paternity were circulated by Marie Narishkina, who was furiously jealous. She quoted the Emperor as denying responsibility for the pregnancy of his wife and it was whispered that a good-looking guards officer named Okhotnikov was the father. Unfortunately for the Empress, the child was a girl. Had it been a son, the Emperor might well have been less anxious to deny his involvement. Meanwhile the baby was christened Elizabeth and became the source of great joy to her mother, who called her 'Lisiska'.

In the Chichagov household there was no such reticence between husband and wife, and by December Elizabeth knew that she was again pregnant. No information about the Chichagov children at this period has survived, but Pavel does refer a few years later to the pleasure of finally being able to enjoy the company of his 'angels' and to teaching his eldest daughter Latin. Similarly, the existence of an abundance of notes in his hand on poetry and literature suggests that he took some interest in their education. In 1806, the eldest, Adèle, who would have been 6 in September, could have entered the boarding school for young noblewomen that had been founded in 1764 by the Empress Catherine at the Convent of Smolny, but as Elizabeth herself had been educated at home, it seems more likely that the Chichagovs did not consider sending their daughters to boarding school. Most probably, the girls passed their days together in the nursery, surrounded by numerous servants and the charming wooden toys that abounded in nineteenth-century Russia. At an early age, the children would have been bilingual, as Elizabeth spoke English at home and the servants spoke only Russian. Later, de Maistre recalls being enchanted by Adèle's childish French.

In early 1807 Pavel was summoned by the Emperor. The Adriatic fleet was to be used against the Turks and Pavel was to forward the relevant instructions immediately to Seniavin, who had taken up his station close to the Dardanelles at Tenedos. He also contacted two French emigrés who were in the service of Russia: the Duc de Richelieu, who was the governor of the southern province of New Russia and the port of Odessa, and the Marquis de Traversay, who, as commander of the Black Sea fleet, was also governor of the port of Nikolayev. Pavel's messages outlined the details of the secret and highly complex naval operation that was planned against the Turks, but he was astounded to receive, a few weeks later, an urgent letter from Seniavin asking for clarification. On the same day that Pavel's message had arrived, Seniavin had received contradictory orders in the name of Budberg and the Emperor. Not unnaturally, Seniavin was confused.

Pavel immediately sought an explanation and soon discovered that Budberg had, without informing him, persuaded the Emperor to cancel his instructions. Instead the Corsican, Pozzo di Borgo, was to be dispatched from Vienna as a special envoy to the Turks with wide-ranging powers over the fleet. At this news, Pavel's anger knew no bounds and when he was asked to retransmit the new orders to Seniavin, he launched into one of his, by now, legendary exchanges with the Emperor. In a letter that paid scant attention to protocol, he pointed out that Budberg's proposal placed the commander of the fleet in the most humiliating position imaginable, since he was, in practice, reduced to executing the caprices of a man who was not only a foreigner, but also an adventurer of uncertain affiliations. Pavel concluded the letter with a declaration that he refused to transmit an order that was so humiliating to the Russians. When he received Pavel's steaming letter, the Emperor may well have considered, momentarily, his father's reactions to Pavel in a more sympathetic light. Not even a sovereign as mild as Alexander could tolerate such expressions from a subject, and the reply that he wrote to Pavel was so severe that Pavel's head began to swim as he read the first lines. Eventually they resolved the matter between them. Pavel submitted to imperial authority, but extracted a face-saving postscript to the orders, in the hand of the Emperor, which stated that all instructions could only be executed with the consent of the commander of the fleet.

In the long term, Pavel's frankness paid off. In a court full of ambitious and sycophantic subjects, his complete disregard for personal gain won him the Emperor's lasting trust and affection. Like Elizabeth, the Emperor had come to know Pavel extremely well. Between 1802 and 1807 the court journal – whose indexes are incomplete – records over three hundred and fifty occasions on which the Emperor and Pavel were together for dinner or meetings. The reality was probably more. During this period, the Emperor had come to appreciate Pavel's unique qualities and, like his wife, had learnt to deal firmly with his tantrums. From this time on, ministers realized that the navy had a redoubtable champion in Pavel, and Budberg may well have regretted trying to double-cross him. A year later, the new Foreign Minister, Rumiantsev, told the French Ambassador that he dared not meddle in naval matters and remarked that 'the navy has a particular chief. This chief is, like the God of Israel, a god jealous of all other gods and on top of that, a rather stubborn god. Don't make me quarrel with him as that would upset the Emperor.'[11]

The proposed naval expedition against Turkey was never realized. In February 1807, a British naval force under Admiral Duckworth tried to enter the Dardanelles and retired with heavy damage. Seniavin arrived too late to assist his ally and failed to persuade the British to make a second attempt. He remained, however, blockading the Dardanelles and in May he repulsed a large Turkish fleet and captured three ships that had run aground. A month later, he inflicted a severe naval defeat on the Turks at Lemnos and captured the Turkish troops that had been landed at Tenedos, but the Russian navy gained little glory for these exploits. The eyes of Russia were already turned westwards where, at Friedland on 14 June 1807, the Russians suffered a crushing defeat at the hands of Napoleon and the Emperor was obliged to ask for peace. Since no written record was kept of their discussion, the meeting between the two emperors at Tilsit, on a raft in the river Neman, has been the subject of much historical speculation. Napoleon is said to have been very taken by the personal and physical charms of the Emperor Alexander and to have treated him with great courtesy. For his part, the Russian Emperor was greatly impressed by the personality of Napoleon and warmed to him as a friend. Two treaties were signed, one public and one secret. In the former, large parts of Prussia were divided up, Napoleon's brothers were acknowledged as the kings of Naples and Westphalia, and the Ionian Islands were handed over to the French. Napoleon also undertook to mediate between Russia and Turkey. In the latter, the full extent of Napoleon's global ambitions was laid bare. Russia was committed to a war against Britain, unless she made peace with France. Similarly, the French would join the Russians against Turkey, if negotiations for peace were unsuccessful.

During the Emperor's absence with the army, Elizabeth went to court on two occasions. On 16 June both the Chichagovs dined at the Tauride Palace at a small party for seventeen given by the Dowager, accompanied by the Grand Duchess Catherine. Two days earlier, Elizabeth had been in attendance on her own, also at the Tauride Palace, when the Dowager made a Sunday visit to the Empress Elizabeth and her baby. It was an anxious time, for the little Princess was ill, but although the Empress missed church, she dutifully received presentations in the garden and the reception hall before retiring to the seclusion of her apartments to dine alone with her sister. As a mother, Elizabeth would have sympathized deeply with the Empress, especially as she knew, from personal experience, the precariousness of infant survival. Mercifully Elizabeth's latest pregnancy had, for once, proceeded smoothly. In a letter of 23 July Pavel tells Vorontsov that 'thanks to Providence and the attentions and talents of Dr. Leighton, everything went very well and she is enjoying better health than ever before.'[12] The baby was another little girl, whom they christened Catherine after her paternal grandmother. However, Elizabeth's good health was not the only reason for celebration. On his return from Tilsit, the Emperor had appointed Pavel a full admiral. In addition, after four and a half years of running the navy, he had been promoted from deputy minister to minister.

Once again, it is Rogerson who passes the news to England, in what may be a garbled version of Pavel's confrontation with Budberg and the Emperor over the Adriatic fleet:

> Mr Tchitchagow is in great favour: everything that he predicted has happened. Also we really need him at the moment and Cronstadt is being fortified as it was during the reign of Paul. He is the only minister who can succeed with the Master: who is very good to him. He believes that he needs him and he is afraid of losing him.
>
> I can't resist telling you an anecdote about him. Since all the instructions for the Mediterranean fall within his competence, Budberg sent him from Tilsit the orders from the Emperor for the unconditional surrender of Cattaro, asking him to countersign them and send them on. He blew up and returned all the papers to him with the most violent comments on their contents and refusing to obey. All this procured him a very gracious letter from the Master who, on his return here, made him a minister. All this is true, but not generally known.[13]

Vorontsov heard of Pavel's success from other sources. In October, in a letter advising Vorontsov to return to Russia, the Minister of Education, Count Zavadovskii, observes that Pavel is enjoying a 'fair wind'.[14] Vorontsov also received a letter from Kochubei, who was about to resign as Minister of the Interior, in which Pavel is described as being on the best possible terms with the Emperor.[15]

In September, the British attack on the Danes at Copenhagen had outraged the Emperor and pushed him further into the arms of Napoleon. Kochubei's letter was written four days after the rupture of diplomatic relations between Russia and Britain and was sent with the departing Leveson-Gower. Kochubei implores Vorontsov to distance himself 'from a country that is at war with your own',[16] but Vorontsov was busy achieving one of his dearest ambitions, namely the marriage of Katinka into the highest echelons of English society. He had no intention of leaving England until her marriage to the Earl of Pembroke was safely accomplished.

The year 1808 opened sadly for Elizabeth. She had already experienced the anguish of finding herself torn between her feelings for her own country and her love and loyalty to her husband at the outset of her marriage, but at that time, Pavel's intense dislike of the Emperor Paul had lessened the conflict. This time the situation was far more distressing. Pavel fully shared the Emperor's anger at Britain's attack on the innocent Danes; a letter to the Emperor bears witness to his fury at Britain's high-handed naval policies and the incursions of the British navy into the Baltic: 'Look at them, masters of the Baltic without a word to anyone, simply because they wish it. British frigates sail all over this sea without one even daring to ask them by what right.'[17] Worse still, Pavel was strongly in favour of the Treaty of Tilsit. While, therefore, Pavel travelled continually on naval business, Elizabeth remained in St Petersburg and during the long dark days of winter, she dreamed of the rolling hills of Kent and the familiar faces of Chatham. She may also have pondered on the words of her father. An entry for January 1808 is one of the few fragments of her daily journal which survives. Her terse comments speak volumes for her state of mind: 'January: Pavel has left for Vyborg and other places with Ponthon and a Piedmontese officer. The sadness of our separation has been increased by the thought that his mission is to defend the coast against the English. God will that it stops there. Pavel has gone to Revel.'[18]

# CHAPTER NINE

# The French

*1808–1809*

Napoleon lost no time in sending an envoy to St Petersburg to ensure that the terms of both treaties of Tilsit were respected. The first ambassador, General Savary, only stayed for a few months before returning to Paris, where he later replaced Fouché as Napoleon's Chief of Police. Porter describes him as carrying himself 'with all the gorgeous parade of the court he represents; and drives about in an equipage more becoming an Eastern Satrap than a hardy soldier'.[1] Pavel soon became acquainted with Savary, but came to know his successor, the Marquis de Caulaincourt,* far better. They had frequent meetings and Caulaincourt regularly attended the Chichagovs' evening parties.

Both ambassadors were implicated in the murder of the Duc d'Enghien, but on his arrival in St Petersburg, Russian society mistakenly believed that Caulaincourt was more guilty than Savary and treated him accordingly. Although Porter, as an Englishman, was not an objective observer he gives us a good example of the ambassador's frosty reception:

> Since I wrote the above, the new Embassador [*sic*] has arrived from Paris to replace the old, who returns to his master. This man is even less polished than his predecessor, or else a bolder professor of the law which makes all means admissible to serve a desired end. Indeed, so little decency has he in vaunting his bloody deeds, that when a lady of rank, the other day, asked him how he could get any persons hard-hearted enough to shoot the Duke d'Enghien, he replied with the greatest coolness, 'O madam, I took care of that.'[2]

Within a very few weeks of his arrival in Russia, Caulaincourt had given Pavel a bust of Napoleon, to whom he made the following report: 'I often see Admiral Tchitchagoff, Minister of the Navy; he is, I believe, one of the most capable men in his country. I am assured that he has always been against the war with France and that he was one of the defenders of M. d'Oubril's treaty.'[3]

---

* Created Duc de Vicence by Napoleon in 1808.

Caulaincourt's chief objective was to encourage Russia to declare war on the pro-British Swedes. The Emperor found the prospect hard to resist. Support from the Danes and the French was forthcoming and the prize was the Russian annexation of Finland. Pavel, who had been entrusted by the Emperor with the defence of the coasts, was closely associated with the naval aspects of the operation. In addition, Caulaincourt brought with him an expert on fortifications, an engineer named Ponthon, and proposed that he should advise the Russians on their coastal batteries. In his early enthusiasm for co-operation with Napoleon, the Emperor directed Pavel to take Ponthon on his tour of inspection of the Baltic and to give him unfettered access to all naval establishments. Ponthon made copious notes and duly reported back to the Emperor. However, detailed plans of Russia's defences were also sent directly to Napoleon. In his memoirs, Pavel claims that he considered it extremely imprudent to reveal so much to a foreigner, and in a letter to his Foreign Minister, Champagny, Caulaincourt complains that Pavel was dragging his feet over the operation against Finland. It is clear, however, from Pavel's correspondence with the Emperor in early January that he favoured the alliance with France and that any delays were being caused by Danish objections to the stationing of French troops in their country.[4] In February 1808, the campaign went ahead successfully; by the end of three months the whole of Finland was under Russian domination and the crucial naval fortress of Sveaborg had fallen without a fight.

Caulaincourt's second concern was the secret aspects of the Treaty of Tilsit and in particular the conquest of Turkey, which, in Napoleon's eyes, was the first step to a glorious oriental campaign that would rival the achievements of Alexander the Great. Caulaincourt soon found himself in tough negotiations with the Emperor, through the mediation of Rumiantsev, on the division of the Ottoman Empire. Even before the cracks started to appear in the Franco-Russian alliance, the Emperor was considering Pavel as a special envoy to Napoleon.

By now, the Emperor had absolutely no doubts about Pavel's loyalty to himself and to Russia; however, he was well aware of Pavel's mixed political reputation. Pavel's support of both treaties with the French – the non-ratified treaty negotiated by d'Oubril and the Treaty of Tilsit – had been based on a desire for peace rather than any political sympathies. After the signing of the treaty, he wrote: 'Another very happy event for Russia in general, and for me in particular, is the end of this war, which if it had not finished now, threatened us with the greatest

170

disasters – ruin, famine, plague, without counting the bloodshed and the very great dishonour which would have followed as an inevitable consequence.'[5]

However, Pavel's early admiration for Napoleon (Caulaincourt claims that he asked for the bust) and his high-profile stance over the aborted d'Oubril treaty had given him a Francophile lustre that made him highly credible in the eyes of the French. It is possible that the Emperor encouraged him in his Francophile stance in order to be able to use his talents in the delicate negotiations that lay ahead, but all who knew Pavel well, including the Emperor, suspected that after Russia, his real sympathies still lay with Britain. Of Pavel's intimates, the perceptive de Maistre, in a letter to the King of Sardinia in January 1808, came closest to the truth:

[He] is an unresolved problem to me, and I have found no one who is any wiser than I am. He is a friend of the French, the bust of Bonaparte sits on his desk, he spends the whole day abusing the English and yet there is not an Englishman who is not presented at his house. The French, on the other hand, never enter it except by dint of their rank. It is now nearly seven years that I have heard his interminable sarcasms against England; but his wife, who is English to the teeth, never replies except by a certain smile which seems to me to say: *Keep on talking, my dear friend, for I am in the secret.*[6]

Meanwhile, the Emperor cautiously explored with Caulaincourt the possibility of Pavel as an envoy. In early January he quizzed Caulaincourt on Pavel:

*The Emperor.* Do you like Tchitchagoff? he is married to an Englishwoman; but nobody is more enthusiastic about the Emperor Napoleon or serves me better in the sense of Tilsit. He is a man who abhors the English.

Caulaincourt's reply was appropriately suave:

*The Ambassador.* He appears to me to be very well disposed and entirely devoted to Your Majesty. Judging from what he says, he does not like the English and we are in such agreement on this point that I see him frequently. *The Emperor.* I am very pleased about this. He is a man who does not let difficulties deter him.[7]

Throughout January, Caulaincourt did all he could to endear himself to the imperial family at St Petersburg. When he discovered that the Empress had searched vainly for a very soft Savonnerie carpet, on which the little Princess could crawl without scratching her knees, he immediately wrote and asked Champagny to send him two – one for the baby and the one for the Empress. These attentions, however, did little to mitigate the diplomatic wranglings. After a dinner at the court in March, the Emperor invited Caulaincourt into his private office to pursue their discussions on the conquest of Turkey and the sensitive subject of Constantinople. Caulaincourt asked the Emperor if he had anyone in mind to send as a special envoy to Napoleon:

> *The Emperor.* Yes I have indeed got someone, but I cannot do without him here. Without him, how shall I make my navy work? It is Tchitchagoff. What do you think of him? Frankly, come on, tell me what you think of him.
> *The Ambassador.* I think well of him, Sire, I have even written to the Emperor telling him that I often see him. He has all that is required to understand the advantages of this important matter. But is he determined enough to conclude? I have known him only such a short time.[8]

As a subject very close to his heart became a further irritant in the relationship between the new allies, Pavel found his position vis-à-vis the French Ambassador increasingly delicate. During Pavel's absence, the Emperor had made an oral commitment to Caulaincourt to put the Adriatic fleet at the disposal of the French. Caulaincourt was now demanding satisfaction. He raised the subject with Rumiantsev, who shrugged off responsibility and told him to talk to Pavel. Pavel played for time and in the course of a lengthy meeting gave Caulaincourt an evasive reply. He dreaded the thought of his precious fleet being blown to bits by the guns of the British navy and he was determined to try and save it. When Caulaincourt next dined at the court, the Emperor, in an indication that the fleet did not come unconditionally, asked him if he had agreed on what was going to be supplied to the Russian squadrons: 'When we were allied with the English, we were supplied with provisions and the maintenance of our ships. This is the practice with auxiliary forces. Your delegation should know this.'[9] Caulaincourt had already argued this out with Pavel without reaching a conclusion. He therefore refused to give any commitment to the Emperor and the subject of the fleet was dropped. But in the end Caulaincourt got his way and Pavel was obliged, with a heavy heart, to hand over instructions to the Russian fleet and these were dispatched to Paris.

Caulaincourt continued to be a regular guest at the Chichagov house, from where, as the brief jottings in her journal reveal, Elizabeth was a close observer of all that was going on: 'April: News of the capture of Gothland by a secret expedition sent by Pavel under the orders of Admiral Bodisko which was a complete success. Thanks to the fog, they were able to disembark without being seen by the inhabitants. There was therefore no bloodshed. On the same evening we also got the news that the governor had promised to surrender Sveaborg, if no help is forthcoming from Sweden. A *Te Deum* for the victory.'[10]

To Elizabeth's relief, relations with England were remarkably unchanged in practical terms. Despite Russia's theoretical adherence to Napoleon's 'Continental System', which forbade the purchase of English goods, a reduced quantity continued to reach Russia through neutral shipping. Nor had the Treaty of Tilsit suddenly effaced the bonds of trade and friendship that had existed for generations between Britain and St Petersburg. Few of the Russian nobility, amongst whom Elizabeth had her friends, had any affection for Napoleon, and many landowners were intensely irritated at the losses they were sustaining in their sales of hemp and flax to England. Elizabeth's greatest deprivation was occasioned by the exodus of her English friends.

On 5 March, Martha Wilmot arrived back in St Petersburg after passing five years away from the capital. The elderly Princess Dashkova, who has been described by historians as 'masculinisée', had developed a passion for the young Irishwoman and, to a lesser extent, for her sister, Catherine. Catherine, to whom Princess Dashkova had given a letter of introduction to Elizabeth, had already gone home, but only political events had enabled Martha to extract herself from the Princess's clutches. Martha's journal makes no mention of Elizabeth on this occasion, but from a later reference, it is clear that they were acquainted and had many friends in common. Amongst these were the wealthy and glamorous George and Elizabeth Pollen, with whom Martha planned to travel by ship to England.

On her arrival in St Petersburg, Martha was intensely disappointed to learn that the Pollens had already departed for the ship which they had purchased for the voyage. She returned to Moscow and did not finally leave until October. Meanwhile tragedy struck the Pollens. Forty miles from the Swedish port of Karlskrona, a storm blew up, but the ship was prevented by ice from putting into the shelter of the island of Öland and was wrecked on a sandbank off the port of Memel. There was great loss of life. Elizabeth Pollen saw her husband drowned before her eyes, but she and a female companion with two children survived thirty-six hours in a shelter on the freezing deck and were saved. Martha Wilmot recounts the extraordinary sequel, in which a casket containing the Pollens' marriage certificate was washed up on the beach and returned to the widow. According to Martha, this find greatly eased matters when Elizabeth Pollen first encountered the parents of her late husband, who had never approved of the match and were disposed to suspect its status.

In May, Elizabeth and the children left St Petersburg for the country house near Peterhof that the Chichagovs rented during the summer. Pavel had to stay behind in the capital, but from his letters Elizabeth learnt that the expedition to Gotland had ended in fiasco. The Swedish fleet was still at large in the Baltic, where it enjoyed the support of the British navy. A Swedish force easily ejected the Russians, while Pavel, constrained by his ministerial duties, could do nothing but fume at the lack of initiative of their commander. That evening, Elizabeth had dinner with the Gur'evs – he was Pavel's long-standing friend who had instructed him in mathematics and was now the Minister of Finance. It was an interesting party, for amongst the guests was Aleksandr Chernyshev, recently arrived from Napoleon's headquarters at Bayonne, where the Spanish royal family had been tricked into abdication.

Before long, Napoleon had a full-scale war with Spain on his hands and his grandiose ideas of oriental conquest were abandoned. The Mediterranean fleet, which Pavel had tried so hard to preserve, was safely within the Tagus, blockaded by a British fleet. In August, Seniavin managed to negotiate the honourable surrender of his ships to Britain in return for a safe passage back to Russia for himself and his men. History does not relate whether or not Pavel had any hand in this eminently practical solution. If he did, he managed to keep up a convincing appearance of irritation. Only two ships of the line and four frigates fell into the hands of the French and Pavel continually badgered Caulaincourt for their return. Meanwhile Pavel maintained ostensibly cordial relations with Caulaincourt who, persisting in his close interest in the Russian navy, made a visit with Ponthon to Kronstadt. Here Pavel threw what Caulaincourt describes as *'une très jolie fête'*[11] aboard his yacht, to which the legations of France, Holland and Denmark were invited. In the course of these diplomatic niceties, Caulaincourt may have sensed a slight cooling in Pavel's manner since their disagreement over the fleet, and he judged that it was the moment to make an appropriate gift. This was raised with Napoleon: 'The various arrangements made for the fleet merit perhaps some mark of distinction or goodwill for the Minister of the Navy. He asked me for a bust of Your Majesty, which is on his desk. Your Majesty has grounds for giving him your portrait on a box, and I can assure you that no present could be more suitably placed or more appreciated: he is a capable man, definite on all occasions, and the Emperor sets great store by him.'[12]

Throughout the summer Elizabeth and Pavel were caught up in a whirl of naval and court activities. Elizabeth had long since resolved the conflicts of loyalty that must have assailed her when Russia and Britain first found themselves on opposing sides. Her journal confirms how closely her thinking was aligned with Pavel's: 'July. Launching of several ships. The first, a ship of 84 guns (*l'Audacieux*), four frigates and a brig. Complete success, beautiful day and a magnificent spectacle to see the Neva covered with ships of the line and vessels of every kind. It is impossible not to perceive the astonishing improvement brought about in the navy since Pavel has been at its head, but perhaps few people here would like to admit it.'[13] Elizabeth had a keen eye in naval matters. She had, after all, grown up in the dockyard that built the best fighting ships in the world.

In May, the sudden death of the little Princess Elizabeth had further confirmed the Empress in her life of semi-seclusion. To add to her sorrows, the imperial mistress gave birth to a little girl, christened Sophie, to whom the Emperor became devoted. Unruffled, the Dowager proceeded as usual with her summer season at Pavlovsk. In the middle of July Elizabeth attended the court. It was a Sunday and after church there was a large party, where, as usual, the ladies were placed together close to the hostess. Elizabeth was seated a few places away from the Grand Duchesses, next to the wife of General Kutuzov. In the evening, a ball took place in the Greek Hall.

Two weeks later, Pavel was able to accompany Elizabeth to Pavlovsk, where they witnessed a programme of royal amusements that recalled the heyday of the court at Versailles. After dinner, the Emperor arrived with the Crown Prince Constantine, and the imperial party repaired to an ornate wooden pavilion known as the Treillage, where they listened to a concert played by the palace huntsmen with singing by the palace choir. Then, since it was still broad daylight, they descended the stone staircase to the Marienthal Pool, where they boarded two small yachts and drifted gently across the placid waters of the lake.[14] The court journal states that these diversions were limited to the imperial family, but in the meantime Elizabeth and Pavel would have enjoyed a rare moment of leisure together. It is possible that they strolled in the palace, much of whose exquisite furniture had been ordered from Paris, or that they conversed with the other guests, but in the sultry humidity that always prevailed at that time of year, they may well have preferred to sit quietly together in the garden. At 9 p.m. the royal family rejoined their guests for supper at round tables which had been placed outside in the open-air dining-room. As the twilight deepened, illuminations appeared in many parts of the garden and Russian and French actors performed theatricals and a ballet. Later there was, once again, dancing in the Greek Hall, which lasted until 2 a.m.

In high summer, Elizabeth would have been dressed in the alluringly low-cut and diaphanous fashion of the period, while Pavel sweltered in the skintight uniform that was insisted upon by the Emperor. There is a portrait of Pavel in court dress at the Hermitage (Plate 10). His expression is a combination of extreme alertness and humour. His fair hair is tousled, and a little smile seems to play around the upturned corners of his lips. The *retroussé* nose, which Adèle was said to have inherited, is very much in evidence. He wears his imperial orders with nonchalance.

Shortly before her name-day celebrations in August, the Dowager moved to Peterhof. Elizabeth and Pavel's summer house was within easy range of the palace and throughout the last week of July, they were in constant attendance at the court. Elizabeth accompanied the royal party on evening walks in the gardens and she was present at a little supper party organized in the intimacy of Mon Plaisir. A ball was given, at which the ladies wore Russian national costumes – although the men were permitted to remain in their usual evening attire. The Dowager's burst of elaborate entertainment was probably not unrelated to the presence of Prince George – the heir to the Duchy of Oldenburg and a suitor of the Grand Duchess Catherine – of whom the Dowager strongly approved. The Dowager's firm views on whom her daughters should marry were later to have enormous political repercussions.

A few weeks later Pavel experienced another naval setback, about which he minded acutely. Despite the military successes of the Russians in Finland, the war with Sweden was by no means over, and the sight of the Swedish fleet cruising freely in the Baltic with its British watchdogs was a constant source of irritation to Pavel. The Emperor had given him 30,000 men to guard the Baltic coast and during his frequent journeys to supervise their positioning, Pavel had observed that the British presence was minimal. He also knew that a well-armed British squadron under the command of Sir James Saumarez was on its way to join the Swedes. Speed was of the essence and the Emperor gave his permission for Pavel to arm and dispatch a naval force to attack the Swedes while they were still virtually unsupported. But the ageing Khanikov, whom Pavel had put in command, dawdled and missed his chance and did not reach the Swedish fleet until two British ships of the line had joined it. Instead of attacking, Khanikov and his force of nine battleships fled in great disorder before the British *Centaur* and *Implacable*. Pavel comments bitterly that the Swedish ships sailed so badly that they remained far behind and he cringed at the image of his compatriots turning tail at the sight of the British. The chase lasted thirty-six hours and concluded when the Russian ships found shelter within the harbour of Baltischport. Only one Russian ship put up a fight, the 74-gun *Vievalod*. She was overtaken and engaged by the *Implacable*. Within twenty minutes she was reduced to silence and later burnt. Shortly afterwards Saumarez arrived and the Russians found themselves blockaded. Unable to bear it any longer, Pavel left St Petersburg and stormed off to the scene of action. Thanks to the recently overhauled coastal batteries, the ships were well protected and after a few weeks the blockading British and Swedish forces withdrew. The Russians returned to Kronstadt and Khanikov was subsequently court-martialled and dismissed from the service.

There can be no doubt that if Pavel had taken the command, which he claims in his memoirs to have contemplated, he would never have refused an engagement. It was, therefore, a mercy for Elizabeth that in the end he decided not to participate personally in an operation which would have inevitably resulted in a direct clash between her husband and her countrymen. Pavel, however, saw this episode as another national disgrace and his memoirs, which are interrupted at this point, close with the following words: 'All these failed expeditions one after another, starting with the one in the Mediterranean, disgusted me and convinced me that with men like Russian sailors, one cannot undertake anything offensive.'[15]

There is no satisfactory explanation for this abrupt break in Pavel's memoirs. Fortunately it is possible to reconstruct much of his and Elizabeth's life from other sources. The existence, however, of a list of headings outlining the events that Pavel considered to be significant during the missing period, which was found amongst his papers after his death, indicates that he either intended to or did write about what happened. There are, however, also grounds for believing that in later life, Pavel wished to draw a veil over certain episodes that took place at this time. His daughter Catherine tells us that her father forced her to burn many pages in his hand before he died.

On the list, which like the memoirs is written in French, one short heading stands out – '*sa maladie*'. Pavel does not specify whose illness, but his long-standing concern for Elizabeth's health makes it highly probable that the reference is to her long period of sickness in April 1809. From the outset of their marriage Elizabeth had shown, intermittently, all the classic symptoms of tuberculosis – an illness to which young women were particularly susceptible until well into the twentieth century. (In 1900 the peak age for female mortality from tuberculosis was 25 to 29 years old.) Although tuberculosis is infectious, it is also an illness in which heredity plays an important role. There was almost certainly unidentified tuberculosis in Elizabeth's family and her father's so-called asthma attacks were most likely symptoms of the disease. The cause of her mother's death is not recorded, but even if it was officially childbirth, she too may have been infected. In his later life, visitors to Elton refer to Lord Carysfort's 'asthma' and to his terrible nocturnal bouts of coughing.

If Elizabeth had contracted tuberculosis at an early age, it would have been greatly aggravated by the climate in St Petersburg, and her bouts of fever and unexplained fatigue, combined with her recurrent cough, make tuberculosis the most likely identity of the 'chronic' or 'mortal' illness to which her acquaintances later refer. At this time, little was known about the disease, except that its sufferers benefited from rest, fresh air and a good climate. The St Petersburg doctors who recommended a cruise for Elizabeth were acting in accordance with contemporary medical beliefs. Similarly, Elizabeth's health always improved in the summer, particularly when she was in the countryside at Peterhof. Whenever he was suffering from depression, Pavel's morbid terror of losing Elizabeth increased, based on the suspicion that she had an incurable illness.

By 1809 Pavel was having problems of his own and the notion that he must save Elizabeth began to offer a perfect moral solution to his subliminal desire to escape from his responsibilities. After seven years of non-stop high-level activity, during which his cruise on the Baltic was his only recorded holiday, the stress of his job and the constant conflicts with his colleagues had reduced this highly strung man to a state of nervous and physical exhaustion. The link between Pavel's bodily health and his state of mind had not escaped de Maistre, who writes to Pavel in 1810: 'Do as you wish, but restore the physical health on which the state of your morale so largely depends.'[16] Throughout his time as head of the navy, Pavel was driven by the completely unrealistic ambition of bringing the Russian navy up to the standard of the British one. He tried to force the pace of reform, cursing the climatic and geographic features of his homeland that inevitably slowed him down and the characteristics of his countrymen, who would never have the same maritime tradition as an island nation. Despite real achievements in many areas, Pavel, as a perfectionist, was never satisfied. His dream was for a naval glory that compared with Nelson's at Trafalgar.

Seen in this light, the abandonment of the important naval attack on Constantinople and the debacles of 1808 were, for Pavel, major disasters. He became profoundly depressed and his vindictive persecution of Khanikov is a symptom of this. In 1809 the elderly Admiral, who had rendered many kindnesses to Pavel and Elizabeth during the early years of their marriage, was court-martialled and found guilty by Pavel of 'unconsidered negligence, weakness of command, slowness and a lack of resolution, for permitting the British ships to link up with the Swedish fleet, for having sought refuge at Baltischport without proper reasons, after having lost the *Vievalod*, burnt by the English'.[17] Fortunately, the Emperor was more merciful and never confirmed the sentence.

Pavel's prickly personality, combined with his impatience, continued to make him many enemies and, never a team player at the best of times, he found the Emperor's preference for working in committees exasperating. A further source of irritation was the rise of a new imperial favourite, Mikhail Speranskii, the son of a village priest. One of the results of the peace was that the Emperor's interests shifted from defence to internal matters and Speranskii, a brilliant bureaucrat, was entrusted with all-encompassing legislative and educational reforms as well as the preparation of taxes. In his propositions to the Emperor, Speranskii outlined the creation of a Duma and of a Council of State as the supreme advisory body to the Emperor. Although Speranskii's proposals for a Duma were never implemented, the Council of State was later established. In meetings Pavel frequently argued against Speranksii because, like most of the established nobility, he disliked Speranskii's egalitarian ideas, but the Emperor ignored his views. Thus when Pavel later wrote venomously about Speranskii to Vorontsov, it was partly out of jealousy.

With the marriage of Katinka in the spring, Vorontsov was even more reluctant to return to Russia. Katinka had become the mistress of the Pembrokes' magnificent country seat at Wilton, where Vorontsov spent much of his time. In a letter which he asks to be shown to Pavel, he makes an elaborate case to his son, Mikhail, on the difficulties and dangers of the journey. The letter closes with a reference to the Pollen shipwreck and the comment that: 'neither the Emperor nor the fatherland could gain any advantage from knowing that some poor old man has been drowned between Memel and Riga.'[18]

In the autumn of 1808 the Emperor, accompanied by a small suite including Speranskii, met Napoleon in the central German city of Erfurt. The outcome was a new Franco-Russian treaty, the Congress of Erfurt, and despite the Emperor's refusal to sign an alliance against Austria, both sides reiterated their warm feelings for each other. Napoleon was already beginning to wonder if one of the Russian Grand Duchesses could not provide him with the longed-for heir. When he returned from Erfurt, Caulaincourt continued his attentions to Pavel and presented him with a diamond-encrusted box bearing the portrait of Napoleon. Pavel also received another decoration from the Emperor, the order of St Vladimir. But these marks of favour did little to raise Pavel's spirits and he and the Emperor had a mild falling out over the purchase of a house for his ministry. Elizabeth was also feeling low. The sight of Martha Wilmot, who describes Elizabeth as 'a very sweet creature',[19] brought on a bout of homesickness. Martha came to tea when she was about to make her second attempt to leave Russia and undertook to carry back to England a letter from Elizabeth to one of her sisters.

The Emperor's court journal reveals that Pavel made only ten appearances at the court during the first six months of 1809, compared with seventy-two for the same period in 1806, eighty-nine in 1807 and thirty-one in 1808, when he was frequently travelling and the Emperor was away with the army. In March Elizabeth was invited to the Winter Palace by Maria Feodorovna. The occasion was the christening in the Palace chapel of a Kutuzov child. The Emperor appeared for the ceremony at which the child was named after him. Later, the Dowager had a supper party and played cards, but Elizabeth returned to Pavel, who was at home and unwell. Throughout March, the Chichagov house was a gloomy place. Pavel was confined to his room for three weeks, but his father was also failing fast. Elizabeth too had fallen ill, perhaps in part owing to the strain of the illnesses of both Pavel and her father-in-law. She outlines events in her journal:

> April: My journal has been neglected for a long time and, during this time, my poor father-in-law died without suffering on 4<sup>th</sup> April, deeply mourned by the family and all who had known him.
>
> His body was laid out until Wednesday, with all the ceremonies that are the custom here. I was too ill to go to the church, but I was able to hear the service at the house, which was attended by the Emperor, the Grand-Duke, the Princes of Weymar and of Oldenburg. His Majesty had him rendered all the military honours imaginable, and was himself at the Newsky [Cathedral] when the cannons were fired.[20]

Pavel had adored and admired his father and he felt the loss deeply. He and Elizabeth had greatly mourned Pavel's youngest brother, who had died at Shklov several years previously, but the passing of Vasilii, with whom Pavel had been closely associated both personally and professionally throughout his life, was an even greater blow. The Emperor, who had also come to visit Pavel at home during his illness, understood Pavel's feelings very well and knew that an imperial tribute to his father would do much to console him. Elizabeth, who suffered from none of Pavel's complexes about the Emperor, notes firmly in her journal: 'He [the Emperor] showed himself, on this occasion, as on all others, full of kindness and attention.'[21]

Elizabeth also records a further and unforeseen honour that was bestowed on the Chichagovs: 'During that time the marriage of the Grand-Duchess Catherine with the Prince of Oldenburg took place. Amongst the different decorations distributed on this occasion, I was included and received the order of St. Catherine, second class. Left in May for Peterhof, my health improved fairly quickly, and I was able to present myself to the Empress to thank her for the order which she had given me.'[22]

The order of St Catherine was the only imperial order exclusively reserved for women and had been originally created by Peter the Great in 1714 to commemorate the services of his wife during the Russo-Turkish war. The Empress was the Grand Mistress of the order and the Grand Duchesses received the Grand Cross of the order (first class) on birth. The first class was restricted to twelve members only, outside royalty, and the second class was limited to ninety-four members, all of whom were maids or ladies of honour. Since Elizabeth had very little contact with the reigning Empress, there can be only two explanations for her award. Either it came from the Dowager, who knew Elizabeth well, or, as is equally probable, it was the Emperor's way of telling Pavel that he shared his respect for Elizabeth. In either case, Elizabeth's inclusion in the order confirms the impression that she was highly regarded in St Petersburg in her own right and that Roxana Sturdza was not the only person who considered her reputation impeccable.

Elizabeth's serious illness, on the heels of his father's death, shook Pavel to the core. It also offered him the perfect pretext for resigning his position, so that he could take her away, at once, from the unhealthy climate of St Petersburg. Pavel wrote to the Emperor and, as on numerous other occasions, the Emperor refused his resignation. There were further misunderstandings and letters, but eventually Pavel's appearance, still convalescent, and the memory of Elizabeth's pitiful condition at Vasilii's funeral made the Emperor reconsider. Since Tilsit and Erfurt, Russia had been a bystander in the bitter war that was still raging in Europe. The Emperor had refused to be drawn in, either for or against Austria, and Napoleon, who was increasingly eyeing him as a potential brother-in-law, was being conciliatory over Poland. Similarly, Russia was playing no part in the Peninsular War battles that were being fought by France and Britain in Spain and Portugal. Closer to home, the pro-British King of Sweden had been ousted by a revolution and the Swedes were making overtures for peace. In the light of all these factors, the Emperor concluded that he could safely give Pavel some holiday. There were currently no urgent tasks for the navy – and anyway the best part of it was in British hands. With his customary generosity, the Emperor gave Pavel unlimited leave of absence from the end of the navigational season on the equivalent of full pay. In September 1809 an order was drawn up in Pavel's favour for a salary of four thousand roubles a year with an additional six thousand roubles of 'table money' annually.

During this last summer in Russia, Pavel's changes of mood were more erratic than ever. He talked violently of leaving Russia for good and began to arrange for the sale of his country properties. Elizabeth was shattered by the speed at which events were moving and tried to reason with him, although she knew that his desire to get away was in part motivated by concerns for her health. Like Pavel, she longed for a holiday, but she had no desire permanently to abandon a world to which she now belonged. Furthermore, Pavel's proposed destination of Paris filled her with dread. As an Englishwoman, she was unenthusiastic about becoming a resident of Napoleon's capital. With Caulaincourt,

Pavel talked of stopping only briefly in Paris and then moving, for health reasons, to the warmer climate of Nice, in the south of France, but when they were alone, Pavel whispered to Elizabeth that there were rumours of a peace treaty between France and England, and that as soon as the political circumstances permitted it, their destination would be England.

For once, Elizabeth and Pavel took no official part in the annual festivities at Peterhof, but de Maistre came to their house to change before fulfilling his diplomatic duties at the court. After the formal dinner, he felt insufferably sad and bored by it all and fled back to the Chichagovs to spend the rest of the evening in their more congenial company. Elizabeth was entertaining some of her women friends, amongst them Mary Shcherbatova, pining for Robert Ker Porter, who had returned to England. It was a perfect summer night and when darkness fell they set off on foot together through the many gardens in the area in the hope of glimpsing the fireworks. The long avenues of the park were lit for miles by thousands of lamps and when the illuminations of the palace and the cascade came into view, they were breathtakingly beautiful. Far out in the Gulf, they could see a line of warships riding at anchor outside Kronstadt. The outlines of their masts and rigging were picked out by dozens of lights. Free from the cares of office, Pavel was, for once, relaxed and with de Maistre he was always at his most witty. They were all close friends and there was much talk and laughter. As they made their way through the trees, Elizabeth's slight figure, in a simple summer gown, slipped in and out of the shadows. The gaiety of the moment had temporarily soothed her concerns about the future and for the first time in many days, she was smiling.

In the middle of September, accompanied by their children and two servants, the Chichagovs set off overland for France. Their friends were scandalized and Roxana Sturdza's comments echo those of many others: 'Admiral Tchitchagoff, still enamoured of Napoleon's glory, wished with all his heart to draw closer to the object of his devotion. In spite of the efforts of the duc de Vicence [Caulaincourt] and the wish of the Emperor, he insisted on resigning and made preparations to go to Paris. His wife, more reasonable, was not able to deflect him from this remarkable folly. My sorrow at their departure was all the greater because Madame Tchitchagoff did not hide the fatal premonitions that overwhelmed her. We parted weeping.'[23]

# CHAPTER TEN

# 'A Deplorable Caprice'

### 1809–1811

Roxana Sturdza had misread Pavel's motives for going to France. It was a practical step that had little to do with his vaunted admiration for Napoleon. At this time, relations between Britain and Russia were such that it was inconceivable for a senior minister of the Russian government to travel there on holiday. On the other hand, Pavel had excellent relations with Caulaincourt, who would furnish him with all the necessary documents that were necessary for travel through the extensive European territories now under French domination. Furthermore, his standing with Caulaincourt assured him a valuable entrée into political circles in Paris, which would increase his chances of negotiating an early passage to England. Even at this time of war, passports from France to England were still being issued to those with the right contacts.

In fact Caulaincourt wrote to Napoleon in August about the departure of the Chichagovs:

> Admiral Tchitchagoff is going to Paris with his wife, and from there to Nice for his health. When everyone wanted war with France, he on the contrary, was against it and maintains this view. His principles have not changed; he is a good Russian and one could say a Frenchman in his admiration of Your Majesty. His wife, born an Englishwoman, restricts herself to household duties. Both of them are ill and are looking for a better climate during the winter; he retains the ministry of the navy, which will be confided *ad interim* to the marquis de Traversé. The Emperor sets great store by Admiral Tchitchagoff, who is one of the most able men in this country.[1]

A notice appeared in the *Journal de Paris* that 'the Minister of the Navy has permission to travel abroad to regain his health'[2] and the former counsellor from the London Embassy, Baron Nikolai, who was in St Petersburg, passed the news on to Vorontsov: 'Admiral Tchitchagov left a fortnight ago with all his family to stay in the south of France. He has sold his lands, his house and all his movable possessions. He retains, however, the title of Minister of the Navy with all its trappings. In the meantime, the marquis de Traversay is fulfilling the functions of minister.'[3]

It had not escaped Pavel that for his replacement, the Emperor had once again chosen a foreigner and he notes tersely: 'I proposed several people, all Russians. He has taken a Frenchman, Traversé.'[4]

There is no record of the route taken by Pavel and Elizabeth to Paris. We do know, however, that they passed through Frankfurt and Karlsruhe, where Pavel delivered a letter from the Empress to her mother. It is most probable that they took the road through Riga and Berlin, the discomforts of which are recorded by many contemporary travellers. Pavel's decision to travel before the snow fell would not only have made their journey slower, but would also have necessitated the perilous crossing by raft of the many large rivers that crossed their route. Their carriage jolted for hours along roads full of potholes and at nights the inns and posthouses often offered the most rudimentary accommodation. Some travellers preferred to sleep in their carriages rather than expose themselves to the squalor and the frequent thefts. The journey took nearly a month and the Chichagovs finally arrived in Paris on 10 October 1809.

Pavel was astonished, but not favourably impressed, by his first sight of the French capital. The Arc de Triomphe, which was still under construction, marked the outer limits of Paris to the west, and to the north Montmartre, which lay outside the gates of the city, was a village clustered around a hill covered with windmills. Apart from the magnificent public buildings and palaces, much of the city was composed of narrow, densely populated and malodorous streets. The spacious boulevards of Baron Haussmann had yet to be created and after the huge, open vistas of St Petersburg, Pavel may well have found Paris oppressive. He regarded it, however, purely as a point of transit and he and Elizabeth moved into temporary accommodation while they planned their next move.

By the autumn of 1809, despite some setbacks in Spain, Napoleon was the supreme master of Europe. He had created his siblings kings and queens and had pushed the frontiers of France to Danzig on the Baltic and to Dalmatia on the Adriatic. When he returned on 26 October to Fontainebleau from his latest victory over the Austrians at Wagram, accompanied by sixty boxes of objets d'art that he had collected on his campaigns, Napoleon found himself in the middle of a domestic crisis. The pregnancy of his Polish mistress, the beautiful Marie Walewska, had confirmed his suspicions that Josephine was responsible for their failure to produce an heir and he had convinced himself that it was his imperial duty to divorce her. Against the backdrop of continual court activities, Napoleon and Josephine were in the painful process of ending their marriage.

The palace at Fontainebleau had been recently redecorated in the sumptuous new style made fashionable by the campaigns in Egypt and, in imitation of his Bourbon predecessors, Napoleon had decreed that his court should move there for the opening of the hunting season. The Russian Ambassador, the enormously stout Prince Kurakin, hurried down to Fontainebleau to pay his respects. The correspondence that was continuing to pass between the courts of Russia and France on the subject of the Grand Duchess assured him a warm reception, although there were difficulties. When the proposed union had first been broached at Erfurt, Napoleon's choice had fallen on the Emperor's favourite sister, Catherine, who had meanwhile married the Prince of Oldenburg. Now the younger Grand Duchess, the 15-year-old Anna, was under scrutiny and the Russian Emperor was being courted accordingly, but Napoleon had failed to take into consideration the influence of Maria Feodorovna. The German-born Dowager's refusal to consider a marriage between her young and innocent daughter and a divorced Corsican of 40 placed her son in a delicate diplomatic situation. All he could do, without giving Napoleon an outright refusal, was to suggest that he wait until the Grand Duchess was a little older. In the autumn of 1809, therefore, Napoleon's attitude to Russia was still shaped by his hope of acquiring a royal Russian bride.

In mid-November, the court returned to Paris and established itself, as usual, in the Tuileries Palace. Very soon after, Pavel and Elizabeth were presented to Napoleon. The lapse in Pavel's memoirs, however, leaves us with no information on his reactions to this first encounter with the man, nearly two years younger than himself, whose achievements had commanded his respect – if not his admiration – for nearly a decade. Similarly, no details of Elizabeth's presentation survive, nor of her emotions when she found herself face to face with England's greatest enemy. Her years of training in St Petersburg doubtless stood her in good stead and she probably gave Napoleon the same cool-eyed gaze that she reserved for Caulaincourt. Thanks to the favour with which Russia was being regarded and to the recommendations of Caulaincourt, the Chichagovs were well received and, judging by the headings in Pavel's memoirs, he and Elizabeth were soon caught up in a court life that was every bit as busy as their schedule in St Petersburg. The isolated comment 'How he [Napoleon] caresses the court ladies'[5] suggests that Pavel was unprepared for Napoleon's sexuality and that he was astounded by the freedom with which he behaved in public. Pavel would have been even more shocked if he had known of Napoleon's letter to

Josephine, in which he suggests that had the good-looking Russian Emperor been a woman, he would have liked him as a mistress.

In December, a letter from Caulaincourt bears the Emperor's thanks to Napoleon for his welcome to Pavel, and rumours of 'the distinctions accorded to Admiral Tchitchagoff'[6] were soon circulating in St Petersburg. Such gossip, recorded by Caulaincourt under the title of *Les Nouvelles et On Dit*, was often surprisingly accurate and therefore the further comment that 'his wife has not been out anywhere because of her health, not even to the theatre'[7] cannot be dismissed. In his letters, Pavel stresses the improvement in Elizabeth's health and says that she was accompanying him everywhere, but an entry in the *Journal de Paris* for 14 December seems to suggest that some of Pavel's socializing with Napoleon and his family may have been done alone. (It is equally possible that wives of non-royalty – even if present – did not rate a mention.)

> The Prince [Marshall Berthier] and Princess of Neuchâtel and Wagram had the honour to receive on Monday, at their chateau of Grosbois: Their Imperial Majesties, the Emperor and Empress; the King of Wurtemberg; the King and Queen of Westphalia; the King and Queen of Naples. Prince Kurakin, Admiral Tchitchagow and a party from the court had been invited. After the hunt, which was very successful and favoured by very good weather, there was dinner, an entertainment and a ball. The gardens and avenues of the Chateau of Grosbois were illuminated. Their Imperial Majesties returned to Paris at eleven p.m.[8]

This must have been one of the last occasions that Napoleon and Josephine attended a social function as a couple, for on 15 December 1809 their divorce proceedings were ceremonially conducted in the throne room of the Tuileries in the presence of the court, and the next day Josephine retired to Malmaison. For the following week Napoleon continued to visit Josephine and he let it be known that he expected her to be accorded all the respect of a dowager empress. But soon he was hunting at Malmaison without bothering to see her and included Pavel amongst the party. During the same period Pavel was invited, at a court gathering, to join Napoleon in a favourite card game of the Bonaparte family called *reversi*. The game was played by four people with a pack from which the tens had been removed. The Queen of Spain, who was born Julie Clary and was the elder sister of Désirée, the future Queen of Sweden, was the third player, but, tantalizingly, history does not relate if Elizabeth made up the fourth. In St Petersburg Caulaincourt was shown

Prince Kurakin's plaintive letters to the Emperor, in which he refers to Pavel's success: 'Prince Kourakine has written that . . . Admiral Tchitchagoff has been invited without him to Malmaison, that he was very well treated by the Emperor, who said to him: "I have not invited Prince Kourakine because he does not like hunting," that then, at a court party, Admiral Tchitchagoff had the honour of joining in the game of cards that His Majesty was playing with the Queen of Spain. He [Kurakin] appears, without complaining however, to be hurt by this preferential treatment: Prince Kourakine is very vain and sets great store by all these distinctions.'[9]

Both Champagny and Napoleon found Pavel's departure from Russia for health reasons unconvincing and Caulaincourt was obliged to reiterate that 'he has not left the Ministry and has only come to France for his own and his wife's health. . . . He has been genuinely ill, and his wife mortally so on several occasions.'[10] Later, Napoleon's suspicions are aroused by Pavel's absence from the list of members of the new State Council established by Speranskii, and Caulaincourt once again had to assure him of Pavel's continuing high standing with the Emperor, observing that 'he has the right to be a member of the Council and it was because of his absence that he was not on the list of those members who are active.'[11] Nevertheless, Pavel's withdrawal from his post remained as puzzling to the French as it did to his friends and compatriots in St Petersburg.

De Maistre wrote copiously to Pavel throughout this period in affectionate and sentimental letters that mix regrets for Pavel and Elizabeth's absence with thinly disguised rebukes for Pavel's abandonment of his post. He refers to Elizabeth as Pavel's 'adorable other half'[12] and complains that 'whatever you say, Monsieur l'Amiral, I am concerned about your other half. It seems to me that she is not well housed and that she is cold. Take my advice, wrap her up well and bring her back to us.'[13] He archly proposes the solution of divorce, suggesting that Elizabeth would return instantly to St Petersburg once she was free and that Pavel would inevitably pursue her. 'Knowing you, Monsieur l'Amiral, you would marry her all over again. I have never tried this, but I cannot imagine anything more delightful than the pleasure of marrying one's wife.'[14] De Maistre's regular letters, with their irrefutable arguments invoking duty and patriotism, were like the voice of inner conscience and can only have contributed to Pavel's unsettled state of mind.

From a letter to Vorontsov in March, it is clear that Pavel was still very depressed and determined to leave France as soon as possible. 'I do not know if you are aware that I am in Paris with my wife and children. The state of our health contributed to, or rather has served as a pretext for, this journey, but my desire to withdraw myself from the depths of disarray, from incompetence, from absurdity and from the most vile slavery has been the true motive for my departure from the country.'[15] He makes veiled references to his disagreements with Speranskii and launches into several pages of furious argument against his innovations. There was also the related problem of the drop in the value of the rouble, which had reduced the Chichagovs' income by more than half since their arrival in France. This depreciation was caused by Russia's enforced adherence to the Continental System and the resulting loss of customs revenues on goods from Britain, but in the eyes of Pavel and many other Russians, Speranskii's increased taxation was also to blame. The letter closes with a statement that leaves no doubt whatsoever of Pavel's real views on England:

> I plan to spend the rest of the time that this war lasts in some isolated spot, close to a spa with peaceful and educated people. I shall probably go to Switzerland for this, if I can find the medical remedies there which we need. I shall, however, do my best not to distance myself too much from the coast, so that if some unforeseen event brings peace with the only country which honours humanity and merits the name of fatherland for those who have the good fortune to belong to it, I can move there with all my family and spend the rest of my days in that earthly paradise. . . . You are the only man to whom I can speak completely openly as I have done. I have no doubts that all this will remain between us, above all my future intentions.[16]

Pavel was always completely frank with Vorontsov, but his letters to St Petersburg, which he knew would be widely circulated, describe a life of *mondaine* amusements and domestic happiness that was deliberately misleading. Without doubt Pavel was enjoying the quiet mornings spent amongst his 'angels' – far from the huge correspondence and constant worries of the Ministry – and the leisurely afternoons with visits to museums and art galleries. Compared with St Petersburg, the quantity of amusements and entertainments available in Paris was overwhelming. An 1810 map of Paris gives a list of eight theatres, twenty entertainment halls ranging from the opera to the circus and forty-six 'establishments' of science and art, which included museums, academies and libraries. But these letters, written for consumption in a gossipy society, were also intended to act as a smoke screen. After nearly six months in Paris, Pavel was growing increasingly anxious to implement his covert plan of a flight to England, but it was difficult to judge the timing.

Napoleon's face-saving decision to marry the Austrian Archduchess Marie-Louise had been announced in February. By March, the new bride was on her way to Paris and Napoleon was immersed in planning a series of sumptuous wedding celebrations to impress the 19-year-old great-niece of Marie-Antoinette. He was concerned, after his sojourns at the palace of Schönbrunn in Vienna, that Marie-Louise would not find the French capital sufficiently grandiose, and drawing on the French genius for stage-setting, he authorized the construction of a huge scaffolding round the foundations of the Arc de Triomphe, which was covered with painted canvas to create a full-size imitation of the projected monument. North of Paris, redecorations were made to the interior of the chateau at Compiègne, where Napoleon, in imitation of Louis XVI and Marie-Antoinette, planned to have his first meeting with Marie-Louise.

The aspect of Napoleonic Paris has been well captured in hundreds of paintings and engravings of the period. The Russian Emperor was so anxious to learn how Napoleon was beautifying his capital and the interiors of his palaces that Caulaincourt arranged for a series of magnificent albums entitled *Des Monuments de Paris*, with engravings by the architects Charles Percier and P. F. L. Fontaine, to be dispatched to St Petersburg from 1809 onwards. Another album of engravings by Percier and Fontaine faithfully records the scenes of the wedding and is accompanied by a text which describes the events – including an official version of those which led up to the triumphal entry into Paris of the bridal pair. According to the text in Percier and Fontaine's album, Napoleon was already in contact with the Archduchess twenty-four hours before their scheduled first meeting on 27 March. On 26 March, he sent a page to her at Nancy with three pheasants which he had just shot – a token of his sporting prowess, whose symbolism may have escaped the innocent 19-year-old.[17]

Napoleon's first hours with Marie-Louise have been recorded with varying degrees of accuracy and propriety. The brief reference in Pavel's memoirs to 'Pauline's account of the first night'[18] suggests that he may have enjoyed a version of events from Pauline Bonaparte. Her own appetite for amorous exploits would have lent the tale a certain piquancy. It was, however, Pauline's sister Caroline who was the eyewitness to what took place. In the pouring rain of 27 March, Napoleon rushed to meet the coach bearing his sister and Marie-Louise and leapt in with the ladies in a soaking overcoat to lavish embraces upon his bride. It was night by the time they reached the château at Compiègne, and Napoleon, who was in a state of high excitement and impatience, cancelled all formalities and ordered a dinner for three in the bedroom suite which had been prepared for the Archduchess. He and Marie-Louise had already been married by proxy in Vienna and once Caroline had withdrawn, Napoleon took advantage of this legal loophole to consummate the marriage without delay.

On 1 April the civil ceremony took place just outside Paris, at the Palace of St Cloud. The capital exploded into a riot of pageantry and a frenzy of officially decreed festivities. Within the city, the ceremony was announced by a celebratory salvo from the canons of Les Invalides. That evening at St Cloud a magnificent dinner was followed by an entertainment and illuminations which were respectfully recorded in the album of Percier and Fontaine: 'The park [and] the gardens were lit up with infinite artistry; the play of the fountains in the midst of the lights produced the most brilliant effects, and the Great Cascade offered a truly magical spectacle. The diversions of all kinds, the dances, the numerous orchestras that were placed in the principal avenues of the garden, gave an extraordinary liveliness and gaiety to this occasion.'[19]

During the night it rained, but as the first canon announced the departure of the matrimonial cortège, the sun appeared. The carriages passed through the immense guard of honour – which stretched three kilometres from Porte Maillot to the Tuileries – and by the time that Napoleon and Marie-Louise had reached the Arc de Triomphe, it was a brilliant day. The text of the album notes that this was seen as a good omen. A huge crowd had gathered round the Arc de Triomphe, which was festooned with garlands and banners, and the entire length of the Champs-Elysées was lined with spectators. At the entrance to the Tuileries Palace, a richly decorated portico had been erected, and the couple passed under this before descending from their carriage to make their way to the Louvre chapel, where the religious ceremony was to be held. The new Empress of France wore a wedding dress made in Paris of satin and ermine and, while she was not a beauty, her glowing cheeks and ample frame seemed to promise Napoleon the fertility that Josephine, with her slender figure and painted face, had so long denied him. At 6 p.m., after the service, a royal banquet was given, to which 'a great number of people of the highest distinction, all dressed with an extraordinary richness',[20] were invited. From the engravings of this occasion, it would appear that while the royal party ate at a large table, the guests gathered in the surrounding balconies and loggias as spectators. After dinner, Napoleon and Marie-Louise received the homage of the crowd from the balcony of the palace. A concert followed and fireworks, after which they retired to bed. Meanwhile in the city the revels continued and 'almost the whole night was consecrated to public joy; the Champs-Elysées was covered with orchestras, theatres, circuses for different displays, dances and games of all sorts.'[21]

Pavel's status as a distinguished foreigner at court suggests that he and Elizabeth were present at the wedding. When the newly-weds returned to Compiègne on 5 April, Pavel, who was well aware that Caulaincourt was their best ally with Napoleon, wrote him a fulsome letter in the unconvincing guise of a courtier: 'I must express to you the happiness that I feel every time that I am fortunate enough to see His Majesty the Emperor Napoleon, who on every occasion deigns to treat me with kindness. We have just celebrated a marriage that so greatly surpassed all the other ceremonies with its splendour and magnificence that the tenor of the entertainment [?endowed] great men with great qualities. The celebrations were accompanied by gratuities, amnesties and pleasures and all arranged and distributed with justice, generosity and liberality.'[22]

Pavel goes on to describe an evening at the Comédie-Française, when he had taken a box in order to see Napoleon's favourite actor, Talma, whose acting he naturally found sublime. He also mentions that they have found a country house near Versailles, but that 'my health and that of my family pressingly demands that we visit some mineral waters and we must, consequently, leave the centre of all resources and the most temperate climate in the world to try to obtain better health elsewhere.'[23] In a slightly contradictory postscript, probably intended to silence the rumours in St Petersburg, he sends Elizabeth's warm thanks for forwarding her mail and adds that 'Now that she accompanies me everywhere, the air of Paris has done her a great deal of good. She has never been in better health.'[24]

However, Pavel's star with Napoleon was waning. Firstly, because Napoleon's feelings towards Russia had cooled with the frustration of his original marriage plans, but secondly, because he was suspicious of Pavel's status and objectives and found his stated reason of ill health implausible. A young Russian diplomat in Paris, Count Karl Nesselrode, in a covert role of which both Rumiantsev and Kurakin were unaware, was keeping the Emperor informed of political developments through a secret correspondence with Speranskii. He had regular meetings with Talleyrand, to whom he refers by various pseudonyms, including 'my cousin Henry'. Amongst the names he had for Pavel, on whom he spied and reported back to St Petersburg, were, 'le marquis Tulipane', 'mon oncle' and 'la trop sensible princesse'. Just after Napoleon's wedding he sent the following to Speranskii:

I have found . . . Mr Tchitchagof here. He has been very well received by the Emperor Napoleon and is enjoying a certain favour in society. This sovereign has had a private conversation with him and has taken to accosting him at diplomatic parties. The last time he spoke to him, it was to tell him how astonished he was that he had not been nominated a member of the new Council and since then, it seems that his attitude has rather cooled towards him. Mr Tchitchagof plans to spend the summer in the Midi of France and those close to him have assured me that he has a project to go to America, but I have difficulty in believing this. For the rest, the same exaggeration in his opinions, perhaps a little less enthusiasm for this country here, but against his own there is always a lot of exasperation which he allows to explode with very little restraint. . . .

I have grounds to suppose that his conversations with the Emperor have only touched on general subjects; I do not think he has done us much harm up to now, although he is quite friendly with Savary, but since I am intimately convinced that his mind and his easily overexcited imagination could give him all the means, I shall miss no opportunity to follow his movements while he is here and will not fail to give you an exact account of them.[25]

The 'gratuities' and 'amnesties' that Napoleon had distributed at the time of his wedding did not extend to Pavel, and in mid-April Pavel received the news that his application for passports to England had been refused. His reactions to this setback were violent. He was furious, but unlike the Emperor Alexander, Napoleon was ruthless. At Pavel and Elizabeth's lodgings a terrible scene took place. All the tensions and frustrations of the past months, and indeed of the past years, took possession of Pavel. Elizabeth could only watch helplessly as he raged and fumed like a madman and she could do nothing to dissuade him from a plan to depart immediately to look for an alternative method of reaching England.

Pavel tells de Maistre that in his and Elizabeth's 'conjugal equation'[26] they were in complete complicity and that in all the views expressed in his correspondence 'I = We.'[27] From its inception, however, the plan to go to

England (of which de Maistre knew nothing) had placed Elizabeth in a dilemma. She was by nature serious and dutiful. Her defiance of her father was not in character and had only been prompted by her passionate love for Pavel. Now all her instincts told her that Pavel was making a terrible mistake. Like de Maistre, she believed that he should return to the service of his country and yet the thought of going back to England was so irresistible that she was half inclined to agree with him. Throughout their time in Paris, Elizabeth had been worried about Pavel's frame of mind; his headaches and his palpitations were the physical symptoms of a deeper malaise. In the intimacy of their bedroom, as he held her tightly to him, he told her that his frequent visits to the Tuileries were simply a masquerade to obtain their freedom and that he hated the constant intrigues of the French court as much as he had hated those of St Petersburg.

Pavel left Paris in a very disturbed state. According to a letter which he later wrote to Caulaincourt,[28] he first visited Dieppe, possibly in the hope of finding a ship to England. From there he claims to have taken a route across Europe which included Baden, Lausanne and Geneva, but Elizabeth meanwhile had no idea of his whereabouts. As the days passed, she became anxious and rumours of Pavel's escapade began to spread. Normally so calm, Elizabeth, too, was feeling the stress. She had very little money and no network of contacts, as she had in St Petersburg. Doubtless the children were asking constantly for their father and eventually the Russian servants would also have become uneasy. On top of it all, she had discovered that she was expecting another baby. The bush telegraph to St Petersburg reported the following, which is faithfully transcribed by Caulaincourt in his *Nouvelles et On Dit*: 'They are saying that Admiral Tchitchagoff, who is in Paris, has gone crazy, that he has asked for a passport to go to England, that he has left Paris, leaving his wife and children there in a state of anxiety, and that he has been arrested in Munich, running around the main streets and behaving like a madman.'[29]

Like all rumours, the reports that reached St Petersburg were doubtless exaggerated, but when Pavel returned to Paris, he withdrew completely from society and followed a strict medical regime. There is, however, a further aspect to this incident which, if she had any suspicion of it, would explain Elizabeth's extreme agitation. Although he does not mention Italy to Caulaincourt, the records of the border police show that on 17 May Pavel entered Switzerland from the Italian city of Genoa. He was travelling on a diplomatic passport and his visa number was fourteen. The following entry, visa number fifteen, is for a Russian woman also travelling on a diplomatic passport and similarly coming from Genoa. She is described as 'La dame Severin'. The name of Madame Severin, the young and very pretty wife of a German merchant in St Petersburg, had been romantically linked with the Emperor's the previous year. The Emperor's eye was not unknown to stray occasionally from Marie Narishkina and the country dacha of Madame Severin was reputed to have been the scene of an imperial dalliance. The common route of Pavel and Madame Severin may have been a coincidence, but the possibility of a brief amorous interlude cannot be dismissed. It would also explain the excessive nature of his subsequent feelings of guilt and remorse over Elizabeth.

We do not know what passed between the Chichagovs when Pavel returned to Paris. His letter to Caulaincourt at this time is subdued in tone and he sounds a little chastened.[30] Pavel was still talking about living in Switzerland, but Elizabeth persuaded him that she could not travel in her present condition. Instead they moved into a small apartment at no. 19 rue Blanche. This was a narrow street running uphill towards Montmartre to the edges of the city, where access was controlled by a gatehouse known as the Barrière Blanche. Formerly the rue Blanche was regularly used by carts bearing plaster from the quarries of Montmartre, which could be the origin of its name. It was on the outer fringes of what was then considered to be residentially acceptable and far less elegant than the nearby rue de la Chaussée d'Antin. The rue Blanche, however, had the advantage of being located close to a large number of public gardens and a well-known thermal bathing establishment. It may have been these amenities, as well as the more modest price, that attracted the Chichagovs to the area.

A map dating from before the Revolution shows that in 1777 much of the land to the west, and some to the east, of the rue Blanche was given over to private parks and gardens. The most elaborate of these was designed for the wealthy financier Simon-Charles Boutin, who called it Tivoli, after the much admired gardens of the Villa d'Este outside Rome. After the Revolution, Boutin's private pleasure garden was acquired by the State and he was guillotined. The gardens were subsequently rented out to successive entrepreneurs, who turned them into a business concern by organizing money-making 'spectacles' and other amusements. In 1799 another garden containing thermal baths was opened close by and this was also known as Tivoli – a name which was to become a generic term for an amusement park.

In his letter to Caulaincourt, Pavel extols the merits of the thermal baths at Tivoli: 'After everything, I am in Paris not far from Tivoli, where we are taking the sulphur baths. For my part, I have been recommended the [illegible] douche which I hope will do me good. . . . The neighbourhood of the baths is enhanced by the good air that one breathes there and by the walks that are available. The regime to which I am obliged to submit has caused me to retire from society in order to [reap] the excellent fruits of exercise, pools and regulated thoughts. This is my mode of living: if all that does not cure me, I shall regard myself as incurable.'[31] He makes some opaque references to the advantages of Paris over London – perhaps a hint to Caulaincourt that he has abandoned, for the time being, the idea of England – and asks Caulaincourt for help with his brother Vasilii's passport for France.

Elizabeth and Pavel had another visitor from Russia, Roxana Sturdza. She disapproved strongly of Pavel's sojourn in Paris and in a letter to de Maistre disparagingly refers to their flat as 'a narrow box'.[32] In his reply, de Maistre, who suspected that Pavel was hiding something from him, analyses his behaviour:

> I am less sure of the rule of three, and even of my esteem for you, than I am of a profound ulcer in the depths of this heart, folded and refolded upon itself, where nothing can be seen. This world is but a performance: everywhere motives are replaced by appearances, so that we do not know the reasons for anything. This ends up by confusing everything; what is true is sometimes mixed with lies. But where? but when? but by how much? That is what we do not know. . . . To return to our friend Tch—f, I know first and foremost that none of the reasons which he gives are the true ones, and I believe, furthermore, that it is a matter of wounded pride. All the rest is a closed book. When two beings in perfect harmony meet each other by chance, when perfect confidence is the result of a long and pleasant experience, when the doors are closed and no one is listening, when the sorrow on one side needs to talk and the goodness on the other needs to listen, then it can happen, as Jacques-Bénigne has said so divinely, that *one of these hearts, leaning towards the other, lets its secret escape.* . . . You may judge if I have the least pretension to discharge those two hearts in the rue Blanche no.19! . . . I pity Madame Tch—f greatly. . . . It is a deplorable caprice, and nothing more.[33]

These were very difficult days for Elizabeth. Despite the proximity of the gardens and regular visits to the baths, the hot summer months spent in a small, airless apartment in Paris were almost as detrimental to her health as the icy winds of St Petersburg. She had been badly shaken by Pavel's disappearance and in her deteriorating condition, she soon had another miscarriage. Since his return, Pavel seemed to depend on her more than ever before and she hoped that the proposed visit of Pavel's brother Vasilii would help to raise his spirits. In the meantime, any weakness that he may have had for Madame Severin had passed and his desire for his wife had never been greater; her growing physical fragility did nothing to cool his ardour. Elizabeth dreaded another pregnancy, but she loved him too much to refuse.

While Pavel and Elizabeth shunned social life, Napoleon and Marie-Louise embarked on a prolonged honeymoon consisting of banquets and balls which were given in their honour during the months following the wedding. On 1 July, the Austrian Ambassador, Prince Schwarzenberg, invited a large number of guests to a ball at the Austrian Embassy, which was situated in the rue de Provence, not far from the rue Blanche. A contemporary newspaper cites an account of what happened:

You must imagine a vast salon accommodating 1,200 people without being crowded. This salon was decorated with an extraordinary magnificence. Festoons of gauze and muslin, shaped into garlands, had been used. The splendour of the salon had been increased by a great number of mirrors of the largest size, 73 chandeliers from the ceiling, each one with 40 candles, without counting the candles that had been placed between the mirrors. It is still not known whether it was by accident or not that one of the garlands went too close to the chandeliers and set fire to the decorations, which were coated with a varnish of wine spirits. Furthermore, the ceiling being covered with waxed canvas, the flames spread in a moment to the four corners of the room, like a fireworks display. The first thing was to make His Majesty the Emperor leave and he had scarcely left when everyone rushed for the exits. There were only three. You can imagine the anguish, the terror, the despair of the women and the cries of 'sauve qui peut'! People pushed, people shoved, people kicked without regard for either sex or rank. In a moment, the ceiling fell, the chandeliers, the blazing joists and boards fell on the men and women who screamed horribly. The mirrors, shattered by the heat, exploded with a noise like pistol shots. His excellency Prince Kourakin, a man of great corpulence, was struck down by the fall of a chandelier, which broke his arm. He was trampled underfoot by the fleeing crowd. Several women suffered the same fate. Others were burned when their gauze and lace dresses were consumed by the flames or torn so that a great number escaped almost naked into the Ambassador's garden, where they hid themselves in the bushes. Other women hoped to escape through an opening that the fire had already made in the panelling, but, pushed by the crowd which followed, and not

197

finding a way out, they perished in a ghastly manner. . . . Many millions of diamonds were lost during the commotion. Prince Kourakin lost a solitaire estimated at 400,000 francs from his hat and while he was on the ground, he lost a very valuable ring and at the same time nearly lost the finger on which it was worn – it is feared that his arm will have to be amputated.[34]

Kurakin was very badly burned and remained out of action for a year, but his personal vanity had saved him from even worse injuries, for the heavy quality of his costly silk coat from Lyon offered him some protection from the flames.

In the autumn, de Maistre, sensing that Elizabeth was responsive to his crusade to bring Pavel back to Russia, began writing to her separately. The gentleness of his letters to Elizabeth differs greatly from the sharp wit of his exchanges with Roxana Sturdza and Pavel: 'When I asked you, in my last letter, not to lean your poor little bosom against the table just to give me the pleasure of reading one of your letters, I did not know it, but your letter of 24th July had already arrived,'[35] and he goes on to assure her that what she calls her 'anglais-français' is a perfect 'français-anglais'. The chief objective of his correspondence, however, was to recruit her influence over Pavel. He encloses in his letter to her a strongly argued text entitled 'Dissertation on the word Fatherland' and asks her to 'press my dissertation on Monsieur l'Amiral, and if you wish, in order to make the accents of reason more penetrating, add to them those of tenderness'.[36] De Maistre, who was a little in love with Elizabeth himself, understood better than anyone else the romantic bonds that united the Chichagovs. His homily to Pavel closes: 'After, therefore, a man distinguished in every way, has had a sufficient change of air, when he has eaten enough peaches and grapes, and his wife has had a boy, *he should return to his homeland.*'[37]

As Elizabeth and Pavel wrestled with their personal predicament, action had not ceased on the world stage. The war between Russia and Turkey dragged on and relations between Russia and France continued to deteriorate as internal economic pressures gradually undermined Russia's adherence to the Continental System. When, therefore, on 22 January 1811, Napoleon provocatively annexed the Duchy of Oldenburg – whose ruler was father-in-law of the Grand Duchess Catherine – the two nations were set on an inevitable course to war. In Spain Napoleonic troops were under pressure from the British and in Paris political intrigues were rife. Ever since the Congress of Erfurt in 1808, the deposed French Foreign Minister, Talleyrand, had been scheming against Napoleon. In early 1809 Napoleon discovered that during his absence, Talleyrand and Fouché, the Minister of Police, had tried to hatch a plot to install a provisional government in Paris. In June 1810 Fouché was replaced by Savary, but in the meantime Caulaincourt was also beginning to share some of Talleyrand's disenchantment with Napoleon and to confide his fears to the Emperor in St Petersburg. Napoleon got wind of this and in the spring of 1811, Caulaincourt left Russia and was replaced by General Lauriston.

As the alliance between Russia and France crumbled, life in Paris was becoming daily less easy for the Russian community. Napoleon was barely on speaking terms with Kurakin, and Champagny had held an angry conversation with Nesselrode at a public dinner before a great number of people. The dearth of letters to or from the Chichagovs at this time is perhaps a reflection of their growing isolation in a country that was virtually at war with their own. As her hopes of reaching England faded, Elizabeth turned for consolation to a study of the Bible, but Pavel preferred Voltaire. Two notebooks in Pavel's hand have survived containing long extracts of Voltaire's *Zadig ou La Destinée* and it is possible that Pavel used this period of inactivity to contemplate the mixed fortunes of Voltaire's oriental hero. He may even have taken comfort in comparing some of Zadig's adventures with his own experiences in the courts of two Emperors.

The deterioration in relations between France and Russia and the impossibility of taking his family to England must also have caused Pavel to reconsider their permanent emigration from Russia, for in March 1811 Caulaincourt reports that the Chichagovs have announced that they will return to St Petersburg in May.[38] Elizabeth, however, was once again expecting a baby. On 20 March 1811 another far more highly publicized pregnancy reached its successful conclusion and a salute of a hundred and one salvos boomed out over Paris to mark the birth of Marie-Louise's son and Napoleon's heir.

Throughout Elizabeth's pregnancy, Pavel was in his usual state of anxiety. She had lost so many babies in the early months, that it was not until the pregnancy was well advanced that Pavel realized that it would be inadvisable to attempt the journey back to St Petersburg. Once again, they would have to pass the months of summer in the stifling heat of their Paris flat. Late in July, Elizabeth went into labour. Her delicate constitution had already been enfeebled over the years by the recurring bouts of illness and frequent miscarriages. From the outset, she was very weak. It was soon apparent that this birth was going to be quite as difficult as any of the previous ones and, as the hours passed, Pavel sent repeated notes for the doctor, but he was no longer in St Petersburg, where his status immediately commanded the best attention available. What contacts he may have had in high places had largely evaporated over the past year and, furthermore, the distraught Russian servant may have had difficulty in conveying the message. Eventually the doctor came. The modest address would have convinced him that the patient was no one of note. They were foreigners. He mounted the stairs. Within the limited confines of the apartment, it had not been possible to protect the children from what was going on, and the three little girls huddled in terror around their nurse, listening to their mother's screams. In a small and airless room, the patient lay on a blood-spattered sheet. Her body writhed in agony at the onset of another wave of the convulsions that had been tearing her apart for hours. Beneath the streaks of sweat, her face was ashen and beside her bed stood a wild-eyed man, whose haggard features betrayed that the world of his nightmares had become a reality. There was little the doctor could do. He knew nothing of Elizabeth's case history and he lacked Dr Leighton's skilful touch. As she struggled to expel the child, Elizabeth's life ebbed away. The baby was stillborn and Elizabeth died shortly afterwards. Despite her sufferings, she had remained lucid to the end and in her last moments with Pavel, she had begged him to return home without delay and to send the children to her sisters in England. Then he was to dedicate himself to the service of his king and country.

# CHAPTER ELEVEN

# The Retreat from Moscow
## 1811–1814

Pavel's reactions to Elizabeth's death were predictably dramatic. As Rogerson had earlier observed, he was a man whose hatreds and affections knew no half measures. He was prostrated by the loss of his adored wife, but he was determined to follow her last wishes to the letter. Since he decided that the most sure way of informing Elizabeth's next of kin was through the Embassy, Pavel wrote to Father Smirnov in London on the day of her death and asked him to inform her sisters, and also Vorontsov and Katinka. The letter took over two weeks to reach Smirnov, but he acted immediately and in his reply, which enclosed a letter of condolence from Beatrice, he assures Pavel that he has 'conveyed, with appropriate care, the news of Elisaveta Carolovna's death to her sisters, Count Simon Romanovitch and Lady Pembroke, who all share in your grief.'[1] A simple notice in the *Gentleman's Magazine* gives the date of her death as 24 July 1811.[2]

By the time Elizabeth's family heard the news, however, Pavel was already on the way to St Petersburg. Travelling with him were the embalmed bodies of Elizabeth and her baby. The news of Elizabeth's death preceded his arrival and was noted by de Maistre in his journal on 15 August. On 1 September, de Maistre wrote to the King of Sardinia that Pavel was 'en route' and 'in despair'.[3] A week later, when Pavel arrived in the capital, he sent at once for his old friend:

> I ran there and he threw himself into my arms in complete desolation. The body of his wife was in the next-door room. What did he not tell me on the subject of his incurable despair and the country from which he has just come! He showed me, in very great confidence, a signed letter that the Emperor had written to him in response to the one that the Admiral had sent to him on arrival. . . . Sire, what a letter! The most tender and sensitive friend could not have written more.[4]

At a time when death in childbirth was a common occurrence and marriages were often made for convenience rather than for love, the prolonged presence of Elizabeth's embalmed body in the house and the intensity and duration of Pavel's grief aroused widespread curiosity. Amongst his few friends, however, there was sympathy. In a letter to a friend, Vorontsov's son, Mikhail, writes: 'The strangeness of this attachment and of this so painfully prolonged affliction pleases me. His return will stop all the abusive rumours spread about him since his departure. I was never able to believe that he would expatriate himself and am very glad that a man of character and ability has been returned to his country. The exaggerated views that he appeared to hold can change and he is in a position to be of service.'[5]

The positive aspects of Pavel's unhappiness did not escape Roxana Sturdza, who describes him at this time as being 'prey to a sombre distress, accusing and hating himself and rejecting the most simple consolations. Such distress inevitably made an impression; it was also the subject of all conversations, and the Emperor, who was naturally inclined to share the emotions of the heart, was very touched by the Admiral's misfortune.'[6]

During his absence in Paris, Pavel's many enemies had attempted on several occasions to injure his relationship with the Emperor, but without success. On his return, the Emperor gave Pavel a warm reception and agreed without demur to his request to be relieved of his post as Minister of the Navy. An imperial ukase was issued to the Senate dated 28 November 1811, in which the Emperor accepted Pavel's resignation with 'goodwill and gratitude for his devoted and caring directorship'.[7] In a similar ukase, Traversay was confirmed as his successor. Meanwhile Pavel was attached 'to the person of the Emperor', a high-ranking and undefined position that had been especially created for him. His 'table money' was raised from six to twelve thousand roubles a year and in addition, he retained his original salary of four thousand. He was also appointed to the State Council. The Austrian envoy, the Count Saint-Julien, reported on the appointment to Metternich, the Austrian Minister for Foreign Affairs, in Vienna: 'The nomination of the previous Minister of the Navy, Tchitchagoff, to the Great Council, attached by ukase to the person of the Emperor, has displeased the majority of the public. His opinions are very suspect. At the moment he affects a hatred for the French government of which two years ago he was the most enthusiastic admirer.'[8]

As the days passed, Pavel's misery increased and the absence of Elizabeth seemed to become harder rather than easier to bear. The only significance to him of his exalted position in the court was that it fulfilled the last wishes of Elizabeth to serve his sovereign. Nothing else seemed to matter. By December, Vorontsov was seriously concerned and wrote from Wilton to his son, Mikhail:

> I have had a letter from poor Chichagov since his return to Russia. This letter cut me to the heart; I have never witnessed such unhappiness, such despair as his on the death of his wife, whom he accuses himself of having killed; for he claims that if he had stayed in St Petersburg, Leithon or Lighton, who knew the constitution of his wife well, would have looked after her better than the ignorant French doctors. If you have not written to him, do so and tell him that you hope that out of attachment for the departed, he will preserve himself in order to devote himself to the education of the children which she left him. He is in such despair that I fear for his life, or what would be worse, that he will go mad.[9]

Pavel's uncontrolled grief can only have increased the suffering of the children. In his first letter, Smirnov had already tried to direct Pavel's sombre thoughts away from death by encouraging him to think of his daughters:

> Nothing but time and your own mind can ease the pain . . . in the belief that everything is ruled and brought to a happy conclusion by benign Providence, your wounds will be healed and you will gain comfort and strength in fulfilling your duty as a father by bringing up your delightful daughters in the heritage of love and purest friendship left by the departed. Looking at your daughters, you will certainly remember that their life depends on your life and life is shortened by overwhelming sorrow. I have no doubt that your passionate love for your daughters will serve as the most persuasive reason for you to limit your grief as much as possible. With God's help, the path that you have chosen – to return to Russia – will assist you greatly.[10]

But Pavel did not believe in Smirnov's 'benign Providence' and he tortured himself day and night with feelings of guilt and self-hatred over the death of Elizabeth. Her death in childbirth made his position all the more painful. There were certainly methods of birth control at the time which could have avoided some of Elizabeth's many pregnancies. Was it his longing for a son that had made Elizabeth and Pavel persist so long, in defiance of medical advice, to have another child? No longer engaged at the Ministry, he spent hours alone, conjuring up her departed presence and leafing through her simple daily journal – her Tag-Rag letters – which at nights he placed under his pillow. In a second letter, forwarding another one from Beatrice, Smirnov tries once again to comfort

Pavel and suggests that he may now be growing 'stronger both in spirit and in body, for the prosperity of your little ones who depend completely on your health',[11] but Pavel had receded too far into his self-created hell to hear him.

The bodies of Elizabeth and her child were buried in the Lutheran cemetery on Vasilevskii Island, barely half a mile from the house where she and Pavel had passed most of their married life. The cemetery covers several acres and was intended for foreigners who were not of Orthodox faith. Many imposing monuments to distinguished members of the German and British communities still line its once-ordered avenues. In summer it is a pleasant place, where the gravestones are shaded by spreading lime and maple trees, and even in winter, when the earth is frozen like iron and the trees stand like blackened skeletons against the sky, it has an aura of peace.

Shortly after Pavel left Paris in August 1811, Kurakin, who had made a partial recovery, was publicly abused by Napoleon at the Tuileries. The stream of insults against Russia to which Kurakin was subjected recalled two earlier occasions on which Napoleon had similarly humiliated the envoys of countries with which he planned to rupture relations. The first occasion had been with the British envoy, Lord Whitworth, before the collapse of the Treaty of Amiens and the second with Metternich in 1809 before the invasion of Austria. This incident was therefore interpreted as an unmistakable statement of intent and, as the prospect of war between Russia and France became inevitable, the nations of Europe fell into yet another configuration of coalitions.

On 24 February 1812, the Prussians made a military alliance with the French; by 14 March Austria, now closely linked to the newly founded Napoleonic dynasty, had followed suit. Russia, on the other hand, had found an unexpected ally in Napoleon's marshal, Bernadotte, who had been elected Crown Prince of Sweden in 1810 and on 5 April a Russo-Swedish alliance was signed, followed by a peace treaty between Sweden and Britain. In May Russia and Britain were negotiating delicately for peace through the British envoy to Sweden, Sir Edward Thornton.

With a French invasion imminent, the Emperor was anxious to secure Russia's southern flank, where the so-called army of the Danube under Kutuzov was still occupying the Rumanian principalities of Moldavia and Wallachia. He felt it was worth making concessions to the Turks to secure a peace treaty before the French attacked and he was irritated by the slowness with which Kutuzov was proceeding with the proposed armistice. He was also disgusted by reports that had reached him of unpunished misdemeanours by Kutuzov's troops against the local population. Ever since their falling out at Austerlitz, the young and energetic Emperor had regarded the elderly, one-eyed general with little affection. Kutuzov, with a lifetime of campaigns behind him, had little thirst for action and directed his battles from a carriage with more cunning than verve. Furthermore, in the eyes of the Emperor, the lethargic Kutuzov was not the instrument with which to realize his extraordinary ambitions in the Balkans, which revived the Byzantine fantasies of his grandmother.

In 1779, when the Empress Catherine named her second grandson Constantine after the last Byzantine emperor, Constantine XI Palaeologus, she was nurturing a dream of liberating the Orthodox Christian principalities of Moldavia and Wallachia from the Turks. Neighbouring Serbia would be given to the Austrians, and the Russian navy, based on the Crimea, would capture Constantinople, whose grateful Greek inhabitants would welcome her grandson as their emperor. In 1812, Alexander began to believe that aspects of his grandmother's vision of a revived Byzantium were within his grasp and in his search for the man to lead such a venture his eye fell on Pavel.

Pavel's favour with the Emperor was increasing daily. His chief opponent in the State Council, Speranksii, had made other enemies at court and in March the Emperor had given in to political pressure and had exiled him to the Urals. The Emperor had always been impressed with Pavel's administrative abilities and his honesty; furthermore, since his return from France, Pavel had shown a new docility and a reawakened zeal for service. Largely German himself, the Emperor found it easier to place confidence in Pavel's Teutonic thoroughness than in Kutuzov's more Slavonic approach. In April 1812, shortly before he left to join the army in Vilnius, the Emperor revealed his ambitions to Pavel and in the course of a long audience decided that Pavel should replace Kutuzov as commander of the army of the Danube. Pavel's first objective was to speed up the signing of the armistice and to persuade the Turks to join an alliance with Russia, but after that a huge panorama unfolded, in which Slavonic Christians from the Balkans would rise up and join their Russian brothers in a march against Austria and France. All the details of these extraordinary plans are outlined in full in a letter of 9 April 1812 from the Emperor, in which Pavel is addressed as the commander of the army of the Danube and the Black Sea fleet.[12]

The Emperor's plans and Pavel's appointment were meant to be completely secret, but they soon leaked out. Nesselrode's new wife, who was the daughter of Pavel's old friend, Gur'ev, wrote to her husband about it only four days later:

> You imagine, perhaps, that I am enjoying the agreeable society of Tchitchagof? Not at all, my good friend. He is leaving next week, not for Vilnius but for far further. He will salute His Highness and try to make a close friend of him; he has very great and full powers, and if he cannot come to agreement in the place where the negotiations are taking place [Bucharest], he has been ordered to continue to the capital [Constantinople]. He is taking a great retinue with him, and so that he may enjoy his pleasures in an oriental style, he has been gratified with fifty thousand roubles and three thousand ducats. He has earned the honour of this mission through an amusing intrigue; the person who is bringing you my portrait will tell it to you, ask him to.[13]

The 'intrigue' to which Marie Nesselrode refers probably included Pavel's explosion of temper with Rumiantsev, who had been ordered by the Emperor to furnish Pavel with all the necessary information and documents concerning the negotiations which Kutuzov was holding with the Turks in Bucharest. Accounts of their altercation resounded around the capital and were repeated by de Maistre to his government:

> This nomination was kept extremely secret. One knew, however, that the Admiral had had a terrible scene with the Chancellor, and that, in the course of this tender conversation, the word *treason* escaped from him; at least that is what is believed. The Chancellor omitted to give the Admiral certain papers, and as he left here first, he sent an order from Vilnius halting Kutuzov, with new instructions relative to his original powers, and a warning saying that *if he did not sign the peace on the spot, it would shortly be signed by Admiral Tchitchagoff who was on the heels of the courier.* . . . It seems impossible to me that this business will not have repercussions.[14]

Another rumour suggests that Kutuzov was warned of his approaching fall from grace by his wife.

Pavel made hasty preparations for his departure. In accordance with the Emperor's Byzantine aspirations, he invited the Sturdzas, father and son, to join his staff. The Sturdzas were not only of Phanariot Greek origin but also closely linked with the powerful Morousi family in Moldavia.* Pavel also obtained Rumiantsev's permission to detach a

---

* The principal Greek families living in Constantinople under Turkish rule were named

brilliant young Corfiote named Capodistrias from the Russian Embassy in Vienna to be the head of his diplomatic chancellery. Apart from his new military responsibilities, Pavel had to make arrangements for his children. Beatrice Cunningham, whose husband was now comfortably established as the commissioner at the dockyards of Deptford and Woolwich, had agreed to receive the three Chichagov girls. However their transportation to England would have to wait until friendly relations were more formally re-established. It was not until mid-July that Rumiantsev was able to give Pavel the go-ahead:

> You do not need to await the signature of the peace to send your children to England. His Majesty has already given his consent, so have the goodness either to send them to Sweden, from where they can embark, or to inform me what other means are to your liking. . . . I will ask Monsieur your brother, if he is in St Petersburg, or some other person whom you consider suitable, to do me the honour of addressing himself to me to ask me for the passports, so that I may know the names of your children and those of the people who will accompany them.[15]

No further details survive of the Chichagov girls' journey to England, but from other references in Rumiantsev's letter, it seems possible that they were transported during the movements, of which Pavel's brother was put in charge, that accompanied the restitution to Russia of Seniavin's fleet.

Pavel reached Bucharest to find that Kutuzov had already concluded the negotiations. Without hesitation, Pavel stepped aside and let him take the credit. In his memoirs, which recommence with the period after his return from Paris, he expresses no disappointment – although Kutuzov was heaped with honours and created a Prince. Kutuzov, however, smarted under the humiliation of Pavel's largesse.

On 24 June 1812, Napoleon's 'Grande Armée' crossed the Neman. The war with France had begun. Seton-Watson calculates that, counting later reinforcements, the army eventually numbered 600,000 men.[16] The troops were composed of Poles, Germans, Italians, Spanish, Portuguese and Croats. Only just over a third were French. Four days later,

the Phanariots, after the Phanar (lighthouse) quarter of the city where they lived. During the period 1711–1821 members of these families were appointed hospodars, or governors, of the Danubian states of Moldavia and Wallachia, then vassal states of the Ottoman Empire. This period of Romanian history is therefore known as the Phanariot period.

Napoleon was in Vilnius, which the Russian Emperor had evacuated a week earlier, and the Napoleonic armies began to move eastwards. The Russians had four smaller armies and ahead of the French two of these, commanded by Barclay de Tolly and the Georgian general Bagration respectively, retired with the intention of uniting in the interior. The third Russian army, under the command of Tormasov, was stationed to the west as a protection against the Austrians, and the fourth was under the command of Pavel in Romania.

Throughout the summer, although both sides had detached forces to the north, Napoleon's main army was drawn deeper and deeper into Russian territory. The Emperor continued to correspond with Pavel, declaring that 'my confidence in you, in your genius and your talents, is very great, and I have no doubt that you will justify it.'[17] Pavel, meanwhile, applied himself with his usual thoroughness to the tasks that had been set him. In the view of many Russians, the Treaty of Bucharest was overgenerous to Turkey. Russia was thereby obliged to give up Wallachia and only retained the eastern part of Moldavia, now known as Bessarabia, but the Sultan still procrastinated for many weeks before giving his ratification. At the same time it became apparent that the Turks would never enter into a military alliance that would permit the Russians to raise an army from the Slavonic population of the Balkans. Unlike Kutuzov, Pavel was a man of action, who found these protracted oriental negotiations frustrating in the extreme, and only the firm veto of the Emperor prevented him from trying to force the hand of the Sultan by marching on Constantinople.

By August, the whole grandiose project in the Balkans had to be abandoned. Pavel received instructions from the Emperor to bring up his army to reinforce Tormasov, as Tormasov was being pressed by a French army under General Reynier which had been sent to support the Austrians. Pavel installed the elder Sturdza as Governor of Bessarabia and on 25 August he left Bucharest. Meanwhile, many miles to the north-east of him, after a fierce engagement at Smolensk, the two main Russian armies continued to retire before the French and public feeling was turning against the Commander-in-Chief, Barclay de Tolly, whose foreign extraction had always been a disadvantage. Bowing to popular pressure, the Emperor recalled Kutuzov to replace Barclay de Tolly. The battle which Napoleon had so long awaited finally took place on 7 September at the village of Borodino, not far from Moscow. But despite huge loss of life on both sides, there was no clear-cut victory. After the battle, the Russian army retired, leaving Moscow undefended, and by 15 September Napoleon had taken up his lodgings in the Kremlin. To his astonishment, he found Moscow all but abandoned and within two days a devastating fire, whose origins have never been established, destroyed two thirds of the city and deprived the French of the winter rations on which they had counted. The handsome mansions of the old nobility were reduced to blackened ruins and of Moscow's three hundred churches, the gilded domes of the Kremlin were amongst the few that survived.

Pavel's sudden transformation from admiral to military commander raised some eyebrows in St Petersburg, but most people had only the vaguest idea that the Emperor's Balkan aspirations included a substantial naval element. Like the Empress Catherine, the Emperor envisaged that the Black Sea fleet would play an important role and he also hoped that there would be close co-ordination with the British navy in the Adriatic. For this and for the complex planning and organization of the operation, Pavel was entirely suitable, but what he could not possess was that instinct for military tactics which comes from personal experience. Pavel's expertise was in anchorages, winds and sails. He knew nothing of cavalry and, city-bred, he would not have had that 'eye for country' so vital in the choosing of ground in military operations.

While Napoleon waited in vain for the Russian Emperor to accept his proposals for peace negotiations, the army of the Danube had marched north and achieved its appointed junction with the army of Tormasov. Pavel took command of the combined force, which succeeded in pushing the Austrian army, under the command of Prince Schwarzenberg, back into Poland. As the days passed, however, fears of a French advance on St Petersburg were beginning to spread. Questions were raised about the prolonged absence of the third and fourth armies from the main theatre of war and sharp tongues mocked the naval origins of their commander: 'The Admiral has no wind,' 'he is at anchor' and 'the wind is against him.' Even Vorontsov voiced doubts: 'In spite of the honourable principles, the courage and the activity of our friend Pavel Vasil'evich, I doubt that he can become a skilful military general all of a sudden, having spent all his life in the service of the navy.'[18]

At a time when the enemy had penetrated deeply into Russian territory, the threat presented by the disaffected population of Poland and by the Austrian forces was not fully appreciated, nor the service that Pavel's army rendered in ensuring that Schwarzenberg's forces never rejoined Napoleon. By 19 October, Napoleon had implemented his decision to retire the troops from Moscow. Peace was not forthcoming, his lines of communication were overextended and there was not enough food. Although the season was far advanced, a spell of unusually fine weather lulled him into thinking that he could brave the Russian winter, but within days, Kutuzov's army to the south had prevented him from taking his chosen route and the French forces were obliged to retrace their steps past the corpses of their countrymen and the burnt-out cities through which they had already passed.

The progress of the retreating army was hindered by a huge quantity of booty and the great number of camp followers. As sickness and hunger took their toll, the closely formed columns dissolved into long lines of stragglers, which were continually attacked by small groups of peasants and Cossacks. Hideous acts of savagery took place – on both sides. The weather became bitterly cold and by the night of 6 November it was -25°C and the snow was falling heavily. Frozen and starving, the army and its followers were reduced to a diet of horse meat. The horses had been rendered virtually useless for transport by the absence of studded shoes to prevent them slipping on the ice. When Napoleon reached Smolensk on 8 November, he found that most of the stores he had left there had already been consumed by the reserve French army that had preceded him. Violence and plundering broke out. There was no choice but to continue the retreat. Throughout, their rearguard was under constant attack from the pursuing army of Kutuzov. From the north, Wittgenstein, with an army earlier detached by Kutuzov, was closing in fast; in the south, Pavel's army was approaching Minsk and was well on its way to block the crossing of the River Berezina. The Grande Armée was caught in a trap.

In June the Emperor had been persuaded to give up the supreme command of the armies in the field. However, he continued to send instructions to Pavel, while urging him to co-operate closely with the other commanders. Pavel's instructions from the Emperor were very clear. Once his and Tormasov's armies had cut off Schwarzenberg, he was to rush to Minsk and from there to move on at top speed to the town of Borisov, on the Berezina, which lay across the main route of the retreating army. He was to establish a position there, making an entrenched camp and fortifying the banks of the river to north and south to prevent the enemy from crossing it. Since his army would shortly be united with the commands of Generals Wittgenstein, Steingell and Härtell, some of his troops should be left to reinforce the army under the command of

General Sacken, in order to keep the Austrians at bay. The Emperor was very confident that the proposed operation would bring about the destruction of Napoleon's army and he specified that while the troops of conquered nations such as the Saxons and the Prussians should be allowed to retreat, 'the French should all be killed to the last man.'[19]

In St Petersburg the Emperor's optimism was echoed by his wife in a letter to her mother:

> The French army is in the neighbourhood of Smolensk. Wittgenstein, our hero (and the one who has done the most in this war), is to the right, the Grande Armée is to the left, and in front, the army of Tchitchagoff is barring the route. If you take a look at the map, you can easily work out this position and judge that it would be quite impossible for Napoleon not to be captured in person; but as for that, I do not believe it, for in some way or other, he will find a means of saving his precious self. [20]

The letters received by Nesselrode from his colleague, d'Anstedt, typify the universally high hopes that were held of Pavel: 'If Tchitchagof can push his success a bit further and manage to release Bobruisk, what a brilliant combination of movements for the outcome of the campaign.'[21] 'What a superb battle General Chichagov should make on his side, if his movements are well devised.'[22] From St Petersburg, Nikolai Longinov, another ex-member of his London staff, wrote to Vorontsov about the engagements between Wittgenstein and Napoleon's reserve army under General Victor: 'It is believed that he [Victor] will turn his advance, supported by other troops from the Smolensk side, towards Minsk, and that Admiral Tchitchagow will be attacked in this way by all the forces of Bonaparte. But no one, however, fears for his army, which is composed of such good troops and commanded by such good generals.'[23]

Minsk, which was in enemy hands, was of great strategic importance, because it contained Napoleon's last remaining food supplies. On 16 November, Pavel's troops marched victoriously into Minsk and deprived the French of the vast warehouses on which they had been counting. By 21 November, they had captured the vital bridgehead at Borisov and had crossed the bridge to take possession of the town. A sudden spell of milder weather disposed events still further in favour of the Russians. The ice that normally at this time of year removed the obstacle presented by the river and its surrounding marshlands had not struck. Without access to a bridge, the Berezina remained a formidable barrier. Pavel established his headquarters on the east bank and sent a small advance guard forward to reconnoitre the position of the French, while he awaited the imminent arrival of Wittgenstein and Kutuzov.

At this point, all the signs were propitious and the optimism in St Petersburg seemed well founded. What most observers had overlooked, however, was that the army which Pavel brought to the Berezina was very much smaller than the 35,000 men who had marched from Romania. The junction with Tormasov had swelled its ranks to 70,000, but Pavel had left more than half of this force behind to contain Schwarzenberg. The union that the Emperor had anticipated with the troops of Wittgenstein, Steingell and Härtell had not taken place. Thus, according to Pavel, when the large number of wounded and sick had been accounted for, the number of fighting men that he brought to the Berezina was only around 20,000, of whom 9,000 were cavalry.

What occurred next and over the following days is one of the most disputed episodes of the fatal retreat from Moscow. Generations of historians have tried to apportion the blame to one side or the other. Tolstoy makes a masterly judgement from the Russian point of view:

> Any plan of cutting off and capturing Napoleon and his army, however carefully thought out, would have been like the action of a gardener who, after driving out a herd of cattle that had been trampling his beds, should run out to belabour the cattle about the head. . . . And besides being absurd, to cut off the retreat of Napoleon's army was also impossible.
>
> It was impossible, in the first place, because . . . the probability that Tchitchagov, Kutuzov, and Wittgenstein would all reach an appointed spot in time was so remote that it practically amounted to impossibility. . . . Secondly, it was impossible, because to paralyse the force of inertia with which Napoleon's army was rebounding back along its track, incomparably greater forces were needed than those the Russians had at their command. . . .
>
> The Russian soldiers did all that could or ought to have been done to attain an end worthy of the people, and half of them died doing it. They are not to blame because other Russians, sitting in warm rooms at home, proposed that they should do the impossible.[24]

The headlong pace of the French retreat had exceeded all Pavel's calculations. Just outside Borisov, his small advance guard collided with the first columns of the Grande Armée under Oudinot and were pushed back to Borisov in confusion. Pavel's only engineer had been wounded during the battle for the bridgehead and there had not been time to entrench their position as instructed. While, therefore, Pavel's artillery was able to cover their retreat, his troops were forced back over the long, narrow bridge. During the crossing a quantity of baggage and several hundred men were lost. Once on the west bank, the troops consolidated their position and destroyed their side of the bridge. Opposite them, the French took possession of Borisov. All through the following days and nights, the huge, desperate mass of the Napoleonic army poured into Borisov. Alone on the other bank stood Pavel – most of his 9,000 cavalry immobilized by the surrounding swamps and forests – with 11,000 men. From his rear, came disturbing rumours of an advance by Schwarzenberg.

Estimates of the number of French troops vary wildly. Seton-Watson suggests that by the time Napoleon was approaching the Berezina his fighting troops had been reduced to 20,000, but that on reuniting with his reserves under Victor and Oudinot, he had about 30,000.[25] A contemporary French account by Guillaume de Vaudoncourt suggests 80,000,[26] while the Marquis de Chambray's figures are more in line with Seton-Watson's.[27] But de Chambray also mentions that the number of military stragglers was almost equal to that of the combatants. Napoleon's army doubtless also gave the impression of being larger than it was, because of its great band of camp followers. Including these, the grand total was probably close to Pavel's reckoning, which was 70,000.

Throughout 23 November, Pavel scanned the opposite banks, where a confused and growing mass of troops and camp followers moved in the smoke of huge campfires. When darkness fell, the light from the many enemy bivouacs illuminated great areas of the night sky. Since there was still no sign of either Wittgenstein or Kutuzov, Pavel's mind was constantly occupied with how he might hold off the enemy until support arrived. His main forces were still opposite Borisov, but he placed a line of troops for some distance to either side in order to report on any attempted crossing. He also detached a force of 4,000 men, who were sent north to guard the road to Zembin, not far from the shallow crossing at Studianka, while another detachment with some of the cavalry went south. During the long hours of waiting, Pavel consulted with his officers. They had few maps and no one could predict the number of the enemy nor where they would cross. But a sudden flurry of messages from Kutuzov and Wittgenstein and rumours of movements by Schwarzenberg suggested to Pavel that the French might have diverted from the main route to cross the river several miles to the south. Acting on this information, on 24 November Pavel left the position opposite Borisov strongly defended under the command of one of his officers and

213

marched southwards with a detachment. That evening a scout delivered a message from Wittgenstein, announcing that he was joining up with Kutuzov's main army behind the French. Pavel's reply pressing him to stick to the original plan never reached him.

On 25 November, Pavel received information of an attempted crossing at Ukoloda, between his new headquarters and the original bridgehead opposite Borisov. Although this proved later in the day to have been a false alarm, Pavel had already dispatched a force. Early on the morning of 26 November, however, a series of urgent messages reached Pavel that the enemy was making a serious crossing at the most northern part of the line, near the village of Studianka. During the previous night Tcharplitz, the commander of Pavel's northern detachment, had observed a massing of the enemy and had sent 300 Cossacks to swim their horses across the river and take prisoners, who would give further information. The local village headman was captured and told Tcharplitz, at one in the morning, that the French were preparing to construct two bridges.

Napoleon had arrived at Borisov late in the afternoon of 25 November and had taken the decision to cross at Studianka. Earlier in the day a party of engineers had created the diversion, which was initially reported to Pavel, but once darkness fell and throughout the night of 25/26 November, the bridge-building team worked frantically at Studianka to assemble material for the two bridges – a light one for infantry and cavalry and a stronger one for wagons and cannons. At 7 a.m. Napoleon himself arrived at the site. Inspired by his presence, the pontoneers redoubled their efforts and worked breast-high in the icy water to finish the first bridge by one o'clock. From first light, Tcharplitz's troops had been able to fire on the men working in the river, but before long the French had installed a powerful battery on the crest of the hill above Studianka, which raked Tcharplitz's position and obliged him to retreat. Things were moving fast. Even before the completion of the bridges, the French had secured a bridgehead by crossing on horses and rafts. As soon as the first bridge was complete, Oudinot crossed it with his troops and launched into an attack on the scanty Russian defences; by four o'clock Napoleon was able to send cannons and wagons over the second one. As he regained his quarters opposite Borisov in the evening of 26 November, Pavel could hear the thunder of the French artillery at Studianka.

All through the night of 26/27 November, French troops poured across the two bridges. The bridge for vehicles collapsed twice and was

out of action for several hours on each occasion. Many of the pontoneers who struggled to repair it later died of exposure, for the
weather had again become bitterly cold and the river was full of ice
floes. On 27 November Pavel arrived at the village of Stakova, a few
miles from the crossing, to which Tcharplitz had withdrawn. Close to
the scene of action, he realized that his march south had cost him dear.
The bridges were already well defended. The moment for attack had
been twenty-four hours earlier. Surveying the terrain, he saw only two
choices: either he must attack now with the force that had accompanied
him, or he must postpone action till the next morning, when he could
make a more effective stand by reuniting troops dispersed along the
riverbanks. Pavel took the latter decision and even as he was taking it,
unbeknown to him, Napoleon, mounted on a horse and accompanied by
the Imperial Guard, was crossing the bridge. By late in the afternoon,
a huge number of stragglers and camp followers with their baggage
trains had poured into Studianka and order began to break down. The
vehicle bridge was once more out of action for two hours and as the
crowd grew denser, the situation grew increasingly ugly. Dangerous
fights broke out and it was only by force that a passage was maintained
for artillery and combatants.

Pavel returned at once to the bridgehead at Borisov to marshal his
troops and as night fell, his ears suddenly caught, far away across the
Berezina behind the enemy lines, the distant roar of guns. The army of
Wittgenstein had at last arrived. A short time later Pavel heard the
sound of a second battery on the other side of the river, which
announced the arrival of Platov and his Cossacks. During the night
couriers passed between the two armies. Pavel told Wittgenstein of his
planned attack at dawn and requested a detachment of two divisions of
infantry. He also asked Wittgenstein to harry the French rearguard.
From another courier Pavel learnt that Kutuzov was still at six days'
march. At first light, Tcharplitz attacked. By eight o'clock Pavel had
joined him with the rest of his forces and throughout the day a furious
battle raged in the forest around Stakova. The French, against all the
odds, succeeded in making a heroic cavalry charge in a forest clearing,
while the legendary French surgeon, Larrey, moved his operating table,
made from the trunk of a tree, from one side of the river to the other.
Later in the day Pavel was joined by Platov, who contributed several
regiments of Cossacks to his force. At two o'clock in the afternoon
Wittgenstein made a call on Pavel, but he brought none of the sorely

needed reinforcements of infantry. His troops remained on the left bank of the river, where they had begun to engage the rearguard of the French.

The approach of Wittgenstein's army increased the desperation of those who were still waiting to cross the river. Up to now, it had been possible to exert some control over the access to the bridges, but as the members of the closely packed crowd found themselves within range of the Russian guns, panic broke out and many made a mad rush for the bridges. In the stampede, hundreds were trampled under foot or were pushed to their deaths into the freezing waters of the Berezina. Once darkness fell and the artillery ceased, the alarm subsided and some sort of order was restored. Victor, who was commanding the rearguard, was able to evacuate his troops over the river, but a large crowd still remained, mostly composed of the wounded, the ill, domestic servants, provision sellers and fugitive families, many of whom were in a state of stunned apathy. Instead of taking advantage of the lull that followed Victor's evacuation, they huddled miserably around their campfires and refused to stir. It was only at 5 a.m., when the news began to spread that Napoleon had given instructions for the bridges to be destroyed, that a fresh wave of panic swept through the crowd. In the short interval that remained before the burning of the bridges at 8.30 a.m., there was a second stampede, in which many men, women and children met a similar fate to those who had tried to cross the previous afternoon. Shortly afterwards Platov's Cossacks arrived to take their booty and to capture the survivors. They left behind them a scene of indescribable carnage. Pavel passed the night in a peasant cabin on the west bank, but he slept little, for throughout the night he could hear the anguished groaning of the large number of French troops that had been stripped naked by the Cossacks on his side of the river and were freezing to death.

The following morning, Pavel's army set off in hot pursuit of the remaining French. Ice had covered the marshes that would have impeded their progress, but in any case Tcharplitz had failed to remove the bridges over them. The route along which the pursuing army passed was littered with the bodies of starving, frozen men, who were dying like flies. At the little town of Smorgoni, between Minsk and Vilnius, Napoleon departed with Caulaincourt and fled to Paris, where there was disturbing news of a conspiracy. He went incognito and was accompanied only by a small retinue, which included his Mameluke bodyguard, Rustam. Throughout this extraordinary journey tête-à-tête, Napoleon talked continually to Caulaincourt, who later recorded his comments: 'So what did Kutusof do?

He compromised his army on the Moscow river [at Borodino] which led to the burning of Moscow. During the retreat when he had no one to fight but inanimate bodies and walking spectres, what did he do? He and Wittgenstein allowed the Admiral to be crushed. All the other Russian generals are worth more than that old dowager Kutusof.'[28]

On 10 December Pavel's troops entered Vilnius and fought a heated engagement with the retiring French – Tolstoy portrays Pavel 'wearing a naval uniform with a dirk, and holding his forage cap under his arm',[29] handing the keys of the city to Kutuzov. By 14 December, only 5,000 French troops, which was all that officially remained of those who had taken the road to Borisov, crossed the Neman into Prussia. Further groups of stragglers, Reynier's army and the troops based at Riga escaped over the following weeks, but historians have calculated that out of the 600,000 enemy troops that were deployed in the Russian campaign, only one sixth survived. Had the Grande Armée succeeded in crossing the Berezina unopposed and in wintering in Minsk as Napoleon had originally planned, the course of history might have been very different.

Casualties had also been very heavy on the Russian side and the horrors that Pavel had witnessed exacerbated his impatience with the Russian leadership, which he later voiced in a letter to Vorontsov: 'The poor good Russian soldier, what could one not do with him, if he were only passably led? But he is sacrificed and exterminated by all the means that inexhaustible ignorance can add to disorder.'[30] Pavel continued to grieve for Elizabeth. In December he learned that Vorontsov and Katinka had been to visit his daughters and he once again pours out his heart in a letter:

> The welcome that you and Lady Pembroke gave to my children reflects even more on the angel for whom I shall mourn as long as my miserable existence endures, because you had not yet received my letter about them. . . . Why have I brought about her misfortune and theirs, and above all my own? What a dreadful situation, my beloved father! I implore you not to speak to me of consolation. It can never exist for me. Sorrow, tears and remorse to my last sigh: that is my lot. I have placed the poor children as well as they can possibly be. . . .
>
> The visit that you hastened to make to see your granddaughters, and the welcome that you gave them, all pierce and rend my soul. . . . Everything wounds me, everything causes me to shed tears of sorrow and remorse. Miserable creature that I am! How can I accept the possibility of being comforted when she foresaw everything, predicted everything, sacrificed

217

everything, even though it was a question of her life? When she never uttered a reproach, except against the complaints that I made against Providence to see her suffering so cruelly? I only exist to be punished, my beloved father, and it can never be long or hard enough. . . . My friends, my brothers, even these children, poor and innocent victims, should only serve to perpetuate my sorrow. I have made my vows. The children are in England. She commanded this, so it could not be otherwise. At the first possible opportunity, I shall bring her there and consequently it is in England that I shall die. I will establish myself close to her and I shall always stay there. A few moments will be sacrificed to see my children; I will come and shed tears with you, because you understand me, but I will not be importunate, because I do not want to disturb your happiness. This is my destiny, will it be for long?

He touches only briefly on a matter that was to become a second source of terrible unhappiness: 'However, as I did not capture Napoleon in person, I believe that they will not be pleased with me; but since there have been the best possible results, I am consoling myself about this, and if this will enable me to retire again, that is what would suit me best.'[31]

At Vilnius Kutuzov imposed a period of inactivity on Pavel, who was raring to pursue the French. The Emperor had rejoined the army and shared Pavel's sentiments, but he was a shrewd enough politician to realize that he must impose his opinions diplomatically on Kutuzov, the idol of the troops. Pavel's and Kutuzov's diametrically opposed views on warfare would have strained their relationship, even without the aggravation of Pavel's usurpation at Bucharest, but there is a further incident, which Pavel glosses over in his memoirs. In early September, when Napoleon was threatening Moscow, first Tormasov and then Pavel received urgent instructions from Kutuzov to abandon the pursuit of Schwarzenberg and to come to his aid. Both commanders – who, at forty-five days' march from Moscow, were far further west than Kutuzov realized – ignored this appeal and proceeded with their joint operation. This act of disobedience doubtless exacerbated Kutuzov's dislike of Pavel and gave rise to the malicious jokes in St Petersburg about his naval background.

In the early days of 1813, when Kutuzov's influence was at its height, the whispering campaign against Pavel augmented. Apart from Kutuzov, Pavel's many enemies at court – those men 'sitting in warm rooms at home' – seized upon his failure to capture Napoleon as a pretext to make him an object of mockery and disgrace. There were even some who suggested that he was a traitor, citing his frequent outbursts against Russia as evidence and referring darkly to his widely publicized admiration for Napoleon. He became the butt of jokes and he was unflatteringly depicted by Krylov in a fable about the Berezina.[32] In February 1813 Longinov was unwise enough to repeat some of the gossip to Vorontsov:

> The Marshal [Kutuzov], as Commander-in-Chief of the Army, commands everyone and everything. This did not prevent Mr Chichagov, full of boundless presumption, from disobeying his orders at the Berezina by placing himself on the opposite bank to the one that was prescribed by the Marshal. The Emperor is too good to punish such an error, which in the army is generally mitigated by the gallantry and steadfastness of character shown in a difficult undertaking and is forgotten when the outcome is successful. Your Excellency will see, however, how dangerous it is to have a man like Chichagov under one's orders, who argues from the viewpoint of an admiral about things that he does not understand (he proved this by his march on Borisov, which he did at his own whim, without taking advice from anyone) and who is capable of disobeying orders when they should be followed to the letter. Now that the Emperor himself is with the army, but still leaves all the honours and decisions to the Marshal, I believe that Chichagov is more tractable.[33]

Longinov got a very dusty reply from Vorontsov, but the Emperor never gave Pavel the public vindication he craved. For Pavel, the injustice and growing humiliation of his position, combined with his continuing sorrow over the loss of Elizabeth, were becoming unbearable. After a brief incursion with his army in January into Prussian-held territories, he resigned his command and retired to St Petersburg. Vorontsov endeavoured to dissuade him from retirement, arguing that he was playing into the hands of his enemies, who would have calculated on his thin skin to achieve their aims. He tried to make Pavel take a more robust view of his situation: 'You ask me: "Why have I got enemies, I have never harmed anyone?" You must have enemies at our court as you would have them in any court in the world where you went to live. A man of talent, probity, candour and high principles is a menace, who will never be countenanced by the courtiers, kingmakers and schemers of any court.'[34]

If Pavel had possessed a different temperament, he might have weathered the storm. By April Kutuzov was dead and Russian and allied troops were campaigning across Europe. In October the French were decisively beaten at Leipzig and less than six months later, on 30 March

1814, the Emperors of Russia and Prussia rode side by side into Paris. But Pavel was too full of his misery over Elizabeth and his anger over the misrepresentations of what happened on the Berezina to listen to the advice of his greatest ally. While winter lasted, he spent his days in a small apartment in the city brooding over the past, the betrayals of Wittgenstein and Kutuzov and the pusillanimity of the Emperor. Throughout 1813, his letters to Vorontsov continued to rehearse the events on the Berezina and above all to lament the loss of Elizabeth. Vorontsov used every means in his power to shake Pavel out of his depression.

> The despair that continues to possess you on the subject of the misfortune which you have had in losing your wife does not conform to the character of the steadfast and reasonable man that I know you to be. Without doubt the loss which you have had is great, even irreparable. This is why you must pull yourself together and learn how to master your emotions, to reason with yourself, to think about what your wife would expect of you and to accomplish her ideas and wishes: for there is no doubt that on dying she took with her the sweet consolation that your children, the precious pledges of your mutual love, would be cared for, and that you would preserve your days in order to consecrate them to the education of these dear children. I would never have believed that you were unable to bear a misfortune, however great. It is shameful of you to desire death: it is cowardice not to know how to bear life, above all when a sacred duty, the wishes of your wife, that which you owe to her memory and to your children, imposes on you the obligation to conserve yourself. Be a man, as you were formerly, and accustom yourself to bear the irrevocable decrees of Providence with a resignation that is worthy of a man.[35]

Vorontzov's rebukes sprang from genuine concern and affection, but de Maistre was less loyal, now that Pavel had become a social outcast. To him the service of one's king was an article of faith, for which he had spent many lonely years in Russia, and his missionary zeal was severely affronted by Pavel's second abdication from public life. De Maistre did not conceal his impatience from the sharp-tongued Miss Sturdza – who had never cared for Pavel: 'What talents, what real virtues, wasted through I do not know what demented and incurable pride.'[36] Nor did he find Pavel good company and visiting him became nothing but a duty: 'He has helped me, he loves me, he is unhappy; that suffices: I will never cease to comfort him like a sick man.'[37] In his darkest hours, Pavel was often alone. The Emperor took some time to agree to Pavel's request to

leave for England and while he was waiting, Pavel passed his days preparing an elaborate mausoleum for Elizabeth, which was erected in the
cemetery. Over the entrance he placed the inscription, which, like all the
wording, is in English: 'My Bliss for ever I have buried here the 24 of
July 1811.' He decorated the top of the monument with an oval, containing Elizabeth's portrait in bas-relief. Below it leans a sorrowful, male
figure, who holds a book in his hand. At the bottom is a sleeping lion.
Beneath the portrait are two hearts, one black and one white, which are
joined by a red thread. On the white heart is inscribed 'My only
Treasure' and on the black 'Poorest P[aul]'. The book which the man is
holding is entitled 'My Journal E. C.' On the granite slab that forms the
base are the following lines:

> *Ceaseless sorrow*
> > *Elizabeth*
> *O! The tender ties close twisted with the fibres of the heart,*
> *Which broken, break them and drain the soul*
> *Of human joy, and make it pain to live,*
> *And is it then to live when such friends [are] far?*
> *Tis the survivor dies.*

Pavel finally received permission to leave St Petersburg and in 1814
he travelled to England. True to his word, however, he did not leave
Elizabeth in Russia. He went to Beddington and placed her ashes in the
country church where fifteen years earlier he and she had first embarked
on their fleeting portion of earthly happiness.

# Epilogue

Pavel never returned to Russia and it took him many years to come to terms with Elizabeth's death. Initially he spent a restless period in England, where the constant memories of their courtship only exacerbated his depression, but in 1816 he embarked on a series of journeys across Europe in search of health and peace of mind. These culminated in prolonged sojourns in Florence and Rome, where his brother, Vasilii, joined him. Meanwhile the three girls remained in England in the care of the Cunninghams and it was not until 1818, when he finally settled in Paris, that Pavel decided that he wished to be reunited with his children.

In an attempt to fill the void left by Elizabeth, Pavel had flung himself into a hectic round of social engagements and amusements. From his correspondence with Vorontsov at this time, it is clear that both Vorontsov and the Cunninghams had doubts about the suitability of Pavel's Parisian ménage for three young girls. Thus initially it was only the 17-year-old Adèle who joined her father in Paris, and Pavel enjoyed taking her to the opera and into society, where her interesting manner and lively wit drew favourable comment. Later on, Julie and Catherine also came to France, but for Pavel the joys of family life began to pall, when first Adèle and then Julie fell in love with men of whom he did not approve.

In 1821 Adèle married a Frenchman, the 20-year-old Baron de St Martin, by whom she had a son, Paul-Émile. However, the couple separated after less than four years and there is no further reference to the child, who must have died in infancy. In 1822 Julie also married a Frenchman, Comte Henri de Crouÿ-Chanel, whose family was of Hungarian origin. Pavel's comments on Henri are every bit as disparaging as those made about him by Charles Proby. 'The second [daughter], a good and gentle victim, has fallen into the most despicable hands, an ignorant braggart and without education, false, grasping, deceitful.'[1] When Julie told her father that Henri was a loving and tender husband, Pavel remarked sourly that this was 'because he is hoping to inherit something after my death'.[2] But the marriage appears to have been happy and fruitful, and although she predeceased her father, Julie was survived by four sons, Frédéric, Charles, Gustave and William, and by a daughter, Henriette. Frédéric and Gustave are the progenitors of the only known descendants of Pavel and Elizabeth alive today and it is therefore through Julie, the tiny premature baby who was not expected to live, that the line has survived and continues to flourish in France to this day.

Catherine, the youngest, was the only one of Pavel's daughters who retained his complete approval throughout her life. He describes her as a 'model of gentleness and docility. She is very talented and scrupulously attentive in fulfilling all her duties, even the most minor. She knows everything that a girl of her age could have learnt about the principles of language and literature, she is an accomplished musician, without having a feeling for music, and she enjoys painting, for which she has a great aptitude.'[3] But despite her father's pride in her attainments, Catherine took rather longer than her sisters to marry. It was not until January 1838, aged 30, that she married Colonel Charles-Marie Naudet, who died just over a year later at the age 52. They had no children. Six years later Catherine remarried. This time her husband was a naval officer named Comte Eugène du Bouzet. Once again there were no children and during the long periods that her husband spent at sea, Catherine devoted much of her attention to her father.

Pavel's fiery temperament mellowed very little with age and he persisted in his love of argument. In the early days of the Bourbon restoration, Paris was full of foreigners, including many members of the Russian nobility. Pavel associated with such people as Count Feodor Rostopchin, the erstwhile Governor of Moscow, who had been obliged to leave Russia because many people believed that he had been responsible for the burning of Moscow in 1812. Rostopchin's letters are sprinkled with references to Pavel and to a social circle full of familiar names like Orlov, Shcherbatov, Narishkin and Demidov – all Russians who were either living in or passing through Paris at this time. But for all his immersion in the distractions of Parisian life, Pavel's letters betray a sense of emptiness. After the episode at the Berezina, he seems to have entered a twilight world from which he never escaped. The growing darkness was also physical, for as early as 1818 Pavel was having trouble with his eyes, and this was beginning to interfere with his ability to read and write.

In 1822 Pavel purchased a charming house and property in the little town of Sceaux, a few miles to the south of Paris.* Here, at last, he found a measure of peace and dreamed of cultivating his garden. His visits to Paris grew rarer and his dislike of the French, which had originally

---

* 7 rue Houdan, still known locally as 'le domaine de l'amiral'.

surfaced during his first visit with Elizabeth, re-emerged. 'I like the countryside so much that I plan to spend nine months of the year there. . . . In an hour I can be in Paris or bring from there whatever I need. Most of the amusements of that city no longer attract me; I have abandoned politics, and as for new acquaintances amongst the French, I find that each new contact only brings new inconveniences and regrets. I seek only foreigners and to keep my old friends.'[4]

Still deeply wounded by the aftermath of the engagements at the Berezina, Pavel had no inclination to return to Russia. However, he continued to receive a handsome pension from the Emperor. In 1825, on the premature death of the Emperor Alexander, Pavel wrote to his successor and was assured by the new Emperor, Nicholas, that he intended to respect his late brother's wishes with regard to Pavel's pension. Nine years later, however, an imperial ukase was issued that threatened to relieve all expatriate Russians of their titles and possessions if they did not return to their homeland. Initially Pavel may have genuinely believed that he was exempted from this stricture through his close relationship with the previous Emperor, but he soon discovered his mistake. After an acrimonious exchange of letters with the Emperor Nicholas, Pavel was deprived of his rank and privileges and was dismissed from imperial service by ukase. His pension and his Russian properties were confiscated, leaving him with few resources.

Pavel's response was typically violent and he took a step which deeply shocked his compatriots. He renounced his Russian nationality and in February 1836 both he and Catherine, professing the Protestant faith and their loyalty and fidelity to the King of England, became naturalized subjects of the United Kingdom. It was this action, rather than his mishaps on the Berezina, that placed Pavel, in the eyes of Russian history, beyond the pale and condemned him for ever to the ranks of the forgotten and the disgraced. To this day his portrait is conspicuously absent from the Gallery of 1812 in the Hermitage, while those of many who played far lesser roles than he did in the struggle against Napoleon are displayed. His importance in reorganizing the Russian navy is now acknowledged in most major Russian biographical dictionaries, but his biography has yet to be written.

By 1836 Pavel was completely blind and spent much of his time with his daughters. He had become reconciled with Adèle, who now lived in England. The Crouÿ-Chanels and their five children were also established in England and Julie died there in 1837. Pavel did not, however, sell the house at Sceaux until 1842 – perhaps because his brother, Vasilii, who had become his closest companion in widowhood, had died there in 1826 and was buried in the nearby cemetery. Pavel also owned a modest house in Brighton, at 12 Devonshire Place, and there is an endearing description of him in old age in *Eastern Europe and the Emperor Nicholas*, which was published in 1846:

> Well known to the inhabitants of Brighton, in which place he long resided, the Admiral is still living. Though deprived of his sight, he is in full possession of his intellectual faculties, – a venerable, intelligent, and plain-spoken old man.
>
> It must not be imagined either that he is one of those morose and disappointed cynics, who view the world and recall the past through the distorted medium of the soured and selfish feelings of a withered heart; – on the contrary, his romantic attachment to his first and only wife appears to have filled his existence with enduring and affectionate regret.[5]

This picture, however, is only partially true, for Pavel continued to feel great bitterness at his treatment by the Emperor Nicholas.

Throughout his long retirement one of Pavel's chief preoccupations was the writing of his memoirs. Among other things, he was determined to record the true version of what happened on the Berezina, although he was convinced his actions would eventually be justified by history. During Pavel's lifetime, his finest defence was written in 1813 by Joseph de Maistre in a dispatch to the King of Sardinia. This dispatch subsequently fell into both British and Russian hands and gives a version of events that not only corresponds closely with the evidence of history but also clearly points the finger at Kutuzov.[6] In 1817, Pavel published a paper in French relating to the action at the Berezina, a copy of which he sent to Lord Carysfort, together with an English translation, entitled *The Retreat of Napoleon*. It would seem also, from the rather garbled biographical details cited in *Eastern Europe and the Emperor Nicholas*, that its author had either seen or been told of certain sections of Pavel's memoirs. When he became blind, Pavel relied on his favourite daughter, Catherine du Bouzet, for help with his papers and he spent his final months with her in Paris.

On 10 September 1849, at the age of 82, Pavel died at Catherine's home in Paris.* He had outlived Elizabeth by thirty-eight years, but he

---

* 41 rue de la Ville l'Evêque.

cherished her memory to the end. In a letter addressed to his two surviving daughters two years earlier, he specifies that he wishes his coffin to be covered with the black velvet cloth that had been used for Elizabeth's funeral, which he had kept for this purpose. During his closing years, Pavel envisaged that he would die with his favourite daughter in France, and he therefore requested to be buried in the cemetery at Sceaux 'as close to my brother as possible'. Their two gravestones lie side by side under the shade of a spreading yew tree, with barely an inch between them.

Thanks to the ukase of the Emperor Nicholas, Pavel's worldly goods were few. In his letter, he leaves his desk to his son-in-law, Henri de Crouÿ-Chanel, his pistols to his four grandsons and his gold watch to Eugène du Bouzet. His manservant was to inherit his linen and his daughters were to decide what should be done with his books. His imperial decorations – the orders of St Alexander Nevsky, St Vladimir, St Anne and St George – were to be returned, together with his letters from Catherine the Great and the Emperor Alexander, to the Emperor Nicholas in St Petersburg. His formal will, which was drawn up in England just a few months before his death, makes lengthy provisions for his granddaughter, Henriette, including the stocks and securities that had been part of his marriage settlement with Elizabeth. But his chief legacy to his descendants was the huge, disordered pile of papers that comprised his memoirs and a love of argument.

Four years after Pavel's death, in late December 1853, Parisian society was titillated by the spectacle of a court case between the daughters of Admiral Chichagov. It was the talk of the town and its proceedings were reported in major French and German newspapers. On one side was Adèle, with three of her Crouÿ-Chanel nephews (Gustave alone refused to be involved) and their sister, Henriette. On the other was Catherine du Bouzet, defended by the celebrated Parisian lawyer, Monsieur Paillet. The dispute centred on the letters which Pavel had received from Catherine the Great and the Emperor Alexander and the possession of the manuscripts of his memoirs – which he had given to Catherine in 1846 and of which he makes no mention in either his letter of 1847 or his will of 1849. In accordance with her father's wishes, Catherine had already sent the signed letters of the Emperor Alexander back to St Petersburg, but her request to have one of them as a family memento had been graciously granted and three letters had been returned. The court ruled that these three letters should be distributed amongst the three branches of the family and that Adèle and the Crouÿ-

Chanels should receive the correspondence from Catherine the Great. Catherine du Bouzet retained possession of the manuscripts, but her victory brought her nothing but trouble.

In 1855 Catherine's brother-in-law, Charles du Bouzet, who had offered to help her sort out the manuscripts, published against her wishes a thirty-five-page article in *La Revue Contemporaine*, which was based on Pavel's account of the battle at the Berezina. Catherine wrote a furious letter to the newspapers disassociating herself from this publication, but worse was to come. Charles du Bouzet, who had literary aspirations, saw the memoirs as a means of establishing his reputation. Later in 1855, a slim volume, hurriedly published in Berlin, made its appearance on the Parisian literary scene.[7] The text was an edited version by Charles du Bouzet of Pavel's account of the Berezina episode. Catherine was outraged and denounced the book from the outset. She also managed to obtain a court order which forbade the further publication of her father's memoirs by Charles du Bouzet. But the book continued to be sold openly and enjoyed such success that a second edition was issued in 1858. In 1862 another volume, containing the same text with additions, was published by Charles du Bouzet in Leipzig.[8] It included a reprint of a biographical note on Pavel, written by M. Émile Chasles and originally published in *L'Athenaeum Française*,[9] together with various other extracts purporting to come from Pavel's papers.

The stress of the affair ruined Catherine's health. She had a nervous breakdown and from 1859 onwards she was confined to bed with paralysis of the legs. However, she continued to work on her father's papers and to battle for his reputation. (She had already written a strong letter to Comte Rodolphe de Maistre in 1853, when he published some of his father's correspondence containing criticisms of Pavel.) By 1862, she had completed the preparation of Pavel's memoirs, except for the final chapter on the Berezina, presumably because some of the relevant papers were still in the hands of Charles du Bouzet. A proof copy of Catherine's version exists in two untitled volumes in the Bibiliothèque Nationale in Paris, but for reasons unknown she never went ahead with the publication. What seems most likely is that Catherine was eventually so overwhelmed by the dimensions of the task she had undertaken that the memoirs were never definitively arranged.

In 1881 this version of the memoirs fell into the hands of a Russian member of the family, Leonid Chichagov. He tells us that Catherine, who died in 1882, entrusted him with the task of translating it into Russian and publishing it in Russia. This resulted in the publication of a series of articles in the Russian journal, *Russkaya Starina*, containing extensive extracts from Pavel's memoirs.[10] It was not until 1909, however, through an extraordinary twist of history, that the fourth and final version of the memoirs was published through the efforts of a Romanian named Charles Lahovary. Lahovary had been working in Bucharest, where he had become acquainted with a prominent political figure and former Prime Minister named Démètre Sturdza, who was none other than the grandson of the man whom Pavel had appointed as Governor of Bessarabia in August 1812. Sturdza was deeply interested in Pavel's role in the history of his family and his country, and he asked Lahovary to try and locate the memoirs on one of his frequent visits to Paris. Lahovary discovered Catherine's volumes in the Bibliothèque Nationale and used them to compile the most orderly version of the memoirs available today.[11]

The numerous editions and the similarity between the initials of Catherine du Bouzet and Charles du Bouzet have led to a persisting debate on the authenticity of the text – a subject which has been addressed in the Appendix. The final verdict on the memoirs, however, will have to wait until Pavel's copious correspondence in the Naval and Foreign Ministry archives in Moscow[12] and other related documents have been properly examined. But for a verdict on Pavel himself, it would be hard to improve upon that of de Maistre in 1813:

> Admiral Tchitchagoff is one of the most remarkable figures in Russia. At the time of writing, there is no one who surpasses him or equals him amongst those with a position, in mind, swiftness of judgement, force of character, justice, love of merit wherever he finds it, disinterestedness and even moral austerity. These fine qualities are obscured by two great blemishes: the first, which one could easily overlook without the second, is a way of thinking about religion which is certainly neither Greek nor Latin; the second is a scorn and even a deep hatred for all the institutions of his country, in which he sees nothing but stupidity, ignorance, robbery and despotism. The Russian, who more than any other man in the world can see what he is lacking, is the least forgiving of those who point it out to him. If one wishes to coexist with him, one must never seem to criticize his country. . . . If one excludes the small number of men who know the Admiral intimately and who render him justice, all the rest have vowed an implacable hatred for him and describe him as a public enemy of his country. But at heart, he is nothing of the sort. He is even a better Russian than the rest; for he certainly does not hate Russia, but only the vices and abuses that dishonour her.[13]

# APPENDIX

# *The Memoirs*

The history of Pavel's memoirs is so convoluted that it merits a separate comment. Doubts of the authenticity of the memoirs first arose through the well-meaning efforts of Catherine du Bouzet who, in her attempts to rebut the accusations of Russophobia that continued to tarnish her father's reputation, threw so much suspicion on the unauthorized versions published by Charles du Bouzet that historians have come to consider them 'apocryphal'.

In fact, there are ample grounds for believing that much of the material in the unauthorized memoirs is genuine. Catherine objected to the liberties which Charles du Bouzet took with his linking text and to his interpretation of events because she felt that they represented her father in an unpatriotic light. In her blind devotion, Catherine also suggested that the extracts from the memoirs contained 'inexactitudes', because she refused to believe that her father could have been so devastatingly critical of his homeland. But since Pavel was famed for his outspoken comments, they are the surest evidence of authenticity. Furthermore, the sentiments and the style of the passages attributed to Pavel – which comprise the bulk of the text – tie in closely with his letters. Many of the details can be verified through historical sources. The integrity of the memoirs is further supported by the accurate rendition of a lengthy letter of instructions to Pavel from Emperor Alexander during the campaign of 1812. A study of the original of this letter,[1] now in the archives of the Russian State Library in Moscow, shows that Charles du Bouzet's French translation follows it word for word. Copies of Charles du Bouzet's memoirs are very rare, but the Berlin edition of 1855 can be found in several libraries in Paris, including the Bibliothèque Nationale under the serial number M. 34303.

More unfortunate still is the similarity in the initials of Catherine and Charles du Bouzet. This has led historians to condemn Catherine's version as well because they have confused it with the unauthorized versions by Charles du Bouzet. The authenticity of Catherine's 'authorized' version of the memoirs has never been in question. Furthermore, its contents can be easily verified by a comparison with Pavel's copious correspondence with Vorontsov, de Maistre and others. The only copies of

Catherine's version that I have found are in the Bibliothèque Nationale, under the serial numbers M. 34304–5, with a note that mistakenly attributes their preparation to Eugène du Bouzet, despite an editorial comment in the second volume signed C. du Bouzet, which clearly refers to 'my father' and 'my mother'.

It has been impossible to trace the date of acquisition by the Bibliothèque Nationale of the volumes containing Catherine's version, but judging from the comments of Leonid Chichagov and later of Charles Lahovary, the current volumes have been considerably tidied up by the librarians. According to Leonid Chichagov, who first saw Catherine's version in 1881 (possibly the manuscript and not the typescript), the papers were at that time so disorganized that it was very difficult to put the memoirs in order. Similarly, Charles Lahovary describes the volumes as containing repetitions and gaps. Today the text is largely consistent with Lahovary's version, which can also be found at the Bibliothèque Nationale under the serial number M. 14818, but it is only available to readers on microfiche.

The original manuscript appears to have been dispersed among the family. The only documented sighting of it is contained in an undated note made by Comte Pierre de Robien* in the front of his copy of the Lahovary version, after he had seen a manuscript in Hungary in the hands of his cousin, Comte André de Crouÿ-Chanel.† The manuscript was incomplete and contained some additional material not included in the Lahovary version. Nevertheless, Comte de Robien concluded that the two texts were sufficiently similar to sustain the authenticity of Lahovary's (and therefore Catherine's) version.

The text of Leonid Chichagov's unfinished translation of Pavel's memoirs in *Russkaya Starina* is consistent with Catherine's and Lahovary's versions, although there are some minor variations in the chapter order. But it only covers part of the memoirs and stops, without explanation, half way through.

---

* 1890–1959, great-great-grandson of Pavel and Elizabeth.
† 1854–1927, great-grandson of Pavel and Elizabeth.

# Notes

*A note about the calendar*

Until 1918, the Julian (Old Style) calendar was used by Russia, rather than the Gregorian (New Style) calendar used in Britain and France. The Old Style [OS] calendar ran eleven days behind the New Style [NS] in the eighteenth century, twelve days behind in the nineteenth and thirteen days behind in the twentieth. Dates in the text are given in New Style; dates in the notes are given in New Style unless otherwise stated. Where the style is uncertain, the most probable style is given with a question mark.

## CHAPTER ONE : ELIZABETH

1. William Laird Clowes, *The Royal Navy: A History from the Earliest Times to the Present* (London, 1899), vol. 3, p. 323.
2. Ibid., p. 324.
3. John Charnock, *Biographia Navalis* (London, 1797), vol. 5, p. 501.
4. Ibid., p. 502.
5. Ibid., p. 487.
6. Charles Proby [CP] to Anson, from the *Medway* at Portsmouth, 19 June 1757, British Library [BL], Add. MS 15956, fos. 317–319v.
7. W. G. Hoskins, *Devon* (Tiverton, 1992), p. 322.
8. *Gentleman's Magazine*, 42 (1772), p. 247.
9. Philip MacDougall, *The Chatham Dockyard Story* (Whitstable, 1987), pp. 64–5.
10. John Ruskin, quoted in MacDougall, *Chatham Dockyard Story*, p. 69.
11. Philip MacDougall, *Royal Dockyards* (Princes Risborough, 1989), p. 11.
12. MacDougall, *Chatham Dockyard Story*, p. 87.
13. CP to Admiralty, Proby Papers, Elton Hall, vol. 14, pp. 77–8.
14. CP to Admiralty, 29 April 1778, Proby Papers, vol. 14, p. 83.
15. Clowes, *Royal Navy*, vol. 4, p. 152.
16. CP to Admiralty, 4 May 1778, Proby Papers, vol. 14, p. 84.

17. For this description I have drawn on James Presnail, *Chatham: The Story of a Dockside Town and the Birthplace of the British Navy* (Chatham, 1952), p. 152.
18. Pownoll W. Phipps, *The Life of Colonel Pownoll Phipps* (London, 1894), pp. 9–10.
19. Marcus Binney, 'Sharpham House, Devon', *Country Life*, 17 April 1969, pp. 952–5.
20. *Gentleman's Magazine*, 53 (1783), part 2, p. 717.
21. CP to Elizabeth Proby [EP], *c.* January–March 1799, Pigott Papers, Heritage Service, Acc. 280, London Borough of Sutton.
22. *Kentish Weekly Post and Canterbury Journal*, 1 (5–12 June 1769), p. 39.
23. CP to EP, *c.* January–March 1799, Pigott Papers.
24. Ibid.
25. Revd J. Eagle to Lady Proby, 15 July 1961, Proby Papers.
26. Clowes, *Royal Navy*, vol. 3, pp. 326–7.
27. C. E. Carrington and J. Hampden Jackson, *A History of England* (Cambridge, 1936), p. 550.
28. William Wordsworth, *The French Revolution*, 1809.
29. Carrington & Hampden Jackson, *History of England*, p. 561.
30. MacDougall, *Chatham Dockyard Story*, p. 97.
31. John Gale Jones, *A Political Tour through Rochester, Chatham, Maidstone, Gravesend, etc.* (1796; reprint, Rochester, 1997), p. vii.
32. Jones, *Political Tour*, pp. vii–viii.
33. John Parkinson, *A Tour of Russia, Siberia and the Crimea 1792–1794*, ed. William Collier (London, 1971), p. 63.
34. Anthony Cross, ed., *Engraved in the Memory: James Walker, Engraver to the Empress Catherine the Great, and his Russian Anecdotes* (Oxford and Providence, R. I., 1993), p. 146.
35. *Life and Letters of Sir Gilbert Elliot* (London, 1874), vol. 1, p. 149.

## CHAPTER TWO : PAVEL

1. Pavel Chichagov [PC] to Vasilii Chichagov, letter received 21 August [OS] 1774, Chichagov Archives, F. 333, K. 2, no. 12, Russian State Library, Moscow. Translated from Russian.
2. Hugh Seton-Watson, *The Russian Empire 1801–1917* (Oxford, 1967), pp. 14–21.
3. Anthony Cross, *By the Banks of the Neva: Chapters from the Lives and Careers of the British in Eighteenth-Century Russia* (Cambridge, 1997), p. 184.
4. Charles Gr. Lahovary, ed., *Mémoires de l'Amiral Paul Tchitchagof, Commandant en Chef de l'Armée du Danube, Gouverneur des Principautés de Moldavie et de Valachie en 1812* (Paris and Bucharest, 1909), vol. 1, p. 105. All quotations from the *Mémoires* have been translated from French by the author.
5. Lahovary, *Mémoires*, vol. 1, p. 129.
6. Catherine the Great to PC, 18 May [OS] 1790, Chichagov Archives, F. 333, K. 2, no. 13. Translated from Russian.
7. All dates of naval engagements in the Baltic have been taken from R. C. Anderson, *Naval Wars in the Baltic* (London, 1910).
8. Lahovary, *Mémoires*, vol. 1, pp. 151–2.
9. Parkinson, *Tour of Russia*, p. 59.
10. Lahovary, *Mémoires*, vol. 1, p. 180.
11. Bezborodko to Simon Vorontsov [SV] 3 July [OS] 1792, *Arkhiv Knyazya Vorontsova* [*AKV*], vol. 13 (Moscow, 1879), p. 260. All quotations from the Vorontsov Archives have been translated from French by the author, unless otherwise stated.
12. Bezborodko to SV, received 1 September 1789, *AKV*, vol. 13, p. 165.
13. SV to Aleksandr Vorontsov, 3 May 1791, *AKV*, vol. 9 (Moscow, 1876), p. 198.
14. Lahovary, *Mémoires*, vol. 1, p. 183.
15. Ibid., p. 190.

## CHAPTER THREE : CHATHAM

1. CP to P. Stephens, from the *Pembroke* in Gibraltar Bay, 17 November 1769, 'Letters of Charles Proby', Proby Papers.
2. Jones, *Political Tour*, p. 9.
3. Ibid.

4. CP to Hanickoff [*sic*], 29 March 1796, 'Promiscuous Letters', Chatham Dockyard Records, CHA/P/I 1793–1803, National Maritime Museum, Greenwich.
5. Ibid.
6. Ibid.
7. CP to Hanickoff, 11 April 1796, 'Promiscuous Letters'.
8. Hanickoff to CP, 12 April 1796. 'Promiscuous Letters'.
9. Hanickoff to CP, 25 April 1796. 'Promiscuous Letters'.
10. John Marshall, *Royal Naval Biography* (London, 1824), vol. 2, p. 77.
11. CP to EP, *c.* January–March 1799, Pigott Papers.
12. Ibid.
13. PC to SV, 14 May 1796, *AKV*, vol. 19 (Moscow, 1881), pp. 5–7.

## CHAPTER FOUR : MUTINY

1. CP to EP, *c.* January–March 1799, Pigott Papers.
2. Carrington and Hampden Jackson, *History of England*, p. 570.
3. Jones, *Political Tour*, p. iii.
4. William Coles Finch, *The Medway River and Valley: The Story of the Medway: Aspects of Life on the Medway: Journeyings on the Medway* (London, [1929?]), p. 100.
5. Marshall, *Royal Naval Biography*, vol. 2, p. 79.
6. CP to EP, *c.* January–March 1799, Pigott Papers.
7. K. Waliszewski, *Paul the First of Russia: The Son of Catherine the Great* (London, 1913), p. 107.
8. PC to SV, 28 February 1797, *AKV*, vol. 19, pp. 7–8.
9. Waliszewski, *Paul the First*, pp. 209–10.
10. PC to SV, 10 September [OS] 1797, *AKV*, vol. 19, p. 13.
11. PC to SV, 20 May 1798, *AKV*, vol. 19, pp. 14–15.
12. EP to CP, delivered 8 January 1799, Pigott Papers.
13. Will of CP, Public Record Office, PROB 11/1323.
14. EP to CP, 9 March 1799, Pigott Papers.
15. CP to EP, *c.* January–March 1799, Pigott Papers.
16. Ibid.

17. EP to CP, 23 March 1799, Pigott Papers.
18. CP to EP, *c.* January–March 1799, Pigott Papers.
19. Will of CP.
20. Lahovary, *Mémoires*, vol. 1, p. 222.
21. Rostopchin to SV, 10 May [OS] 1799, *AKV*, vol. 8 (Moscow, 1876), p. 212.
22. Waliszewski, *Paul the First*, p. 121.
23. Ibid., p. 118.
24. Lahovary, *Mémoires*, vol. 1, p. 226.
25. Rostopchin to SV, 3 July [OS] 1799, *AKV*, vol. 8, p. 228.

CHAPTER FIVE : MARRIAGE

1. Lahovary, *Mémoires*, vol. 1, p. 234.
2. PC to SV, 12 September 1799, *AKV*, vol. 19, p. 16.
3. SV to Aleksandr Vorontsov, 8 October 1799, *AKV*, vol. 10 (Moscow, 1876), p. 60.
4. PC to SV, 3 November 1799, *AKV*, vol. 19, p. 17.
5. 'Lady Carysfort's Notes', vol. 1, pp. 13, 20, Proby Papers.
6. Marshall, *Royal Naval Biography*, vol. 2, p. 80.
7. Waliszewski, *Paul the First*, pp. 327–8.
8. Ibid., p. 331.
9. PC to SV, 18 June 1800, *AKV*, vol. 19, p. 19.
10. Waliszewski, *Paul the First*, p. 331.
11. PC to SV, 18 June 1800, *AKV*, vol. 19, p. 19.
12. Ibid., pp. 19–20.
13. PC to SV, 25 June 1800, *AKV*, vol. 19, p. 22.
14. Ibid.
15. PC to SV, 28 June 1800, *AKV*, vol. 19, pp. 24–5.
16. Cross, *Banks of the Neva*, pp. 172–3.
17. Ibid., p. 68
18. Waliszewski, *Paul the First*, p. 332.
19. Cross, *Banks of the Neva*, p. 65.
20. Robert Ker Porter, *Travelling Sketches in Russia and Sweden during the years 1805, 1806, 1807, 1808* (London, 1813), vol. 1, p. 15.
21. PC to SV, 12 September 1800, *AKV*, vol. 19, p. 29.
22. Waliszewski, *Paul the First*, p. 412.
23. PC to SV, 18 November 1800, *AKV*, vol. 19, p. 32.
24. Lahovary, *Mémoires*, vol. 1, p. 245.

25. Waliszewski, *Paul the First*, p. 449.

CHAPTER SIX : ST PETERSBURG

1. Parkinson, *Tour of Russia*, pp. 59, 248 (n. to p. 59).
2. Seton-Watson, *Russian Empire*, p. 25.
3. Ibid.
4. Lahovary, *Mémoires*, vol. 1, p. 206.
5. Will of CP.
6. PC to SV, 9 June 1801, *AKV*, vol. 19, p. 45.
7. Porter, *Travelling Sketches*, vol. 1, pp. 25–6.
8. Nelson to St Vincent, 5 May 1801, *The Dispatches and Letters of Vice Admiral Lord Viscount Nelson*, ed. Sir Nicholas Harris Nicholas (London, 1845), vol. 4, pp. 354–5.
9. Nelson to Pahlen, 9 May 1801, Nicholas, *Dispatches and Letters*, vol. 4, p. 364.
10. Nicholas, *Dispatches and Letters*, vol. 4, p. 377.
11. Nelson to Admiralty, 24 May 1801, Nicholas, *Dispatches and Letters*, vol. 4, p. 389.
12. Ibid.
13. PC to SV, 9 June 1801, *AKV*, vol. 19, p. 44.
14. SV to Mikhail Vorontsov, 3 May 1801, *AKV*, vol. 17 (Moscow, 1880), p. 11.
15. Rogerson to SV, 20 May [?OS] 1801, *AKV*, vol. 30 (Moscow, 1881), p. 151.
16. Elizabeth Chichagova [EC] to 'Joey', 27 March 1802, Proby Papers.
17. PC to SV, 21 January 1804, *AKV*, vol. 19, p. 103.
18. Bezborodko to SV, 26 May [?OS] 1798, *AKV*, vol. 13, p. 392.
19. *The Life of Reginald Heber, D. D., Lord Bishop of Calcutta, by his Widow . . . together with a Journal of his Tour in Norway, Sweden, Russia, Hungary and Germany . . .* (London, 1830), vol. 1, p. 130.
20. The Marchioness of Londonderry, ed., *The Russian Journals of Martha and Catherine Wilmot* (London, 1934), pp. 30–1.
21. Ibid., pp. 209–10.
22. Anthony Cross, ed., *An English Lady at the Court of Catherine the Great: The Journal of Baroness Elizabeth Dimsdale, 1781* (Cambridge, 1989), pp. 68–9.

23. *Life of Reginald Heber*, vol. 1, p. 127.
24. Ibid.
25. Cross, *Banks of the Neva*, p. 17.
26. Ibid., p. 18.
27. Ibid., p. 16.
28. Cross, *An English Lady*, p. 51.
29. Ibid.
30. Londonderry, *Russian Journals*, pp. 202–3.
31. Porter, *Travelling Sketches*, vol. 1, pp. 231–3.
32. Revd Thomas Bentham, *A History of Beddington* (London, 1923), p. 63.
33. PC to Charlotte Ferrers, *c.* June 1801, Proby Papers.
34. PC to SV, 15 December 1801, *AKV*, vol. 19, p. 60.
35. Panin to SV, 2 May [?OS] 1801, *AKV*, vol. 11 (Moscow, 1877), p. 123.
36. SV to Panin, 11 November 1801, *AKV*, vol. 11, p. 252.
37. Rogerson to SV, 27 February [?OS] 1804, *AKV*, vol. 30, p. 212.
38. Lahovary, *Mémoires*, vol. 2, p. 280.
39. Porter, *Travelling Sketches*, vol. 1, pp. 109–12.
40. Joseph de Maistre [JM] to Chevalier de Maistre, 19 January 1808, *Lettres et Opuscules Inédits du Comte Joseph de Maistre*, ed. Comte Rodolphe de Maistre, 2nd ed. (Paris, 1853), vol. 1, p. 173. All quotations from Joseph de Maistre have been translated from French by the author.
41. EC to 'Joey', 27 March 1802, Proby Papers.

CHAPTER SEVEN : THE RISE OF PAVEL

1. *Life of Reginald Heber*, vol. 1, pp. 123–4.
2. Archives Nationales de Paris [ANP], *Mission de Général Savary à S. Petersbourg du 6 août au 23 Xbre 1807*, AF/IV/1697. Translated from French by the author.
3. Lahovary, *Mémoires*, vol. 2, p. 276.
4. Grand Duc Nicolas Mikhaïlowitch, *Le Tsar Alexandre 1er* (Paris, 1931), p. 59. All works written and edited by Mikhaïlowitch have been translated from French by the author.
5. *Mémoires de la Comtesse Edling* (Moscow, 1888), p. 38. All quotations from the memoirs of the Comtesse Edling have been translated from French by the author.
6. K. Waliszewski, *Le Règne d'Alexandre 1er* (Paris, 1923), vol. 1, p. 441.
7. The Empress Elizabeth to her mother, 6 September 1809, *Lettres de l'Impératrice Elizabeth*, ed. Grand Duc Nicolas Mikhaïlowitch (St Petersburg, 1909), vol. 2, p. 343.
8. Leveson-Gower to Lady Bessborough, 9 May 1805, *Lord Granville Leveson Gower (First Earl Granville): Private Correspondence 1781–1821*, ed. Castalia Countess Granville (London, 1916), vol. 2, p. 78.
9. Cross, *Banks of the Neva*, pp. 295–6.
10. Anthony Cross, 'By the Banks of the Thames': Russians in Eighteenth Century Britain (Newtonville, Mass., 1980), p. 160.
11. PC to SV, 25 March 1803, *AKV*, vol. 19, p. 79.
12. Ibid., p. 80.
13. Rogerson to SV, no. 49, 27 February [?OS] 1804, *AKV*, vol. 30, p. 212.
14. Cross, *Banks of the Neva*, p. 295.
15. Laurence Kelly, ed., *St Petersburg: A Travellers' Companion* (London, 1981), p. 267.
16. Porter, *Travelling Sketches*, vol. 1, p. 134.
17. Ibid. p. 119.
18. Ibid. p. 120.
19. Leveson-Gower to Lady Bessborough, 14 November 1809, Granville, *Private Correspondence*, vol. 1, p. 499.
20. Adams Diary, 28 November 1809, *The Diary of John Quincy Adams 1794–1845*, ed. Allan Nevins (New York, 1951), pp. 68–9.
21. Adams Diary, 30 November 1810, Nevins, *Diary*, pp. 77–8.
22. PC to SV, 22 April 1803, *AKV*, vol. 19, p. 91.
23. Londonderry, *Russian Journals*, pp. 27, 37.
24. Leveson-Gower to Lady Bessborough, 6 November 1804, Granville, *Private Correspondence*, vol. 1, p. 485.
25. Lahovary, *Mémoires*, vol. 2, p. 318.
26. Adams Diary, 25 January 1811, Nevins, *Diary*, p. 80.
27. JM to Chevalier de Rossi, 21 August 1804, *Mémoires Politiques et Correspondance Diplomatique de J. de*

*Maistre*, ed. Albert Blanc (Paris, 1858), p. 116.

28. JM to King of Sardinia, January 1808, Blanc, *Mémoires Politiques*, p. 308.

29. JM to King of Sardinia, 22 November 1812, *Correspondance Diplomatique de Joseph de Maistre 1811–1817*, ed. Albert Blanc (Paris, 1860), vol.1, p. 249.

30. Ibid.

31. Ibid.

32. JM to PC, 27 May 1818, *Lettres et Opuscules Inédits du Comte Joseph de Maistre*, ed. Comte Rodolphe de Maistre, 4th ed. (Paris, 1861), vols. 1 and 2, pp. 497–8.

33. JM to King of Sardinia, January 1808, Blanc, *Mémoires Politiques*, p. 307.

34. JM to PC, 26 December 1814, Rodolphe de Maistre, *Lettres et Opuscules Inédits*, 4th ed., vols. 1 and 2, p. 314.

35. JM to King of Sardinia, January 1808, Blanc, *Mémoires Politiques*, p. 308.

36. Rogerson to SV, early 1804, *AKV*, vol. 30, pp. 209–10.

37. Zavadovskii to SV, 11 April [?OS] 1803, *AKV*, vol. 12 (Moscow, 1877), p. 273.

38. PC to SV, 25 March 1803, *AKV*, vol. 19, pp. 86–7.

39. PC to SV, 22 April 1803, *AKV*, vol. 19, pp. 89–90.

40. PC to SV, 22 May 1803, *AKV*, vol. 19, p. 93.

41. See Elizabeth's letter to 'Joey' on p. 124.

42. Lahovary, *Mémoires*, vol. 2, pp. 297–8.

43. Rogerson to SV, 30 April [?OS] 1804, *AKV*, vol. 30, pp. 215–6.

44. PC to SV, 25 April 1804, *AKV*, vol. 19, p. 105.

45. Porter, *Travelling Sketches*, vol. 1, p. 13.

46. PC to SV, 22 September 1804, *AKV*, vol. 19, p. 108.

47. Ibid., p. 114.

48. *Zametki Admirala P. V. Chichagova*, Chichagov Archives, F. 333, K. 3, no. 20. Translated from French by the author.

49. PC to Aleksandr Vorontsov, *c*. October/November 1804, *AKV*, vol. 19, p. 306.

50. PC to SV, 6 December 1804, *AKV*, vol. 19, p. 119.

51. Alexander I to PC, 27 July [OS ] 1805, Chichagov Archives, F. 333, K. 2, no. 15. Translated from Russian.

52. Cross, *Banks of the Neva*, p. 287.

53. PC to SV, 22 September 1804, *AKV*, vol. 19, p. 111.

54. Campbell, *Carron Company*, quoted in Cross, *Banks of the Neva*, p. 255.

55. Londonderry, *Russian Journals*, p. 340.

56. William S. Childe-Pemberton, *The Baroness de Bode 1775–1803* (London, 1900), p. 269.

57. Rogerson to SV, 13 November 1805, *AKV*, vol. 30, p. 226.

## CHAPTER EIGHT : WAR

1. Leo Tolstoy, *War and Peace*, trans. Constance Garnett (New York, 1994), pp. 324–5.

2. PC to SV, 14 February [?OS] 1806, *AKV*, vol. 19, p. 155.

3. Ibid., p. 156.

4. Ibid., p. 153.

5. *Mémoires de la Comtesse Edling*, pp. 22–3.

6. Granville, *Private Correspondence*, vol. 2, p. 234.

7. Londonderry, *Russian Journals*, p. 174.

8. PC to SV, 28 May 1806, *AKV*, vol. 19, p. 158.

9. SV to Stroganov, 4 August 1806, Grand Duc Nicolas Mikhaïlowitch, *Le Comte Paul Stroganov*, trans. F. Billecocq (Paris, 1905), vol. 3, p. 96.

10. Baron P. A. Nikolai to SV, 19 September 1806, *AKV*, vol. 22 (Moscow, 1881), p. 336.

11. Armand de Caulaincourt [AC] to Napoleon, 10 March 1808, Grand Duc Nicolas Mikhaïlowitch, *Les Relations Diplomatiques de la Russie et de la France d'après les rapports des ambassadeurs d'Alexandre et de Napoléon* (St Petersburg, 1905), vol. 1, p. 219.

12. PC to SV, 23 July 1807, *AKV*, vol. 19, pp. 165–6.

13. Rogerson to SV, 27 August [?OS] 1807, *AKV*, vol. 30, pp. 245–6.

14. Zavadovskii to SV, 30 October [?OS] 1807, *AKV*, vol. 12, p. 310. Translated from Russian.

15. Kochubei to SV, 11 November 1807, *AKV*, vol. 14 (Moscow, 1879), p. 199.

16. Ibid., p. 197.

17. PC to Alexander I, 4 September 1807, Ministerstvo Inostrannykh Del SSSR, *Vneshnyaya Politika Rossii XIX i Nachala*

*XX Veka* (Moscow, 1965), p. 47.
Translated from French by the author.
18. Lahovary, *Mémoires*, vol. 2, p. 346.

### CHAPTER NINE : THE FRENCH

1. Porter, *Travelling Sketches*, vol. 2, p. 72.
2. Ibid., p. 74.
3. AC to Napoleon, 15 January 1808, Mikhaïlowitch, *Relations Diplomatiques*, vol. 1, p. 49.
4. PC to Alexander I, 11 January 1808, *Vneshnyaya Politika Rossii*, pp. 147–9. Translated from Russian.
5. PC to SV, 23 July 1807, *AKV*, vol. 19, p. 166.
6. JM to King of Sardinia, January 1808, Blanc, *Mémoires Politiques*, p. 308.
7. AC to Napoleon, 7 January 1808, Mikhaïlowitch, *Relations Diplomatiques*, vol. 1, p. 57.
8. AC to Napoleon, 1 March 1808, Mikhaïlowitch, *Relations Diplomatiques*, vol. 1, pp. 190–1.
9. AC to Napoleon, 12 March 1808, Mikhaïlowitch, *Relations Diplomatiques*, vol. 1, p. 221.
10. Lahovary, *Mémoires*, vol. 2, p. 347.
11. AC to Champagny, 29 June 1808, Mikhaïlowitch, *Relations Diplomatiques*, vol. 2, p. 216.
12. AC to Napoleon, 9 August 1808, Mikhaïlowitch, *Relations Diplomatiques*, vol. 2, p. 266.
13. Lahovary, *Mémoires*, vol. 2, p. 347.
14. This scene is depicted in a watercolour entitled *View of the Palace from the Marienthal Pool* by A. Bugreyev, 1803, reproduced in *Pavlovsk Palace and Park* (Leningrad: Aurora, 1975), p. 13.
15. Lahovary, *Mémoires*, vol. 2, p. 344.
16. JM to PC, 3 April 1810, Joseph de Maistre, *Oeuvres Complètes de J. de Maistre* (Lyon, 1885), vol. 11, Correspondance 3, p. 443.
17. Footnote to AC's report to Champagny, 18 September 1808, Mikhaïlowitch, *Relations Diplomatiques*, vol. 2, p. 352.
18. SV to Mikhail Vorontsov, 6 July 1808, *AKV*, vol. 17, p. 176.
19. Londonderry, *Russian Journals*, p. 391.
20. Lahovary, *Mémoires*, vol. 2, p. 348.
21. Ibid.
22. Ibid.
23. *Mémoires de la Comtesse Edling*, pp. 38–9.

### CHAPTER TEN : 'A DEPLORABLE CAPRICE'

1. AC to Napoleon, 19 August 1809, Mikhaïlowitch, *Relations Diplomatiques*, vol. 4, p. 51.
2. *Journal de Paris*, no. 263, 22 September 1809.
3. Nikolai to SV, 26 September 1809, *AKV*, vol. 22, p. 406.
4. Lahovary, *Mémoires*, vol. 2, p. 345.
5. Ibid., p. 346.
6. 'Les Nouvelles et On Dit de Caulaincourt', 5 January 1810, Mikhaïlowitch, *Relations Diplomatiques*, vol. 6, p. 94.
7. Ibid.
8. *Journal de Paris*, no. 348, 14 December 1809.
9. AC to Champagny, 5 February 1810, Mikhaïlowitch, *Relations Diplomatiques*, vol. 4, p. 273.
10. AC to Champagny, 6 January 1810, Mikhaïlowitch, *Relations Diplomatiques*, vol. 4, p. 242.
11. AC to Napoleon, 4 February 1810, Mikhaïlowitch, *Relations Diplomatiques*, vol. 4, p. 269.
12. JM to PC, 3 April 1810, Joseph de Maistre, *Oeuvres Complètes*, vol. 11, Correspondance 3, p. 440.
13. JM to PC, 29 January 1810, Joseph de Maistre, *Oeuvres Complètes*, vol. 11, Correspondance 3, p. 394.
14. Ibid.
15. PC to SV, 26 March 1810, *AKV*, vol. 19, p. 168.
16. Ibid., p. 173.
17. Charles Percier and P. F. L. Fontaine, *Descriptions des Cérémonies et des Fêtes qui ont eu lieu pour le mariage de S. M. L'Empereur Napoléon avec S. A. I. l'Archiduchesse Marie Louise d'Autriche à Paris le 2 avril 1810* (Paris, 1810), p. 19.
18. Lahovary, *Mémoires*, vol. 2, p. 346.
19. Percier and Fontaine, *Descriptions*, p. 25. Translated from French by the author.
20. Ibid, p. 37.
21. Ibid, p. 38.
22. PC to Duc de Vicence [AC], 5 April 1810, ANP, Archives Privées, *95 AP,

Fonds Caulaincourt, 'Correspondance du duc de Vicence, ambassadeur', no. 6, dossier 17. Translated from French by the author.

23. Ibid.

24. Ibid.

25. Nesselrode to Speranskii, 24 April 1810, *Lettres et Papiers du Chancelier Comte de Nesselrode 1760–1850*, ed. Comte A. de Nesselrode (Paris, n.d.), vol. 3, p. 251. All quotations from *Lettres et Papiers* have been translated from French by the author.

26. JM to PC, 6 May 1810, Joseph de Maistre, *Oeuvres Complètes*, vol. 11, Correspondance 3, p. 449.

27. Ibid.

28. PC to AC, 24 July 1810, 'Correspondance du duc de Vicence', no. 6, dossier 17.

29. 'Les Nouvelles et On Dit de Caulaincourt', 4 August 1810, Mikhaïlowitch, *Relations Diplomatiques*, vol. 6, p. 148.

30. PC to AC, 24 July 1810, 'Correspondance du duc de Vicence', no. 6, dossier 17.

31. Ibid. Translated from French by the author.

32. Roxana Sturdza to JM, n.d., Rodolphe de Maistre, *Lettres et Opuscules Inédits*, 2nd ed., vol. 2, p. 36.

33. JM to Roxana Sturdza, n.d., Rodolphe de Maistre, *Lettres et Opuscules Inédits*, 2nd ed., vol. 2, pp. 35–6.

34. *Gazette de Munich*, 30 July 1810. Translated from French by the author.

35. JM to EC, 13 September 1810, Joseph de Maistre, *Oeuvres Complètes*, vol. 11, Correspondance 3, p. 476.

36. Ibid., p. 479.

37. JM to PC, 13 September 1810, Joseph de Maistre, *Oeuvres Complètes*, vol. 11, Correspondance 3, p. 486.

38. 'Les Nouvelles et On Dit de Caulaincourt', 4 March 1811, Mikhaïlowitch, *Relations Diplomatiques*, vol. 6, p. 187.

CHAPTER ELEVEN : THE
RETREAT FROM MOSCOW

1. Smirnov to PC, 24 August 1811, Chichagov Archives, F. 333, K. 3, no. 29.

2. *Gentleman's Magazine*, 81 (1811), part 2, p. 193.

3. JM to King of Sardinia, 1 September 1811, Blanc, *Correspondance Diplomatique*, vol. 1, p. 20.

4. JM to King of Sardinia, 9 September 1811, Blanc, *Correspondance Diplomatique*, vol. 1, p. 22.

5. Mikhail Vorontsov, 11 October [?OS] 1811, *AKV*, vol. 35 (Moscow, n.d.), p. 107.

6. *Mémoires de la Comtesse Edling*, pp. 50–1.

7. Instructions of Alexander I, 28 November 1811, Chichagov Archives, F. 333, K. 2, no. 16. Translated from Russian.

8. Saint-Julien to Metternich, 3 January 1812, Grand Duc Nicolas Mikhaïlowitch, *L'Empereur Alexandre 1er: Essai d'Étude Historique* (St Petersburg, 1912), vol. 1, p. 454.

9. SV to Mikhail Vorontsov, 8 December 1811, *AKV*, vol. 17, pp. 199–200.

10. Smirnov to PC, 24 August 1811, Chichagov Archives, F. 333, K. 3, no. 29. Translated from Russian.

11. Smirnov to PC, 28 December 1811, Chichagov Archives, F. 333, K. 3, no. 29. Translated from Russian.

12. Alexander I to PC, 9 April [?OS] 1812, Chichagov Archives, F. 333, K. 2, no. 16.

13. Comtesse Nesselrode to Comte Nesselrode, 13 April [?OS] 1812, A. de Nesselrode, *Lettres et Papiers*, vol. 4, pp. 15–16.

14. JM to Chevalier de Rossi, 9 May [?OS] 1812, Blanc, *Correspondance Diplomatique*, vol. 1, pp. 99–100.

15. Rumiantsev to PC, 30 June [?OS] 1812, Chichagov Archives, F. 333, K. 3, no. 24. Translated from French by the author.

16. Seton-Watson, *Russian Empire*, p. 127.

17. Alexander I to PC, 2 May [OS] 1812, A. de Nesselrode, *Lettres et Papiers*, vol. 4, p. 209.

18. SV to Mikhail Vorontsov, 6 November 1812, *AKV*, vol. 17, p. 253.

19. Instructions from Alexander I to PC [August/September 1812], Chichagov Archives, F. 333, K. 2, no. 16 (no. 6). Translated from Russian.

20. The Empress Elizabeth to her mother, 22 November 1812, Mikhaïlowitch,

*Lettres de l'Impératrice Elizabeth*, vol. 2, p. 545.

21. D'Anstedt to Nesselrode, 14 October [?OS] 1812, A. de Nesselrode, *Lettres et Papiers*, vol. 4, p. 105.

22. D'Anstedt to Nesselrode, 15 October [?OS] 1812, A. de Nesselrode, *Lettres et Papiers*, vol. 4, p. 110.

23. Longinov to SV, 11 November [?OS] 1812, *AKV*, vol. 23 (Moscow, 1882), pp. 206–7.

24. Tolstoy, *War and Peace*, pp. 1221–2.

25. Seton-Watson, *Russian Empire*, pp. 139–40.

26. Guillaume de Vaudoncourt, *Relation Impartiale du Passage de la Bérézina, par l'Armée Française, en 1812, par un Témoin Oculaire* (Paris, 1814), p. 37.

27. The Marquis de Chambray, *L'Histoire de l'Expédition de Russie* (Paris, 1823), vol. 2, bk. 4, pp. 298–300.

28. Jean Hanoteau, ed., *Mémoires du Général de Caulaincourt, Duc de Vicence* (Paris, n.d.), vol. 2, pp. 220–1. Translated from French by the author.

29. Tolstoy, *War and Peace*, p. 1252.

30. PC to SV, 27 September 1813, *AKV*, vol. 19, p. 213.

31. PC to SV, 17 December 1812, *AKV*, vol. 19, pp. 174–7.

32. Ivan Krylov, *The Pike and the Cat.*

33. Longinov to SV, 21 January [?OS] 1813, *AKV*, vol. 23, pp. 232–3.

34. SV to PC, 3 March 1813, *AKV*, vol. 19, p. 289.

35. Ibid., pp. 287–8.

36. JM to Roxana Sturdza, 1813, Rodolphe de Maistre, *Lettres et Opuscule Inédits*, 2nd. ed., vol. 2, p. 38.

37. Ibid., p. 39.

## EPILOGUE

1. PC to SV, 22 May 1825, *AKV*, vol. 19, p. 276.

2. Ibid.

3. Ibid.

4. PC to SV, no. 81, 8 October 1824, *AKV*, vol. 19, p. 273.

5. C. Hennigsen, *Eastern Europe and the Emperor Nicholas* (London, 1846), vol. 1, p. 137.

6. JM to King of Sardinia, 14 June 1813, *AKV*, vol. 15, (Moscow, 1880), pp. 483–503.

7. Charles du Bouzet, ed., *Mémoires Inédits de l'Amiral Tchitchagoff: Campagnes de la Russie en 1812 contre la Turquie, l'Autriche et la France* (Berlin, 1855).

8. Charles du Bouzet, ed., *Mémoires de l'Amiral Tchitchagoff (1767–1849): Avec une notice biographique: D'après des documents authentiques* (Leipzig, 1862).

9. Émile Chasles, *Étude Biographique sur l'Amiral Tchitchagoff* (Mâcon, n.d.). Originally published in *L'Athenaeum Française*, 29 April 1854. The text was also published with an account of the court case between the sisters: Émile Chasles, *Documents relatifs à la Vie et au Testament de l'Amiral Tchitchagoff* (Paris, 1854).

10. Leonid Mikhailovich Chichagov, ed., 'Zapiski Admirala Pavla Vasil'evicha Chichagova', *Russkaya Starina*, vol. 50, May (1886), pp. 221–52; June (1886), pp. 463–86; vol. 51, August (1886), pp. 247–70; September (1886), pp. 487–518; vol. 52, October (1886), pp. 25–44; November (1886), pp. 239–58; vol. 55, July (1887), pp. 35–54; September (1887), pp. 523–44; vol. 58, June (1888), pp. 535–61; vol. 59, July (1888), pp. 1–21; August (1888), pp. 225–48; September (1888), pp. 463–81; vol. 60, pp. 35–60.

11. Lahovary, *Mémoires.*

12. K. Waliszewski locates the correspondence of Pavel with the Emperor Alexander in the State Archives of the Russian Ministry of Foreign Affairs, sect. 5, no. 207.

13. JM to King of Sardinia, 14 June 1813, *AKV*, vol. 15, pp. 491–2.

## APPENDIX : THE MEMOIRS

1. Alexander I to PC, 1812, August/September 1812, Chichagov Archives, F. 333. K. 2, no. 16 (no. 6).

# Biographical Notes

ADAMS, John Quincy. 1767–1848. American diplomat, politician and sixth U. S. President. Born in Massachusetts and admitted to the bar at the age of 23. He completed several diplomatic missions and was Minister to Russia, 1809–14. U. S. Secretary of State, 1817–25. President, 1825–9.

ALEXANDER I (Grand Duke Alexander). 1777–1825. Eldest of the four sons of the Emperor Paul and Maria Feodorovna. His policies were initially liberal, influenced by the teachings of his Swiss tutor, Frédéric-César de La Harpe, but after the defeat of Napoleon he became increasingly reactionary. Fell into extreme mysticism during the last years of his life.

BAGRATION, Petr Ivanovich. 1765–1812. Military figure, general and prince. Descended from an ancient Georgian princely family. In military service from 1782 and commanded the advance guard in Suvorov's Italian and Swiss campaigns of 1799. Became a hero of the war of 1812, when he commanded the left wing of the Russian army at the battle of Borodino and died of his wounds, having shown great skill and personal bravery.

BARCLAY DE TOLLY, Mikhail Bogdanovich. 1761–1818. Field marshal and prince. Descended from an old Scottish family that settled in Riga in the 17th century. Replaced by Kutuzov as Commander-in-Chief of the Russian forces in 1812 because his tactical retreat before the French was unpopular with the nobility, but fought with great courage at the battle of Borodino in 1812. Successfully commanded the Russo-Prussian army during the foreign campaigns of 1813–14.

BENNIGSEN, Levin August. 1745–1826. Russian military figure, general, baron and count. Officer in the Hanoverian army who entered Russian service in 1773. Participated in the 1801 conspiracy and assassination of the Emperor Paul. Held a number of senior military positions and was Commander-in-Chief when the Russian army was defeated by the French at the battle of Friedland, 1807. Commanded an army during the foreign campaigns of 1813–14 and commanded the second (southern) Russian army, 1814–18, before being discharged for incompetence in 1818.

BEZBORODKO, Aleksandr Andreevich. 1747–99. Statesman and prince (1797). Descendant of a Ukranian Cossack officer. Became secretary to Catherine the Great in 1775 and from 1784 was de facto head of the College of Foreign Affairs. Received the rank of Chancellor in 1797.

BUSH, Catherine. ?–1817. Daughter of the imperial gardener, John Bush, and married the architect Charles Cameron in 1784. They had one daughter.

BUSH, John. c.1730–95. Imperial gardener. A Hanoverian who had a celebrated nursery garden in Hackney. Recruited by Catherine the Great in 1771 and worked at Tsarskoe Selo, 1774–89, when he returned to England.

CAMERON, Charles. 1746?–1812. A London-born Scottish architect and landscape designer, who entered the service of Catherine the Great in 1779. During Catherine's reign he worked at Pavlovsk and Tsarskoe Selo, where he built the 'Cameron Gallery'.

Fell into disfavour under the Emperor Paul (1796–1801) but was appointed architect to the Admiralty in 1802. Dismissed in 1805 for reasons unknown. Died in St Petersburg.

CAPODISTRIAS, Ioannis. 1776–1831. Greek statesman and count. Born in Corfu. Invited to Russia by the Emperor Alexander in 1809 and worked in the Russian diplomatic service until 1827. Elected President of Greece in 1827 by the national assembly during the Greek war of independence. Victim of a plot and assassinated in 1831.

CATHERINE II (Catherine the Great). 1729–96. Born Sophia Frederika Augusta von Anhalt-Zerbst. She came from a poor German princely family. Married in 1745 to the heir to the Russian throne, the future Peter III, and became the Empress of Russia in 1762, after overthrowing her husband with the support of the Preobrazhenskii Regiment.

CAULAINCOURT, Armand-Augustin-Louis (created Duc de Vicence in 1808). 1773–1827. French statesman, diplomat and marquis. Came from an aristocratic family but enjoyed complete confidence of Napoleon. Sent to St Petersburg in 1801 to congratulate the Emperor Alexander on his accession to the throne. French ambassador to Russia, 1807–11, and attempted to dissuade Napoleon from invading Russia. Continually with Napoleon during the campaign of 1812. Napoleon's Foreign Minister during the Hundred Days. Barred from state activity after the Bourbon restoration.

CHERNYSHEV, Aleksandr Ivanovich. 1786–1857. Military and state figure, general, count (1826) and grand duke (1849). Carried out important diplomatic assignments in France and Sweden, 1808–12, and served as a military and diplomatic agent in Paris. Served closely with the Emperor Alexander in the campaign of 1812.

CHICHAGOV, Vasilii Iakolevich. 1726–1809. Navigator and admiral. Joined the Russian navy in 1742 and commanded the Baltic fleet during the Russo-Swedish war of 1788–90. Several geographical features have been named in his honour.

CONSTANTINE, Grand Duke. 1779–1831. Second son of the Emperor Paul and Maria Feodorovna. Took command of the Polish army after a military career and became de facto viceroy of the Kingdom of Poland, 1815–31. Renounced his right to the throne in 1823 because of his morganatic marriage in 1820 to the Polish countess J. Grudzinska (later Duchess Lowicz).

CZARTORYSKI, Adam Jerzy. 1770–1861. Polish and Russian state and political figure. Prince. Born in Warsaw of a Polish princely family. Close friend of the Emperor Alexander and member of the 'unofficial committee'. Rumoured to have been the lover of the Empress Elizabeth. Foreign Minister, 1804–6.

DASHKOVA, Ekaterina Romanova. 1743/4–1810. Literary figure and director of the St Petersburg Academy of Sciences from 1783. Sister of Simon and Aleksandr Vorontsov. Participated actively in the 1762 coup d'état, which brought Catherine the Great to the throne.

DIMSDALE, Elizabeth. 1732–1812. Diarist. Married Baron Thomas Dimsdale in 1781 and accompanied him to Russia within a few months of their marriage. She recorded her experiences in a journal.

DIMSDALE, Thomas. 1712–1800. A Quaker physician from Hertford and a pioneer in the field of smallpox inoculation. Invited to Russia in 1768 to inoculate Catherine the Great and the Grand Duke Paul. He was created a baron and returned to Russia in 1781, with his third wife, Elizabeth, to inoculate the Grand Dukes Alexander and Constantine. Died in Hertford.

DU PLESSIS, Armand-Emmanuel (Duc de Richelieu). 1766–1822. French and Russian state figure. Joined the Russian army in 1790 and settled in Russia in 1795. Governor of Odessa, 1803–14. Also Governor of Novorossiia, 1805–14. Transformed Odessa into a major trade city and developed northern Black Sea region. Returned to France in 1814 and served as Prime Minister to Louis XVIII, 1815–18 and 1820–1.

GASCOIGNE, Charles. 1738–1806. Scottish armaments expert, formerly employed at the Carron factory in Scotland, who went to Russia in 1786. Appointed head of the Aleksandrovskii cannon works and the Konchezerskii iron foundry at Petrozavodsk. Became involved in many other projects, including the Izhora works at Kolpina and amassed a fortune. Honoured by Catherine the Great and the Emperor Paul.

GREIG, Samuel Charles. 1736–88. Scotsman and Russian admiral. Transferred from the British to the Russian navy in 1764 and led the Russian fleet to victory at the battle of Çeshme in 1770. Became commander of Kronstadt in 1775 and an admiral in 1882. Commanded the Baltic fleet in the early stages of the Russo-Swedish war of 1788–90, and died of a fever at Revel.

HEBER, Reginald. 1783–1826. Traveller, cleric and hymn writer. Visited St Petersburg in 1805 as part of an extensive tour of northern and eastern Europe. Ordained in 1807 and appointed Bishop of Calcutta in 1823. Died of a sudden illness while on tour.

KOCHUBEI, Viktor Pavlovich. 1768–1834. Diplomat, statesman, count (1799) and prince (1831). Close friend of the Emperor Alexander and member of his 'unofficial committee'. Minister of Foreign Affairs, 1802–7 and 1819–23.

KRYLOV, Ivan Andreevich. 1769–1844. Author, fabulist and journalist. First book of fables came out in 1809. Created fables that were satires or comic episodes and brought the genre to the peak of its development.

KURAKIN, Aleksandr Borisovich. 1752–1818. Statesman, diplomat and prince. Brought up with the future Emperor Paul. Headed Board of Foreign Affairs,1796–1802. Russian Ambassador to France, 1808–12.

KUTUZOV, Mikhail Illarionovich. 1745–1813. Military commander, field marshal (1812) and prince. Came from a military family and served with distinction in a variety of military positions. Endowed with great military abilities and became the idol of the troops. Commander-in-Chief of the Russian forces in the struggle against Napoleon, 1812 and 1813.

LEVESON-GOWER, Lord Granville. 1773–1846. Diplomat. Third son of the 1st Marquis of Stafford. Appointed British Ambassador to St Petersburg in 1804, but returned to England in 1805. Reappointed to Russia in spring 1807, but left after a few months, when Russia declared war on Britain following the signing of the Treaty of Tilsit. Created Viscount Granville in 1815 and Earl Granville in 1833. British Ambassador to France, 1824–41 (with a short interval in 1834). Addicted to cards, he is reputed to have lost £23,000 at one sitting.

LOMONOSOV, Mikhail Vasil'evich. 1711–65. First Russian natural scientist of world importance. Son of a peasant who worked as a fisherman. One of the founders of physical chemistry, a poet, artist, historian and advocate of Russian education. Moscow University, which now bears his name, was founded according to his plans in 1755.

MAISTRE, Joseph Marie de. 1753–1821. Diplomat, political figure , religious philosopher and count. A native of Savoy and educated by the Jesuits. Envoy of the King of

Sardinia to St Petersburg, 1802–17, where he wrote his major philosophical works. De Maistre's political views were determined by his idea of establishing a new world order based on religion.

MORDVINOV, Nikolai Semenovich. 1754–1845. Admiral, statesman, economist, public figure and count (1834). Member and Vice-President of the Admiralty, 1799–1801, and briefly Minister of the Navy in 1802. Worked closely with Speranskii in drafting a plan for the improvement of Russia's financial system. A major landowner, he advanced a plan for the gradual liquidation of serfdom and wrote a number of important works on economic matters.

NESSELRODE, Karl Vasil'evich. 1780–1862. Statesman, diplomat and count. Son of a Russian diplomat. Began his diplomatic career in 1801 and was attached to the army in 1812. Minister of Foreign Affairs, 1816–56. Member of the State Council, 1821, Vice-Chancellor, 1828, and Chancellor, 1845. Forced into retirement in 1856 after Russia's defeat in the Crimean War.

NICHOLAS I, 1796–1855. Third son of the Emperor Paul and Maria Feodorovna. Ascended the throne on the sudden death of his brother, the Emperor Alexander. His rule saw the apex of absolute monarchy. Introduced rigid censorship and subjected progressive Russians to persecution and repression. Died shortly after the defeat of Russia in the Crimean War.

NOVOSIL'TSEV, Nikolai Nikolaevich. 1768–1838. Statesman, President of the St Petersburg Academy of Sciences, 1803–10, and count (1833). Enjoyed the Emperor Alexander's special trust and was a member of the 'unofficial committee'. Carried out diplomatic assignments in Europe, 1804–9, including London.

ORLOV, Aleksei Grigor'evich. 1737–1807. Army officer, statesman and count (1762). Played a prominent part in the coup d'état of 1762, which placed Catherine the Great on the throne. Commander of the Russian naval squadron in the battle of Çeshme in 1770.

ORLOV, Grigorii Grigor'evich. 1734–83. Military and state figure, brother of Aleksei Orlov. Had a son from his liaison with the future Catherine the Great and participated actively in the 1762 coup d'état which placed her on the throne.

PAHLEN, Petr Alekseevich von der. 1745–1826. Military figure, general and count (1799). Member of the Baltic nobility. Appointed military governor of St Petersburg in 1798. One of the chief organizers of the conspiracy against the Emperor Paul in March 1801. Banished in June 1801 to his Courland estate by the Emperor Alexander.

PANIN, Nikita Petrovich. 1770–1837. Military and court figure, general and diplomat. In 1797, Ambassador in Berlin, where he tried to draw the Prussian government into actively fighting the French. Vice-Chancellor in 1799 and one of the organizers of the 1801 conspiracy against the Emperor Paul. He directed foreign policy briefly under the Emperor Alexander, but was disgraced and banished from St Petersburg in 1804.

PARKINSON, John. 1754–1840. Oxford don and diarist. Visited Russia, 1792–4, as tutor and companion to Edward Bootle-Wilbraham (later 1st Lord Skelmersdale). Kept a travel diary which gives an illuminating picture of life in St Petersburg.

PAUL I. 1754–1801. Emperor, 1796–1801. Officially the son of Catherine the Great and Peter III but his father may have been Catherine's lover, Sergei Saltykov. Alarmed by the French Revolution, he pursued a repressive regime, which made him very unpopular. Murdered by conspirators in 1801.

PETER I (Peter the Great). 1672–1725. Only son of Tsar Aleksei Mikhailovich by his second wife, N. K. Narishkina. Came to the throne with his half-brother, Ivan V. Alekseevich, in 1682. His half-sister, Sofia Alekseevna, acted as regent until 1689. Endowed with intelligence, a strong will, energy, breadth of vision, purposefulness, curiosity and a great capacity for work, Peter the Great established the Russian navy, founded St Petersburg and was one of Russia's most outstanding rulers.

PETER III. 1728–62. Russian Emperor, 1761–2. Son of Charles Frederick, Duke of Holstein-Gottorp, and Anna Petrovna, daughter of Peter the Great. Deposed in 1762 by an opposition movement headed by his wife, Catherine the Great, and later murdered.

PLATOV, Matvei Ivanovich. 1751–1818. Cossack leader, cavalry general and count (1812). Commanded the Don Cossack Corps in the war of 1812 and contributed largely to the defeat of Napoleon. Accompanied the Emperor Alexander to England in 1814 and was awarded an honorary doctorate by Oxford University.

PORTER, Robert Ker. 1777–1842. Painter and traveller. Appointed historical painter to the Emperor Alexander and lived in St Petersburg, 1804–6. Painted a number of pictures for the Hermitage Museum and Admiralty. Published an account of his travels in Russia and Sweden in 1809. In 1812, after further travels, he married Princess Mary Shcherbatova. Returned to England and was knighted in 1813. British Consul in Venezuela, 1826–41. Died in St Petersburg.

POTEMKIN, Grigorii Aleksandrovich. 1739–91. Statesman, military figure, diplomat, field marshal and prince (1787). The son of an army officer who, as Catherine the Great's favourite, became the most powerful man in Russia.

RIBAS, José de. 1749–1800. Russian admiral of Spanish nationality born in Naples. Entered the service of Russia in 1772 at the invitation of Aleksei Orlov, with whom he was implicated in the deception and abduction in Italy of 'Princess' Tarakanova.

ROGERSON, John. 1741–1823. Scottish doctor and Russian court figure. Went to Russia in 1766. He was made court physician in 1776 by Catherine the Great and retained this position until his return to Scotland in 1816.

ROSTOPCHIN, Feodor Vasil'evich. 1763–1826. Statesman and count (1799). Virtual head of the College of Foreign Affairs, 1798–1801. Governor-General of Moscow, 1812–14, and widely believed to have started the fire, although he later denied this.

RUMIANTSEV, Nikolai Petrovich 1754–1826. Statesman, diplomat and count. Foreign Minister, 1807–14. Chairman of the State Council, 1810–12, and retired in 1814. Subsidized scholars and amassed a huge library, which in 1925 served as the basis for the Lenin State Library (now Russian State Library).

SENIAVIN, Dmitrii Nikolaevich. 1763–1831. Naval commander and admiral. Commanded the Russian fleet in the Adriatic in 1806 and prevented the French seizure of the Ionian Islands. Commanded the fleet which blockaded the Dardanelles and defeated the Ottoman fleet in 1807. Negotiated the safe return of Russian crews after his fleet was impounded by the British in Lisbon in 1808. Demoted to a minor position in 1811 by the Emperor Alexander for his independent action and retired in 1813.

SHEREMETEV, Petr Borisovich. 1713–88. High chamberlain, general, senator and prominent state figure during the reigns of the Empress Elizabeth and Catherine the Great. Hugely wealthy, he built various palaces and supported peasant theatres, choruses and orchestras. Amassed a valuable art collection.

SMIRNOV, Iakov Ivanovich. 1754–1840. Son of a village priest from Ukraine. Chaplain to the Embassy in London, 1780–1837, but carried out many other embassy-related duties. Widely respected by the Russian community in London and consulted by many English travellers to Russia.

SPERANSKII, Mikhail Mikhailovich. 1772–1839. Statesman and count (1839). Son of a priest. Directed a department of Ministry of Internal Affairs, 1803–7. Secretary of State to the Emperor Alexander, 1807, and Deputy Minister of Justice in 1808. Established the State Council in 1810. His reforms displeased the conservatives, who brought about his disgrace and exile in 1812.

STROGANOV, Pavel Aleksandrovich. 1772–1817. State and military figure, general (1814) and count. Formed a close friendship with the future Emperor Alexander in 1796 and later helped him to create the 'unofficial committee', of which he was a member. Senator in 1802 and deputy minister of the interior, 1802–7. Entered military service in 1807 and commanded a combined grenadier division which distinguished itself at the battle of Borodino in 1812. Retired in 1814.

STURDZA, Roxana. 1786–1844. Wrote memoirs. Born in Constantinople of Phanariot Greek origin. Her mother was a member of the powerful Morousi family. In 1792 her parents emigrated to Russia and settled in White Russia. In 1801 the family moved to St Petersburg. She became a maid of honour to the Empress Elizabeth in about 1811 and married Count Edling in 1818. Settled on her husband's estates in Bessarabia in 1824, devoting the rest of her life to good works. She died in Odessa.

SUVOROV, Aleksandr Vasil'evich. 1729–1800. Military commander and theorist, count (1789), prince of Italy (1799), generalissimo (1799). One of the best educated Russian military figures of the 18th century. His military theories and practice are reflected in an enormous literary legacy. An enlightened and humane commander, he became a popular hero after his legendary Italian and Swiss campaigns against the French in 1799. Constantly humiliated by the Emperor Paul, who objected to his independent views.

TARAKANOVA, Elizaveta Alekseevna (known as 'Princess' Tarakanova; also known as Fräulein Frank or Madame Tremouille). 1745–75. Adventuress and impostor, she claimed to be the daughter of the Empress Elizabeth (daughter of Peter the Great) and Count A. G. Razumovskii and heiress to the Russian throne. She died of tuberculosis as a prisoner in the Peter and Paul Fortress.

TORMASOV, Aleksandr Petrovich. 1752–1819. Military commander, general and count (1816). Commanded the Russian Third Army in 1812 and was acting Commander-in-Chief during the illness of Kutuzov in 1813. Governor-General of Moscow in 1814 and did much to restore the city after the fire.

TRAVERSAY, Jean-Baptist de. 1754–1831. French marquis and Russian admiral. Born on his mother's sugar plantation in Martinique and entered the French naval school at Rochefort in 1766. In 1790, after an active naval career, he was invited by Catherine the Great to serve in the Russian navy. Promoted to admiral in 1802 by the Emperor Alexander and Commander-in-Chief of the Black Sea Fleet, 1802–9. Acting Minister of the Navy, 1809–12. Minister of the Navy, 1812–28. Died in Russia.

VORONTSOV, Aleksandr Romanovich. 1741–1805. Statesman and diplomat, brother of Simon Vorontsov. Served as chargé d'affaires in Vienna (1761) and minister pleni-potentiary in England (1762–4) and Holland (1764–8). President of the College of

Commerce, 1773–94, becoming a senator in 1779. Retired from government service under the Emperor Paul but returned to serve as Chancellor to the Emperor Alexander, 1802–4.

VORONTSOV, Mikhail Semenovich. 1782–1856. Statesman, field marshal (1856) and prince. Son of Simon Vorontsov. Commanded a division in 1812 and the Russian corps of occupation in France, 1815–18. Close to members of the Decembrist movement. Held prominent government positions in the Black Sea region, 1823–44, and was Vice-Regent to the Caucasus and Commander-in-Chief of the Separate Caucasian Corps, 1844–54.

VORONTSOV, Simon Romanovich. 1744–1832. Count, diplomat and statesman. Russian Ambassador to Venice (1782–4) and London (1784–1806), where he pursued policy of strengthening economic and political ties with England. In 1800 he was forced into temporary retirement by the Emperor Paul but he returned to serve under the Emperor Alexander until 1806. He retired in England.

VORONTSOVA, Catherine Simonovna ('Katinka'). 1784–1856. Only daughter of Simon Vorontsov. In 1808 she married the 11th Earl of Pembroke, as his second wife, and became a leading figure in London society. Their eldest son was Sidney Herbert (later 1st Baron Herbert of Lea), who, as Minister of War at the outset of the Crimean War, supported the work of Florence Nightingale.

WARREN, Sir John Borlase. 1753–1822. Baronet, English admiral and diplomat. Served with distinction in various naval commands throughout the Napoleonic wars. In 1802 he was nominated a member of the Privy Council and British Ambassador to St Petersburg, where he served until 1805. He returned to naval service in 1806 and was promoted to the rank of admiral in 1810.

WILMOT, Catherine. 1773–1824. Diarist. Born in Ireland and visited Russia, 1805–7, where she joined her younger sister, Martha, as the guest of Princess Dashkova. Wrote letters which admirably portray the daily life of the leisured classes in Russia at the time of her visit. Died unmarried, of consumption, in Paris.

WILMOT, Martha. 1775–1873. Diarist. Born in Ireland and younger sister of Catherine. Visited Russia, 1803–8, as the guest of Princess Dashkova, who became devoted to her. She wrote a journal and letters which give a lively account of her life in Russia. While returning to Ireland, she survived a shipwreck off the coast of Finland. She married the Revd William Bradford, who later became chaplain to the British Embassy in Vienna.

WITTGENSTEIN, Ludwig Adolf Pieter. 1769–1843. Military commander, count, field marshal and prince (1834). Descended from an aristocratic German family. Named Commander-in-Chief of the Russian army in April 1813 after the death of Kutuzov, but because of defeats in May 1813 was replaced by Barclay de Tolly.

ZUBOV, Platon Aleksandrovich. 1767–1822. State figure and last favourite of Catherine the Great. Enjoyed immense power despite his limitations as an administrator. Received vast estates and tens of thousands of serfs from the Empress. His career ended with her death in 1796.

# Selected Bibliography

## 1. MANUSCRIPT SOURCES

Elton Hall, Peterborough. Proby Papers. Various manuscript and typescript copies of Charles Proby's correspondence and other family correspondence. Typescript copies of the letters from Pavel Chichagov to Charlotte Ferrers of *c.* June 1801 and from Elizabeth Chichagova to 'Joey' of 27 March 1802.

London, Borough of Sutton, Central Library. Pigott Papers, Heritage Service, Acc. 280. Letters and drafts of letters between Elizabeth Proby and Charles Proby.

—, British Library. Add. MS 15956, fos. 317–319v. Letter from Charles Proby to Lord Anson.

—, Greenwich, Library of the National Maritime Museum. 'Promiscuous Letters', Chatham Dockyard Records, CHA/P/I 1793–1803. Letters between Commissioner Charles Proby and Admiral Khanikov.

—, House of Lords Record Office. Copies of the 1836 naturalization papers relating to Pavel and Catherine Chichagov.

—, Public Record Office. Will of Charles Proby, PROB 11/1323

—, Senate House, School of Slavonic and East European Studies Library. Chichagov Collection. Photographs and typescript notes supplied by Dinah Dean.

Moscow, Russian State Library. Chichagov Archives, F. 333, K. 2 & K. 3. Letters to and from Pavel and Vasilii Chichagov and various notebooks.

Paris, Archives Nationales de Paris. Archives Privées. *95 AP, 6. Fonds Caulaincourt. 'Correspondance du duc de Vicence, ambassadeur.' Dossier no. 17. Letters from Admiral Chichagov to the Duc de Vicence.

—. *Journaux Étrangers*, AF/IV/1567, *Gazette de Munich*, 30 July 1810. Description of the fire at the Austrian Embassy.

—. *Mission de Général Savary à S. Petersbourg du 6 août au 23 Xbre 1807*, AF/IV/1697. Description of the Russian court.

Plymouth, City of Plymouth Archives & Records. Copies of marriage and birth certificates of the Pownoll family.

## 2. PRINTED WORKS

Anderson, R. C. *Naval Wars in the Baltic*. London: C. Gilbert-Wood, 1910.

*Arkhiv Knyazya Vorontsova*. Vol. 8. Moscow: Tipografiya I. K. Gracheva, 1876. Vol. 9. Moscow: Tipografiya I. K. Gracheva, 1876. Vol. 10. Moscow: Tipografiya I. K. Gracheva, 1876. Vol. 11. Moscow: Tipografiya I. K. Gracheva, 1877. Vol. 12. Moscow, Tipografiya Lebedeva, 1877. Vol. 13. Moscow: Tipografiya Lebedeva, 1879. Vol. 14. Moscow: Tipografiya Lebedeva, 1879. Vol. 15. Moscow, Tipografiya Lebedeva, 1880. Vol. 17. Moscow: Tipografiya A. Gattsuka, 1880. Vol. 19. Moscow: 1881. Vol. 22. Moscow: Ve Universitetskoi Tipografii (M. Katkov), 1881. Vol. 23. Moscow: Ve Universitetskoi Tipografii (M. Katkov), 1882. Vol. 30. Moscow: Ve Universitetskoi Tipografii (M. Katkov), 1881. Vol. 35. Moscow: Universitetskaya Tipografiya, n.d.

Benoist de la Grandière, Edmée. 'Pavel, Vassilevitch Tchitchagoff 1767 (Saint Petersbourg) – 1849 (Paris).' *Bulletin des Amis de Sceaux*, no. 14, 1997.

Bentham, Revd Thomas. *A History of Beddington*. London: John Murray, 1923.

Binney, Marcus. 'Sharpham House, Devon', *Country Life*, 17 April 1969.

Blanc, Albert, ed. *Correspondance Diplomatique de Joseph de Maistre 1811–1817*. Vol. 1. Paris: Michel Lévy Frères, 1860.

—, ed. *Mémoires Politiques et Correspondance Diplomatique de J. de Maistre*. Paris: Librairie Nouvelle, 1858.

Borenius, Tancred, and the Rev. J. V. Hodgson, with a preface by Granville Proby. *A Catalogue of the Pictures at Elton Hall in Huntingdonshire in the Possession of Colonel Douglas James Proby*. London: The Medici Society Limited, 1924.

Bouzet, Charles du, ed. *Mémoires inédits de l'Amiral Tchitchagoff: Campagnes de la Russie en 1812 contre la Turquie, l'Autriche et la France*. Berlin: F. Schneider et Comp. 1855.

—, ed. *Mémoires de l'Amiral Tchitchagoff (1767–1849): Avec une notice biographique: D'après des documents authentiques*. Bibliothèque Russe, Nouvelle Série, vol. 7. Leipzig: A. Franck'sche Verlags Buchhandlung, 1862.

*Burke's Peerage, Baronetage & Knightage*, 100th ed. London: Burke's Peerage Ltd, 1953.

Carrington, C. E., and J. Hampden Jackson. *A History of England*. Cambridge: Cambridge University Press, 1936.

Chambray, The Marquis de. *L'Histoire de l'Éxpedition de Russie*. 2 vols. Paris: Chez Pillet Ainé, 1823.

Charnock, John. *Biographia Navalis*. Vol. 5. London, 1797.

Chasles, Émile. *Documents relatifs à la Vie et au Testament de l'Amiral Tchitchagoff*. Paris, 1854.

—. *Étude Biographique sur l'Amiral Tchitchagoff*. Extrait de *L'Athenaeum Française* du 29 avril 1854. Mâcon: Imprimerie d'Émile Protat, n.d.

Chatenet, Madeleine du. *Traversay: Un Français ministre de la Marine des Tsars*. Paris: Éditions Tallandier, 1996.

Chichagov, Leonid Mikhailovich, ed. 'Zapiski Admirala Pavla Vasil'evicha Chichagova.' *Russkaya Starina*, vols. 50, 51, 52, 55, 58, 59 and 60 (1886–8).

Childe-Pemberton, William S. *The Baroness de Bode 1775–1803*. London: Longmans, Green, and Co., 1900.

Clowes, William Laird. *The Royal Navy: A History from the Earliest Times to the Present*. Vol. 3. London: Sampson Low, Marston and Company, 1899.

Coad, Jonathan. *Historic Architecture of Chatham Dockyard, 1700–1850*. National Maritime Museum in conjunction with the Society for Nautical Research, 1982.

Cross, Anthony. *By the Banks of the Neva: Chapters from the Lives and Careers of the British in Eighteenth-Century Russia*. Cambridge: Cambridge University Press, 1997.

—. *'By the Banks of the Thames': Russians in Eighteenth Century Britain*. Newtonville, Mass.: Oriental Research Partners, 1980.

—, ed. *An English Lady at the Court of Catherine the Great: The Journal of Baroness Elizabeth Dimsdale, 1781*. Cambridge: Crest Publications, 1989.

—, ed. *Engraved in the Memory: James Walker, Engraver to the Empress Catherine the Great, and his Russian Anecdotes*. Oxford and Providence, R. I.: Berg Publishers, 1993.

Duckett, M. W., ed. *Dictionnaire de la Conversation et de la Lecture*. Vol. 16. Paris: Chez Michel Lévy Frères, 1858.

Finch, William Coles. *The Medway River and Valley: The Story of the Medway: Aspects of Life on the Medway: Journeyings on the Medway*. London: The C. W. Daniel Company, [1929?].

*Gentleman's Magazine*, 42 (1772), 53 (1783), 81 (1811).

Gmeline, Patrick de. *Dictionnaire de la Noblesse Russe*. Paris: Editions Contrepoint, n.d.

Granville, Castalia Countess, ed. *Lord Granville Leveson Gower (First Earl Granville): Private Correspondence 1781–1821*. 2 vols. London: John Murray, 1916.

*Great Soviet Encyclopedia*. 31 vols. New York and London: Macmillan, Inc., 1983. Originally published as *Bolshaya Sovetskaya Entsiklopediya* (Moscow: Izdatel'stvo 'Sovetskaya Entsiklopediya', 1981).

Hanoteau, Jean, ed. *Mémoires du Général de Caulaincourt, Duc de Vicence, Grand Écuyer de l'Empereur*. Vol. 2. Paris: Librairie Plon, n.d.

Hasted, Edward. *The History and Topographical Survey of the County of Kent*. Canterbury: Printed for the author, by Simmons and Kirkby, 1782.

Hennigsen, C. *Eastern Europe and the Emperor Nicholas*. Vol. 1. London: T. C. Newby, 1846.

Hoskins, W. G. *Devon*. Commemorative edition. Tiverton: Devon Books, 1992.

Jane, Fred T. *The Imperial Russian Navy*. London: W. Thacker & Co., 1899.

Jones, John Gale. *A Political Tour through Rochester, Chatham, Maidstone, Gravesend, etc.* 1796. Reprint. Rochester: Baggins Book Bazaar in association with Bruce Aubry, 1997.

*Journal de Paris*, nos. 263 (1809), 348 (1809).

*Kamerfur'erskii tseremonial'nyi zhurnal' 1801–1813*. St. Petersburg, 1903–4.

Kelly, Laurence. *St Petersburg: A Travellers' Companion*. London: Constable, 1981.

*Kentish Weekly Post and Canterbury Journal* 1, 5–12 June, 1769.

*Lady's Magazine*, January 1785.

Lahovary, Charles Gr., ed. *Mémoires de l'Amiral Paul Tchitchagof, Commandant en Chef de l'Armée du Danube, Gouverneur des Principautés de Moldavie et de Valachie en 1812*. 2 vols. Paris: Plon-Nourrit et Cie, 1909; Bucharest: Socec et Cie, 1909.

Langlois, Gilles-Antoine. *Folies, Tivolis et Attractions, les premiers parcs de loisirs parisiens*. Paris: Imprimerie Aleçonnaise, 1991.

*Life and Letters of Sir Gilbert Elliot*. Vol. 1. London: Longmans, Green, & Co., 1874.

*The Life of Reginald Heber, D. D., Lord Bishop of Calcutta, by his Widow with Selections from his Correspondence, Unpublished Poems, and Private Papers; together with a Journal of his Tour in Norway, Sweden, Russia, Hungary and Germany and a History of the Cossaks*. London: John Murray, 1830.

Londonderry, The Marchioness of, ed. *The Russian Journals of Martha and Catherine Wilmot*. London, Macmillan and Co., Ltd., 1934.

MacDougall, Philip. *The Chatham Dockyard Story*. Whitstable: Meresborough Books, 1987.

——. *Royal Dockyards*. Shire Album 231. Princes Risborough, Shire Publications, 1989.

Maistre, Comte Rodolphe de, ed. *Lettres et Opuscules Inédits du Comte Joseph de Maistre*. 2nd ed. 2 vols. Paris: A. Vaton, 1853.

——, ed. *Lettres et Opuscules Inédits du Comte Joseph de Maistre*. 4th ed. Vols. 1 and 2. Paris: A. Vaton, 1861.

Maistre, Joseph de. *Les Carnets du Comte Joseph de Maistre: Livre Journal 1790–1817*. Paris and Lyon: Librairie Catholique Emmanuel Vitte, 1923.

——, *Oeuvres Complètes de J. de Maistre*. Vol. 11, Correspondance 3. Lyon: Vitte et Perrussel, 1885.

Marshall, John. *Royal Naval Biography*. Vol. 2. London: Longman, Hurst, Rees, Orme, Brown and Green, 1824.

*Mémoires de la Comtesse Edling*. Moscow: Imprimerie du St. Synode, 1888.

Mikhaïlowitch, Grand Duc Nicolas. *Le Comte Paul Stroganov*. Translated by F. Billecocq. Vol. 3. Paris: Imprimerie Nationale, 1905.

—. *L'Empereur Alexandre 1er: Essai d'Étude Historique*. Vol. 1. St. Petersburg: Manufacture des Papiers de l'État, 1912.

—. *Le Tsar Alexandre 1er*. Translated by the Baronne N. Wrangel. Paris: Payot, 1931.

—, ed. *Les Relations Diplomatiques de la Russie et de la France d'après les rapports des ambassadeurs d'Alexandre et de Napoléon*. 6 vols. St. Petersburg: Manufacture des Papiers de l'État, 1905.

—, ed. *Lettres de l'Impératrice Elizabeth*. Vol. 2. St Petersburg: Manufacture des Papiers de l'État, 1909.

—, ed. *Peterburgskii Nekropol'*. St Petersburg: Tipografiya M. M. Ctasyulevicha, 1913.

Ministerstvo Inostrannykh Del SSSR. *Vneshnyaya Politika Rossii XIX i Nachala XX Veka*. Moscow: Izdatel'stvo Politicheskoi Literatury, 1965.

Nesselrode, Comte A. de, ed. *Lettres et Papiers du Chancelier Comte de Nesselrode 1760–1850*. Vols. 3 and 4. Paris: A. Lahure, n.d.

Nevins, Allan, ed. *The Diary of John Quincy Adams 1794–1845: American Diplomacy, and Political, Social, and Intellectual Life, from Washington to Polk*. New York: Charles Scribner's Sons, 1951.

Nicholas, Sir Nicholas Harris, ed. *The Dispatches and Letters of Vice Admiral Lord Viscount Nelson*. Vol. 4. London: Henry Colburn, 1845.

Parkinson, John. *A Tour of Russia, Siberia and the Crimea 1792–1794*. Edited by William Collier. London: Frank Cass & Co. Ltd., 1971.

Percier, Charles, and P. F. L. Fontaine. *Descriptions des Cérémonies et des Fêtes qui ont eu lieu pour le mariage de S. M. L'Empereur Napoléon avec S. A. I. l'Archiduchesse Marie Louise d'Autriche à Paris le 2 avril 1810*. Paris: 1810.

Phipps, Pownoll W. *The Life of Colonel Pownoll Phipps*. London: R. Bentley and Son, 1894.

Porter, Robert Ker. *Travelling Sketches in Russia and Sweden during the years 1805, 1806, 1807, 1808*. 2 vols. London: John Stockdale, 1813.

Presnail, James. *Chatham: The Story of a Dockyard Town and the Birthplace of the British Navy*. Chatham, Corporation of Chatham, 1952.

Preston, J. M. *Industrial Medway: an historical survey*. Chatham: W. & J. Mackay, 1977.

*Private Papers of British Diplomats 1782–1900*. Royal Commission on Historical Manuscripts, London, Her Majesty's Stationary Office, 1985.

*Russkii Biograficheskii Slovar'*. St Petersburg: Tipografiya I. N. Skorokhodova, 1905.

Seton-Watson, Hugh. *The Russian Empire 1801–1917*. Oxford, Clarendon Press, 1967.

Shvidkovsky, Dimitri. *The Empress and the Architect*. New Haven and London: Yale University Press, 1996.

Stephen, Leslie, and Sidney Lee, eds. *Dictionary of National Biography*. London: Smith, Elder & Co., 1908.

Syrett, David, and R. L. DiNardo, eds. *The Commissioned Sea Officers of the Royal Navy 1660–1815*. Published by Scolar Press for the Navy Records Society, 1994.

Tolstoy, Leo. *War and Peace*. Translated by Constance Garnett. New York: The Modern Library, 1994.

Vaudoncourt, Guillaume de. *Relation Impartiale du Passage de la Bérézina, par l'Armée Française, en 1812, par un Témoin Oculaire*. Paris: Chez Barrois l'aîné, 1814.

Waliszewski, K. *Le Règne d'Alexandre 1er: La Bastille Russe et La Révolution en Marche (1801–1812)*. Vol. 1. Paris: Librairie Plon, 1923.

—. *Paul the First of Russia: The Son of Catherine the Great*. London: W. Heinemann, 1913.

Walter, Richard. *Anson's Voyage round the World*. London: Martin Hopkinson Ltd.; Boston: Charles E. Lauriat Co., 1928.

*Wright's Topography of Rochester, Chatham, Strood, Brompton, etc. and Directory of the Clergy, Gentry, Tradesmen, etc.* Published by I. G. Wright, Chatham Hill, 1838.

# Index

Adams, John Quincy 134, 137
Addington, Henry 142
Alexander I, Emperor of Russia
and Austria 144, 205, 208, 209, 211
and Britain 142, 144, 156, 161, 166, 167,
168, 170, 204
and Caulaincourt 170, 171, 172, 190
and France 119–20, 139, 144, 154, 156–7,
162, 163, 167, 170–2, 174, 182, 198–9
and Italy 136
and Kutuzov 154, 204–5, 218
and Napoleon 154, 161–2, 166, 180, 187,
190
and Pavel 104, 118–19, 120, 130, 141,
143, 149–50, 156, 162, 164–5, 167, 180,
182, 205, 210, 219, 221
and Sweden 97, 106, 120, 144, 161, 170,
173, 174, 176–7, 179, 192, 204
and Turkey 157, 163, 164, 165–6, 170,
198, 204, 205, 206, 208
as Grand Duke 68, 89, 93, 98, 99, 100, 109
at court 123, 127, 158–9, 160, 180
Balkan aspirations 205, 209
character 122
final campaign against Napoleon 207–20
kindness to Pavel 143, 145, 149–50, 181,
182, 201, 202, 224
liaisons 128–9, 175, 195
reforms 104, 119, 126, 130–1, 141
relations with Empress Elizabeth 128,
129, 130, 163–4
Amelia, Princess 127
Amiens, Treaty of 120, 204
Anna, Grand Duchess 159, 186
Anson, Commodore George 1–2, 3
Anstedt, d' 211
Aumon, Monsieur 28
Austen, Jane 1, 7
Austerlitz 154, 156, 157, 161, 162, 205

Babaiev 27
Bagration, General Petr 208
Baratynskii 69, 79
Barclay de Tolly, Field Marshal Mikhail 208
Beddington 24, 73, 85, 115, 221
Bennigsen, General Levin 99
Bentham, Samuel 161
Berezina 210, 211–16, 219, 220, 224, 225
Pavel's views on 218, 225
Bessarabia 208, 228
Bessborough, Lady 160

Bezborodko, Count Aleksandr 39, 40, 43,
77, 109
Binns, John 20
Bligh, Captain 61
Bonaparte, Caroline 190–1
Bonaparte, Napoleon, see Napoleon
Bonaparte
Bonaparte, Pauline 190
Borisov 210, 211, 212–15, 217
Borodino 208
Boutin, Simon-Charles 195
Bouzet, Charles du 227–8, 229
Bouzet, Comte Eugène du 223, 226
Bouzet, Comtesse du, see Chichagova,
Catherine
Brenna, Vincenzo 159
Brighton 225
Budberg, General 163, 164–5, 167
Burke, Edmund 18
Burslem, Fanny 73, 146, 148, 150
Bush, John 113
Bush, Mrs 114
Byng, Admiral John 3

Cameron, Catherine (née Bush) 113, 114,
132, 150, 151
Cameron, Charles 113, 121, 130, 141, 151,
159
Campo Formio, Treaty of 63, 71
Canning, George 142
Capodistrias, Ioannis 207
Carl, Prince of Sweden 36-7, 38
Carysfort, John Joshua, 1st Earl of 14, 21–2,
61, 87, 103, 126, 178
as ambassador in St Petersburg 106, 110,
120, 121
as visitor in Russia 22-3, 135
marriages 4, 23
Carysfort, John, 1st Baron 3, 4, 11, 22
Carysfort, Lady (née Elizabeth Allen) 4
Carysfort, Lady (née Elizabeth Grenville)
23, 24, 86, 96
Catherine I, Empress of Russia 26
Catherine II (the Great), Empress of Russia
27, 113, 121, 151
and Britain 19, 34, 93
and serfdom 27, 102
and Sweden 19, 34–40, 41
at court 22, 31, 32, 40, 41, 130
bestowal of honours 37, 39, 40, 41
death and burial 61, 68

Catherine II (*cont.*)
  influence on family 98, 128, 205
  liaisons 31, 42, 67
  naval affairs 30, 33, 34, 35, 36, 45, 161
  Reynolds painting 23
Catherine, Grand Duchess 158, 159, 160,
  166, 176, 181, 186, 198
Caulaincourt, Marquis de (Duc de Vicence)
  69–70, 171, 183, 187, 188, 199, 216
  and Alexander I 170, 171, 172, 190
  and Napoleon 168, 170, 171, 172, 180,
    184, 187, 188, 190, 192, 199, 216
  and Pavel 169, 170, 171, 172–3, 174–5,
    180, 194
  correspondence with Pavel 192, 194, 195,
    196
Çeshme 29, 34, 48
Chambray, Marquis de 213
Champagny, Jean-Baptiste Nompère (Duc de
  Cadore) 170, 172, 188, 199
Chancellor, Richard 92
Chapman, Frederik 45, 49, 120
Charles Emmanuel IV, King of Sardinia 136
Chasles, Émile 227
Chatham Dockyard 6, 7, 8, 9, 19–20, 21
Chernyshev, Count Aleksandr 174
Chichagov, Grigorii 36
Chichagov, Jacob 25
Chichagov, Leonid 227, 230
Chichagov, Pavel
  and Alexander I 117, 118–19, 120, 122,
    126, 130, 149
  and Caulaincourt 169, 170, 171, 172–3,
    174–5, 180, 184
  and Charles Proby 48–9, 50, 52, 54–6,
    58–60, 62–3, 66, 71, 72–7, 222
  and Kushelev 78–9, 80
  and Kutuzov 162, 206, 207, 208, 218–19,
    220
  and Napoleon 139, 142, 144, 146, 162,
    171, 184, 186–8, 192, 193, 219
  and Paul I 79–80, 95, 97–8
  as father 116–17, 164, 207, 217–18, 222
  at court 121, 122, 130, 158–9, 166, 175–6,
    180
  at French court 186, 187, 188, 192
  at Kronstadt 91, 94, 97–8, 101, 104, 126,
    130
  attempts to go to England 77, 183, 189,
    190, 193–4
  attitude towards Russia 36, 43, 53, 70, 83,
    84, 146–7, 148, 155, 156, 224
  attitude towards the English 34, 42, 43,
    46, 53, 139, 155, 168, 171, 189
  battle of Borodino 208–9
  battle on the Berezina 210–17
  campaign in Balkans 205–8
  career 30, 79, 96, 118, 130, 131, 133, 149,
    156, 157, 167, 202, 205–6, 209

character 30, 32–3, 49, 54, 131–2, 139,
  157, 158, 165, 179, 223
childhood 25, 28, 51
correspondence with Caulaincourt 192,
  194, 195, 196
correspondence with Elizabeth 60, 61, 62,
  69–70
critics of 40, 69, 79–80, 130–1, 139–40,
  179, 202, 209, 218–19
death and burial 225–6
disgrace in Russia 219, 224
education 29–30, 31, 42, 43, 45
entertaining 135, 158, 169, 174
family dispute after his death 226
father's death 181
finances 102, 103, 110, 119, 147, 182, 202,
  224
friendship with de Maistre 137–9, 146,
  183, 220
grief over Elizabeth's death 201, 202–4,
  217–18, 219, 221, 223
holiday 145–6, 182–3
honours 37, 39, 40–1, 119, 131, 149, 180,
  226
ill health 81–2, 147, 178–9, 180, 193–4,
  223, 224
imprisonment 80–1
in Switzerland 194–5
letters to Vorontsov 61, 67, 68, 69, 70, 83,
  89, 90, 96, 107, 120, 135, 140–1, 146,
  147, 148, 152, 155, 156, 160, 166, 179,
  188–9, 217, 220
marriage 85–6
meeting with Nelson 106–7, 117
memoirs 102, 103, 128, 190
  lapses in them 186, 207
  on Elizabeth 58, 67, 145, 178
  on Kutuzov and the Berezina 218, 225,
    227
  on naval and military matters 50, 80,
    83, 106, 170, 177–8, 207, 218
  various posthumous versions of 227–8,
    229–30
  writing of them 225
naval action and manoeuvres 30, 35, 36,
  37, 46–7, 176
naval reform 36, 97, 118–19, 126, 130–1,
  140–1, 161, 224
relationship with Elizabeth 56–7, 58, 84,
  96, 138–9, 153
relationship with Vorontsov 43–4, 46, 61,
  77, 132, 142, 144, 148, 149, 156, 189,
  220
residence with Elizabeth in Paris 185, 195
resignations 69, 101, 147, 149, 182, 202,
  219
visits to England 41–2, 44, 47, 83
will 226–7
Chichagov, Peter 27, 30, 41n, 69, 109

Chichagov, Vasilii (Pavel's brother) 41, 44,
  69, 109, 196, 197, 222
  death and burial 225, 226
Chichagov, Vasilii (Pavel's father) 25, 43,
  94–5, 96, 118
  career 27, 28–9, 34–5, 68, 69
  character 27, 32, 36, 109
  death 181
  honours and rewards 29, 37, 39, 40, 41,
    102
  naval action 30, 34–5, 36-8, 39, 40
Chichagova, Adelaide (Adèle) 224, 226–7
  as a child 95, 97, 102, 113, 125, 132, 164
  marriage and son 222
Chichagova, Catherine (Pavel and
  Elizabeth's daughter) 178, 222, 224,
  225
  birth 167
  marriages 223
  her father's papers and memoirs 178,
    226–8
  family dispute 226–9
  ill health 227
Chichagova, Catherine (Pavel's mother) 27,
  32, 36, 41
Chichagova, Elizabeth (née Proby) 16, 168
  at court 121, 122, 130, 158–9, 160, 166,
    175–6, 180
  at French court 186, 187, 192
  attitude towards Russia 91, 93–4, 124–5,
    142
  bestowal of honour 181–2
  birth 1, 6
  childbirths 95, 132, 142–3, 167, 199–200
  childhood 7, 11, 16
  correspondence with Pavel 60, 61, 62,
    69–70, 174
  death and burial 200, 204, 221
  education 14
  entertaining 135, 169
  friendships 86, 113, 136, 137–9, 146, 151,
    173
  her father's will 72–3, 103
  holiday 145–6, 182–3
  ill health 66, 95, 121, 131, 133, 143, 145,
    161, 178, 180, 182, 187, 196–7
  journal entries 168, 173, 175, 181
  letters to her father 72, 73, 74, 75–6
  life in Kronstadt and St Petersburg 93–4,
    95, 101, 107–113, 122
  love of music 51–2, 73
  marriage 85–6
  monument to 221
  mother's death 13
  portraits of 5, 157
  pregnancies 87, 90, 94, 95, 126, 132, 164,
    166, 194, 197, 199
  relationship with her father 52, 59, 62–3,
    66, 71–7

relationship with Pavel 53–4, 56–7, 58,
  67, 70, 84, 96, 124, 138–9, 153, 157,
  193–4
residence in Paris 185, 195
Chichagova, Julie
  birth 132
  death 224
  marriage and children 222, 223
Clowes, William 1, 2, 17
Clyde 57, 64–5, 87
Constantine, Grand Duke 68, 93, 98, 128,
  129, 160, 205
Crouÿ-Chanel children 226–7
Crouÿ-Chanel, Comte André de 230
Crouÿ-Chanel, Comte Henri de 222, 226
Crouÿ-Chanel, Comtesse de, see Chichagova,
  Julie
Cunningham, Beatrice (née Proby) 17, 52,
  60, 64, 103, 201, 203
  care of Chichagov nieces 207, 222
  childhood 7, 8, 12, 14
  marriage 57–8
Cunningham, Captain Charles 57–8, 64–5,
  87, 207
Czartoryski, Prince Adam 104, 128, 154,
  163

Dalrymple, Mrs James (née Anne
  Gascoigne) 152
Dashkova, Princess 42, 110, 114, 173
Demidovs 110, 223
Didham, Mrs 7, 12, 49, 60
Dimsdale, Baroness Elizabeth 111, 114
Dimsdale, Baron Thomas 93, 111
Dolgorukov, Prince 81
Duckworth, Admiral Sir John 165
Duncan, Adam, Admiral Viscount 46–7, 65

Edling, Countess, see Sturdza, Roxana
Elizabeth Alexievna, Empress of Russia
  126, 127, 128, 129, 130, 158, 171–2,
  211
  child of 163–4, 166, 172, 175
Elizabeth Petrovna, Empress of Russia 121
Elliot, Gilbert 23
Elton Hall 4, 14, 21, 22
Enghien, Duc d' 144, 169
Erfurt, Congress of 180, 182, 198
Essen, General 83, 84, 88

Ferrers, Charlotte (née Proby) 18, 24, 50, 52,
  57, 60, 66, 74, 103
  childhood 7, 8, 12, 14
  children 116–17
  marriages 17, 85, 115
Ferrers, Revd John Bromfield 115–16
Fouché, Joseph (Duc d'Otrante) 169, 199
French Revolution 17, 18, 19, 20, 21, 36, 64,
  68, 136

Gagarina, Princess 98, 99
Galloway, Dr 95
Gascoigne, Charles 92, 151–2
*Gentleman's Magazine* 7, 13, 14–15, 62, 201
George of Oldenburg, Prince 176, 181
Golitsina, Princess Eudoxie 159
Greig, Admiral Samuel 34, 35, 92
Grenville, Thomas 120
Grenville, William Wyndham, 1st Baron 155
Gur'ev, Semen 31, 41, 44, 119, 174, 206
Gustav, King of Sweden 34, 38, 39

Hanway, Thomas 3
Hargrave, Diana and Fanny 86
Härtell, General 210, 211
Heber, Reginald 110, 112, 126
Hermann, General 84
Hood, Samuel, Admiral 1st Viscount 20, 57
Howe, Richard, Admiral 1st Earl 63

Jones, John Gale 20, 55
Josephine, Empress of France 185, 187

Khanikov, Vice-Admiral 43, 46, 47, 55, 56, 61, 91, 177, 179
Kochubei, Prince Viktor 79, 89, 104, 167
Kozlanianov, Vice-Admiral 40, 43
Kronstadt 25, 27, 29, 30–1, 35, 130, 174
    fortifications at 33, 45, 91–2, 97, 104, 118–119, 126
    home of Pavel and Elizabeth 93–4, 95, 101
Kruze, Vice-Admiral 37-8, 43
Krylov, Ivan 219
Kurakin, Prince Aleksandr 111, 186, 188, 192, 197–8, 199, 204
Kushelev, Grigorii 68, 69, 78–9, 80, 97, 101, 118, 119, 130
Kutaisov 98
Kutuzov, Field Marshal Prince Mikhail 154, 162, 180, 204–5, 206, 208, 219
    battle on the Berezina 210–11, 212, 213–14, 215, 216–17
    conflict with Pavel 206, 207, 218–19, 225

La Harpe, Frédéric-César de 104, 109
Lahovary, Charles 228, 230
Lane, Edward 91
Lauriston, General 199
Leighton, Dr 167, 200
Leopold, Grand Duke of Tuscany 30
Leveson-Gower, Lord Granville (later 1st Earl Granville) 129, 134, 135, 159–60, 167
Lizakevich 88, 93, 145–6
Lomonosov , Mikhail 27
Longinov, Nikolai 211, 219
Lopukhin, Prince 78
Louis XVI 19

Maistre, Comte Rodolphe de 227
Maistre, Count Joseph de 123, 136–7, 142, 164, 171, 179, 193–4, 196, 206
    disappointment with Pavel 220
    friendship with Pavel and Elizabeth 137–9, 183, 188, 198
    sympathy over Elizabeth's death 20
    verdict on Pavel 225, 228
Maistre, Xavier de 138, 141
Malta 70–1, 88, 93, 142
Makarov, Rear-Admiral 67, 78, 81, 83
Maria Feodorovna, Empress of Russia 98–9, 100, 150, 182
    at court 126, 127, 130, 158–9, 160, 166, 175–6, 180
    influence 67, 126–7, 128, 176, 186
Marie-Louise, Empress of France 190–2, 197, 199
Markov, Count 140, 142
Marthus 41
Menshikov, Prince Aleksandr 26
Metternich, Prince 202, 204
Mikhail, Grand Duke 159
Minsk 210, 211, 216, 217
Moldavia 163, 204, 205, 206, 207n, 208
Mordvinov, Admiral Nikolai 130–1, 140
Moscow 208–9, 210, 212, 217, 218, 223

Napoleon Bonaparte 20, 63, 154, 199
    and Austria 154, 185, 197, 204, 208
    and Britain 120–1, 162, 166, 204
    and Prussia 154, 161, 163, 204
    and Russia 70–1, 136, 142, 144, 154–5, 157, 161, 162, 163, 166, 169–72, 180, 182, 198–9, 204
    and Spain 174
    and Sweden 204
    and Turkey 71, 157, 163, 164, 166, 170, 204, 205
    at court 186, 187, 192
    attitude towards Pavel 188, 192–3
    conspiracies against 144, 199, 216
    march into Russia 207-9
    marriage to Marie-Louise 190–2, 197
    retreat from Moscow 210–17
Narishkin, Dmitrii 129, 223
Narishkina, Madame Marie 128–9, 137, 163, 175, 195
Nassau-Siegen, Prince of 35, 40
Naudet, Colonel Charles-Marie 223
Navy Board 10, 11, 21
Nelidova, Catherine 68
Nelson, Horatio, Admiral Viscount 57, 71, 87, 104–7, 153
Nesselrode, Count Karl 192–3, 199, 211
Nesselrode, Marie 206
Nicholas I, Emperor of Russia 224, 225, 226
    as Grand Duke 159
Nicholas Mikhailovich, Grand Duke 128

Nikolai, Baron P. A. 162, 184
Novosil'tsev, Nikolai 104, 144, 155

Ochakov Crisis 19n, 92
Okhotnikov 164
Oranienbaum 91, 101, 118, 130, 150, 151
Orlov, Count Aleksei 29, 31, 48
Orlov, Count Grigorii 29, 31, 42, 151
Oubril, Baron d' 161, 169, 170, 171
Oudinot, General Nicolas-Charles (Duc de
    Reggio) 212, 213, 214

Pahlen, Count Petr 80, 81, 97, 99, 100, 105,
    120
Palliser, Hugh 2, 3
Panin, Count Nikita 89, 96, 101, 104, 120
Panov 27
Parker, Richard 64–5
Parkinson, John 41
Paul I, Emperor of Russia 67, 69, 93, 102,
    128, 159
    and Britain 88, 93, 97, 105
    and the Chichagovs 69, 77, 79–80, 95, 97
    and France and Italy 60–1, 136
    conspiracy against 89, 96, 98, 99–100
    death 100, 105, 144
    instability 67–8, 79–80, 98
    on serfdom 102
Pavlovsk 67, 78, 113, 126, 158, 159, 160, 175
Pembroke, Countess of ('Katinka'. nee
    Catherine Vorontsova) 42, 86, 96, 121,
    149, 167, 180, 201, 217
Pepys, Samuel 8
Peter I (the Great), Emperor of Russia 19,
    25, 29, 80, 108, 115, 160, 181
    and reform 26, 133
    and the Russian navy 33, 91
Peter III, Emperor of Russia 27, 31, 42, 67n,
    68
Peterhof 118, 126, 150, 160, 174, 176, 178,
    181, 183
Petrozavodsk 151, 152
Pigott, Admiral James 17, 24, 66, 85, 86
Pigott, Sarah (née Proby) 17, 24, 85, 86
    childhood 7, 8, 12, 14
    children 18, 66, 115
    marriage 17
Pitcairn, Colonel Thomas 17, 24, 53, 65
Pitcairn, Charlotte, see Ferrers, Charlotte
Pitt, William (the Younger) 20, 21, 42–3,
    56, 63. 97, 142, 155
Platov, Count Matvei 215–16
Pollen, George 152, 173–4, 180
Pollen, Elizabeth (née Gascoigne) 152, 173–4
Ponthon 170, 174
Porter, Robert Ker 94, 103, 114–15, 122–3,
    133–4, 145, 169, 183
Potemkin, Prince Grigorii 23, 31–2
Povalishin 43

Pownoll, Jane 12, 13, 15
Pownoll, Jacob 5
Pownoll, Captain Philemon 4, 5, 12–13, 17,
    22
Pownoll, Philemon 4–5
Pozzo di Borgo, Count Charles 135–6, 165
prison ships 8, 20
Proby, Baptist (Elizabeth's brother) 5, 6–7
Proby, Baptist (Elizabeth's cousin) 13, 24
Proby, Beatrice, see Cunningham, Beatrice
Proby, Catherine 24
Proby, Captain Charles
    as Commissioner 9, 10, 11, 21, 48, 55–6
    as parent 12, 15–16, 58
    attitude towards Pavel 48–9, 54, 56, 59,
        62, 66, 71–7, 222
    childhood 4
    death and funeral 77
    letters to Elizabeth 74–5, 76–7
    naval career 1–2, 3
    portraits of 3
    relationship with Elizabeth 52, 62–3, 66,
        71
    wife's death 13
    will and codicil 72–3, 103
Proby, Charles (Elizabeth's brother) 5, 6–7,
    13, 17, 18, 21, 24
Proby, Charlotte, see Ferrers, Charlotte
Proby, Elizabeth, see Chichagova, Elizabeth
Proby, Francis Henry 7, 14, 66
Proby, Granville 87
Proby, Jane (née Leveson-Gower) 4
Proby, Sarah (née Pownoll) 4–5, 6, 9, 11, 12,
    13
Proby, Sarah, see Pigott, Sarah
Proby, Sir Peter 4
Proby, Sir Thomas, Bart. 4
Proby, Susan 17, 18, 24

Rastrelli, Bartolomeo Francesco 121
Retvisan 45, 46, 47, 48, 49, 51, 54, 60–1, 69,
    88, 90
Revel 27, 33, 35, 45, 81, 91, 141
Reynier, General 208
Reynolds, Sir Joshua 3, 5, 23
Ribas, Admiral José de 96
Richelieu, Duc de 164
Robien, Comte Pierre de 230
Rogerson, Dr John 93, 95, 132, 142–3,
    152–3, 158
    letters to Vorontsov 107, 121, 139–40,
        144, 152–3, 167
Rostopchin, Count Feodor 78, 81, 89, 223
Rousseau, Jean-Jacques 36, 53, 62, 116n
Rumiantsev, Count Nikolai 165, 170, 172,
    192, 206–7

Sacken, General 211
St Helens, Alleyne Fitzherbert, Lord 120

St Vincent, John Jervis, Earl of 105
Saint-Julien, Count 202
Saltykov, Sergei 67, 109
Sandwich, Lord 9
Saumarez, Sir James 177
Savary, General (Duc de Rovigo) 127, 129,
    169, 193, 199
Sceaux 223, 225, 226
Schwarzenberg, Prince 197, 209, 210, 211,
    213, 218
Sebastiani, General 163
Seniavin, Admiral Dmitrii 149, 156, 157,
    164–5, 166, 174
Seven Years War 2, 5
Severin, Madame 195, 197
Shairp, Stephen 93
Shcherbatova, Princess Mary 134, 183
Sheremetev, Count Petr 92, 103
Shishkov 69, 130
Shklov 69, 91, 94, 96, 102
Sierra Capriola, Duke of 22, 135
Smirnov, Father Iakov 86, 93, 201, 203–4
Smolensk 208, 210, 211
Smorgoni 216
Snow, Mrs Sarah 112
Spencer, George John, 2nd Earl 78
Speranskii, Mikhail 179, 180, 188, 189, 193,
    205
Stakova 215
Steingell, General 210, 211
Stroganov, Count Pavel 96, 101, 103, 104,
    140
    as ambassador to London 155, 156, 162
Studianka 213, 214
Sturdza (father) 206, 208
Sturdza, Aleksandr (son) 206
Sturdza, Démètre 228
Sturdza, Roxana (Countess Edling) 129,
    157-8, 183, 184, 196, 198, 202, 220
Suvorov, General Aleksandr 71, 84, 136, 138

Talleyrand, Count Charles-Maurice de
    (Prince de Bénévent) 161, 193, 198–9
Tarakanova, 'Princess' Elizaveta 80, 96
Taylor, Sir Robert 5
Tcharplitz General 214–216
Texel 47, 61, 65, 84
Tilsit, Treaty of 139, 166, 167, 169, 170,
    173
Tolstoy, Count Leo 1, 154, 212, 217
Tormasov General Aleksandr 208, 209, 210,
    211, 218
Traversay, Marquis de 164, 184–5, 202
Tsarskoe Selo 31, 113, 114, 151, 158–9
Turkish-Russian relations 19, 29, 33, 34, 40,
    42, 43, 48, 71, 161, 181; see also under
    Alexander I

Vaudoncourt, Guillaume de 213

Victor, General Claude (Duc de Bellune)
    211, 213, 216
Victory 6, 7, 10, 20
Vilnius 205, 206, 208, 216, 217, 218
Voltaire 31, 36, 199
Vorontsov, Count Aleksandr 42, 43, 84, 120,
    130, 148, 149, 155
Vorontsov, Count Mikhail (later Prince) 42,
    86, 107, 149, 180, 202, 203
Vorontsov, Count Simon 126, 180
    as ambassador to London 42–3, 46, 47,
        84, 92, 101, 144
    and Chichagov children 96, 203, 217, 220
    concern over Pavel's grief 203, 217
    correspondence with Pavel 61, 67, 68, 69,
        83, 89, 135, 140–1, 144, 146, 149, 156,
        219, 220, 222
    disagreements with Pavel 142, 144, 148,
        162, 209
    friendship with Pavel 43–4, 86, 132, 220
    letter from Bezborodko 109
    letter from Kochubei 167
    letter from Zavadovskii 167
    letters from counsellor Nikolai 162, 184
    letters from Longinov 211, 219
    letters from Rogerson 107, 121, 139–40,
        144, 152–3, 167
    letters from Rostopchin 78, 81
    political influence 120, 155–6
    resignation 88, 89
    retirement 155
    support for Pavel and Elizabeth 77, 78,
        85, 89, 107, 120, 121
Vorontsova, Countess Catherine ('Katinka'),
    see Pembroke, Countess of
Vorontsova, Countess Elizabeth 42
Vyborg, battle of 37, 38, 39, 40, 41

Walewska, Marie 185
Waliszewski 67, 93 ?
Wallachia 163, 204, 205, 207n, 208
Warren, Lady 135, 136, 137, 153
Warren, Admiral Sir John 135
Whitworth, Sir Charles (later Earl) 93, 204
Wilmot, Catherine 111, 114, 160, 173
Wilmot, Martha 110–11, 114, 135, 152, 173,
    174, 180
Winter Palace 31, 40, 108, 121–2, 123, 180
Wittgenstein, General Ludwig 210, 211–12,
    213–16, 220
Wordsworth, William 18

York and Albany, Frederick Augustus, Duke
    of 56, 78, 84

Zakharov, Andreian 141
Zavadovskii, Count Petr 140, 167
Zubov brothers 99, 100
Zubov, Prince 45, 49, 99